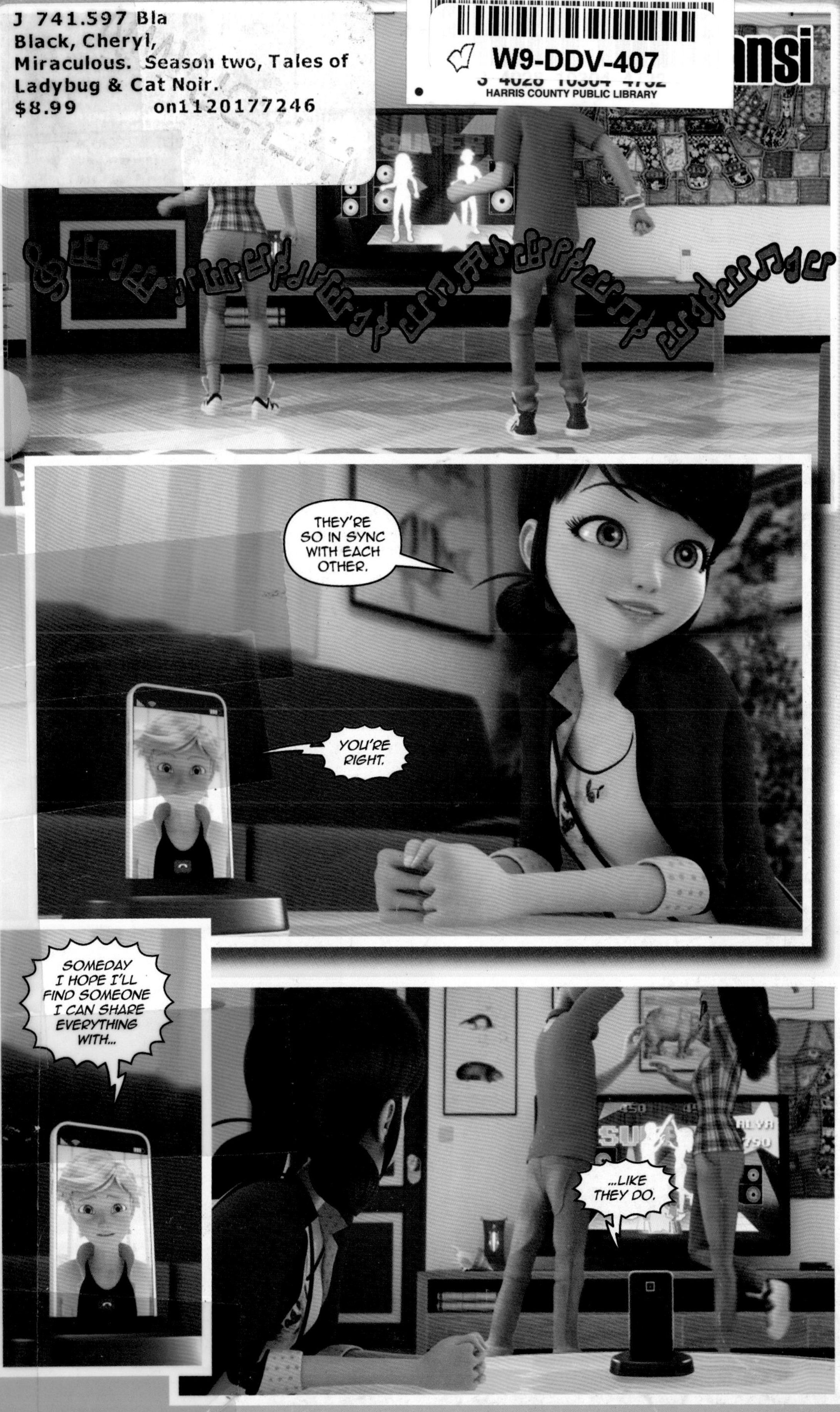
THEY'RE SO IN SYNC WITH EACH OTHER.
YOU'RE RIGHT.
SOMEDAY I HOPE I'LL FIND SOMEONE I CAN SHARE EVERYTHING WITH...
...LIKE THEY DO.

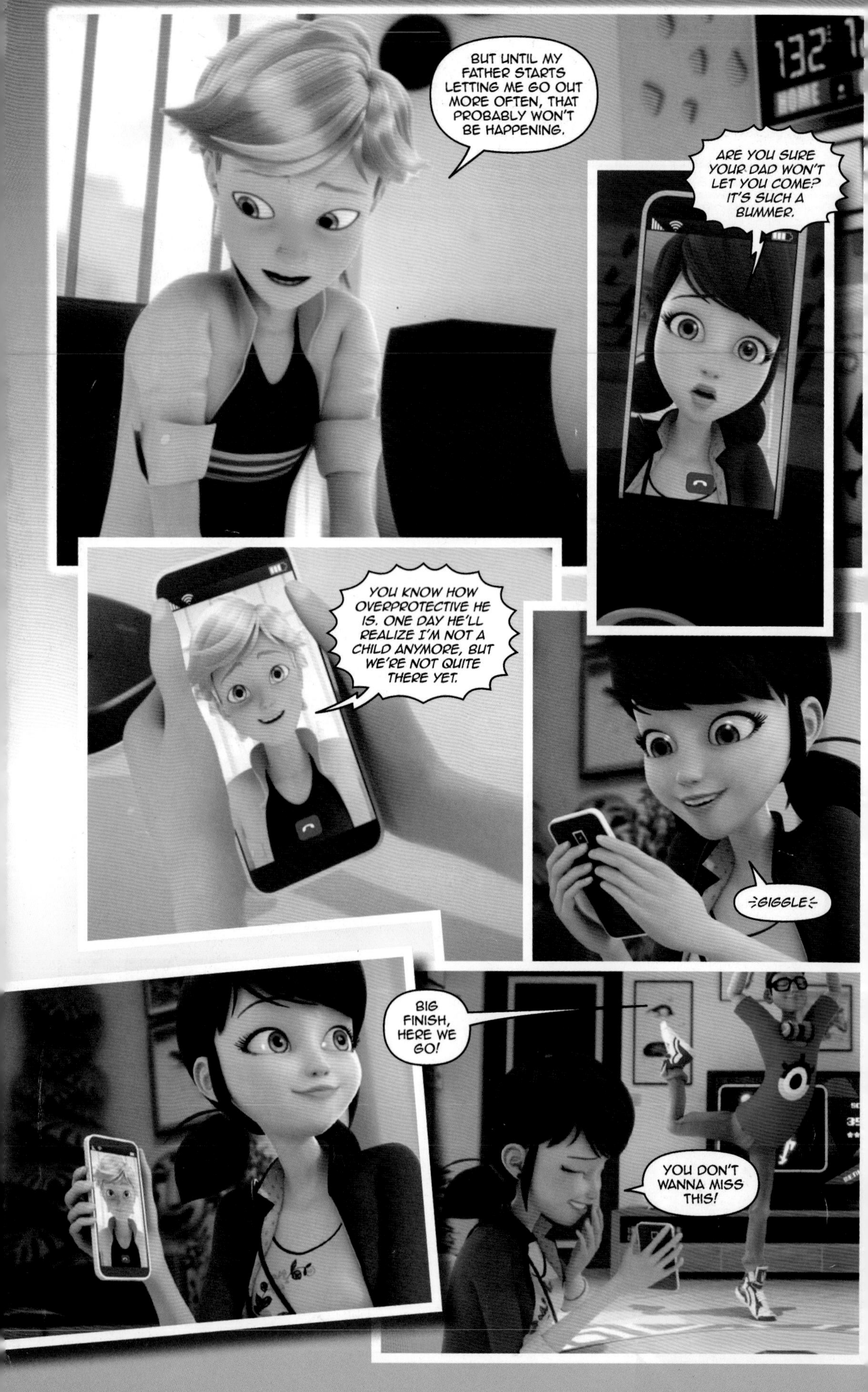
BUT UNTIL MY FATHER STARTS LETTING ME GO OUT MORE OFTEN, THAT PROBABLY WON'T BE HAPPENING.
ARE YOU SURE YOUR DAD WON'T LET YOU COME? IT'S SUCH A BUMMER.
YOU KNOW HOW OVERPROTECTIVE HE IS. ONE DAY HE'LL REALIZE I'M NOT A CHILD ANYMORE, BUT WE'RE NOT QUITE THERE YET.
GIGGLE
BIG FINISH, HERE WE GO!
YOU DON'T WANNA MISS THIS!

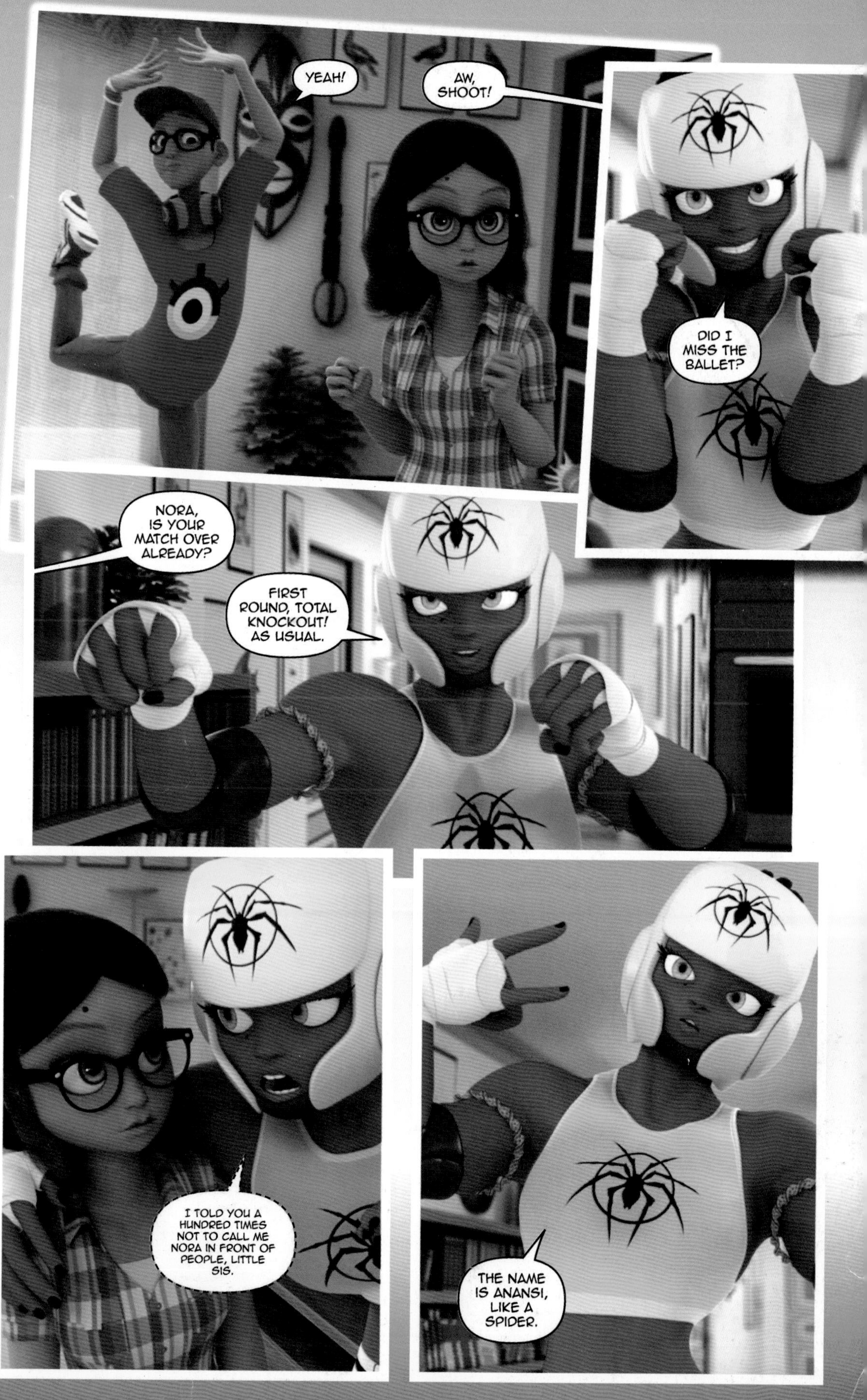
YEAH!
AW, SHOOT!
DID I MISS THE BALLET?
NORA, IS YOUR MATCH OVER ALREADY?
FIRST ROUND, TOTAL KNOCKOUT! AS USUAL.
I TOLD YOU A HUNDRED TIMES NOT TO CALL ME NORA IN FRONT OF PEOPLE, LITTLE SIS.
THE NAME IS ANANSI, LIKE A SPIDER.

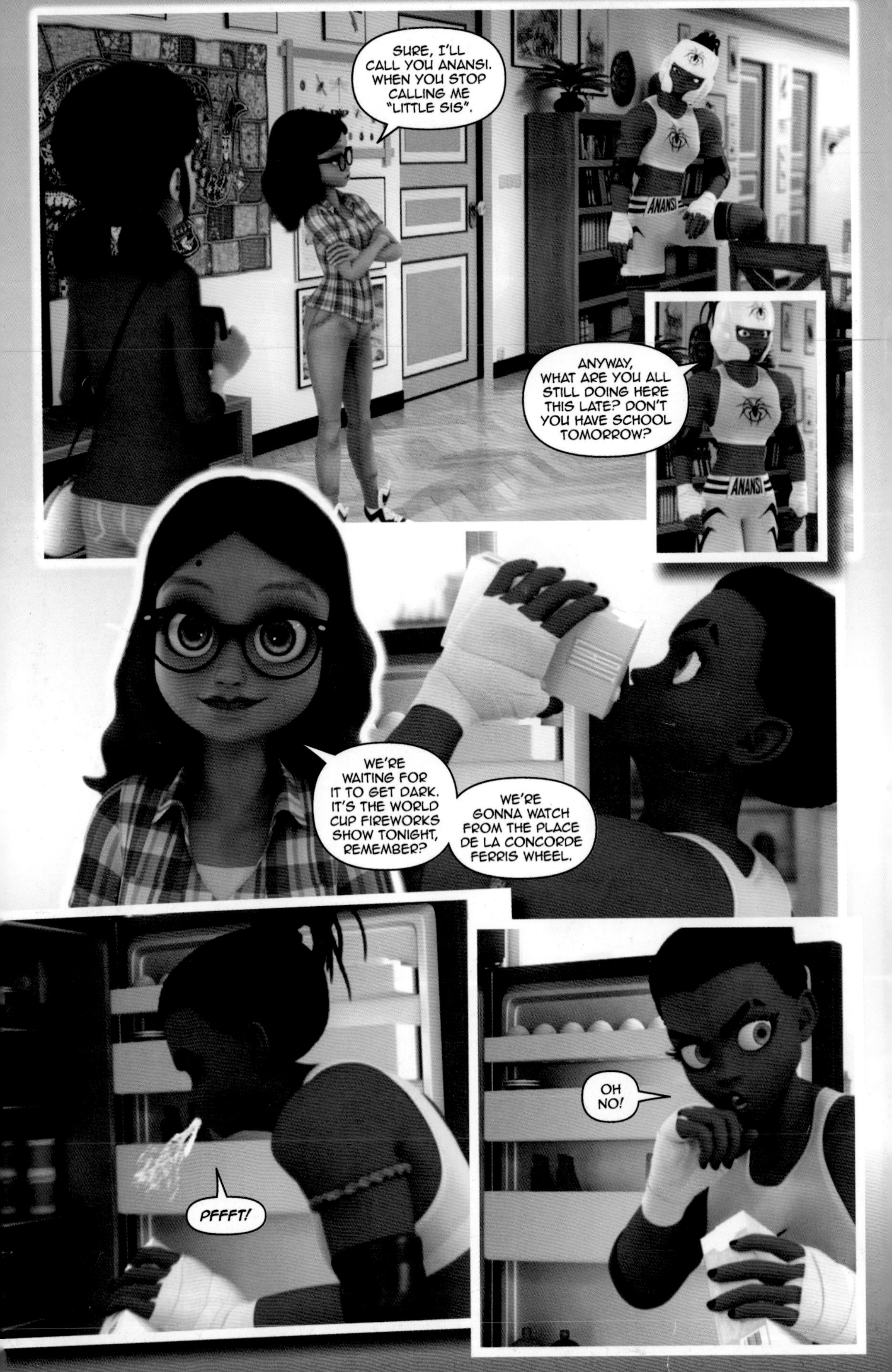
SURE, I'LL CALL YOU ANANSI. WHEN YOU STOP CALLING ME "LITTLE SIS".
ANANSI
ANYWAY, WHAT ARE YOU ALL STILL DOING HERE THIS LATE? DON'T YOU HAVE SCHOOL TOMORROW?
ANANSI
WE'RE WAITING FOR IT TO GET DARK. IT'S THE WORLD CUP FIREWORKS SHOW TONIGHT, REMEMBER?
WE'RE GONNA WATCH FROM THE PLACE DE LA CONCORDE FERRIS WHEEL.
PFFFT!
OH NO!

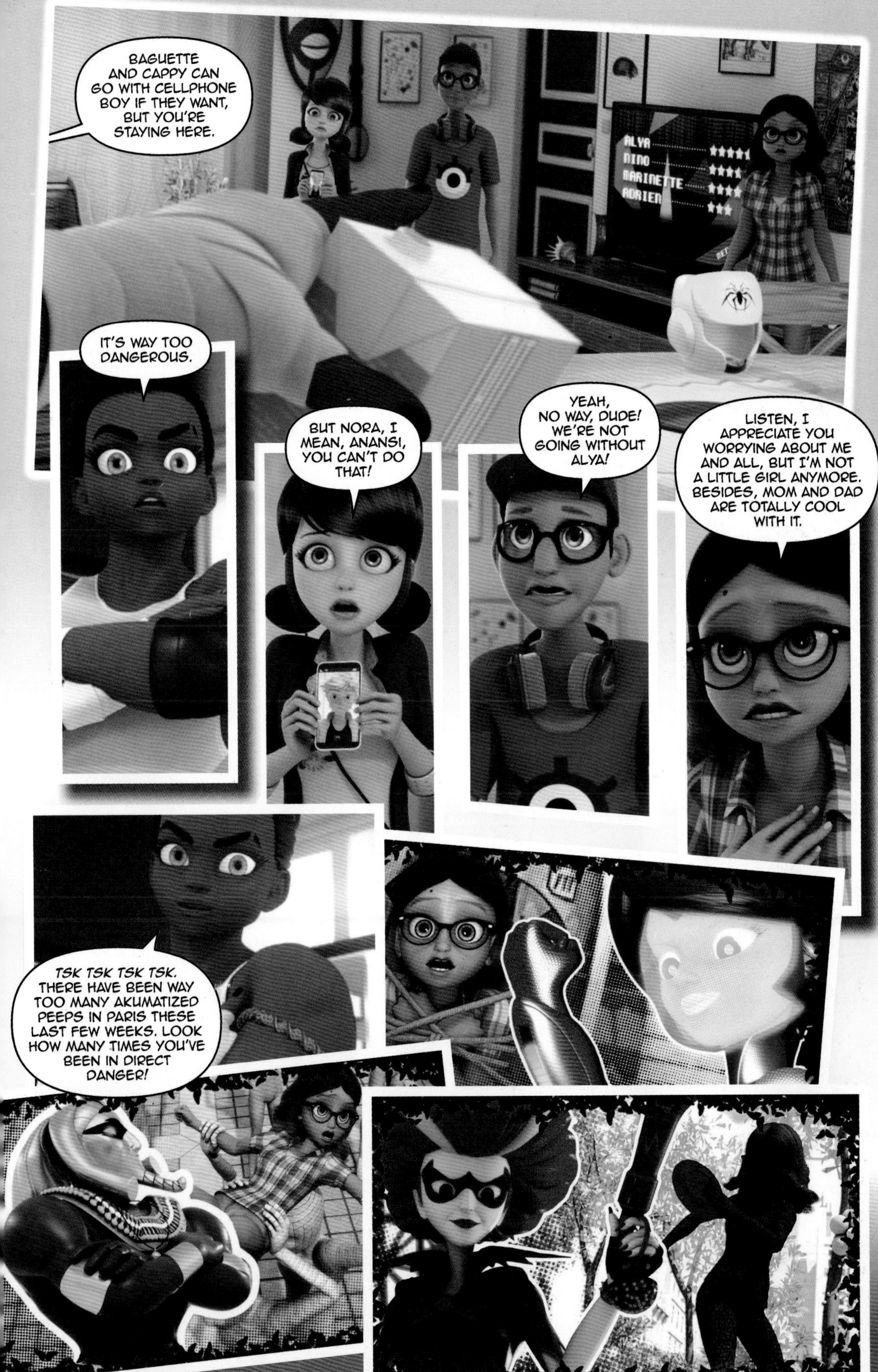
BAGUETTE AND CAPPY CAN GO WITH CELLPHONE BOY IF THEY WANT, BUT YOU'RE STAYING HERE.
ALYA
NINO
MARINETTE
ADRIEN
IT'S WAY TOO DANGEROUS.
BUT NORA, I MEAN, ANANSI, YOU CAN'T DO THAT!
YEAH, NO WAY, DUDE! WE'RE NOT GOING WITHOUT ALYA!
LISTEN, I APPRECIATE YOU WORRYING ABOUT ME AND ALL, BUT I'M NOT A LITTLE GIRL ANYMORE. BESIDES, MOM AND DAD ARE TOTALLY COOL WITH IT.
TSK TSK TSK TSK. THERE HAVE BEEN WAY TOO MANY AKUMATIZED PEEPS IN PARIS THESE LAST FEW WEEKS. LOOK HOW MANY TIMES YOU'VE BEEN IN DIRECT DANGER!

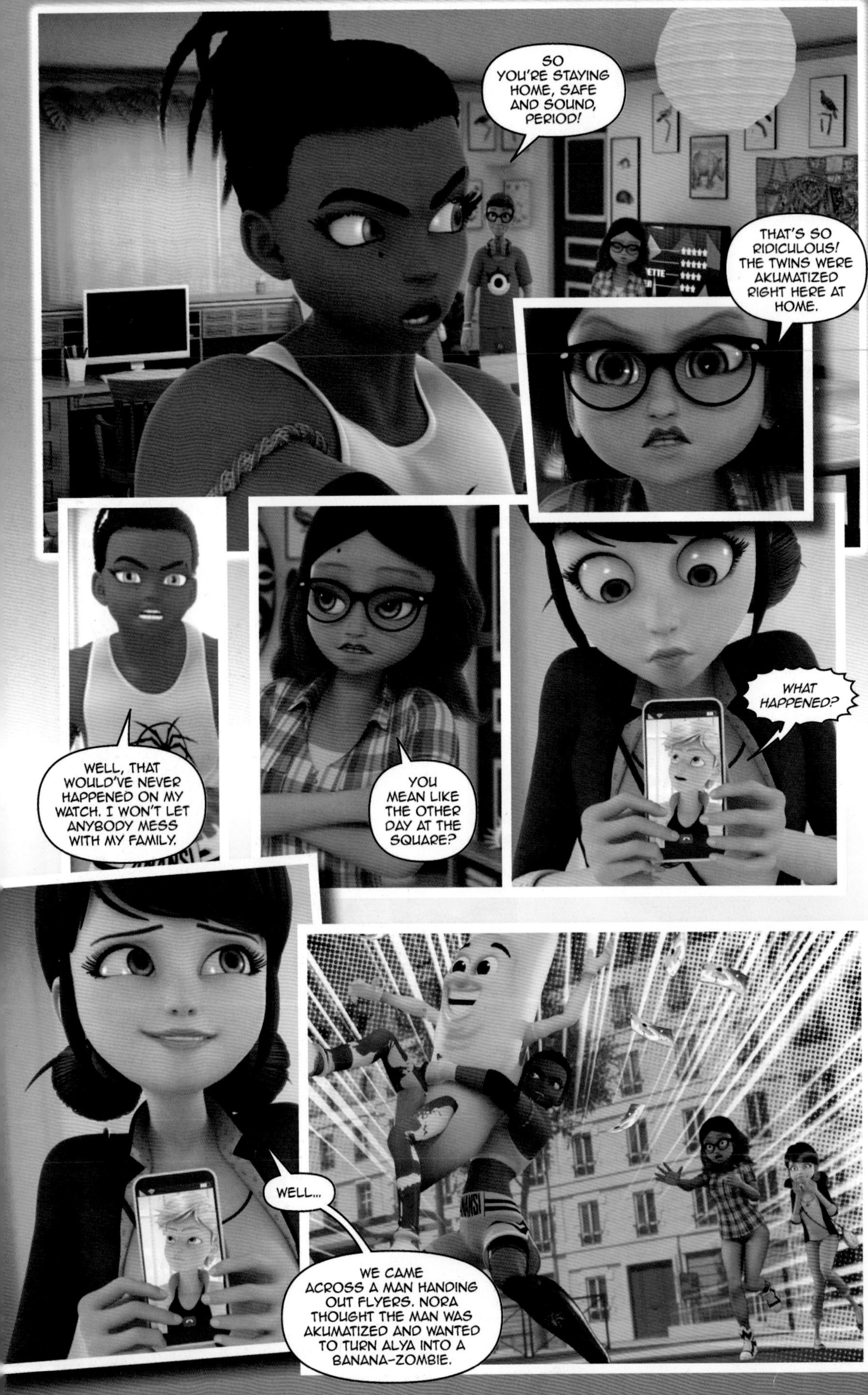
SO YOU'RE STAYING HOME, SAFE AND SOUND, PERIOD!
THAT'S SO RIDICULOUS! THE TWINS WERE AKUMATIZED RIGHT HERE AT HOME.
WELL, THAT WOULD'VE NEVER HAPPENED ON MY WATCH. I WON'T LET ANYBODY MESS WITH MY FAMILY.
YOU MEAN LIKE THE OTHER DAY AT THE SQUARE?
WHAT HAPPENED?
WELL...
WE CAME ACROSS A MAN HANDING OUT FLYERS. NORA THOUGHT THE MAN WAS AKUMATIZED AND WANTED TO TURN ALYA INTO A BANANA-ZOMBIE.

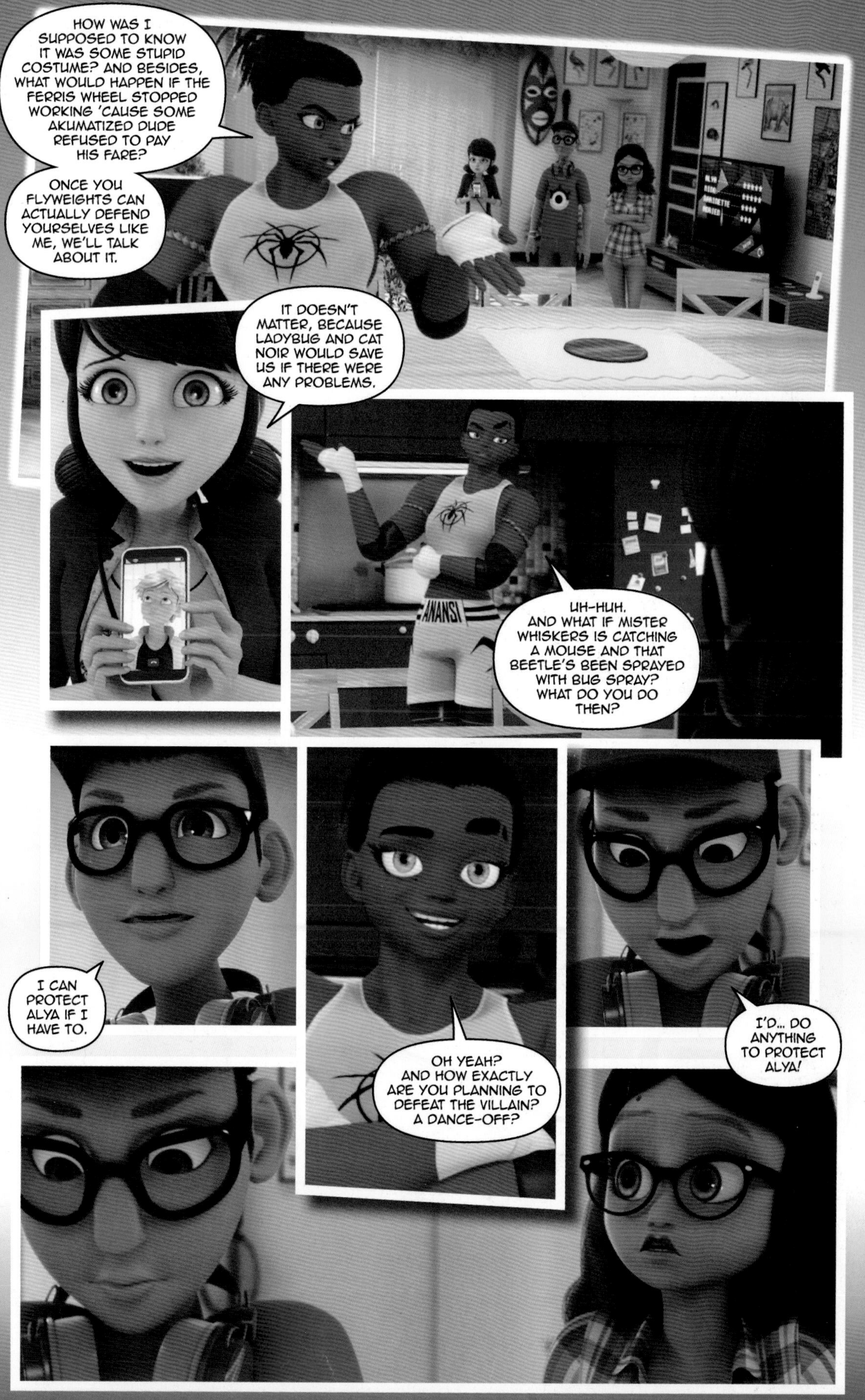

HOW WAS I SUPPOSED TO KNOW IT WAS SOME STUPID COSTUME? AND BESIDES, WHAT WOULD HAPPEN IF THE FERRIS WHEEL STOPPED WORKING 'CAUSE SOME AKUMATIZED DUDE REFUSED TO PAY HIS FARE?
ONCE YOU FLYWEIGHTS CAN ACTUALLY DEFEND YOURSELVES LIKE ME, WE'LL TALK ABOUT IT.
IT DOESN'T MATTER, BECAUSE LADYBUG AND CAT NOIR WOULD SAVE US IF THERE WERE ANY PROBLEMS.
ANANSI
UH-HUH. AND WHAT IF MISTER WHISKERS IS CATCHING A MOUSE AND THAT BEETLE'S BEEN SPRAYED WITH BUG SPRAY? WHAT DO YOU DO THEN?
I CAN PROTECT ALYA IF I HAVE TO.
OH YEAH? AND HOW EXACTLY ARE YOU PLANNING TO DEFEAT THE VILLAIN? A DANCE-OFF?
I'D... DO ANYTHING TO PROTECT ALYA!

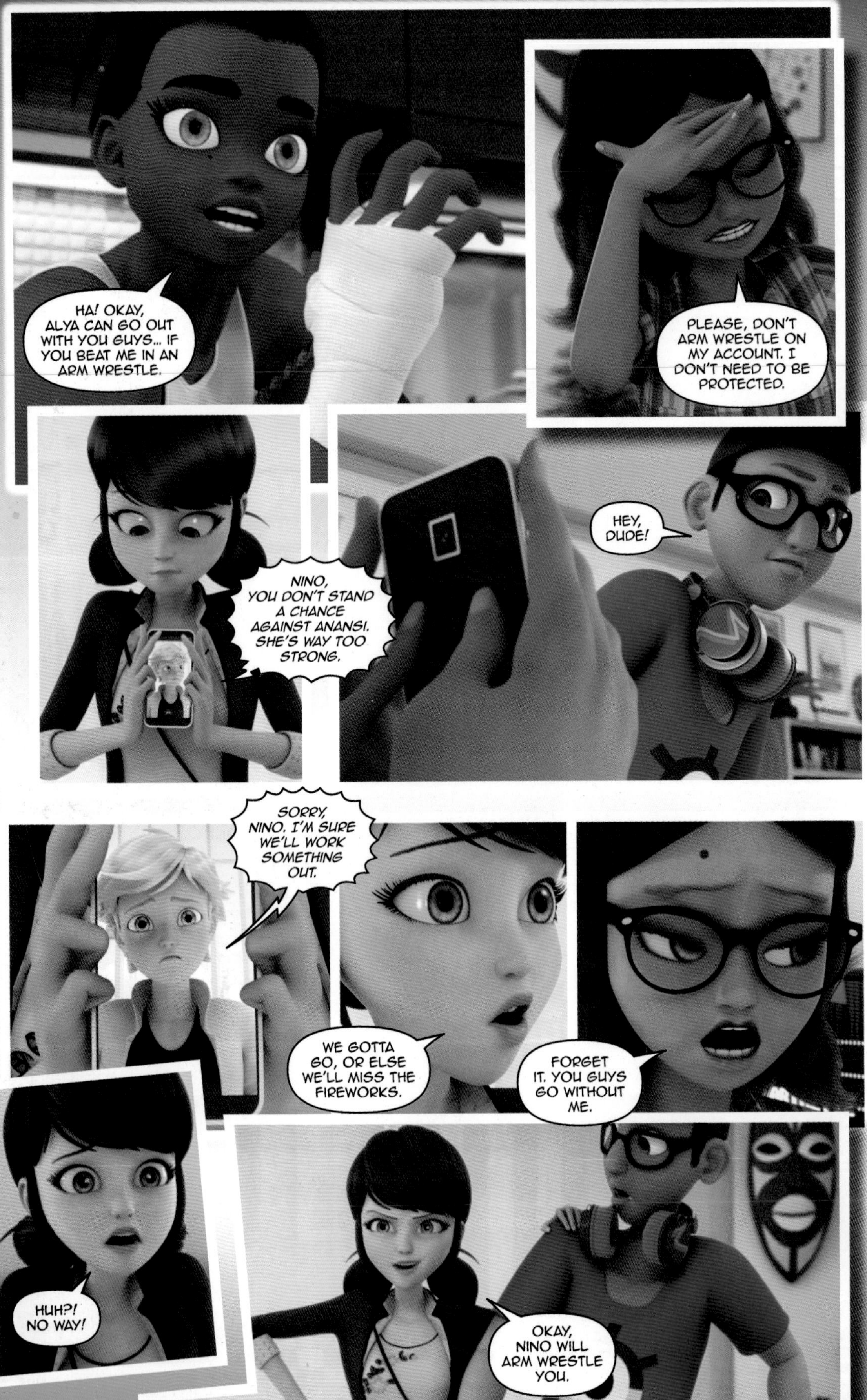
HA! OKAY, ALYA CAN GO OUT WITH YOU GUYS... IF YOU BEAT ME IN AN ARM WRESTLE.
PLEASE, DON'T ARM WRESTLE ON MY ACCOUNT. I DON'T NEED TO BE PROTECTED.
NINO, YOU DON'T STAND A CHANCE AGAINST ANANSI. SHE'S WAY TOO STRONG.
HEY, DUDE!
SORRY, NINO. I'M SURE WE'LL WORK SOMETHING OUT.
WE GOTTA GO, OR ELSE WE'LL MISS THE FIREWORKS.
FORGET IT. YOU GUYS GO WITHOUT ME.
HUH?! NO WAY!
OKAY, NINO WILL ARM WRESTLE YOU.

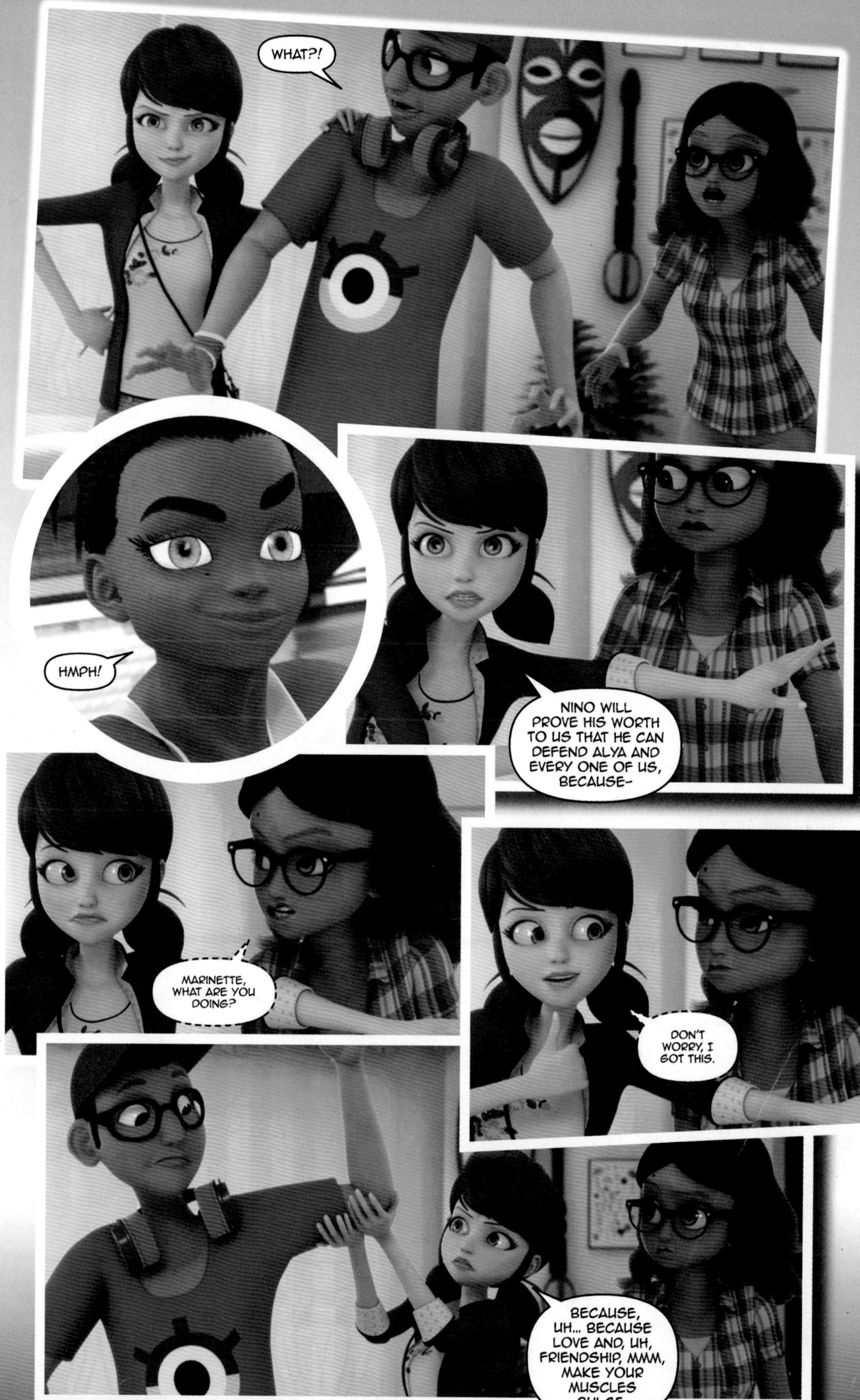
WHAT?!
HMPH!
NINO WILL PROVE HIS WORTH TO US THAT HE CAN DEFEND ALYA AND EVERY ONE OF US, BECAUSE-
MARINETTE, WHAT ARE YOU DOING?
DON'T WORRY, I GOT THIS.
BECAUSE, UH... BECAUSE LOVE AND, UH, FRIENDSHIP, MMM, MAKE YOUR MUSCLES BULGE.

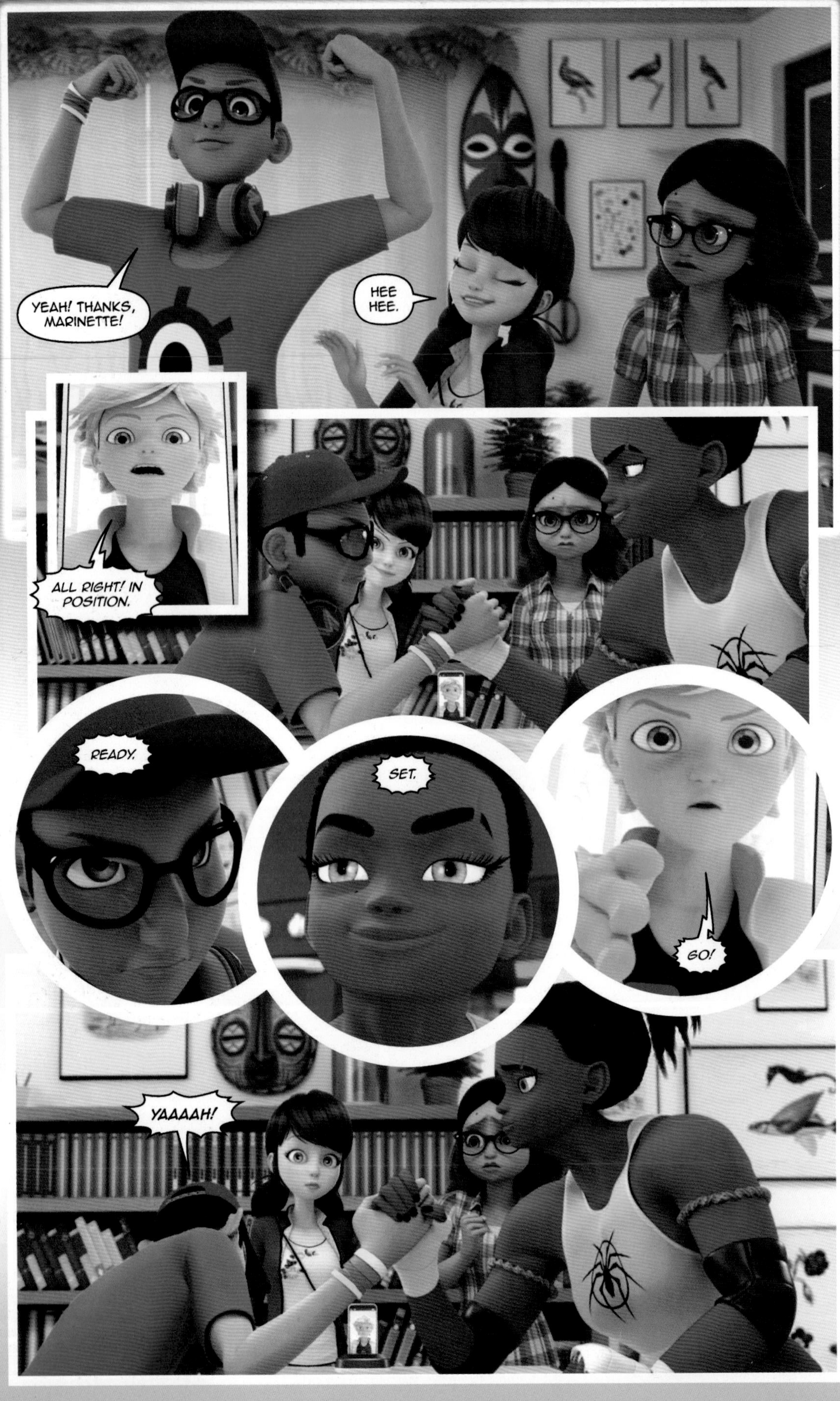
YEAH! THANKS, MARINETTE!
HEE HEE.
ALL RIGHT! IN POSITION.
READY.
SET.
GO!
YAAAAH!

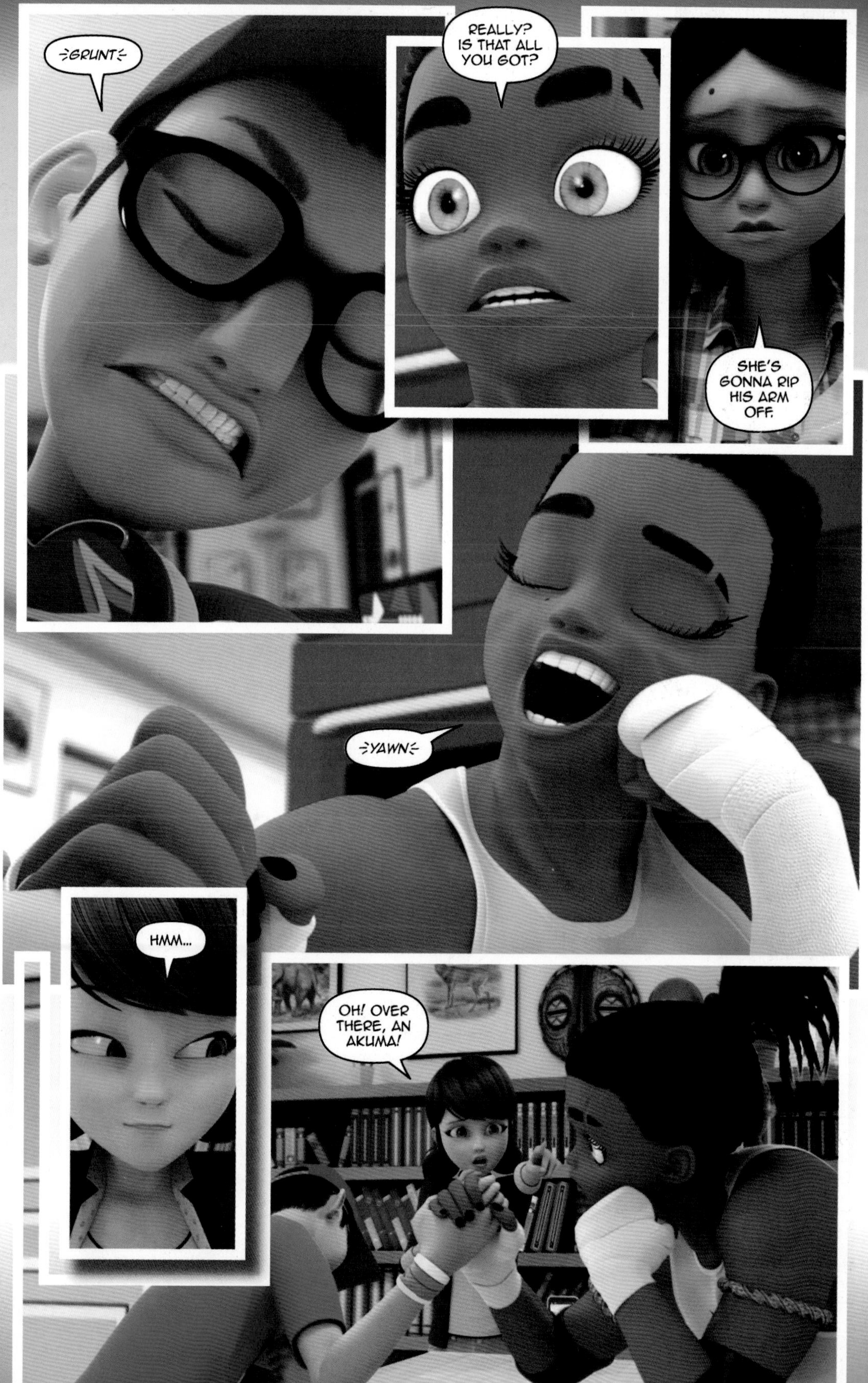

⋟GRUNT⋞
REALLY? IS THAT ALL YOU GOT?
SHE'S GONNA RIP HIS ARM OFF.
⋟YAWN⋞
HMM...
OH! OVER THERE, AN AKUMA!

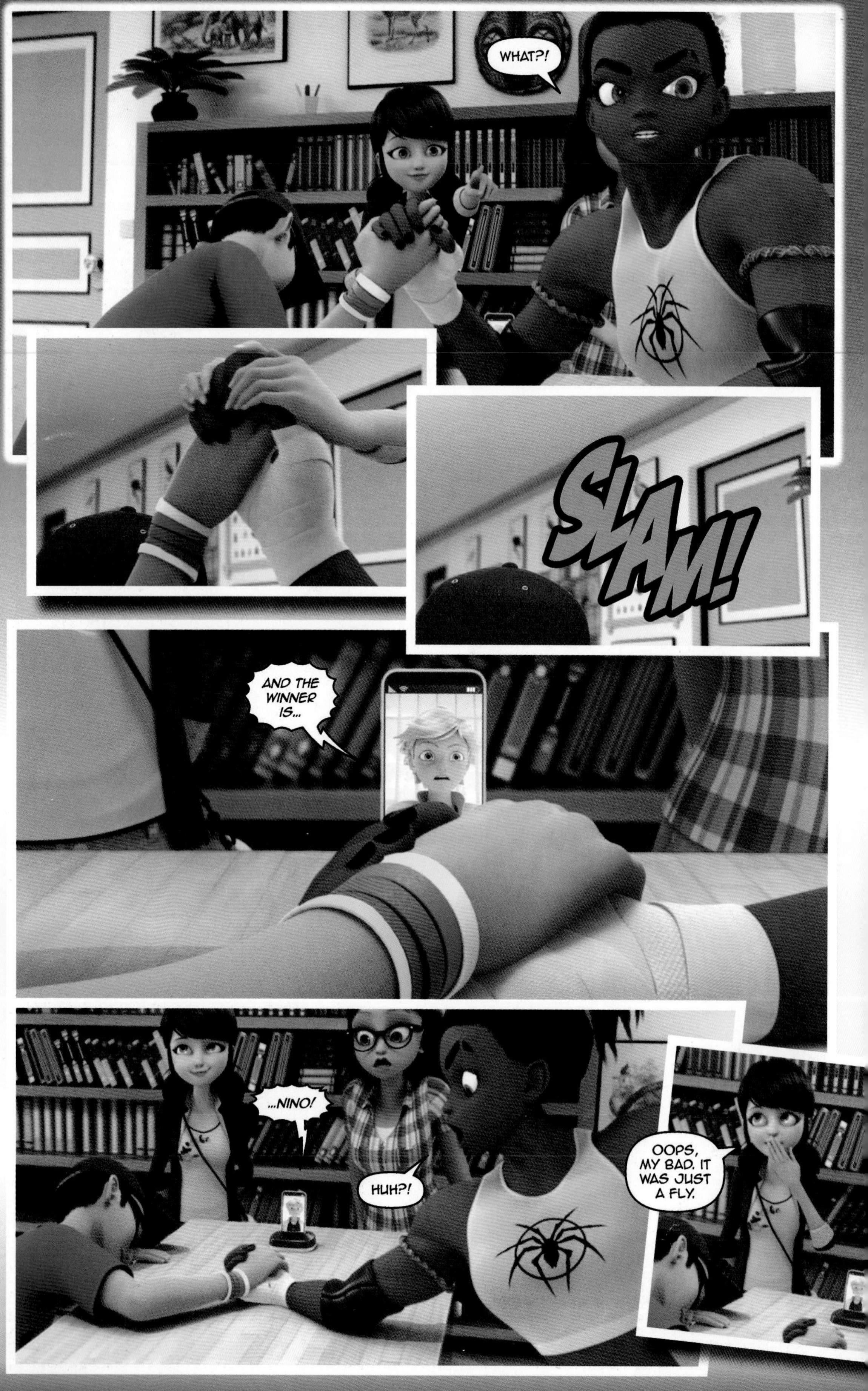
WHAT?!
SLAM!
AND THE WINNER IS...
...NINO!
HUH?!
OOPS, MY BAD. IT WAS JUST A FLY.

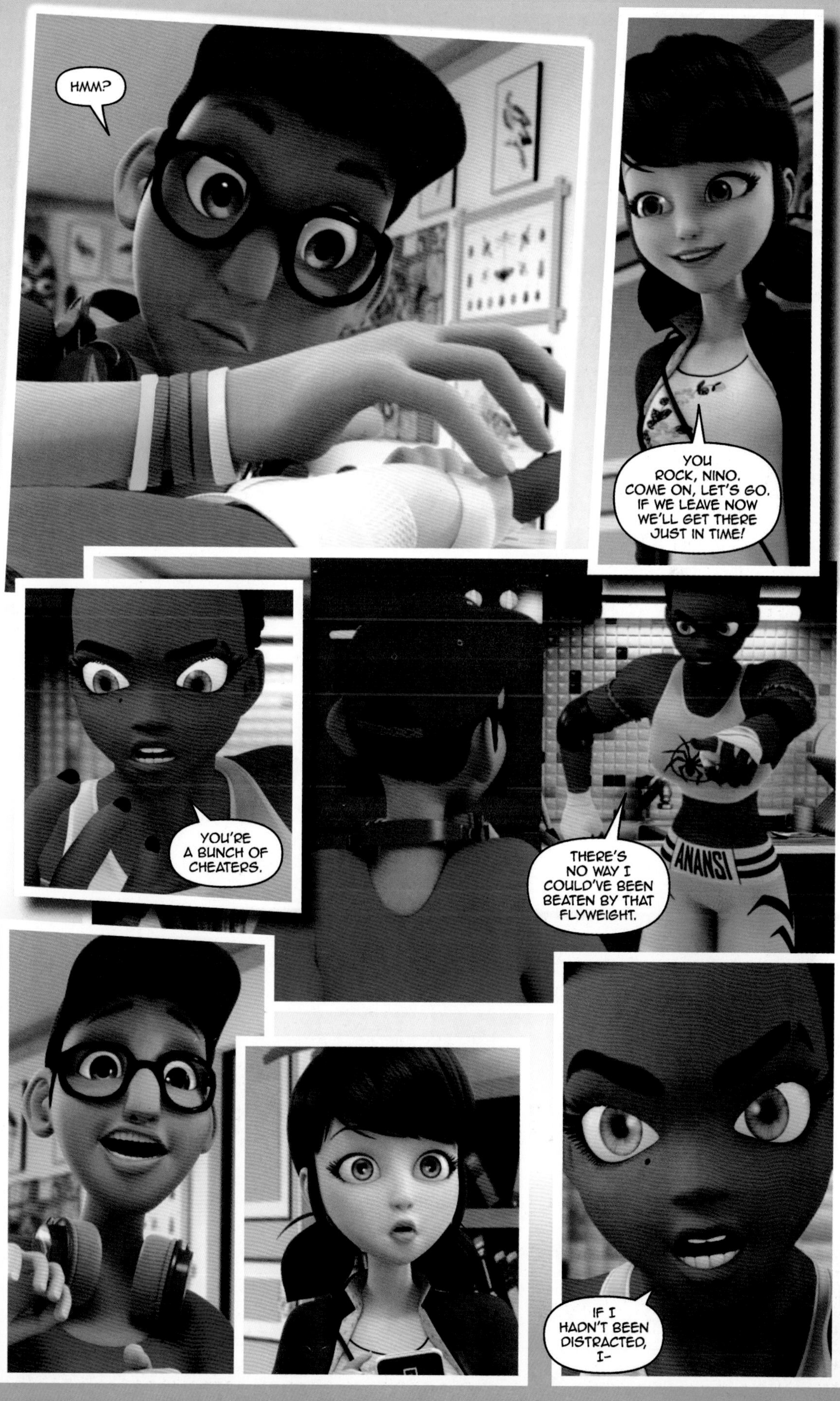
HMM?
YOU ROCK, NINO. COME ON, LET'S GO. IF WE LEAVE NOW WE'LL GET THERE JUST IN TIME!
YOU'RE A BUNCH OF CHEATERS.
THERE'S NO WAY I COULD'VE BEEN BEATEN BY THAT FLYWEIGHT.
ANANSI
IF I HADN'T BEEN DISTRACTED, I-

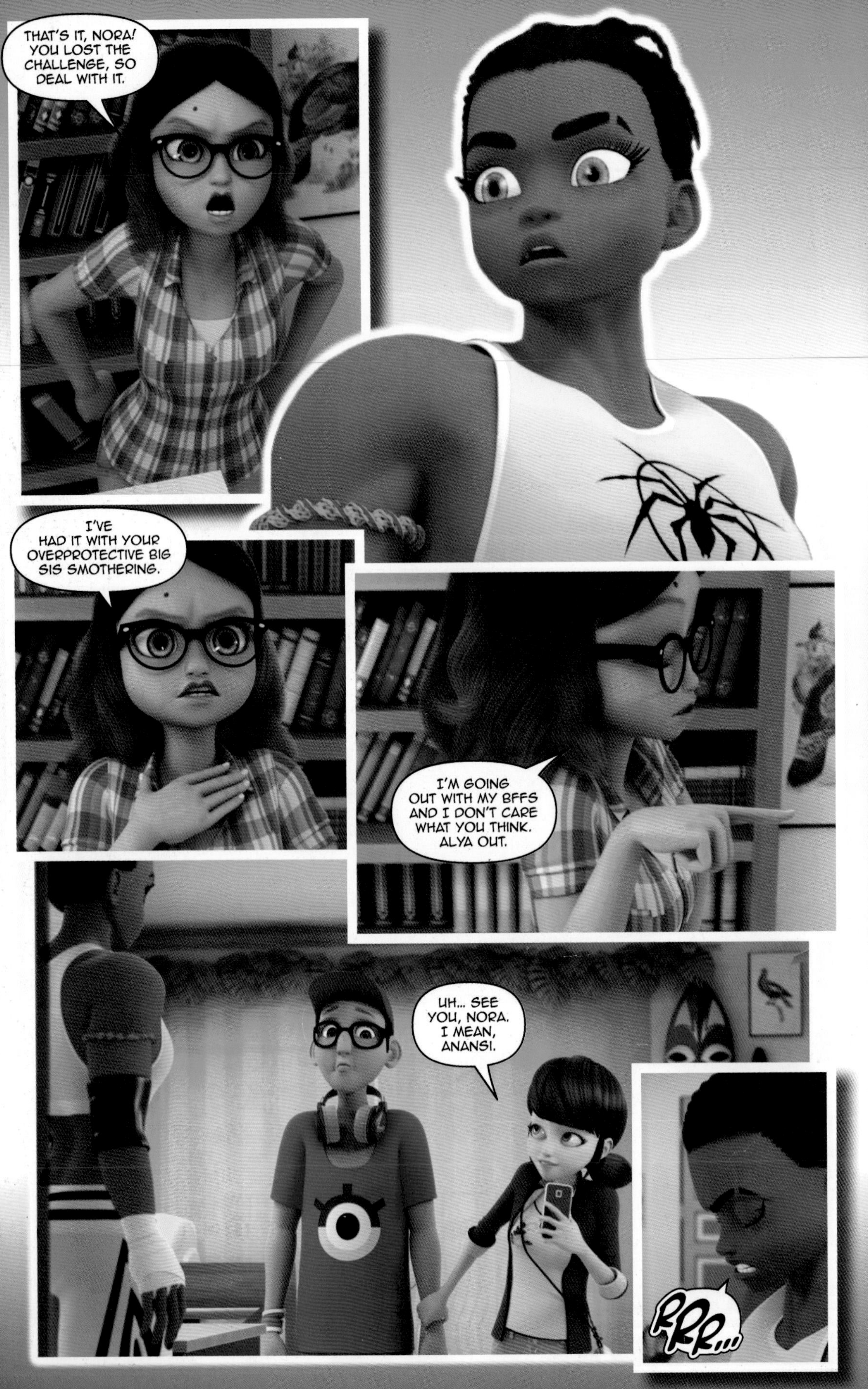
THAT'S IT, NORA! YOU LOST THE CHALLENGE, SO DEAL WITH IT.
I'VE HAD IT WITH YOUR OVERPROTECTIVE BIG SIS SMOTHERING.
I'M GOING OUT WITH MY BFFS AND I DON'T CARE WHAT YOU THINK. ALYA OUT.
UH... SEE YOU, NORA. I MEAN, ANANSI.
RRR...

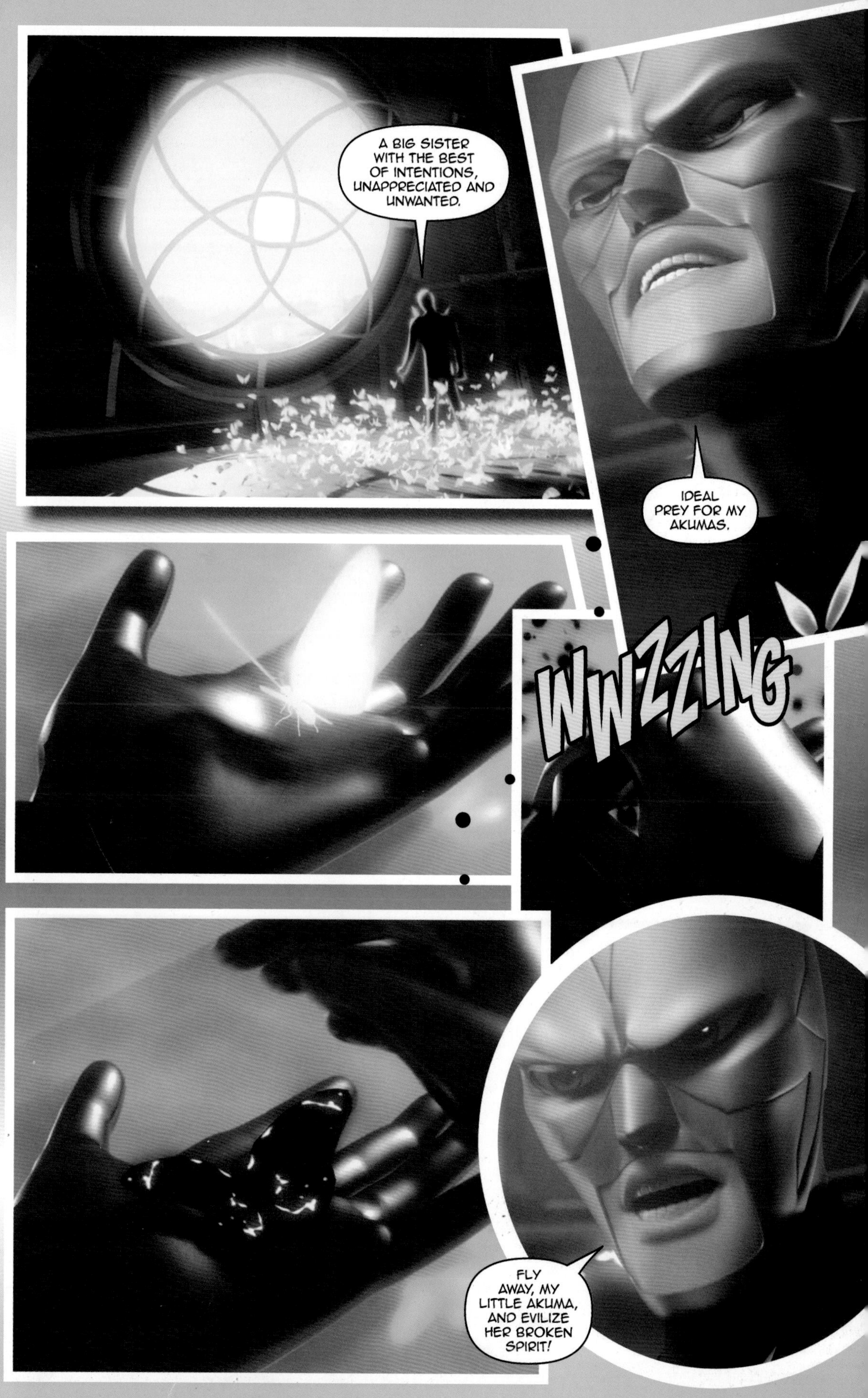
A BIG SISTER WITH THE BEST OF INTENTIONS, UNAPPRECIATED AND UNWANTED.
IDEAL PREY FOR MY AKUMAS.
WWZZING
FLY AWAY, MY LITTLE AKUMA, AND EVILIZE HER BROKEN SPIRIT!

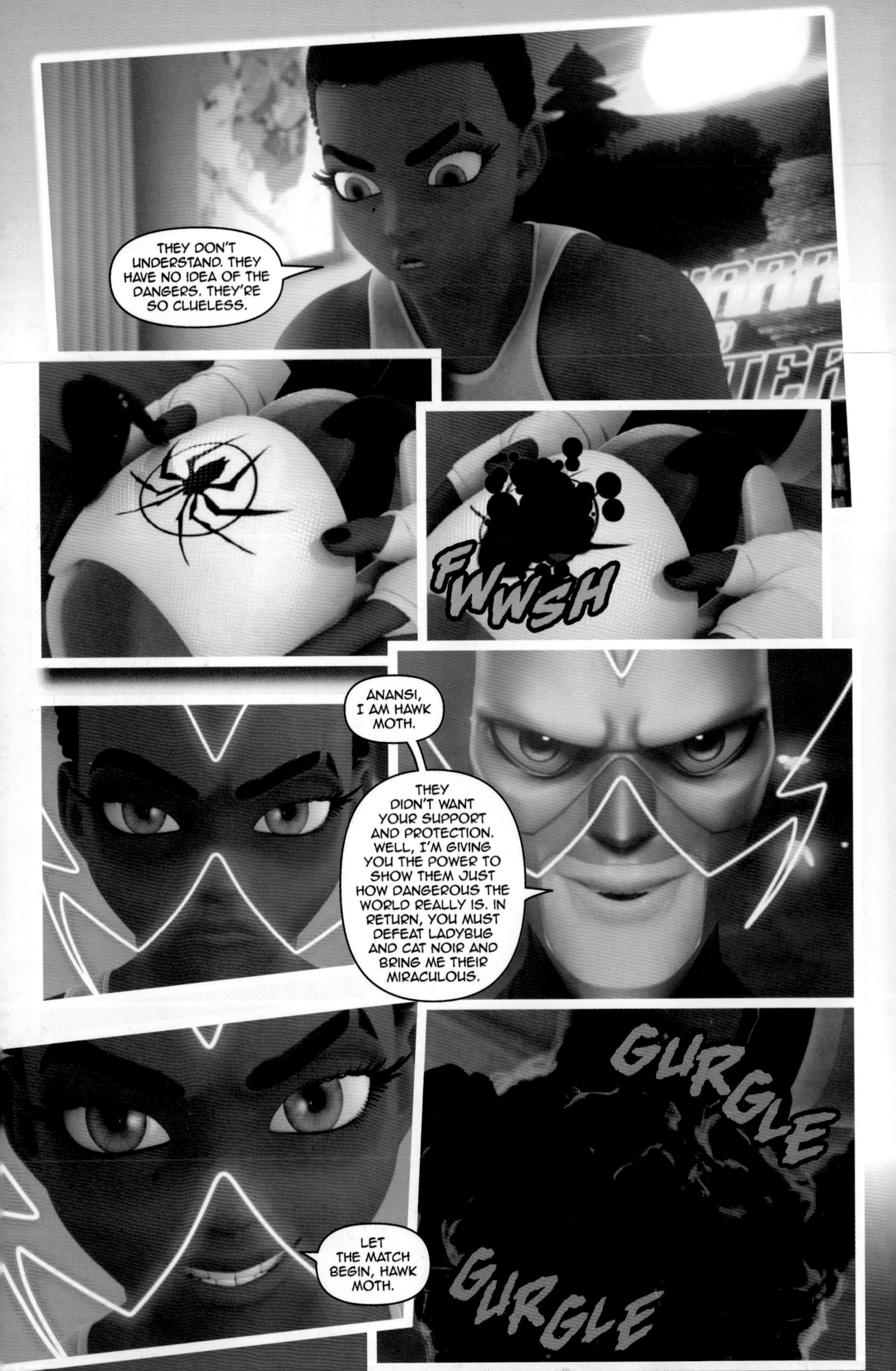
THEY DON'T UNDERSTAND. THEY HAVE NO IDEA OF THE DANGERS. THEY'RE SO CLUELESS.
FWWSH
ANANSI, I AM HAWK MOTH.
THEY DIDN'T WANT YOUR SUPPORT AND PROTECTION. WELL, I'M GIVING YOU THE POWER TO SHOW THEM JUST HOW DANGEROUS THE WORLD REALLY IS. IN RETURN, YOU MUST DEFEAT LADYBUG AND CAT NOIR AND BRING ME THEIR MIRACULOUS.
LET THE MATCH BEGIN, HAWK MOTH.
GURGLE
GURGLE

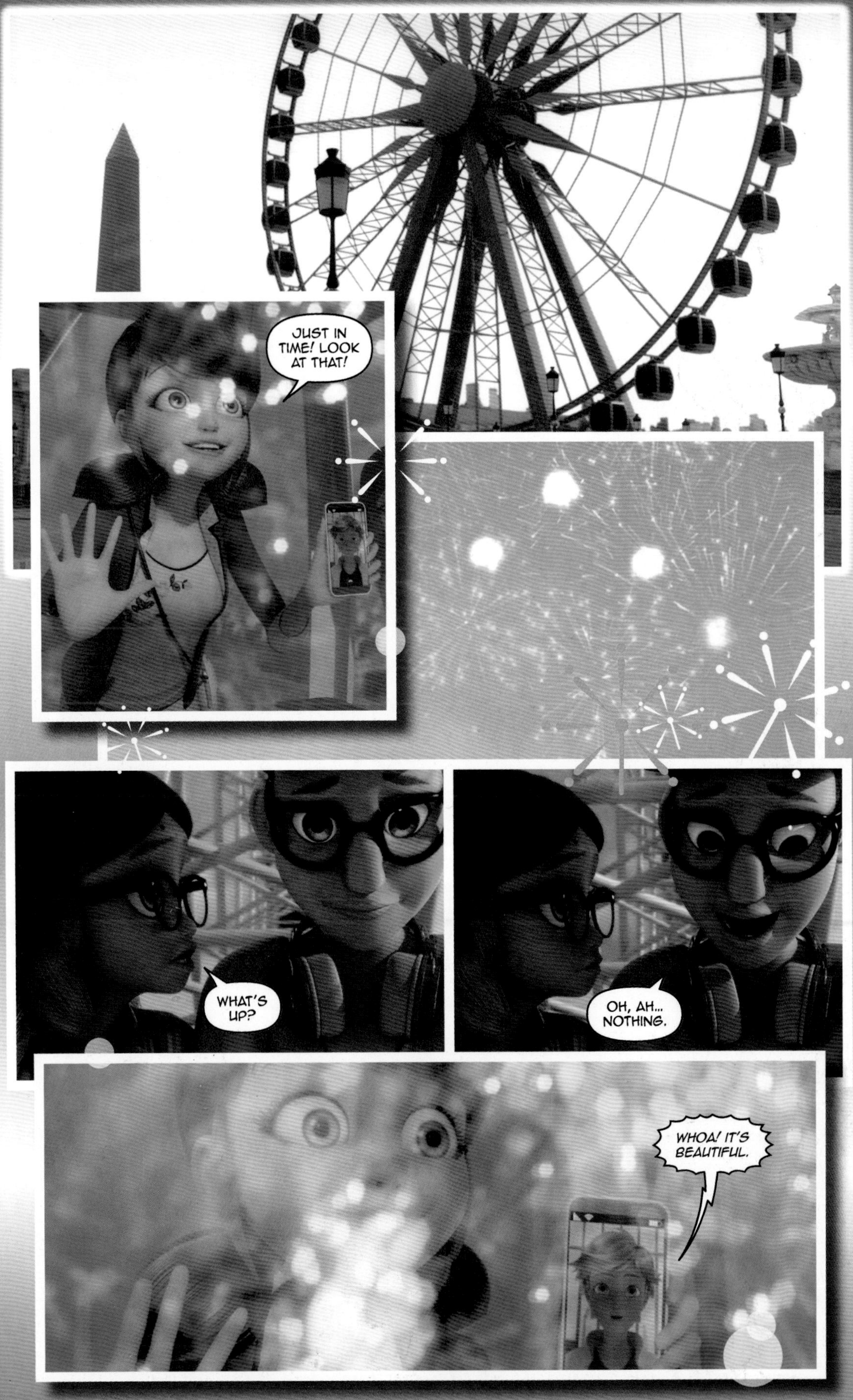
JUST IN TIME! LOOK AT THAT!
WHAT'S UP?
OH, AH... NOTHING.
WHOA! IT'S BEAUTIFUL.

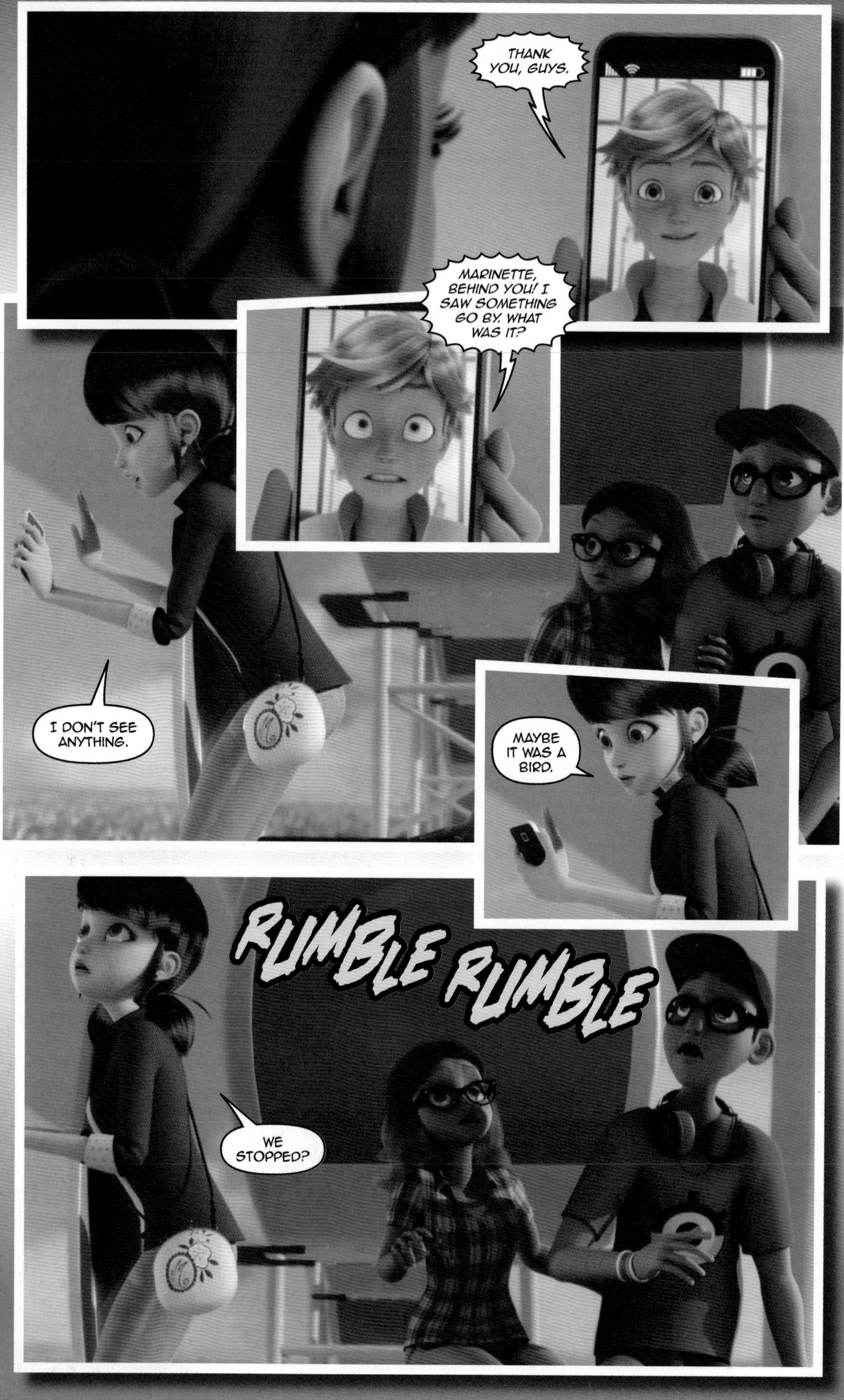
THANK YOU, GUYS.
MARINETTE, BEHIND YOU! I SAW SOMETHING GO BY. WHAT WAS IT?
I DON'T SEE ANYTHING.
MAYBE IT WAS A BIRD.
RUMBLE RUMBLE
WE STOPPED?

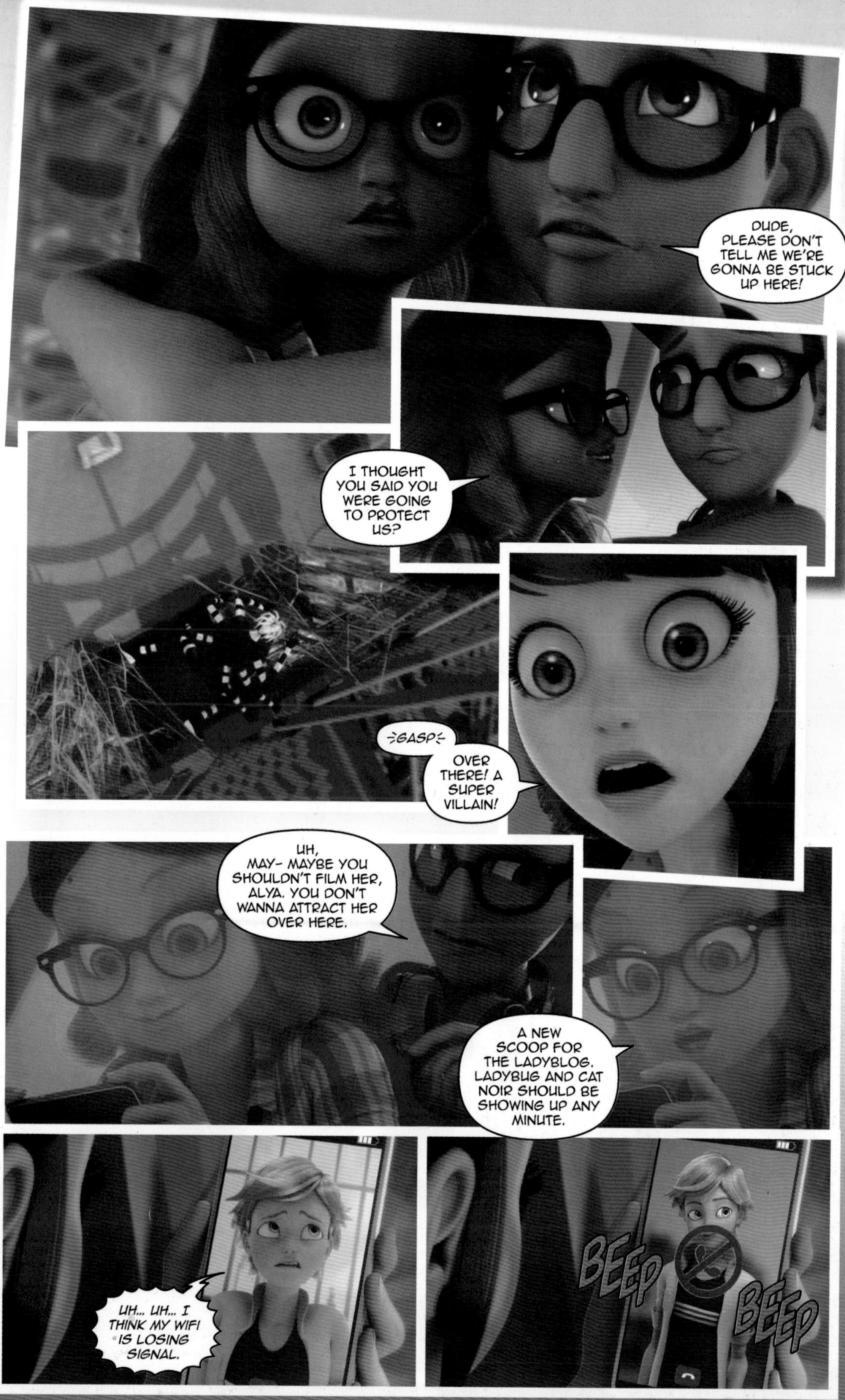
DUDE, PLEASE DON'T TELL ME WE'RE GONNA BE STUCK UP HERE!
I THOUGHT YOU SAID YOU WERE GOING TO PROTECT US?
GASP
OVER THERE! A SUPER VILLAIN!
UH, MAY- MAYBE YOU SHOULDN'T FILM HER, ALYA. YOU DON'T WANNA ATTRACT HER OVER HERE.
A NEW SCOOP FOR THE LADYBLOG. LADYBUG AND CAT NOIR SHOULD BE SHOWING UP ANY MINUTE.
UH... UH... I THINK MY WIFI IS LOSING SIGNAL.
BEEP
BEEP

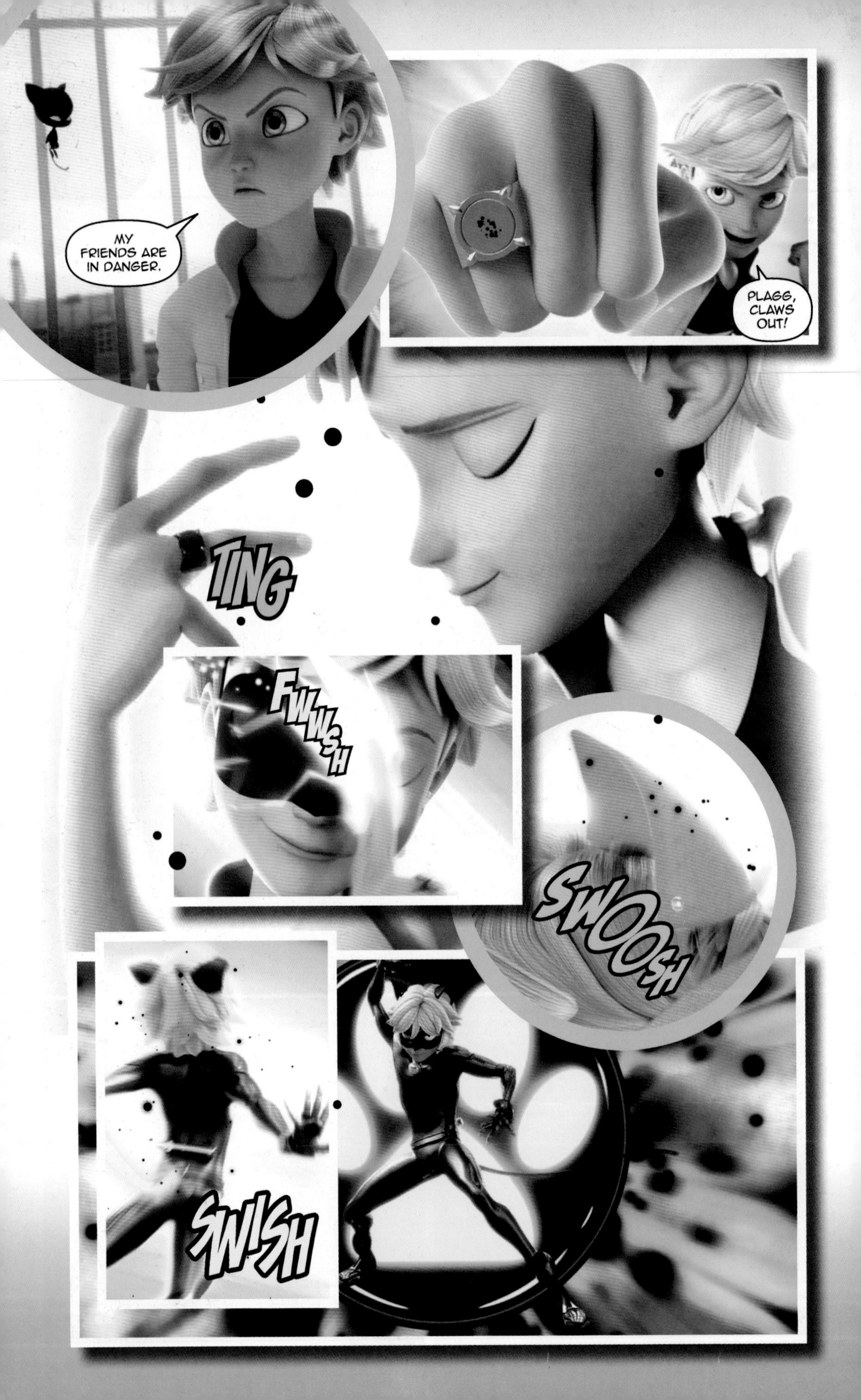
MY FRIENDS ARE IN DANGER.
PLAGG, CLAWS OUT!
TING
FWWSH
SWOOSH
SWISH

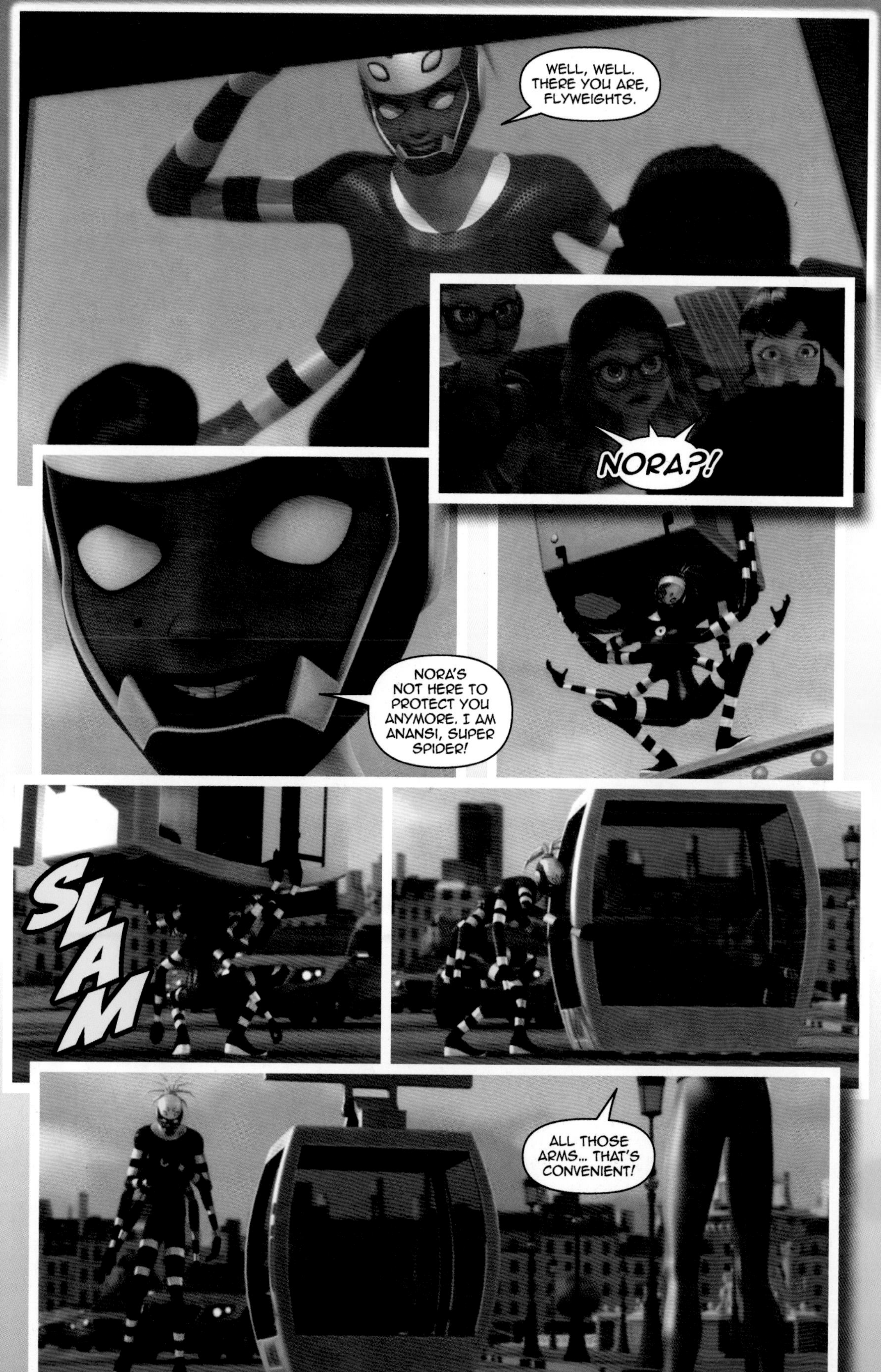
WELL, WELL. THERE YOU ARE, FLYWEIGHTS.
NORA?!
NORA'S NOT HERE TO PROTECT YOU ANYMORE. I AM ANANSI, SUPER SPIDER!
SLAM
ALL THOSE ARMS... THAT'S CONVENIENT!

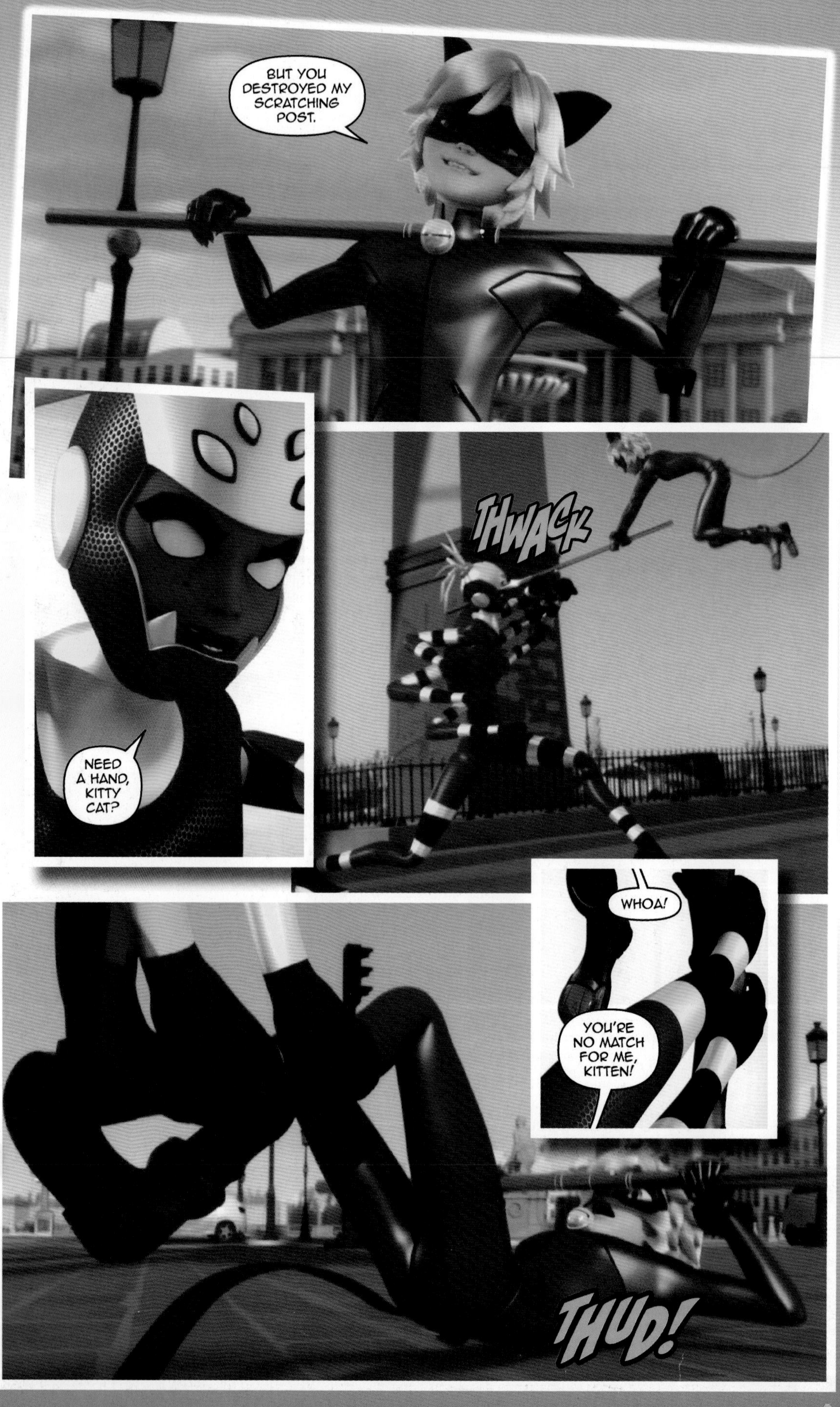
BUT YOU DESTROYED MY SCRATCHING POST.
NEED A HAND, KITTY CAT?
THWACK
WHOA!
YOU'RE NO MATCH FOR ME, KITTEN!
THUD!

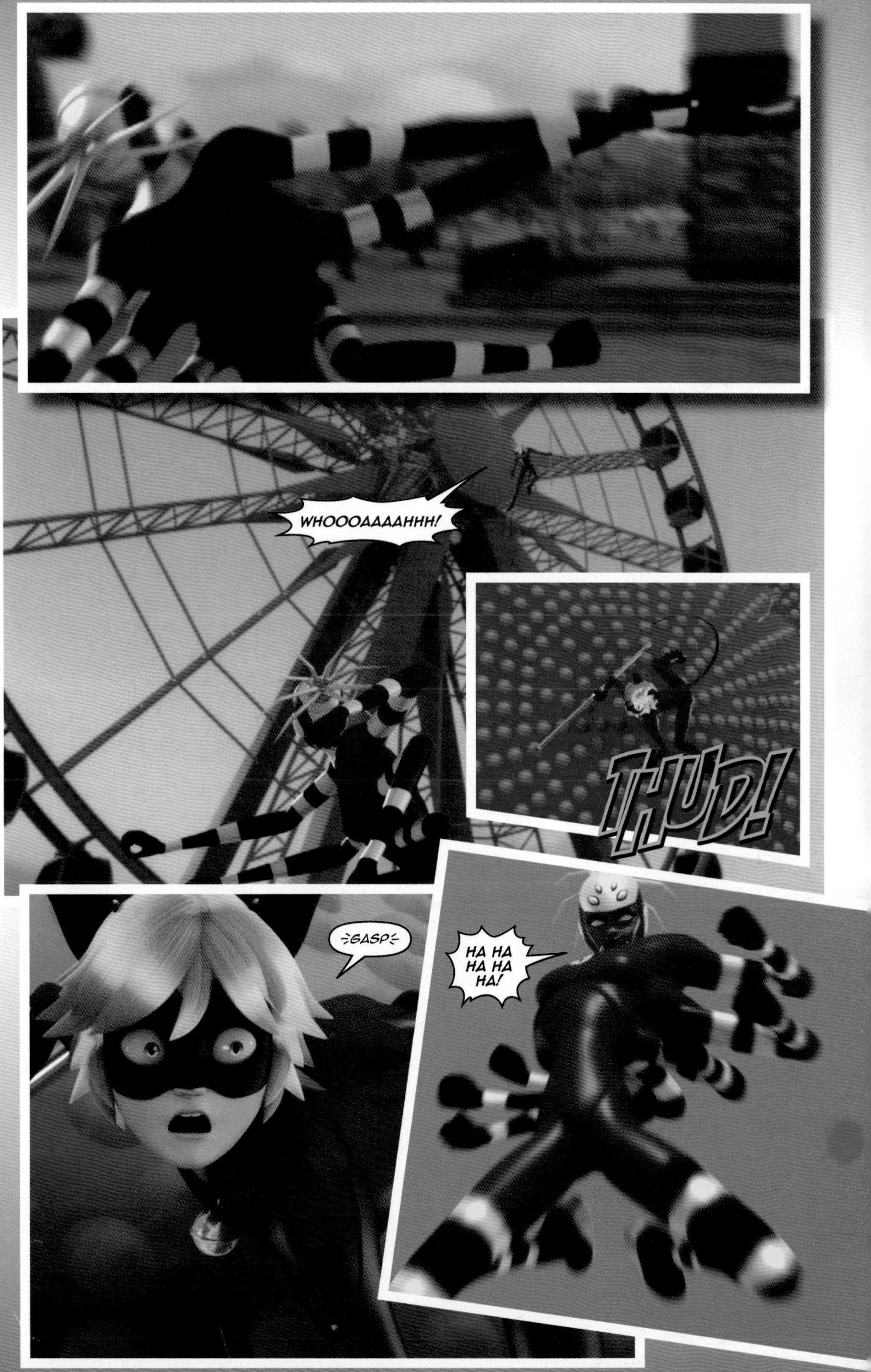
WHOOOAAAAHHH!
THUD!
GASP
HA HA HA HA HA!

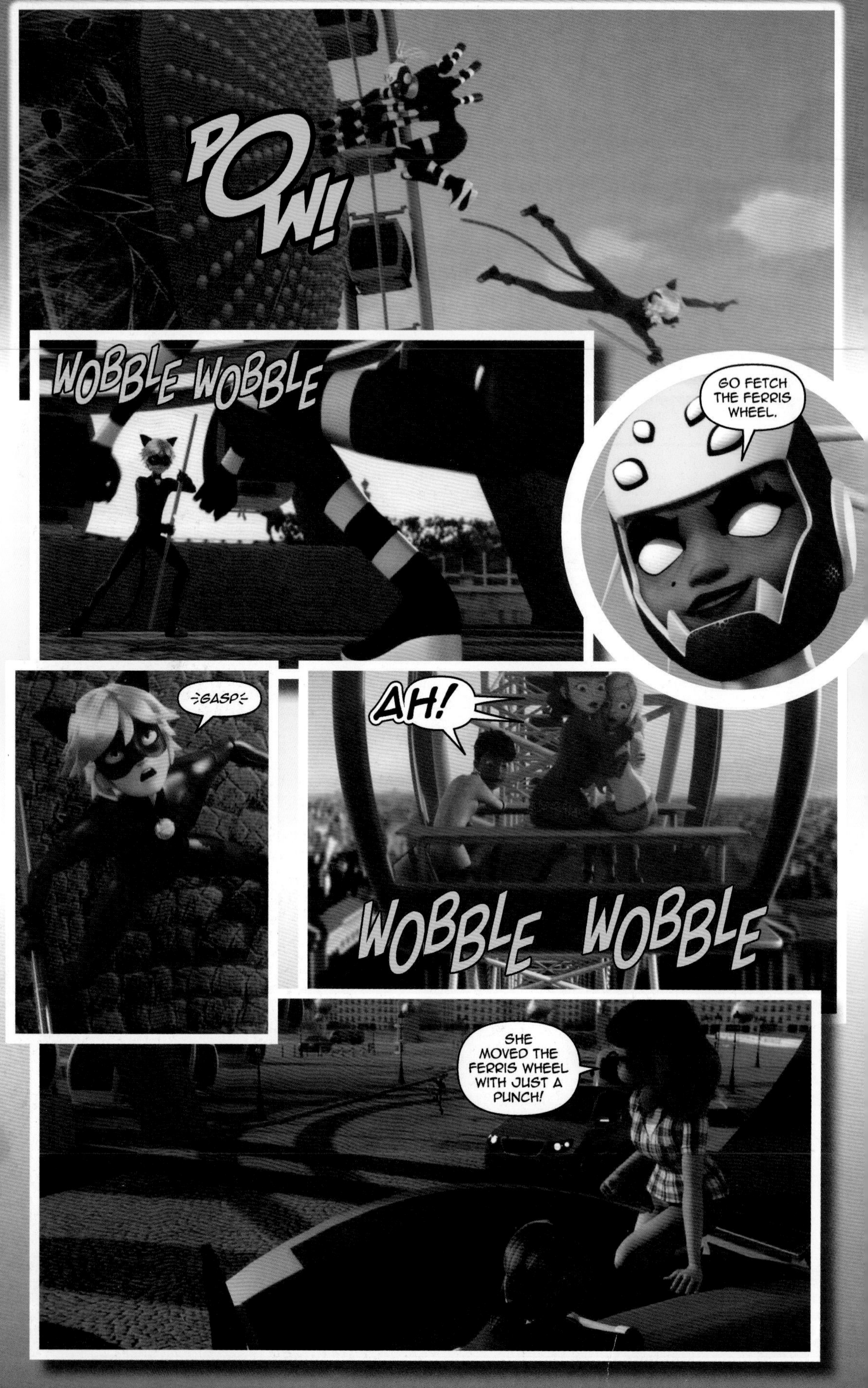
POW!
WOBBLE WOBBLE
GO FETCH THE FERRIS WHEEL.
GASP
AH!
WOBBLE WOBBLE
SHE MOVED THE FERRIS WHEEL WITH JUST A PUNCH!

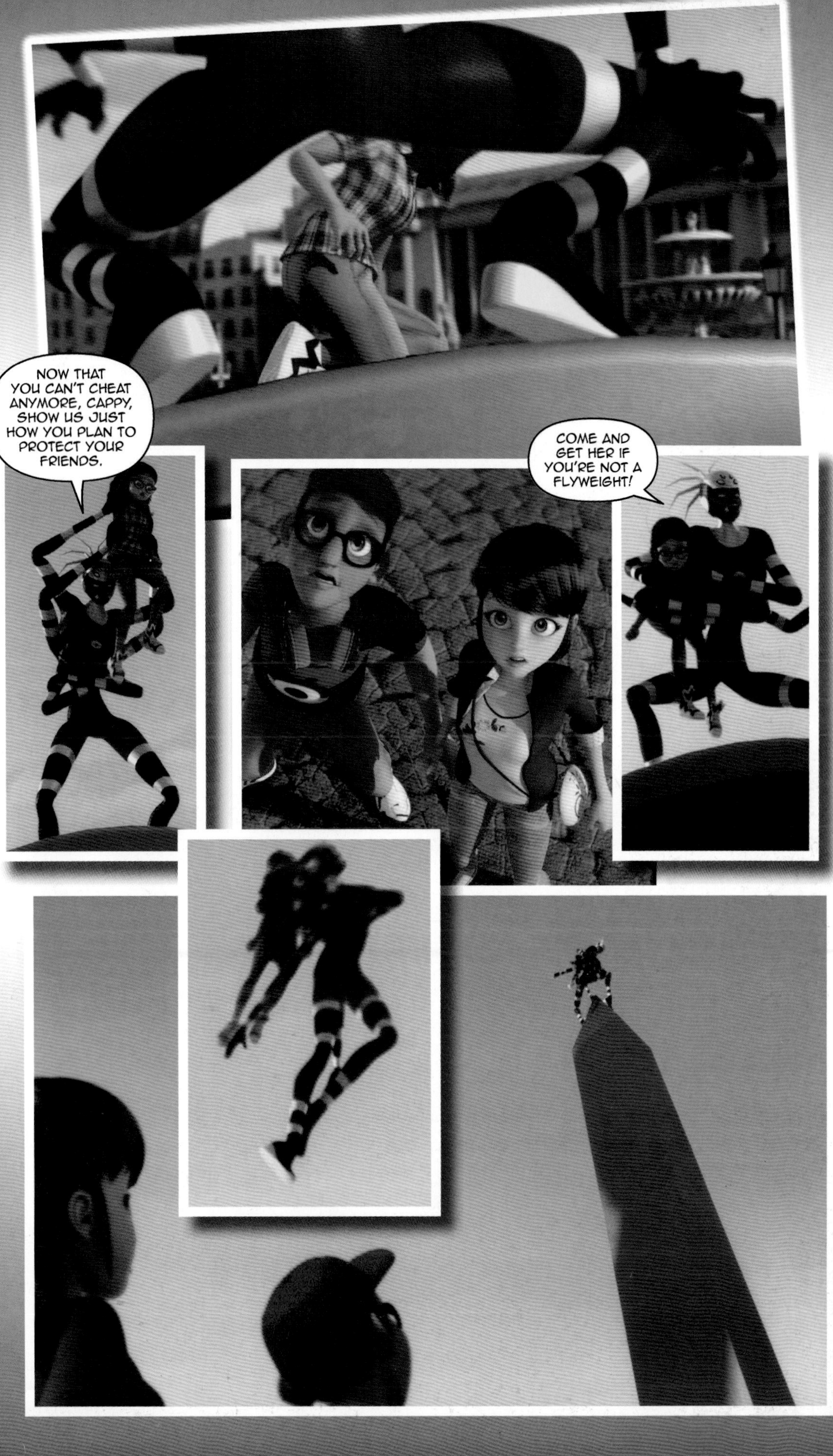
NOW THAT YOU CAN'T CHEAT ANYMORE, CAPPY, SHOW US JUST HOW YOU PLAN TO PROTECT YOUR FRIENDS.
COME AND GET HER IF YOU'RE NOT A FLYWEIGHT!

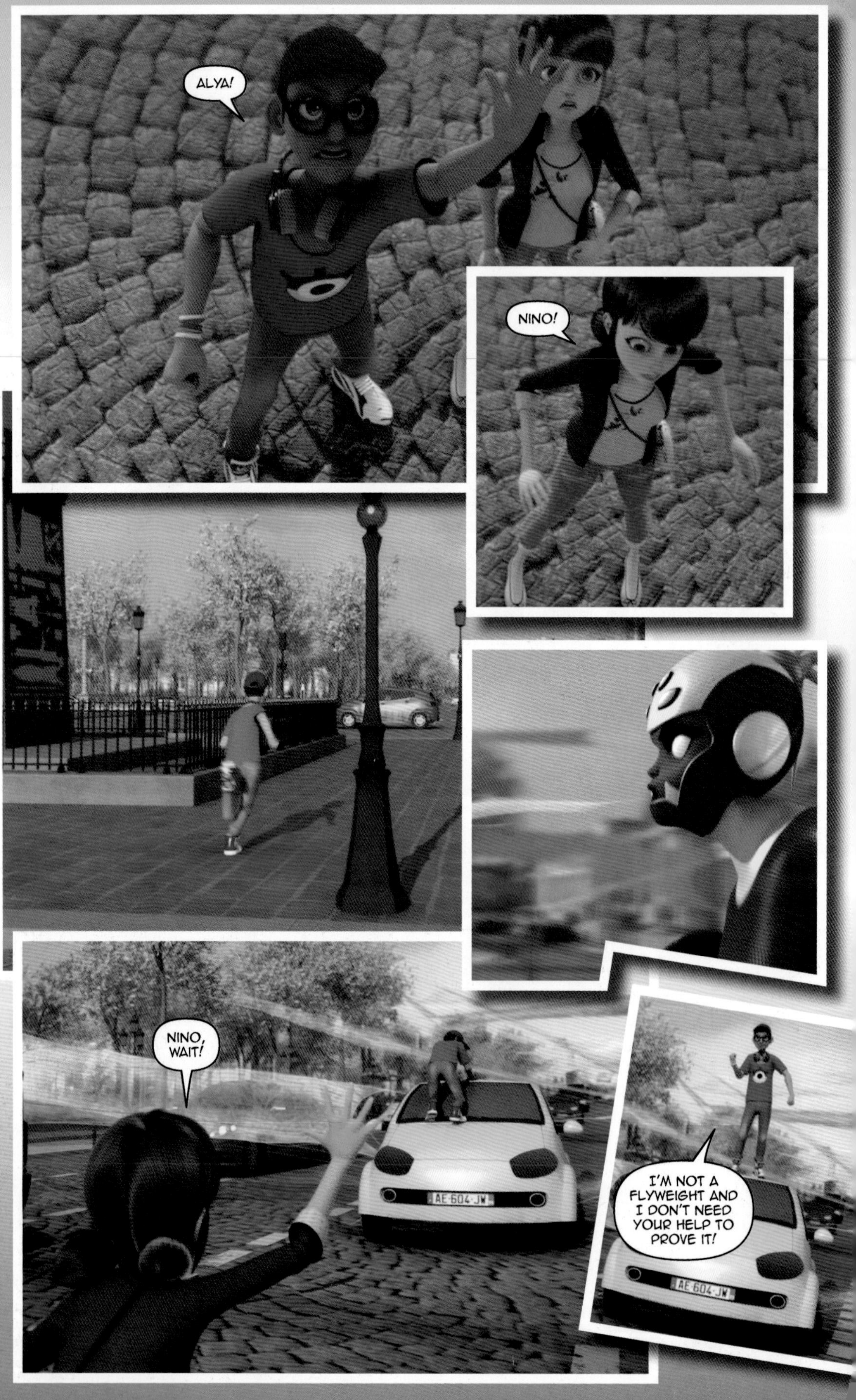
ALYA!
NINO!
NINO, WAIT!
I'M NOT A FLYWEIGHT AND I DON'T NEED YOUR HELP TO PROVE IT!

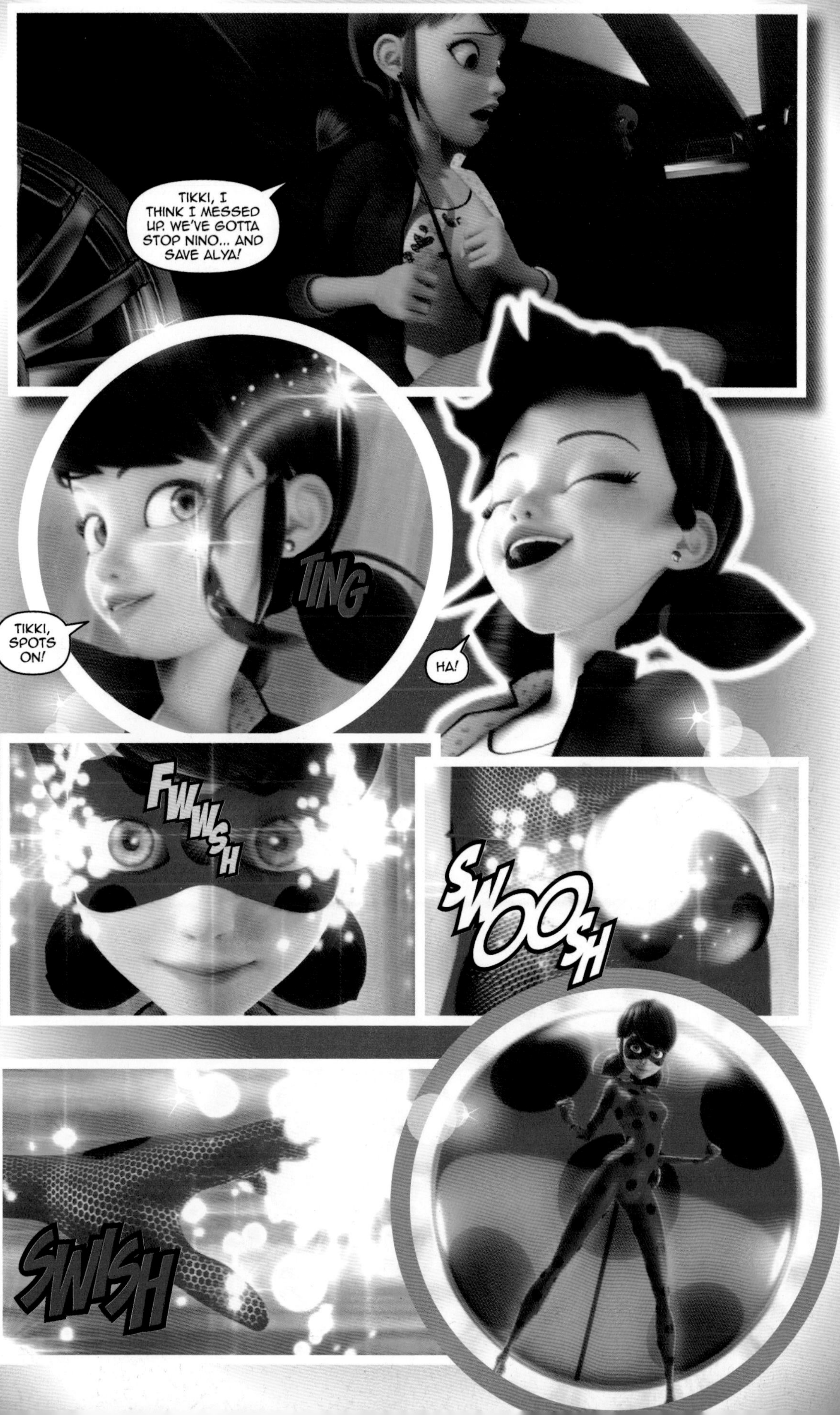
TIKKI, I THINK I MESSED UP. WE'VE GOTTA STOP NINO... AND SAVE ALYA!
TIKKI, SPOTS ON!
TING
HA!
FWWSH
SWOOSH
SWISH

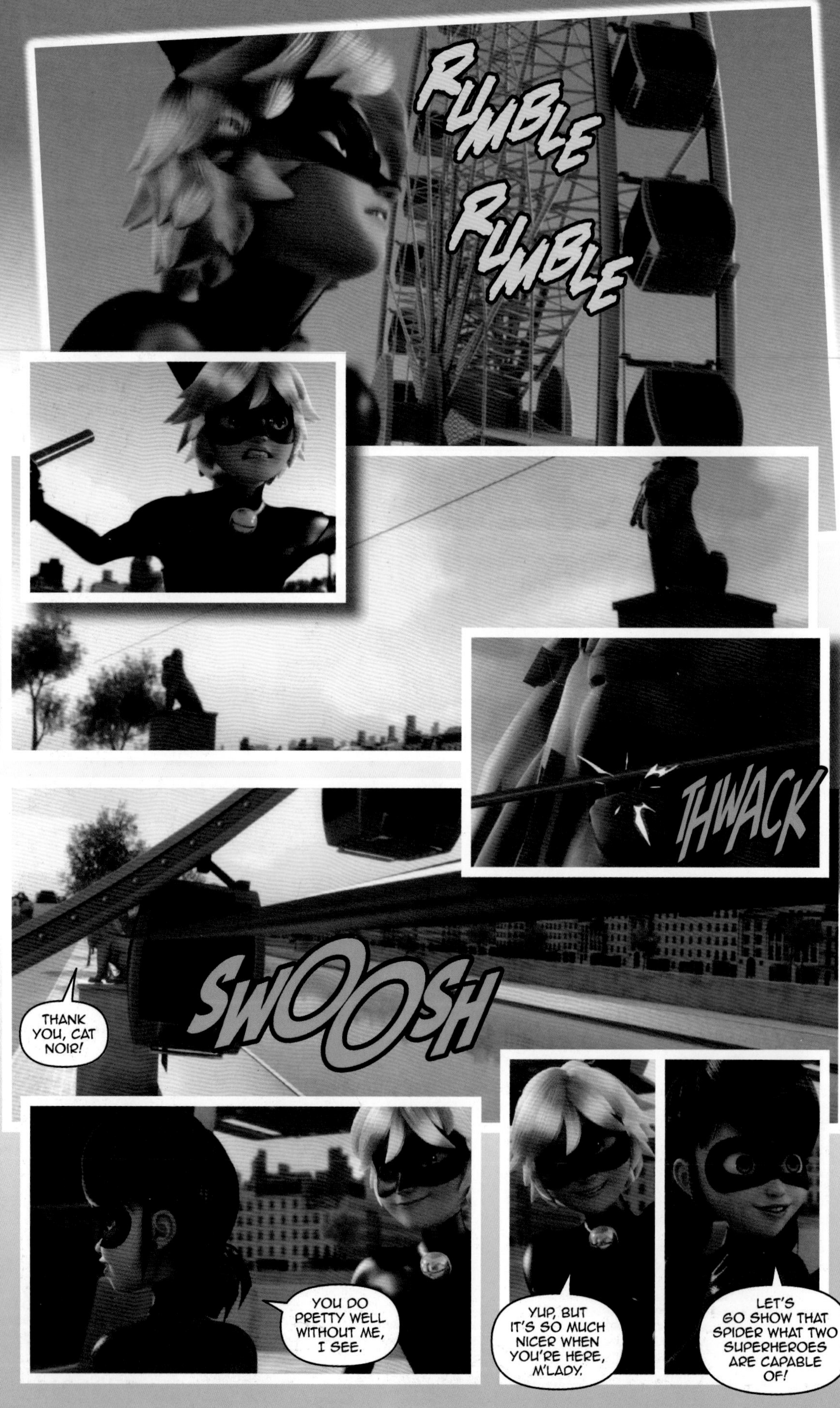
RUMBLE
RUMBLE
THWACK
SWOOSH
THANK YOU, CAT NOIR!
YOU DO PRETTY WELL WITHOUT ME, I SEE.
YUP, BUT IT'S SO MUCH NICER WHEN YOU'RE HERE, M'LADY.
LET'S GO SHOW THAT SPIDER WHAT TWO SUPERHEROES ARE CAPABLE OF!

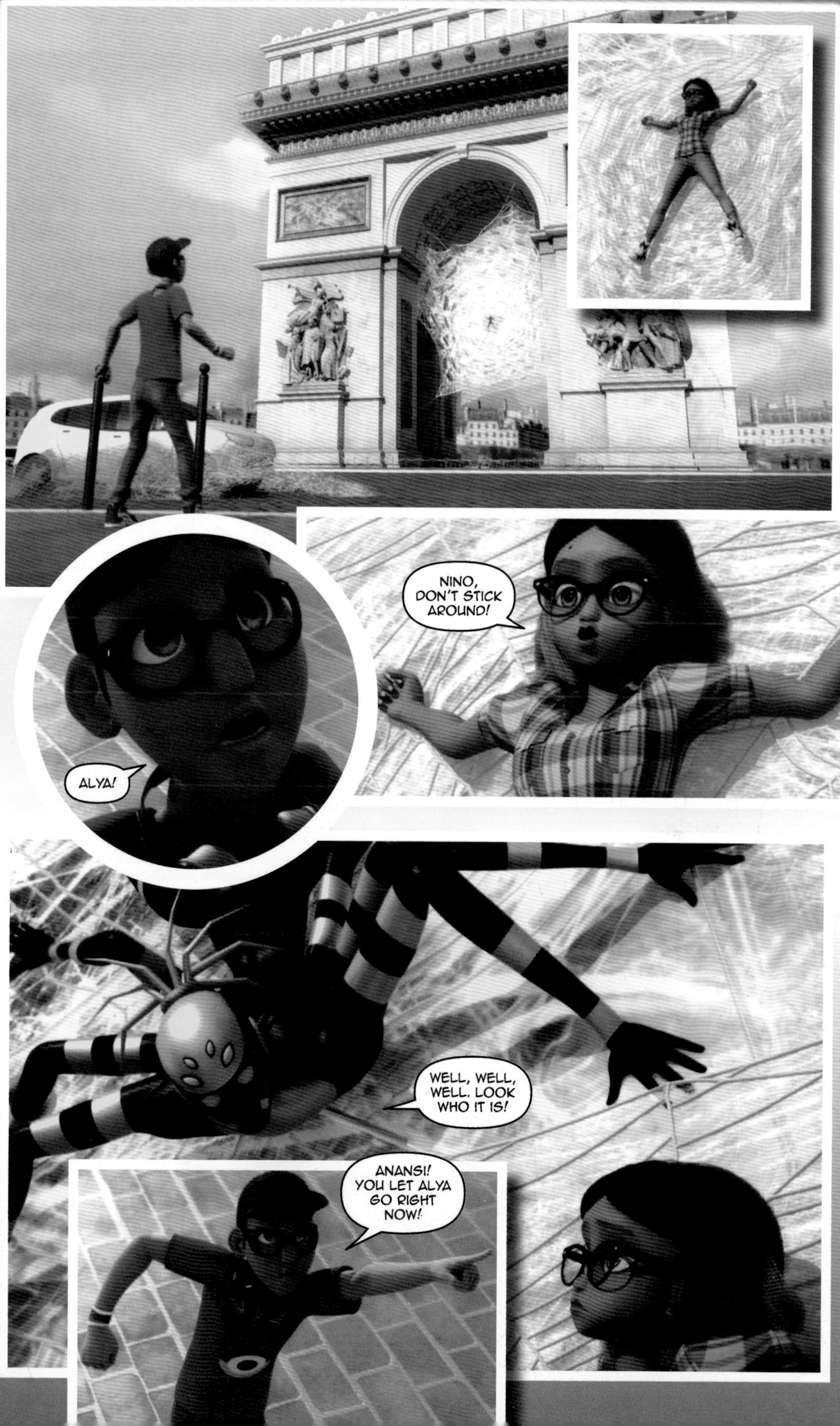
NINO, DON'T STICK AROUND!
ALYA!
WELL, WELL, WELL. LOOK WHO IT IS!
ANANSI! YOU LET ALYA GO RIGHT NOW!

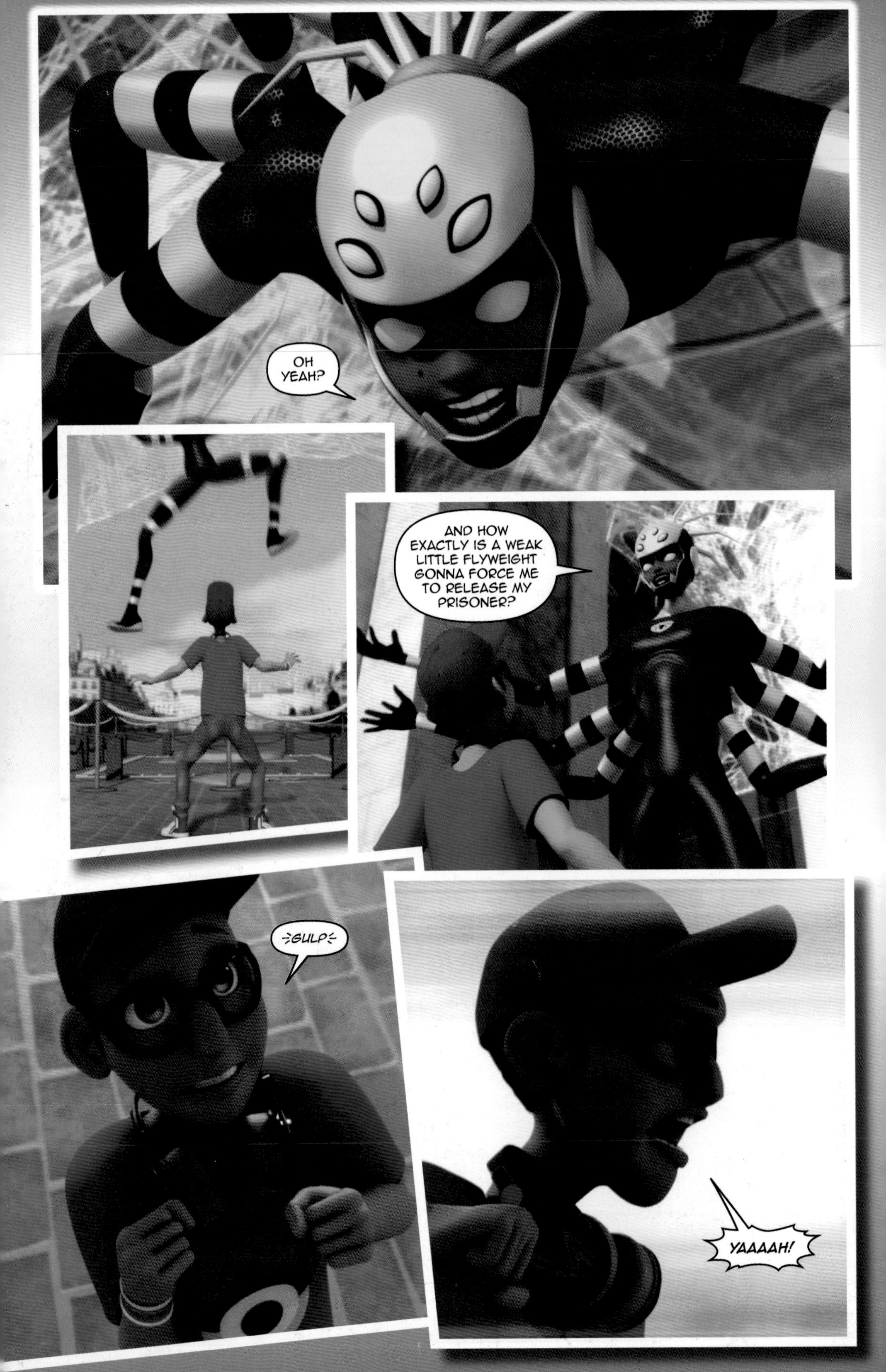
OH YEAH?
AND HOW EXACTLY IS A WEAK LITTLE FLYWEIGHT GONNA FORCE ME TO RELEASE MY PRISONER?
GULP
YAAAAH!

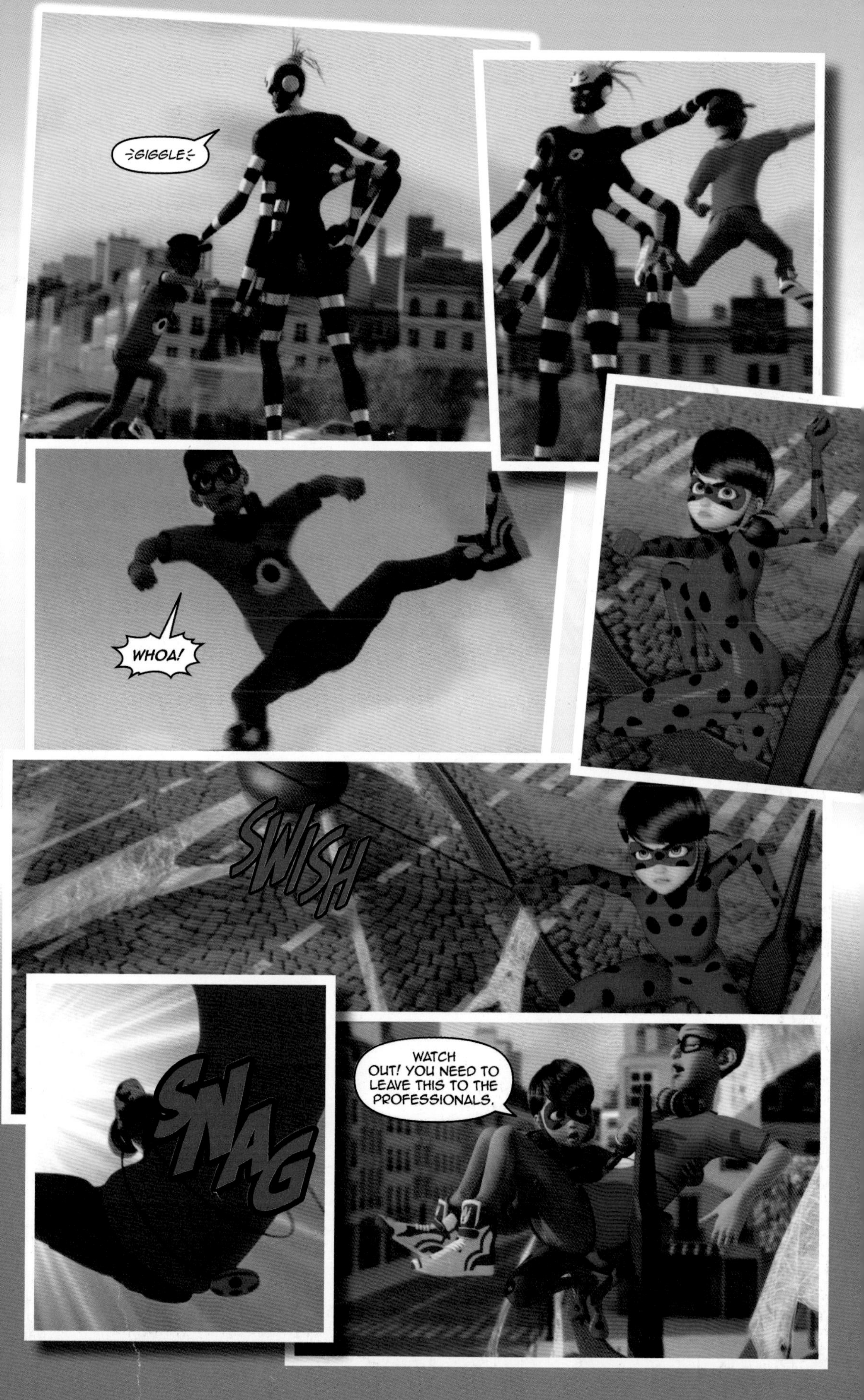
GIGGLE
WHOA!
SWISH
SNAG
WATCH OUT! YOU NEED TO LEAVE THIS TO THE PROFESSIONALS.

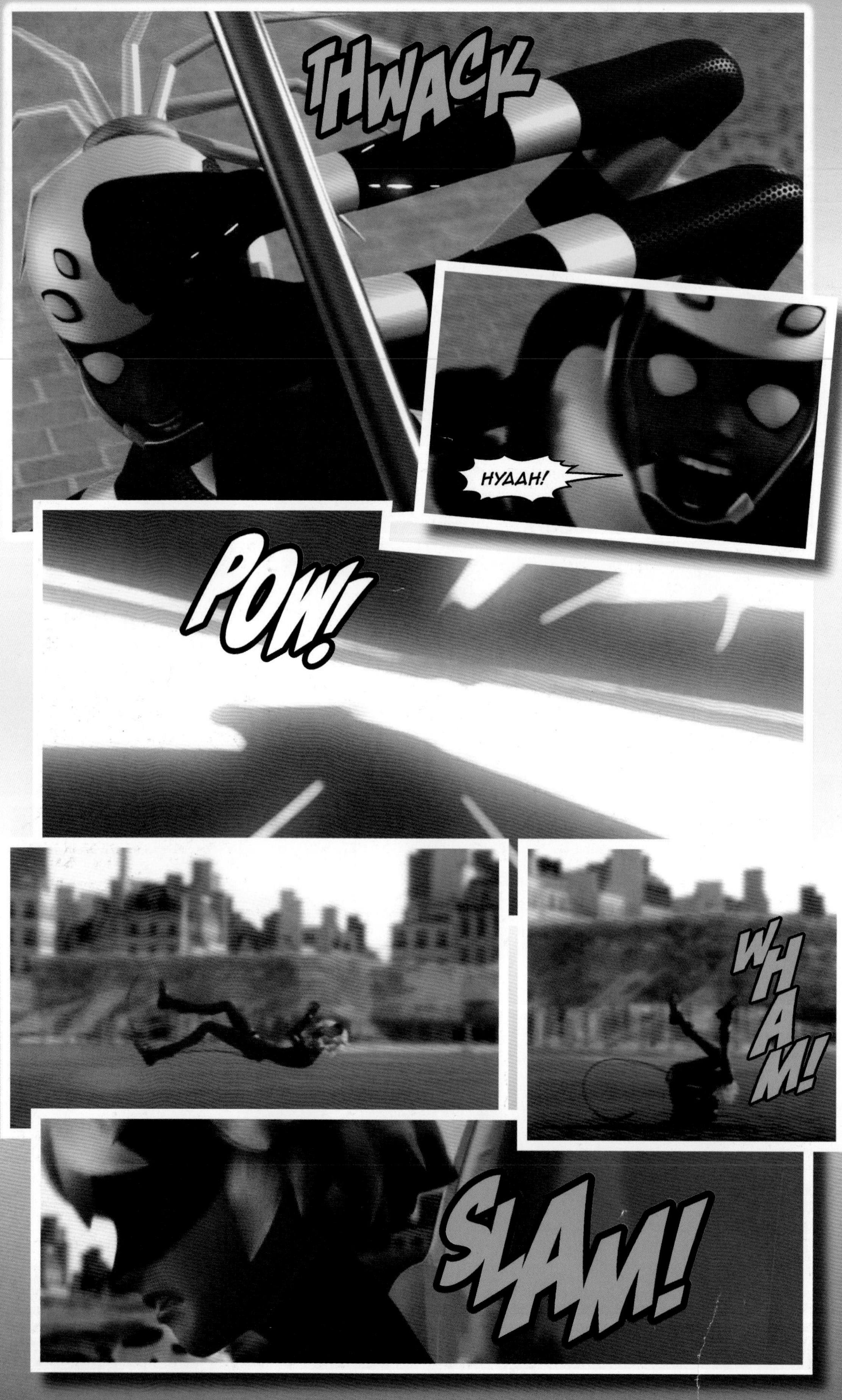
THWACK
HYAAH!
POW!
WHAM!
SLAM!

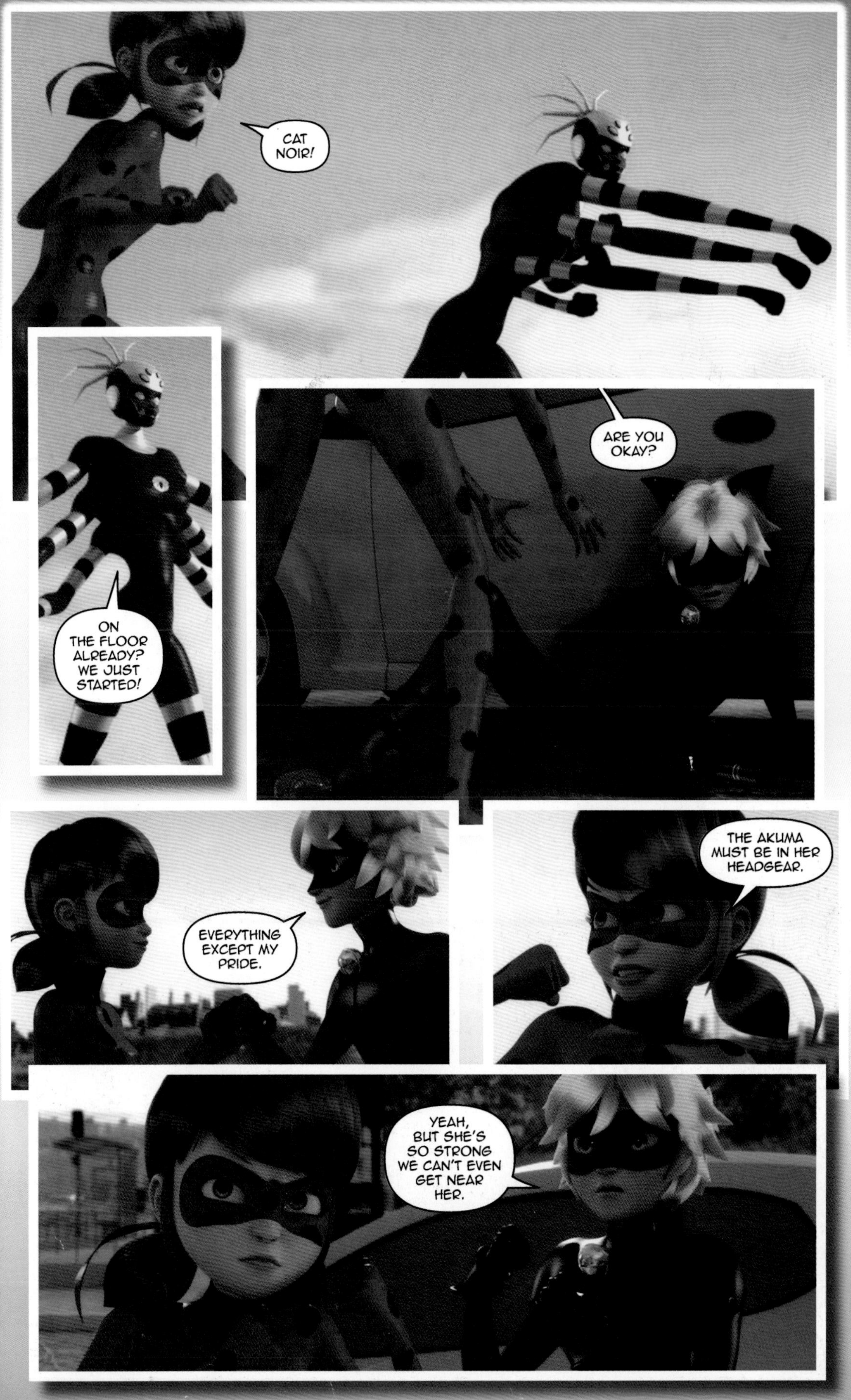
CAT NOIR!
ON THE FLOOR ALREADY? WE JUST STARTED!
ARE YOU OKAY?
EVERYTHING EXCEPT MY PRIDE.
THE AKUMA MUST BE IN HER HEADGEAR.
YEAH, BUT SHE'S SO STRONG WE CAN'T EVEN GET NEAR HER.

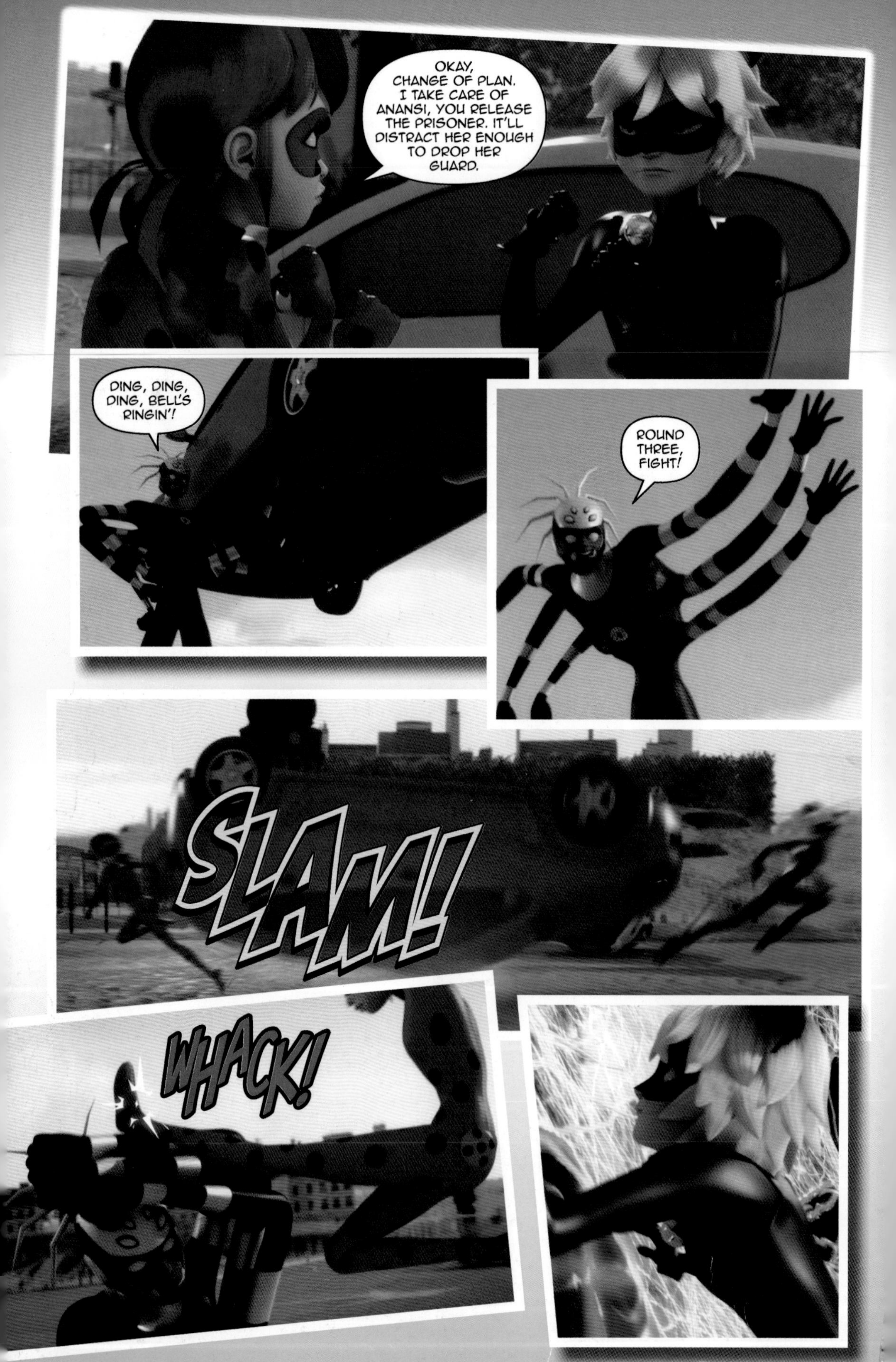
OKAY, CHANGE OF PLAN. I TAKE CARE OF ANANSI, YOU RELEASE THE PRISONER. IT'LL DISTRACT HER ENOUGH TO DROP HER GUARD.
DING, DING, DING, BELL'S RINGIN'!
ROUND THREE, FIGHT!
SLAM!
WHACK!

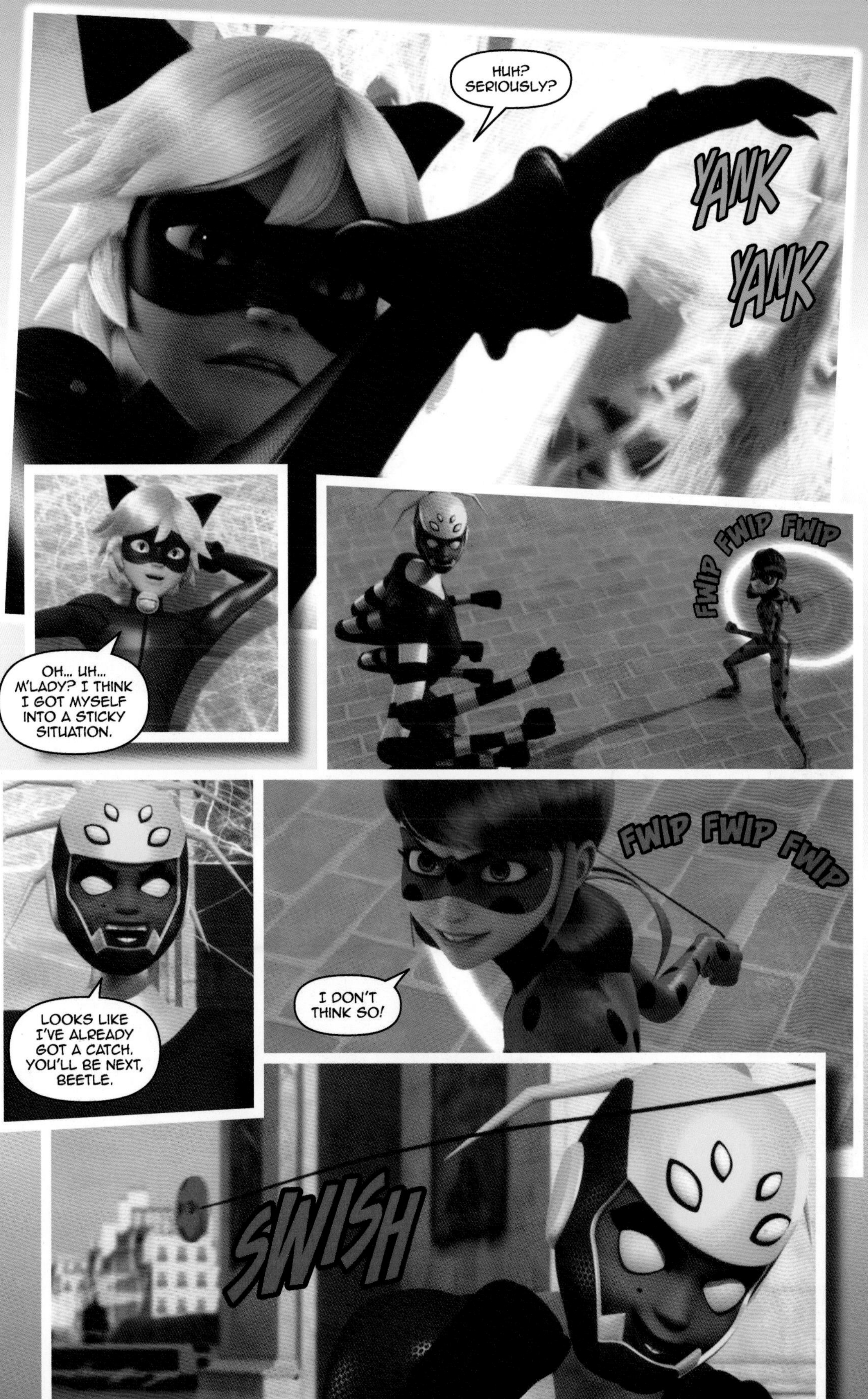
HUH? SERIOUSLY?
YANK
YANK
OH... UH... M'LADY? I THINK I GOT MYSELF INTO A STICKY SITUATION.
FWIP FWIP FWIP
LOOKS LIKE I'VE ALREADY GOT A CATCH. YOU'LL BE NEXT, BEETLE.
FWIP FWIP FWIP
I DON'T THINK SO!
SWISH

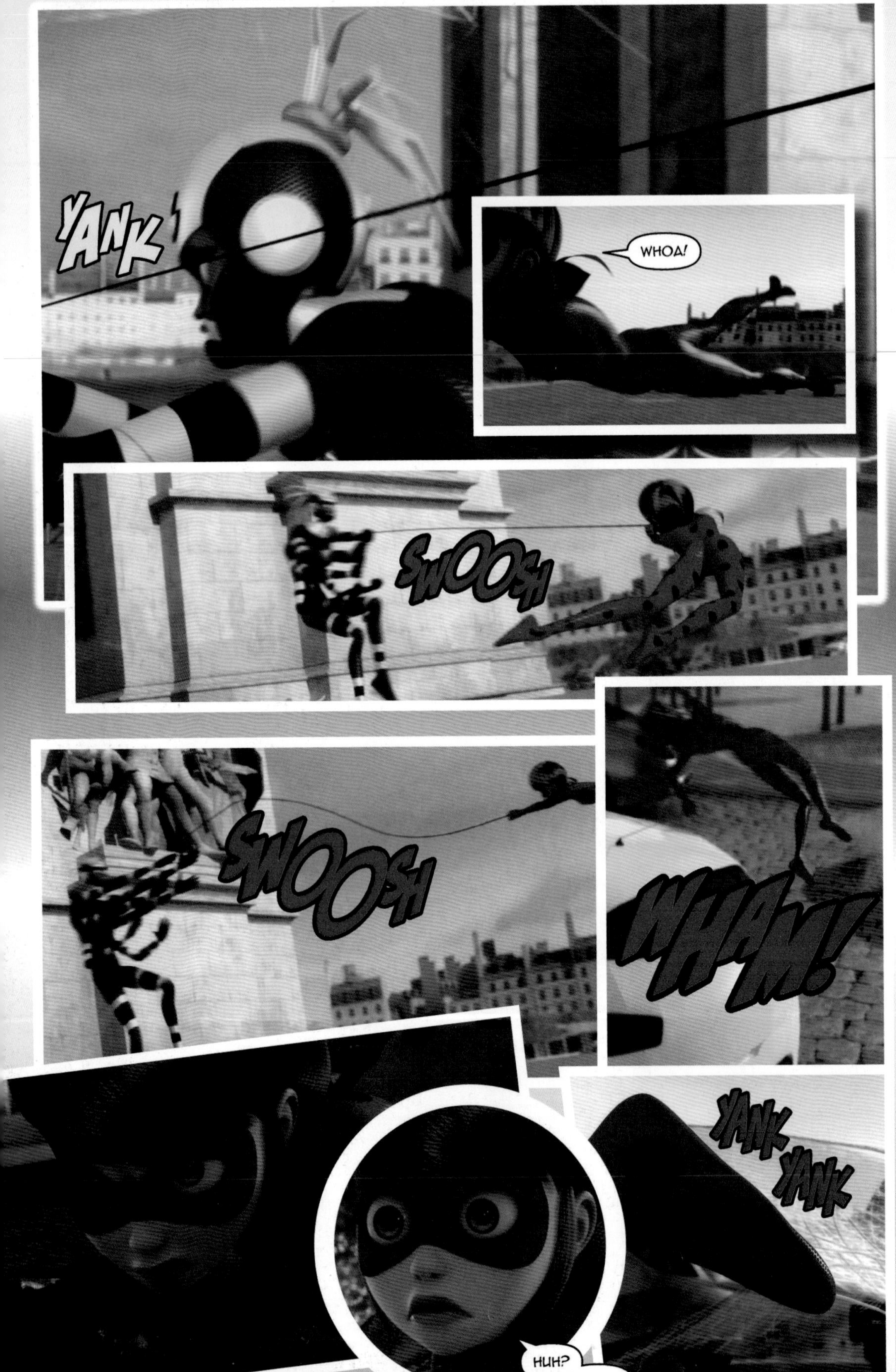
YANK
WHOA!
SWOOSH
SWOOSH
WHAM!
YANK YANK
HUH?
I'M STUCK!

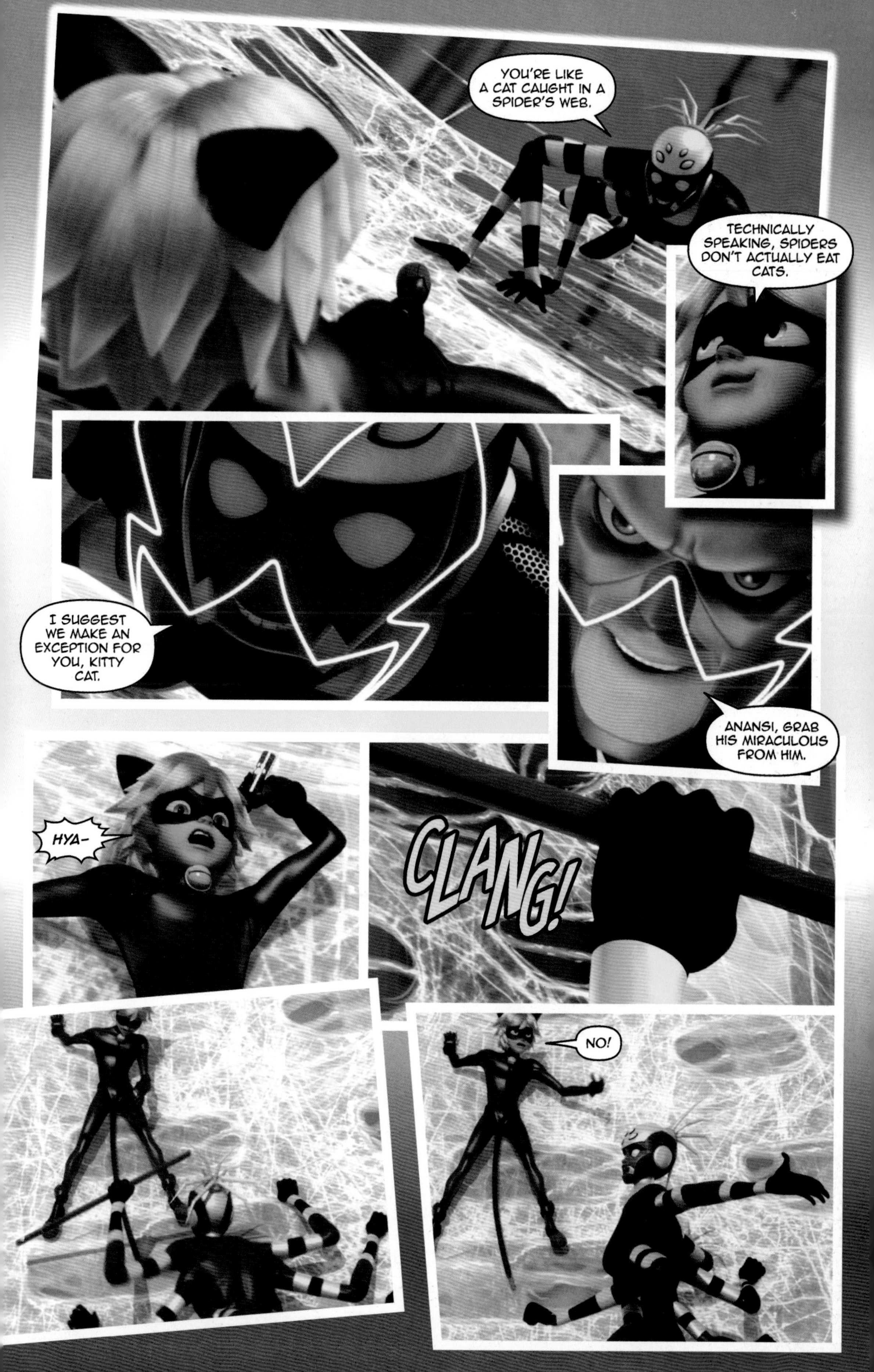
YOU'RE LIKE A CAT CAUGHT IN A SPIDER'S WEB.
TECHNICALLY SPEAKING, SPIDERS DON'T ACTUALLY EAT CATS.
I SUGGEST WE MAKE AN EXCEPTION FOR YOU, KITTY CAT.
ANANSI, GRAB HIS MIRACULOUS FROM HIM.
HYA-
CLANG!
NO!

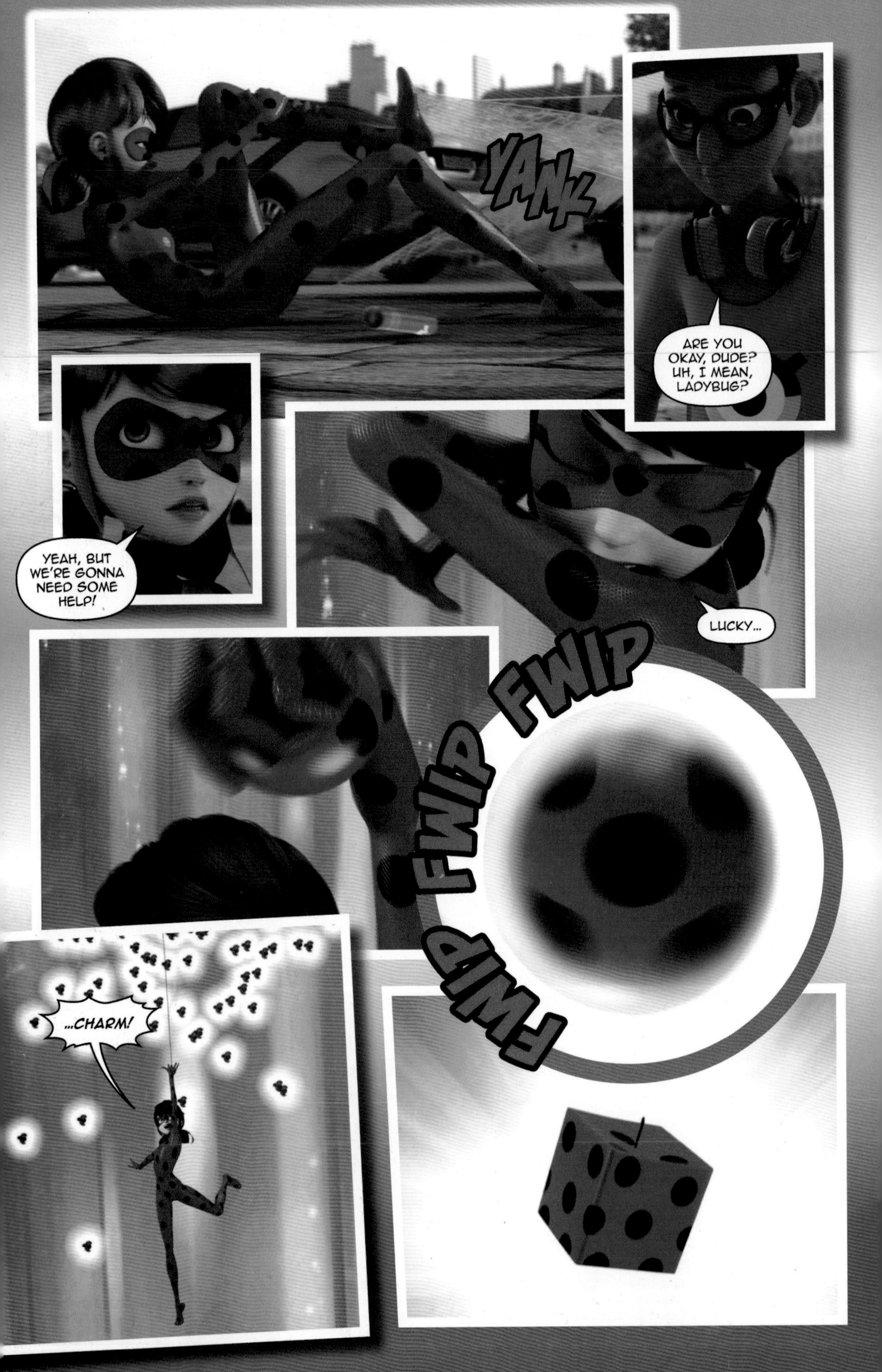
YANK
ARE YOU OKAY, DUDE? UH, I MEAN, LADYBUG?
YEAH, BUT WE'RE GONNA NEED SOME HELP!
LUCKY...
FWIP FWIP FWIP FWIP
...CHARM!

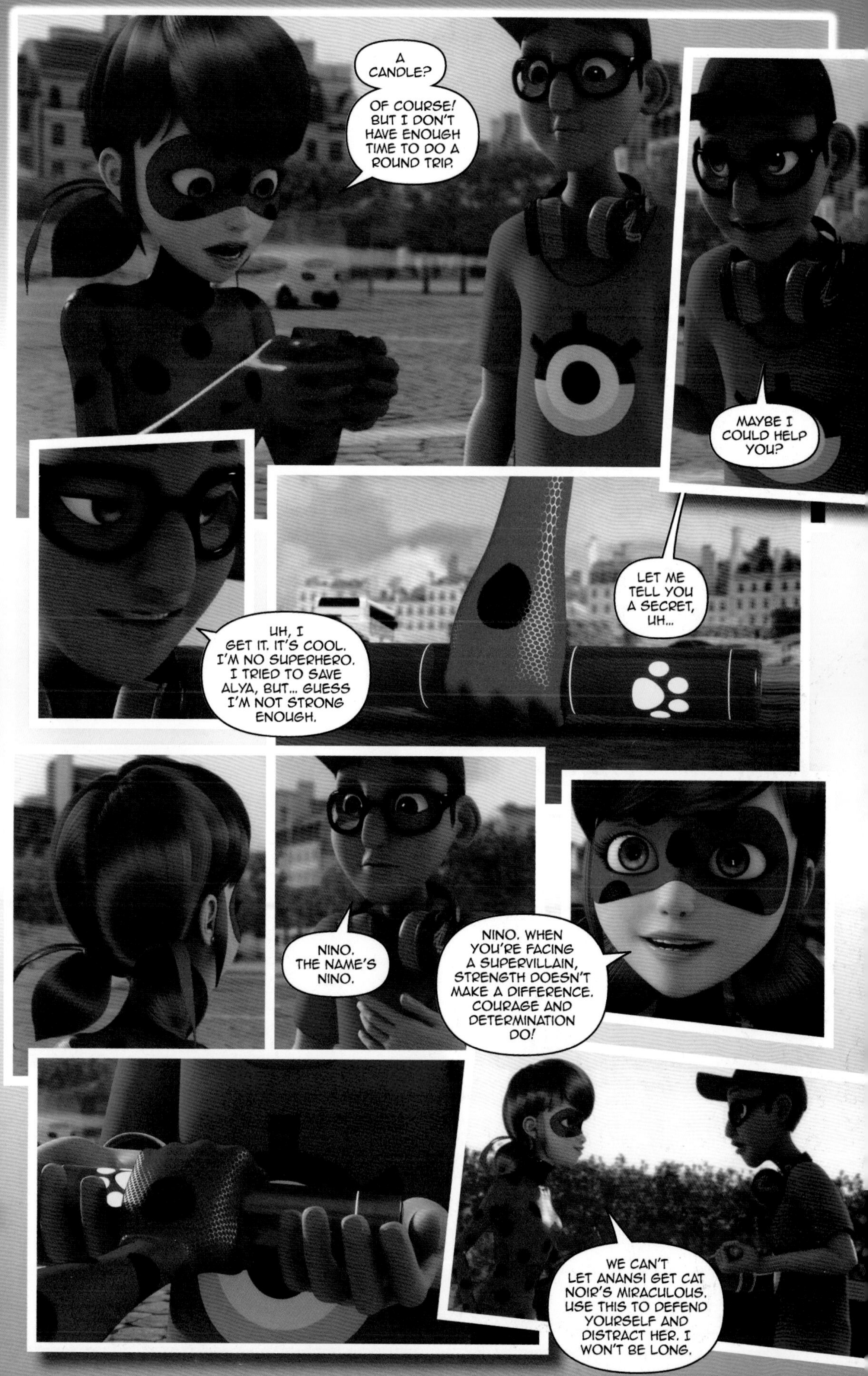
A CANDLE?
OF COURSE! BUT I DON'T HAVE ENOUGH TIME TO DO A ROUND TRIP.
MAYBE I COULD HELP YOU?
UH, I GET IT. IT'S COOL. I'M NO SUPERHERO. I TRIED TO SAVE ALYA, BUT... GUESS I'M NOT STRONG ENOUGH.
LET ME TELL YOU A SECRET, UH...
NINO. THE NAME'S NINO.
NINO. WHEN YOU'RE FACING A SUPERVILLAIN, STRENGTH DOESN'T MAKE A DIFFERENCE. COURAGE AND DETERMINATION DO!
WE CAN'T LET ANANSI GET CAT NOIR'S MIRACULOUS. USE THIS TO DEFEND YOURSELF AND DISTRACT HER. I WON'T BE LONG.

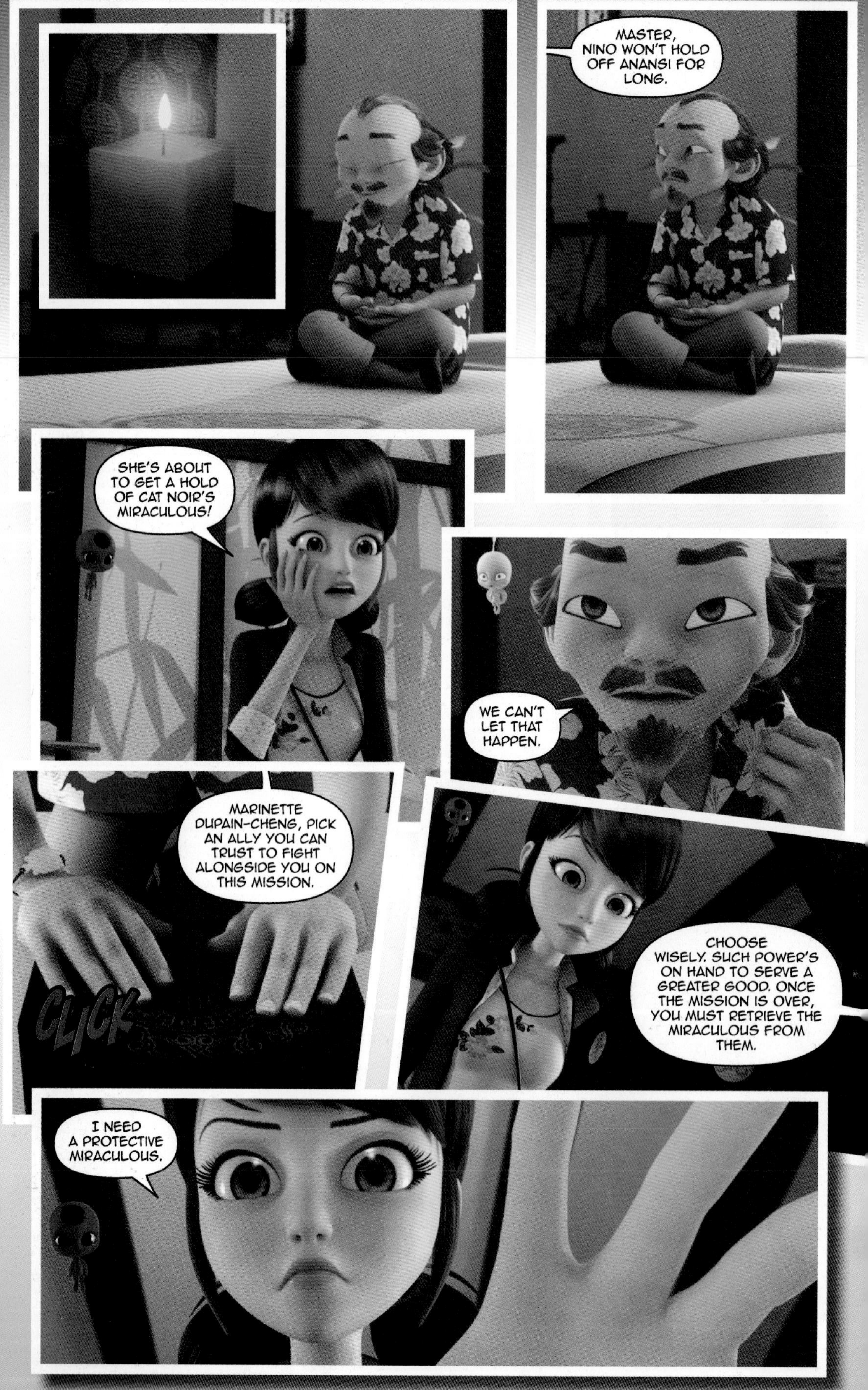
MASTER, NINO WON'T HOLD OFF ANANSI FOR LONG.
SHE'S ABOUT TO GET A HOLD OF CAT NOIR'S MIRACULOUS!
WE CAN'T LET THAT HAPPEN.
MARINETTE DUPAIN-CHENG, PICK AN ALLY YOU CAN TRUST TO FIGHT ALONGSIDE YOU ON THIS MISSION.
CLICK
CHOOSE WISELY. SUCH POWER'S ON HAND TO SERVE A GREATER GOOD. ONCE THE MISSION IS OVER, YOU MUST RETRIEVE THE MIRACULOUS FROM THEM.
I NEED A PROTECTIVE MIRACULOUS.

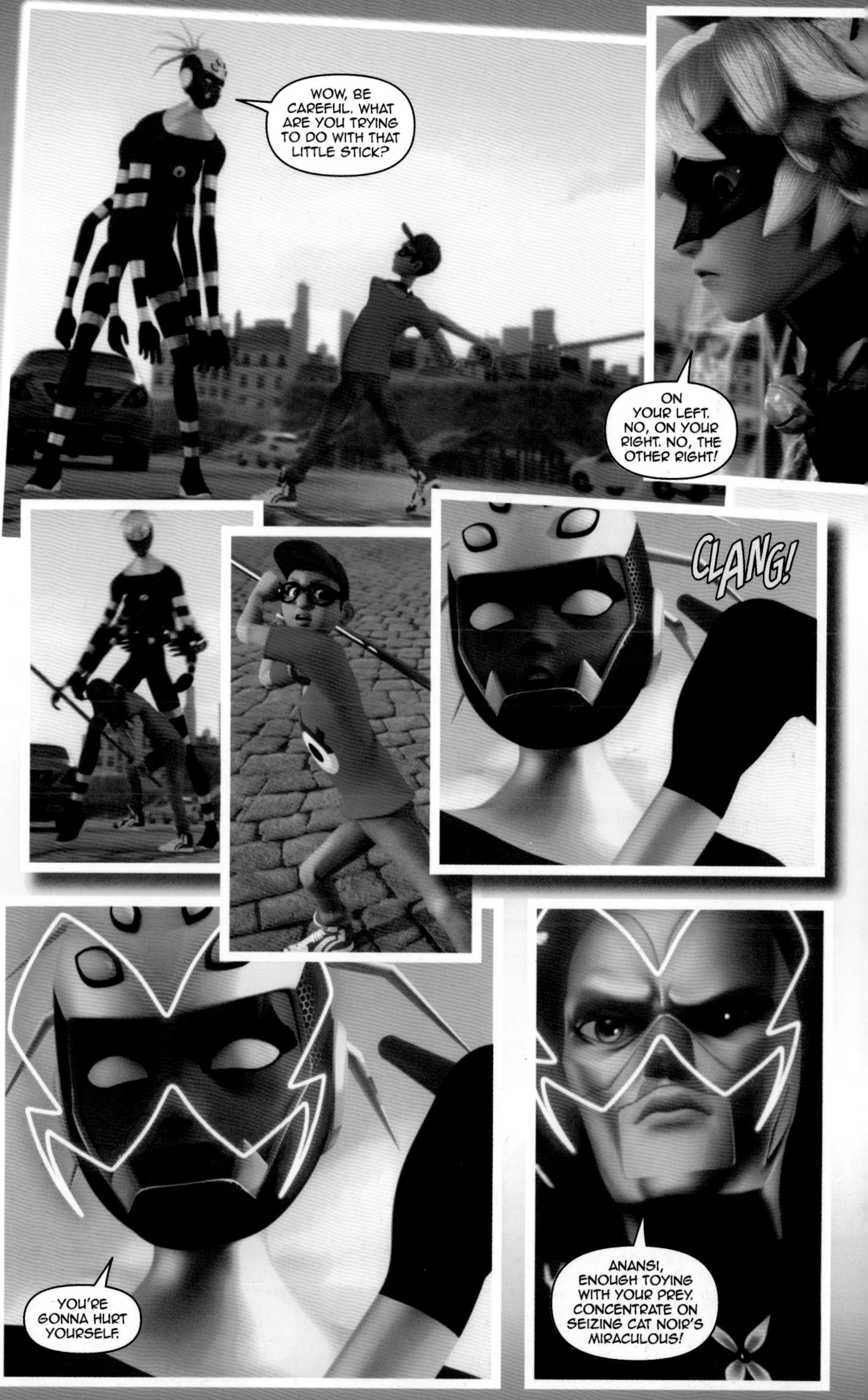
WOW, BE CAREFUL. WHAT ARE YOU TRYING TO DO WITH THAT LITTLE STICK?
ON YOUR LEFT. NO, ON YOUR RIGHT. NO, THE OTHER RIGHT!
CLANG!
YOU'RE GONNA HURT YOURSELF.
ANANSI, ENOUGH TOYING WITH YOUR PREY. CONCENTRATE ON SEIZING CAT NOIR'S MIRACULOUS!

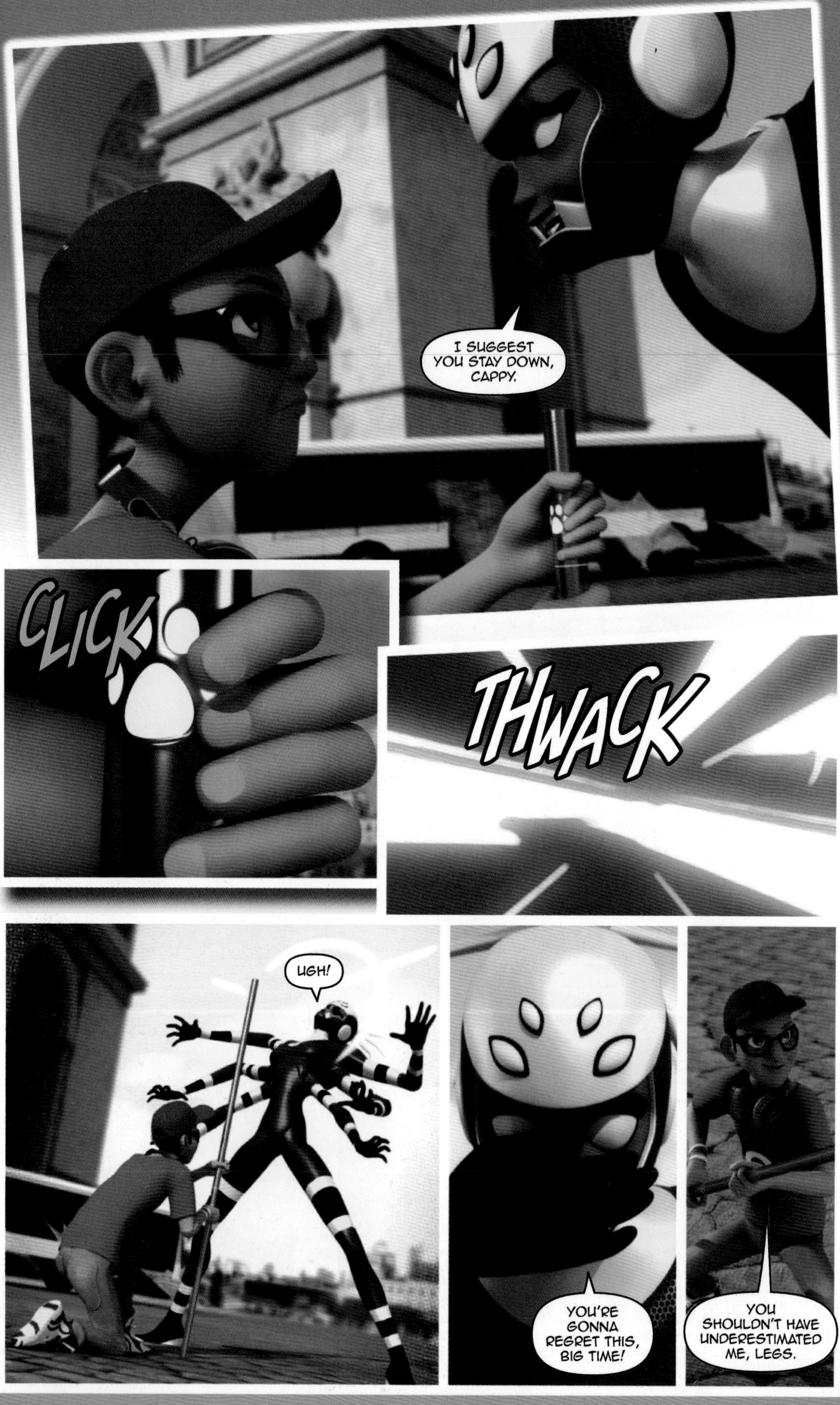
I SUGGEST YOU STAY DOWN, CAPPY.
CLICK
THWACK
UGH!
YOU'RE GONNA REGRET THIS, BIG TIME!
YOU SHOULDN'T HAVE UNDERESTIMATED ME, LEGS.

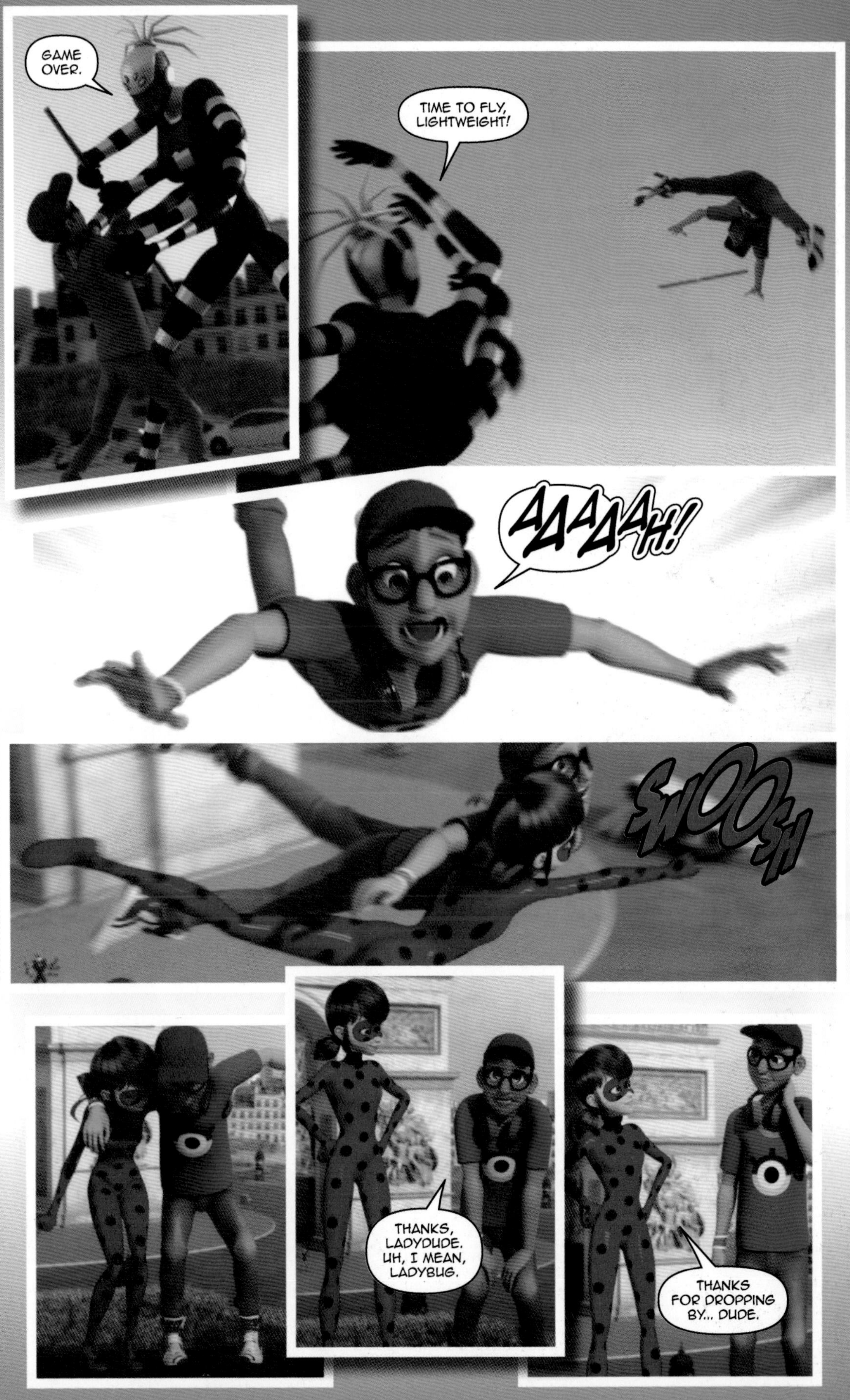
GAME OVER.
TIME TO FLY, LIGHTWEIGHT!
AAAAAH!
SWOOSH
THANKS, LADYDUDE. UH, I MEAN, LADYBUG.
THANKS FOR DROPPING BY... DUDE.

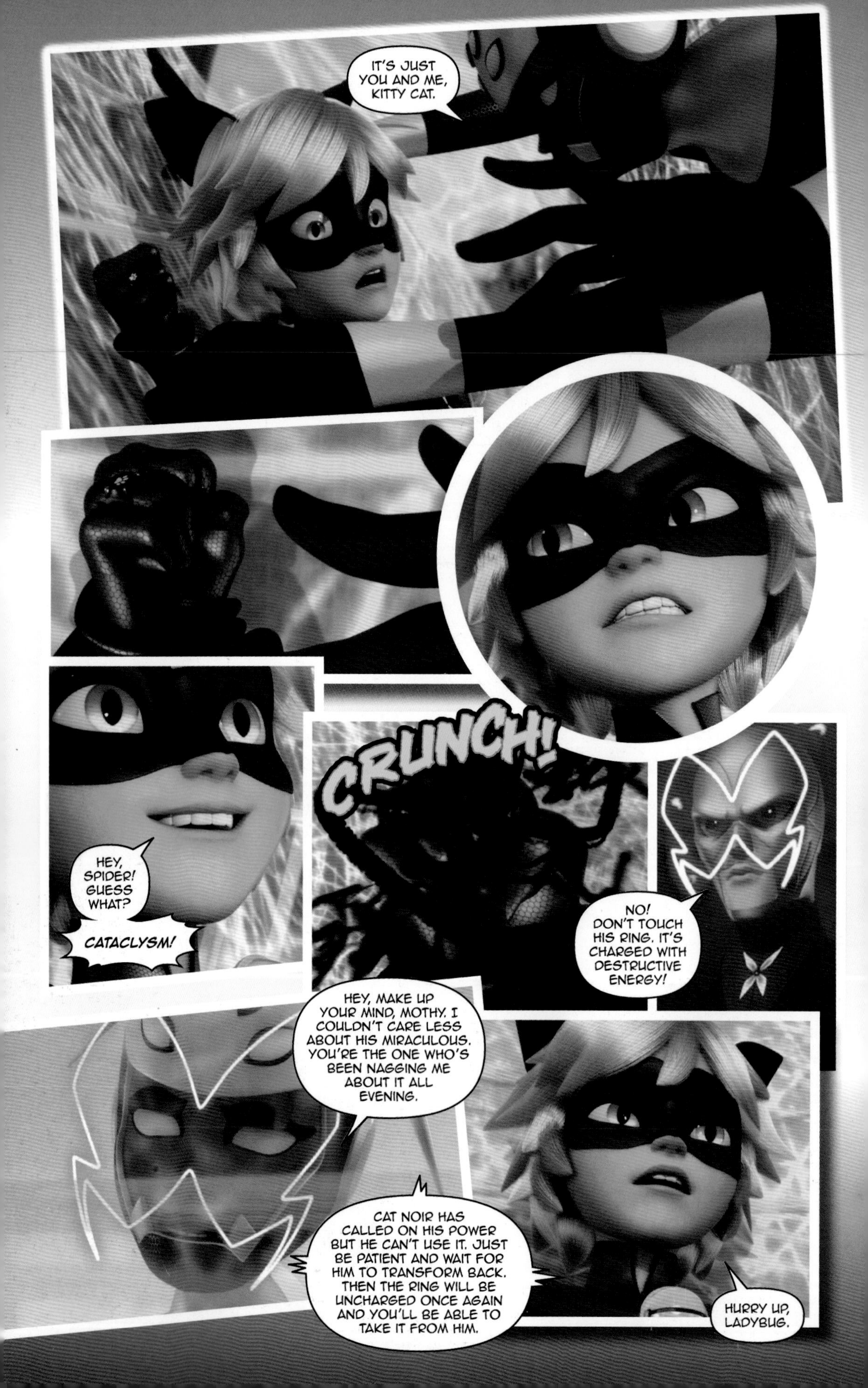
IT'S JUST YOU AND ME, KITTY CAT.
CRUNCH!
HEY, SPIDER! GUESS WHAT?
CATACLYSM!
NO! DON'T TOUCH HIS RING. IT'S CHARGED WITH DESTRUCTIVE ENERGY!
HEY, MAKE UP YOUR MIND, MOTHY. I COULDN'T CARE LESS ABOUT HIS MIRACULOUS. YOU'RE THE ONE WHO'S BEEN NAGGING ME ABOUT IT ALL EVENING.
CAT NOIR HAS CALLED ON HIS POWER BUT HE CAN'T USE IT. JUST BE PATIENT AND WAIT FOR HIM TO TRANSFORM BACK. THEN THE RING WILL BE UNCHARGED ONCE AGAIN AND YOU'LL BE ABLE TO TAKE IT FROM HIM.
HURRY UP, LADYBUG.

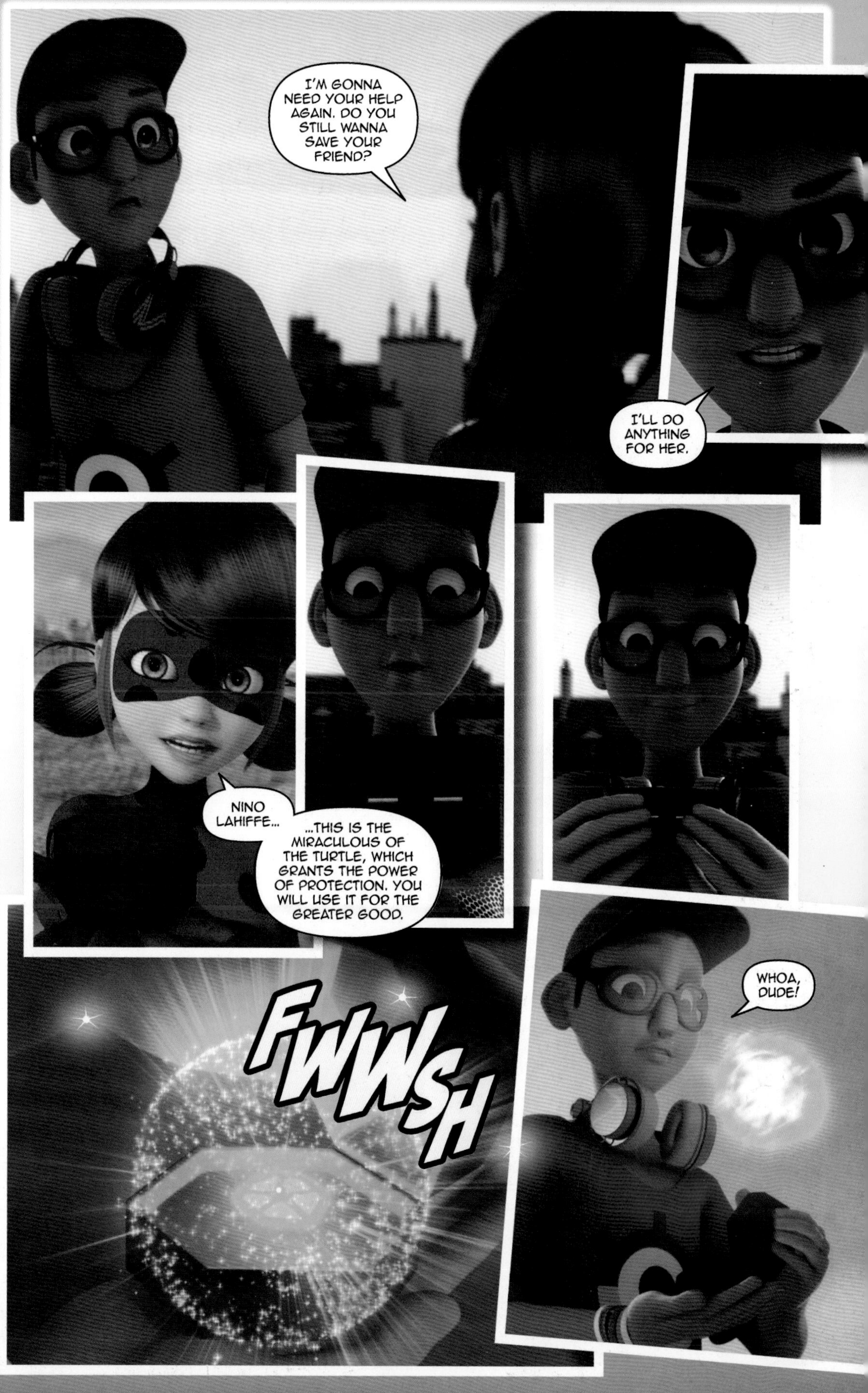
I'M GONNA NEED YOUR HELP AGAIN. DO YOU STILL WANNA SAVE YOUR FRIEND?
I'LL DO ANYTHING FOR HER.
NINO LAHIFFE...
...THIS IS THE MIRACULOUS OF THE TURTLE, WHICH GRANTS THE POWER OF PROTECTION. YOU WILL USE IT FOR THE GREATER GOOD.
FWWSH
WHOA, DUDE!

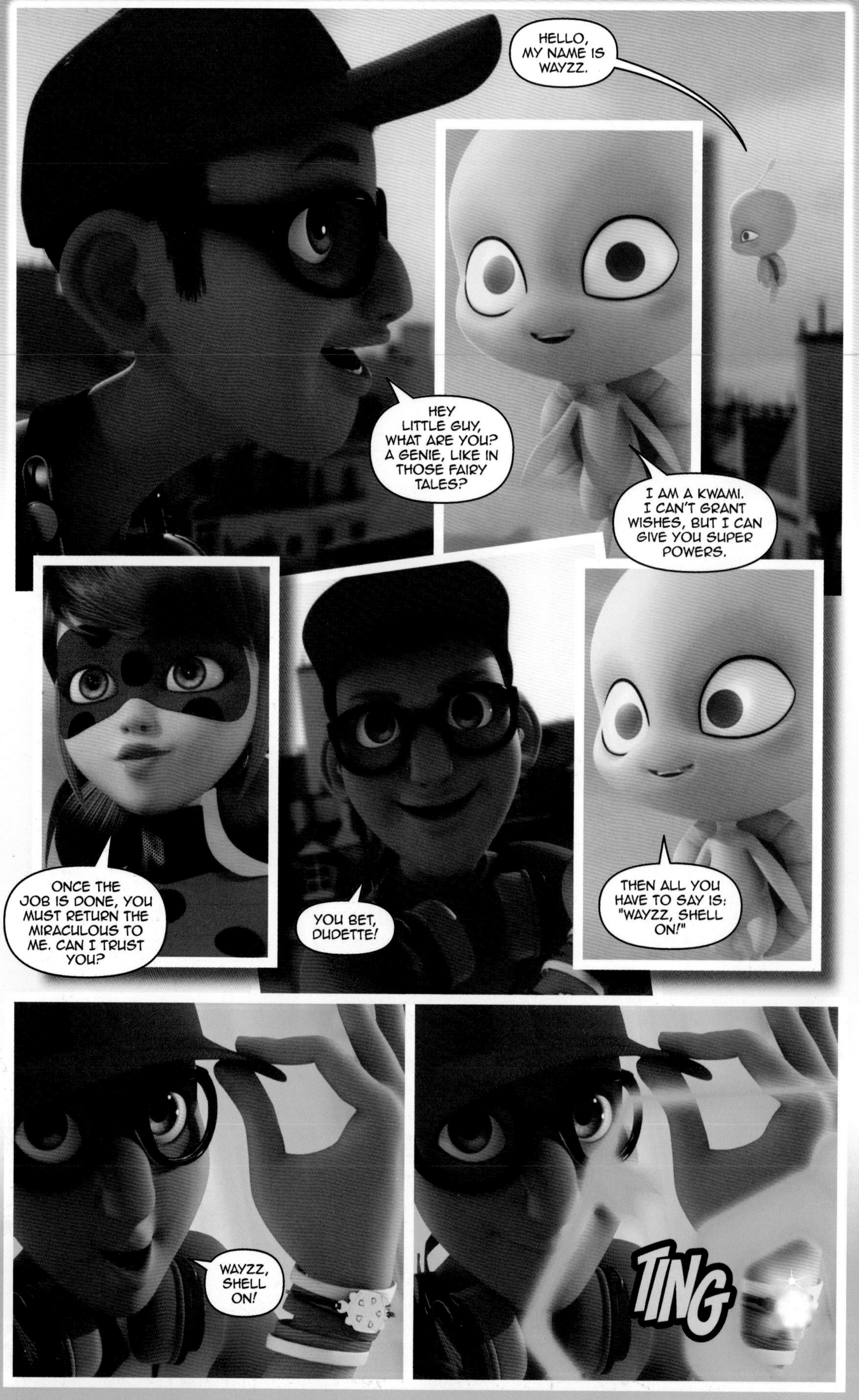
HELLO, MY NAME IS WAYZZ.
HEY LITTLE GUY, WHAT ARE YOU? A GENIE, LIKE IN THOSE FAIRY TALES?
I AM A KWAMI. I CAN'T GRANT WISHES, BUT I CAN GIVE YOU SUPER POWERS.
ONCE THE JOB IS DONE, YOU MUST RETURN THE MIRACULOUS TO ME. CAN I TRUST YOU?
YOU BET, DUDETTE!
THEN ALL YOU HAVE TO SAY IS: "WAYZZ, SHELL ON!"
WAYZZ, SHELL ON!
TING

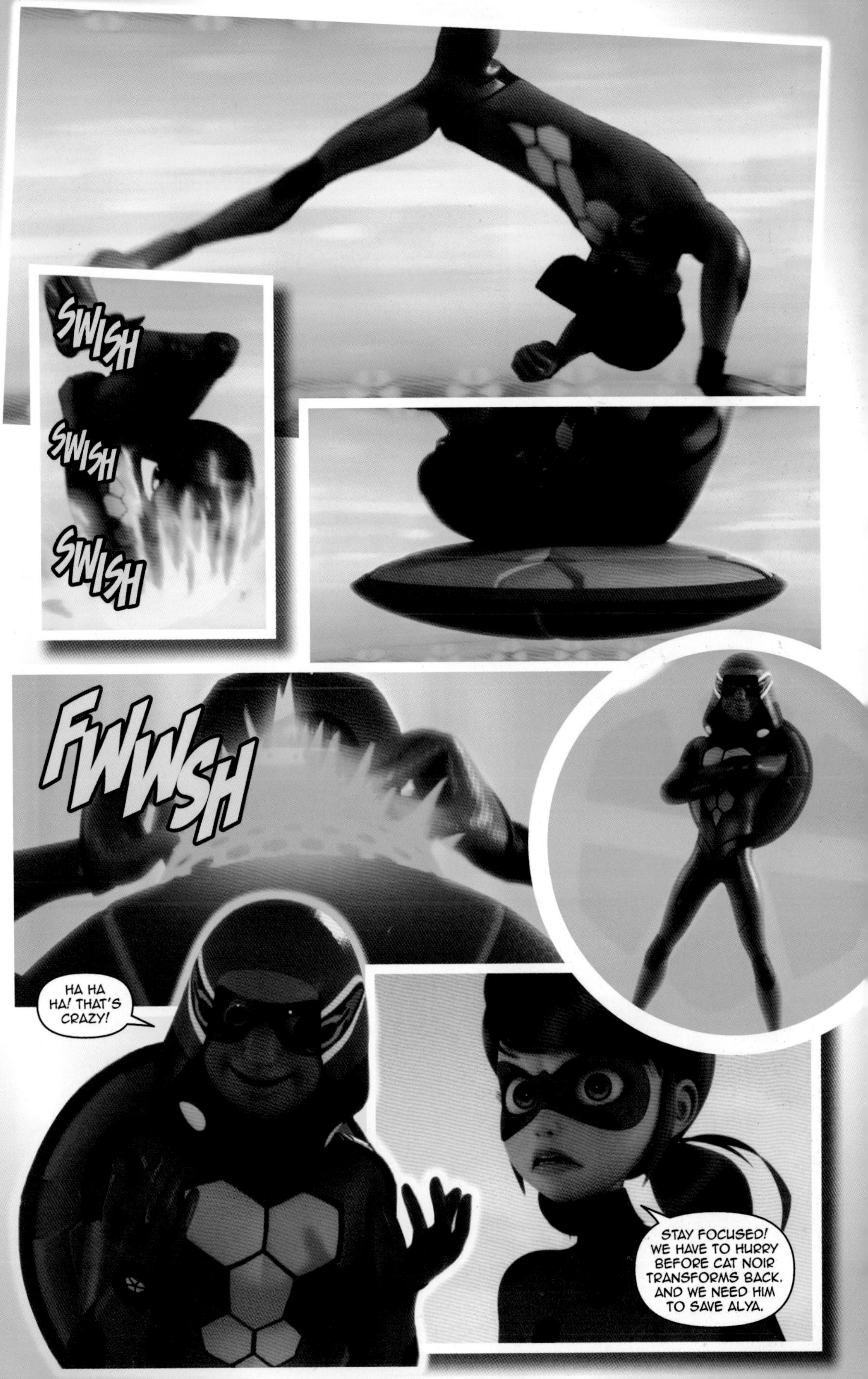
SWISH
SWISH
SWISH
FWWSH
HA HA HA! THAT'S CRAZY!
STAY FOCUSED! WE HAVE TO HURRY BEFORE CAT NOIR TRANSFORMS BACK. AND WE NEED HIM TO SAVE ALYA.

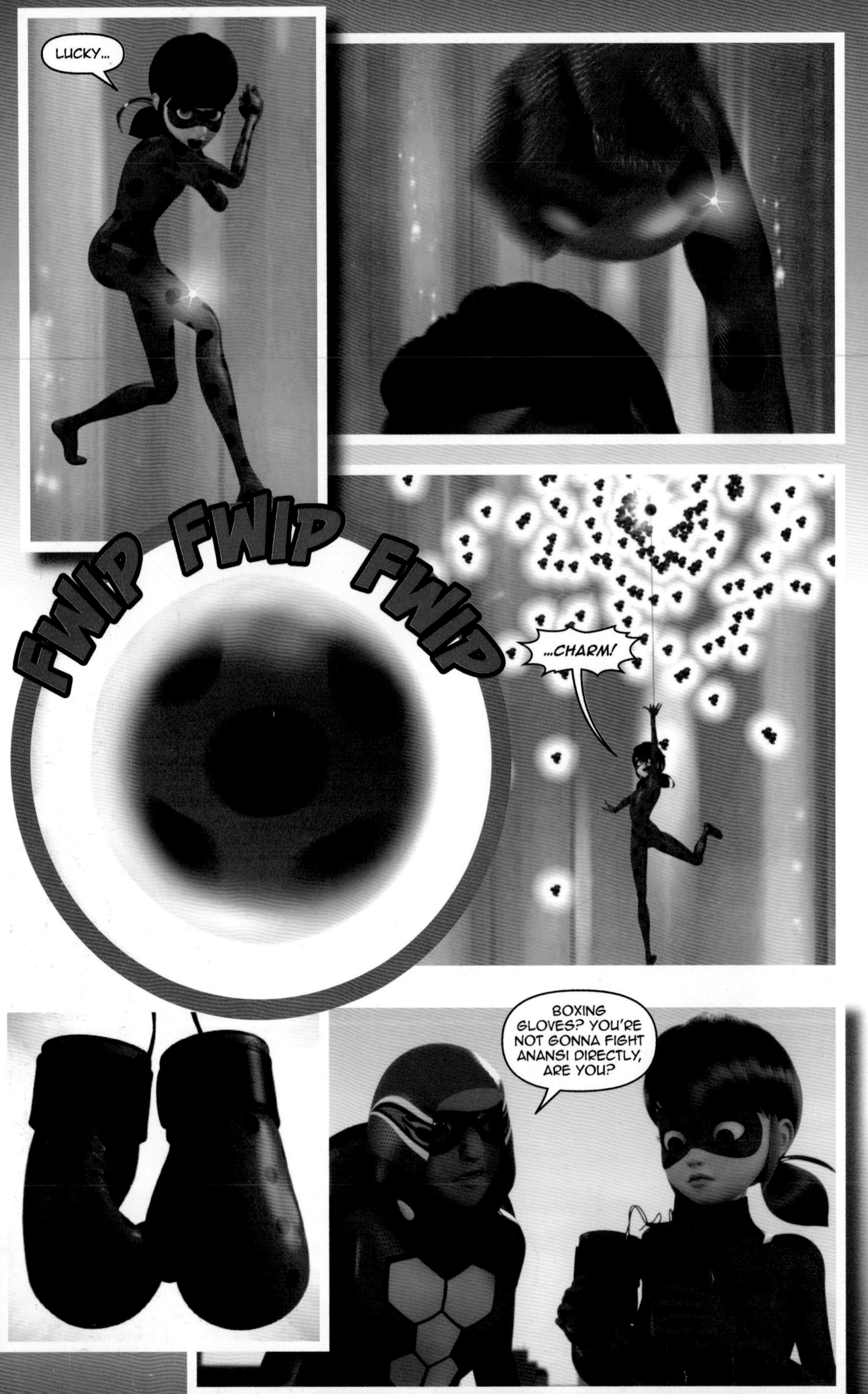
LUCKY...
FWIP FWIP FWIP
...CHARM!
BOXING GLOVES? YOU'RE NOT GONNA FIGHT ANANSI DIRECTLY, ARE YOU?

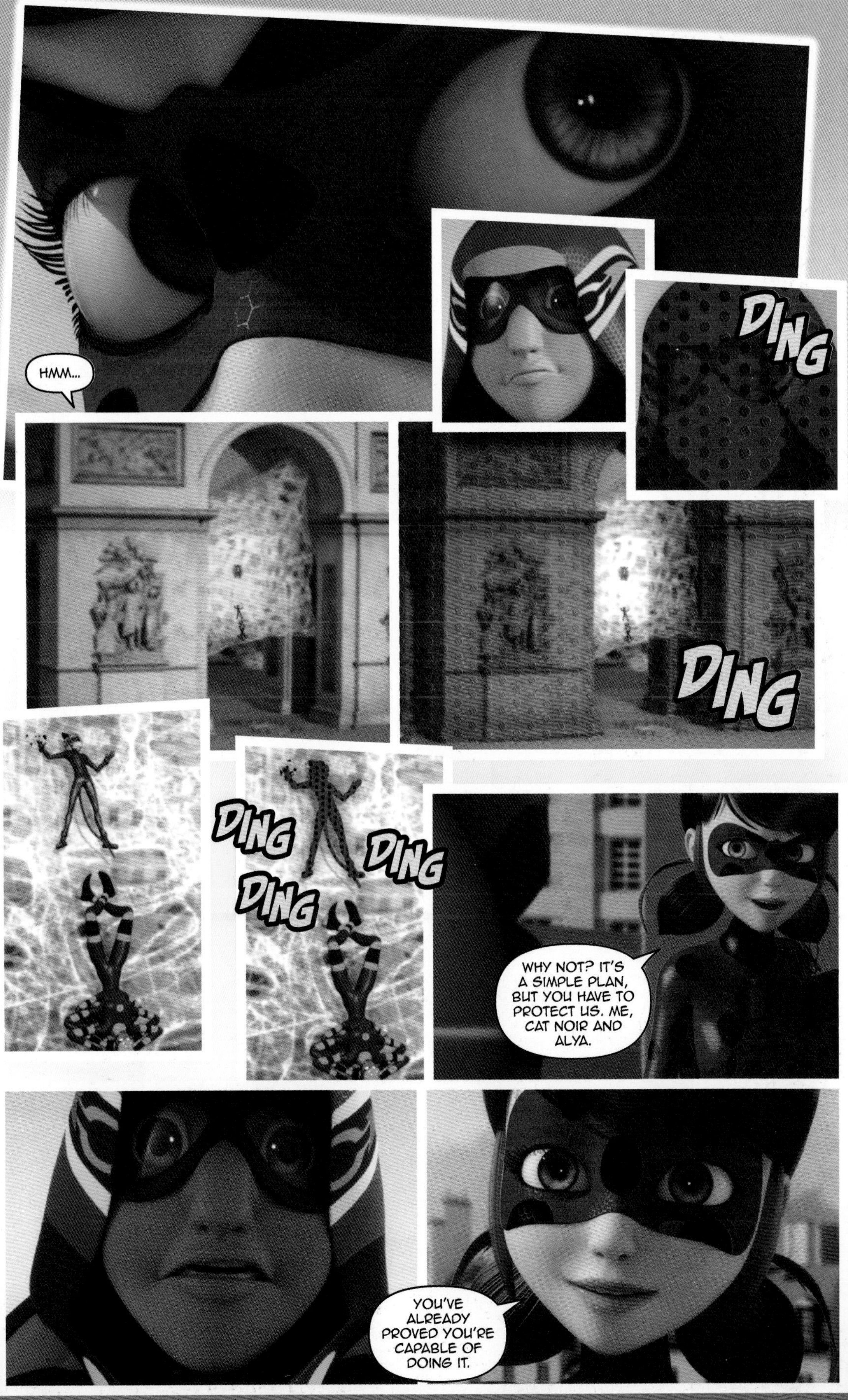
HMM...
DING
DING
DING
DING
DING
WHY NOT? IT'S A SIMPLE PLAN, BUT YOU HAVE TO PROTECT US. ME, CAT NOIR AND ALYA.
YOU'VE ALREADY PROVED YOU'RE CAPABLE OF DOING IT.

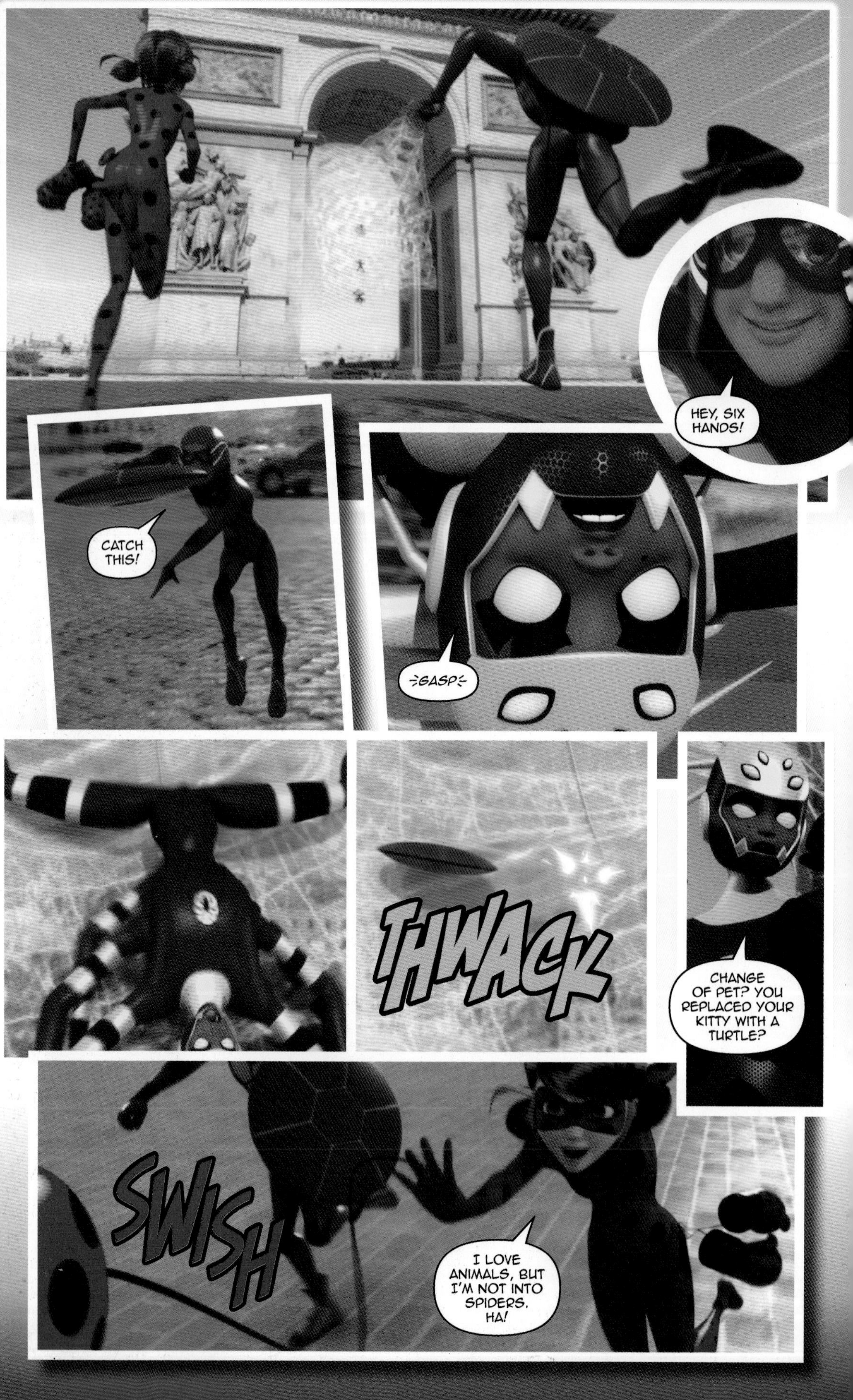
HEY, SIX HANDS!
CATCH THIS!
GASP
THWACK
CHANGE OF PET? YOU REPLACED YOUR KITTY WITH A TURTLE?
SWISH
I LOVE ANIMALS, BUT I'M NOT INTO SPIDERS. HA!

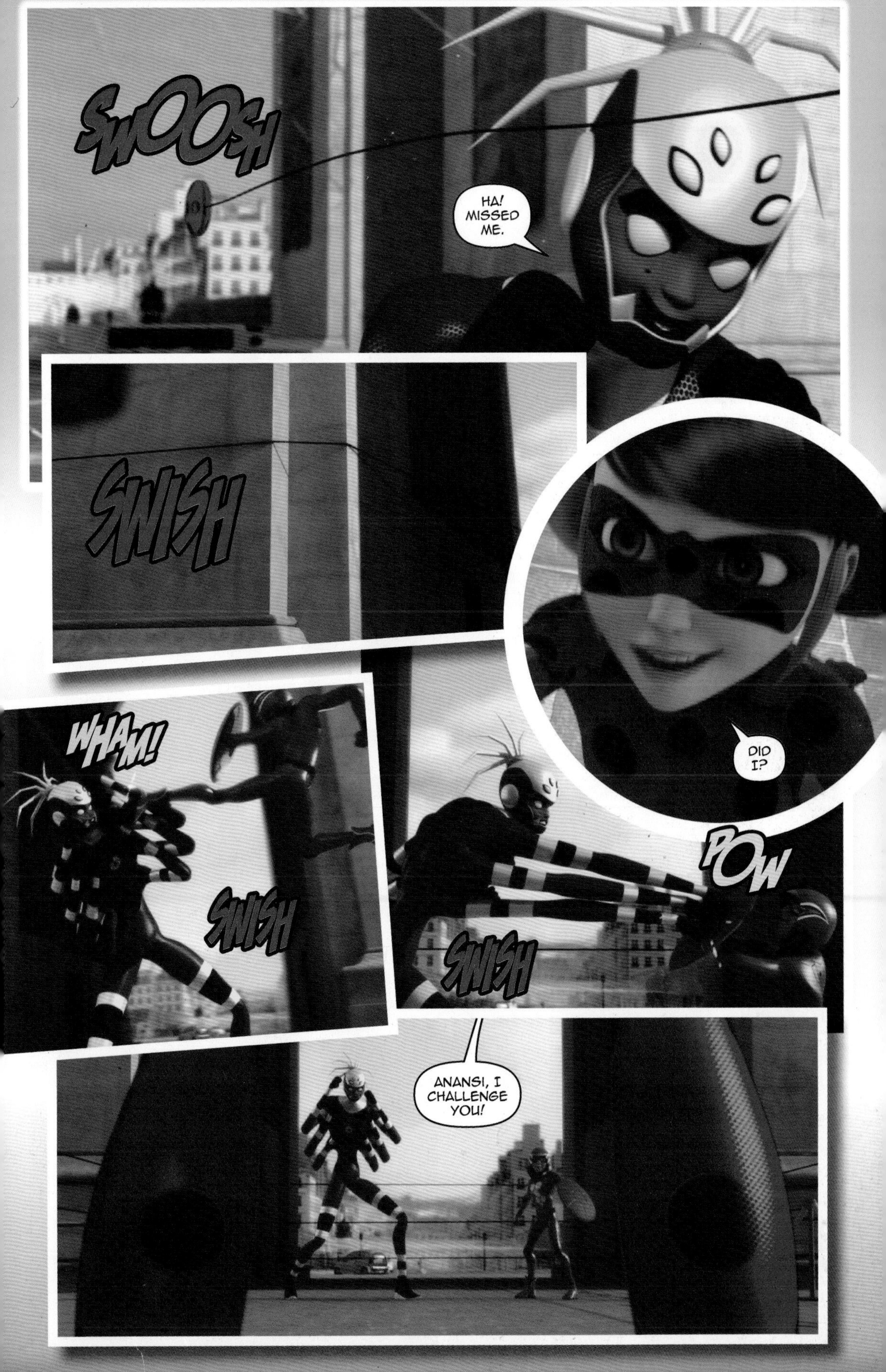
SWOOSH
HA! MISSED ME.
SWISH
DID I?
WHAM!
SWISH
POW
SWISH
ANANSI, I CHALLENGE YOU!

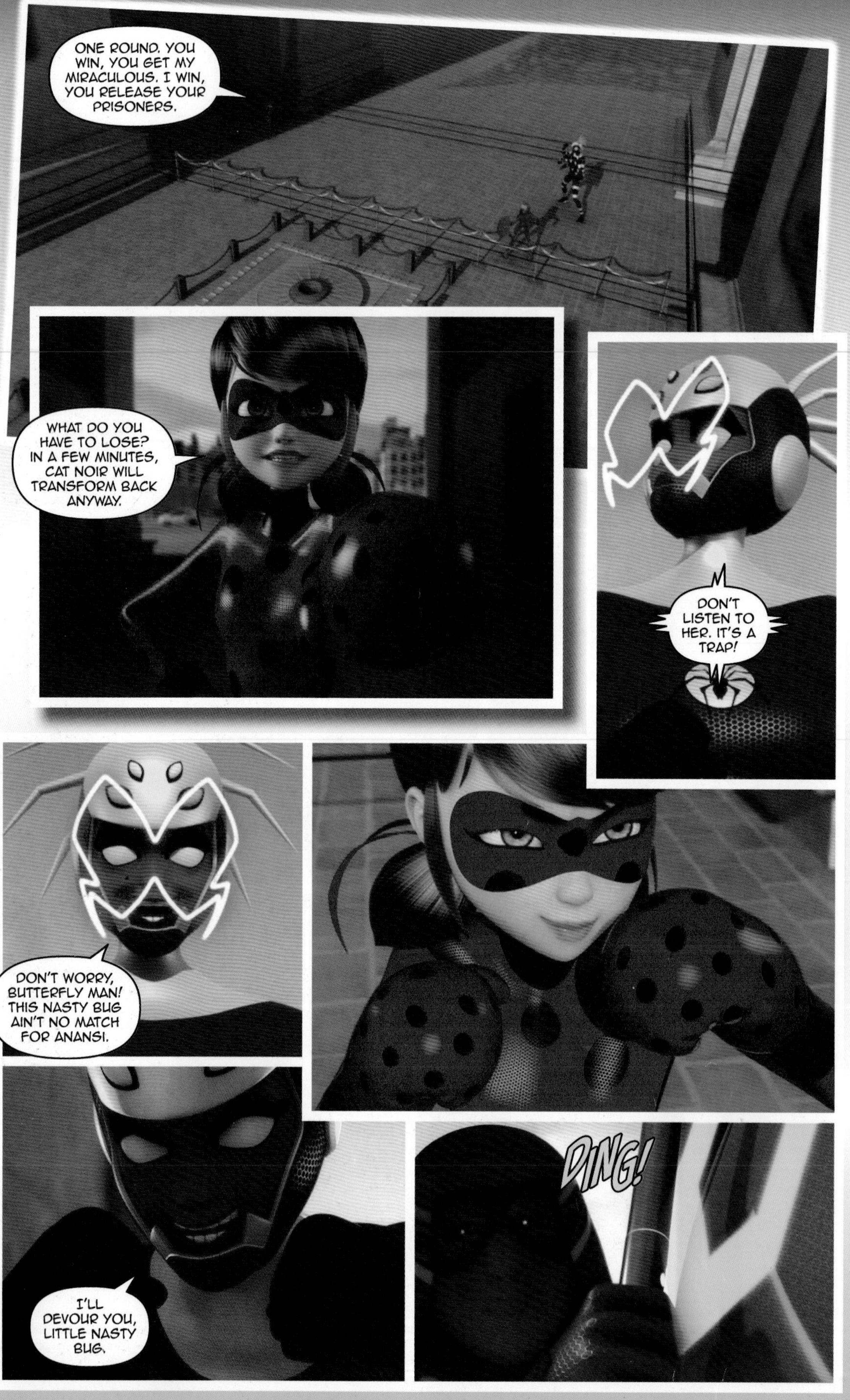
ONE ROUND. YOU WIN, YOU GET MY MIRACULOUS. I WIN, YOU RELEASE YOUR PRISONERS.
WHAT DO YOU HAVE TO LOSE? IN A FEW MINUTES, CAT NOIR WILL TRANSFORM BACK ANYWAY.
DON'T LISTEN TO HER. IT'S A TRAP!
DON'T WORRY, BUTTERFLY MAN! THIS NASTY BUG AIN'T NO MATCH FOR ANANSI.
I'LL DEVOUR YOU, LITTLE NASTY BUG.
DING!

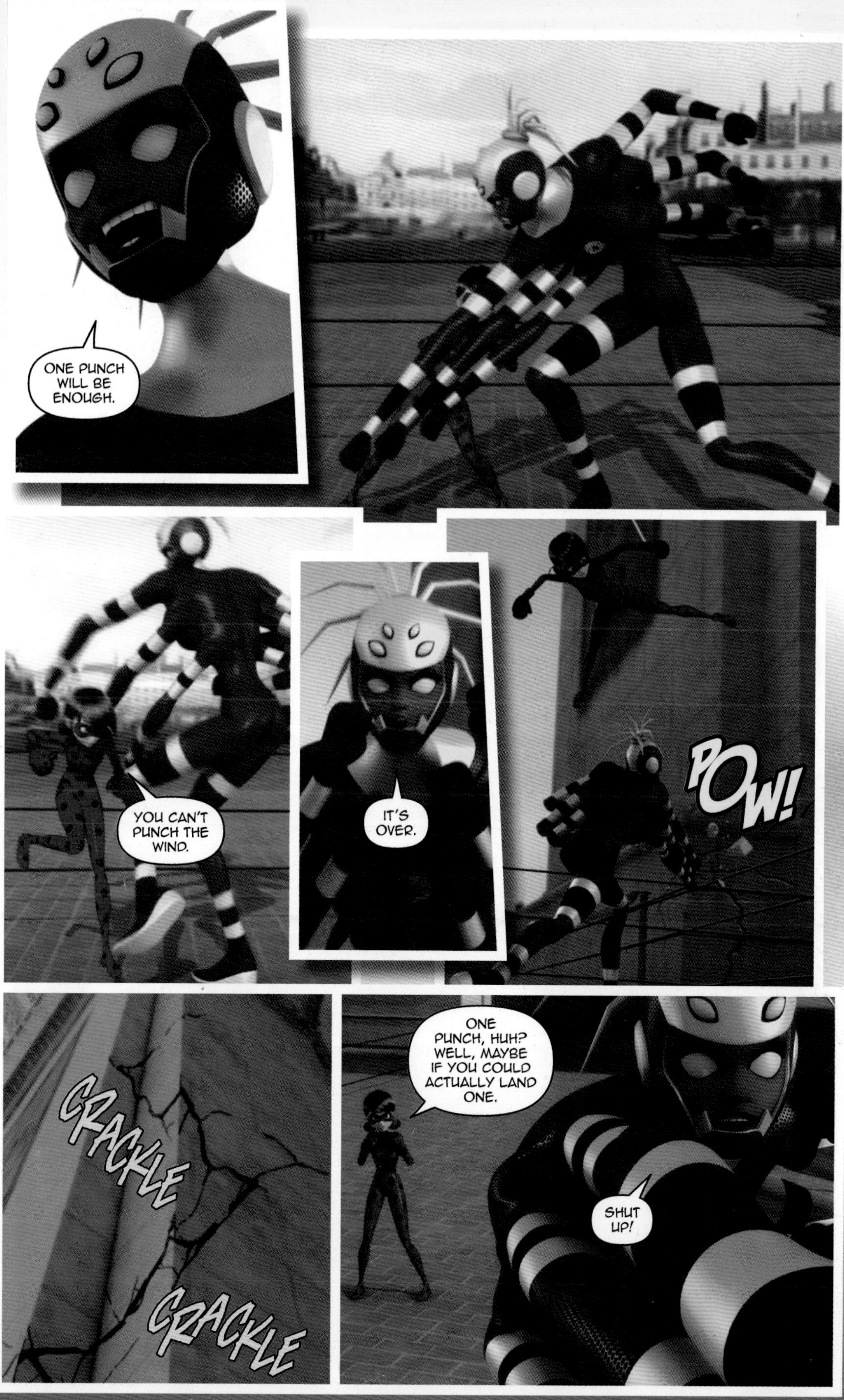
ONE PUNCH WILL BE ENOUGH.
YOU CAN'T PUNCH THE WIND.
IT'S OVER.
POW!
CRACKLE
CRACKLE
ONE PUNCH, HUH? WELL, MAYBE IF YOU COULD ACTUALLY LAND ONE.
SHUT UP!

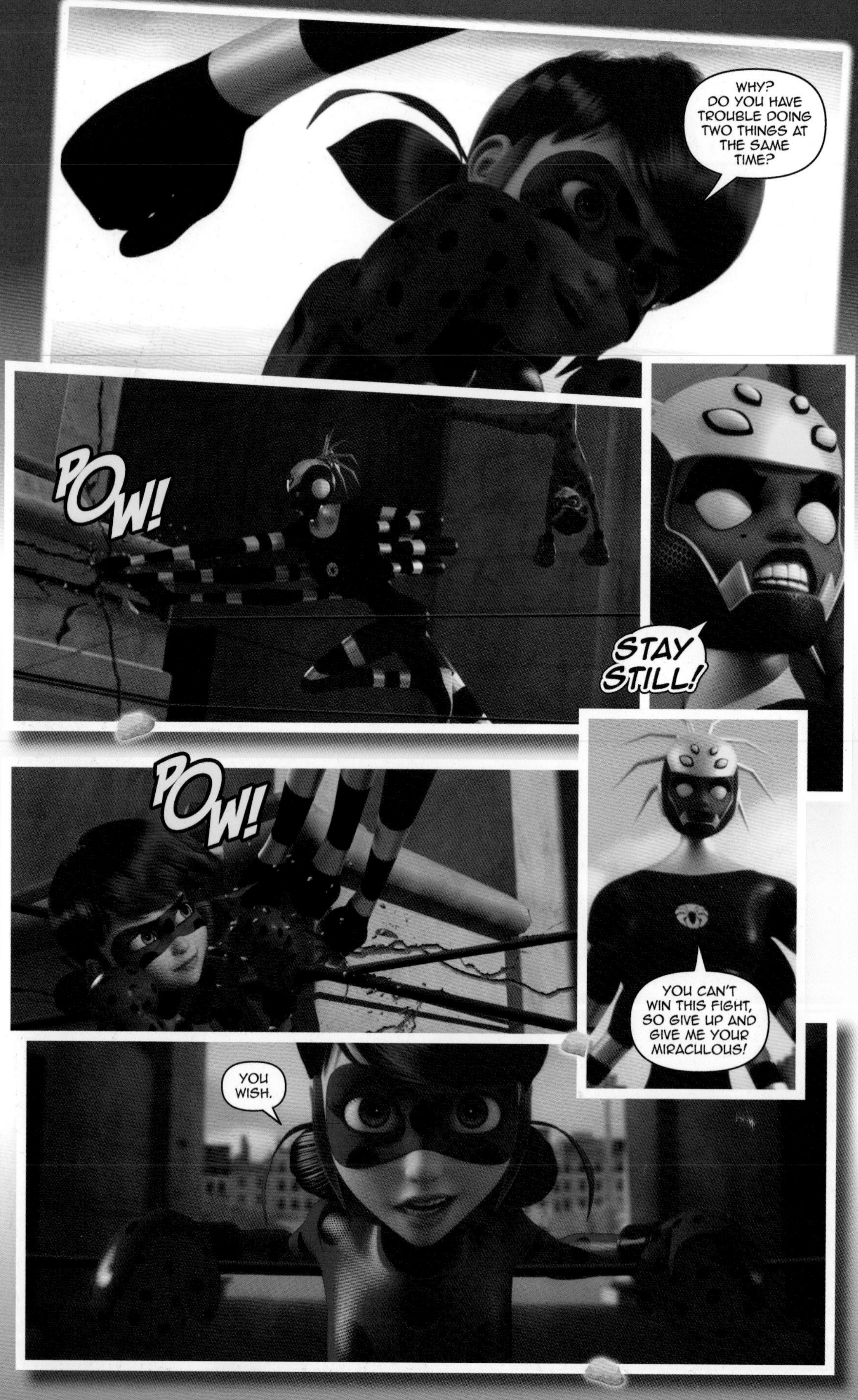
WHY? DO YOU HAVE TROUBLE DOING TWO THINGS AT THE SAME TIME?
POW!
STAY STILL!
POW!
YOU CAN'T WIN THIS FIGHT, SO GIVE UP AND GIVE ME YOUR MIRACULOUS!
YOU WISH.

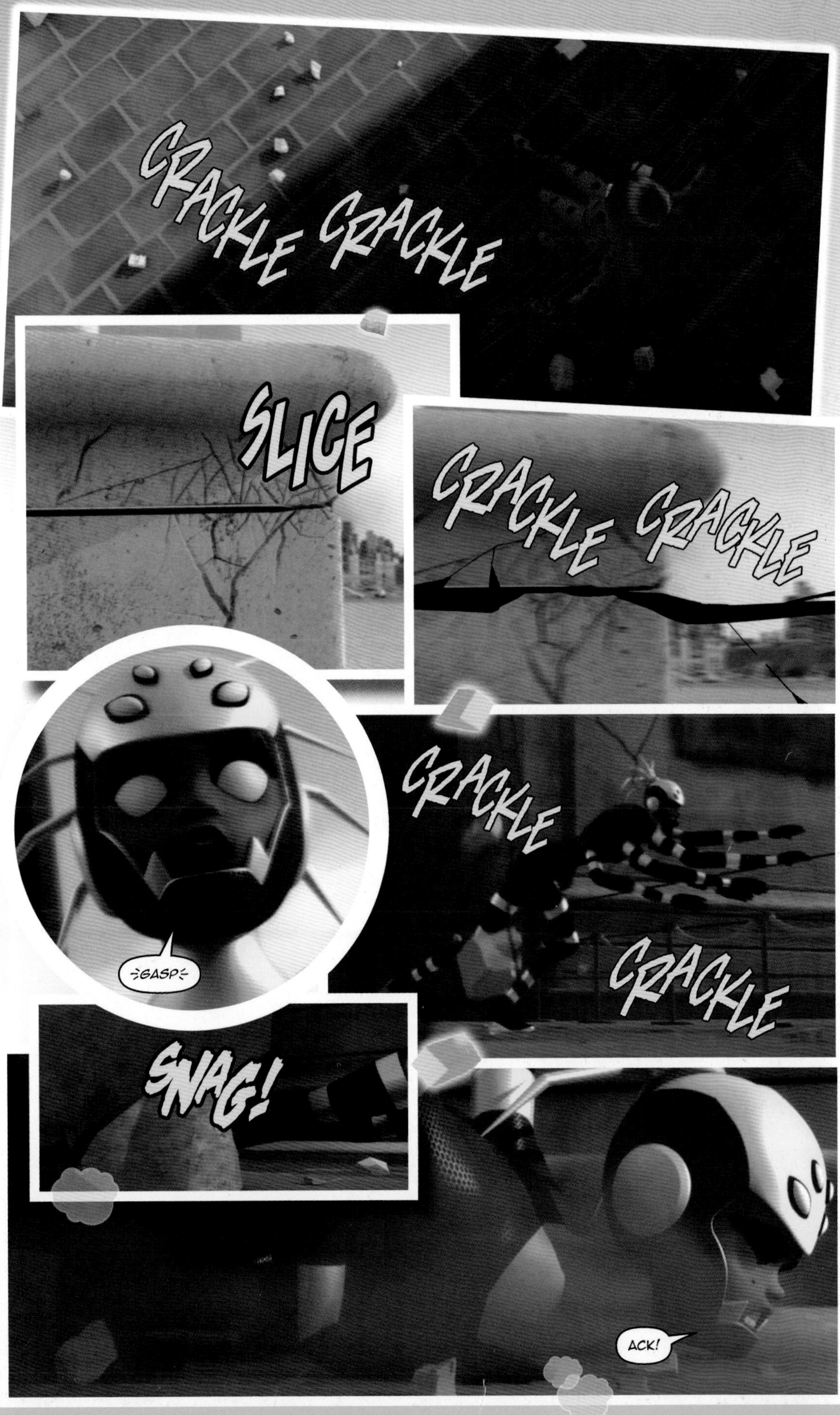
CRACKLE CRACKLE
SLICE
CRACKLE CRACKLE
GASP
CRACKLE
CRACKLE
SNAG!
ACK!

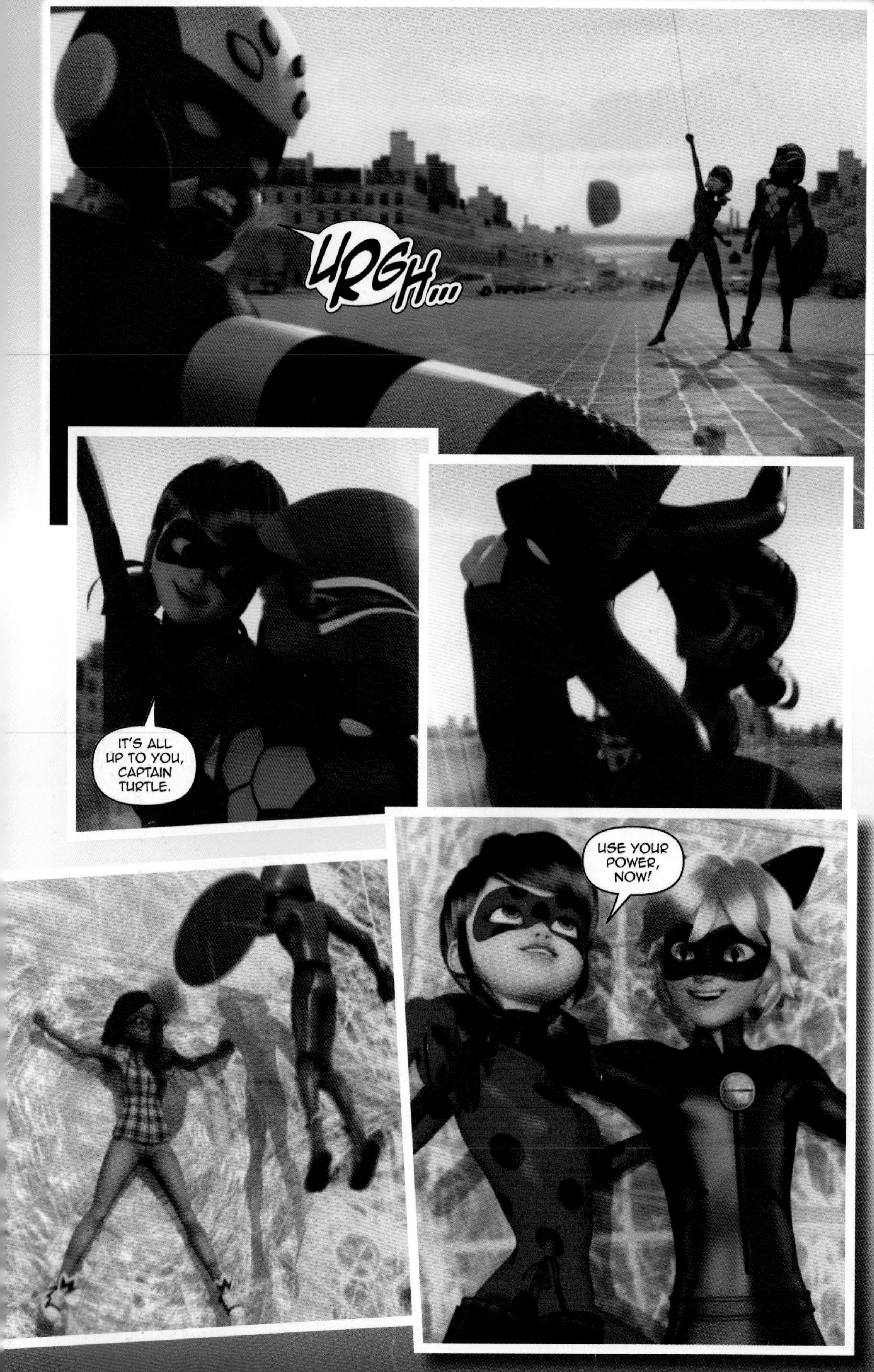
URGH...
IT'S ALL UP TO YOU, CAPTAIN TURTLE.
USE YOUR POWER, NOW!

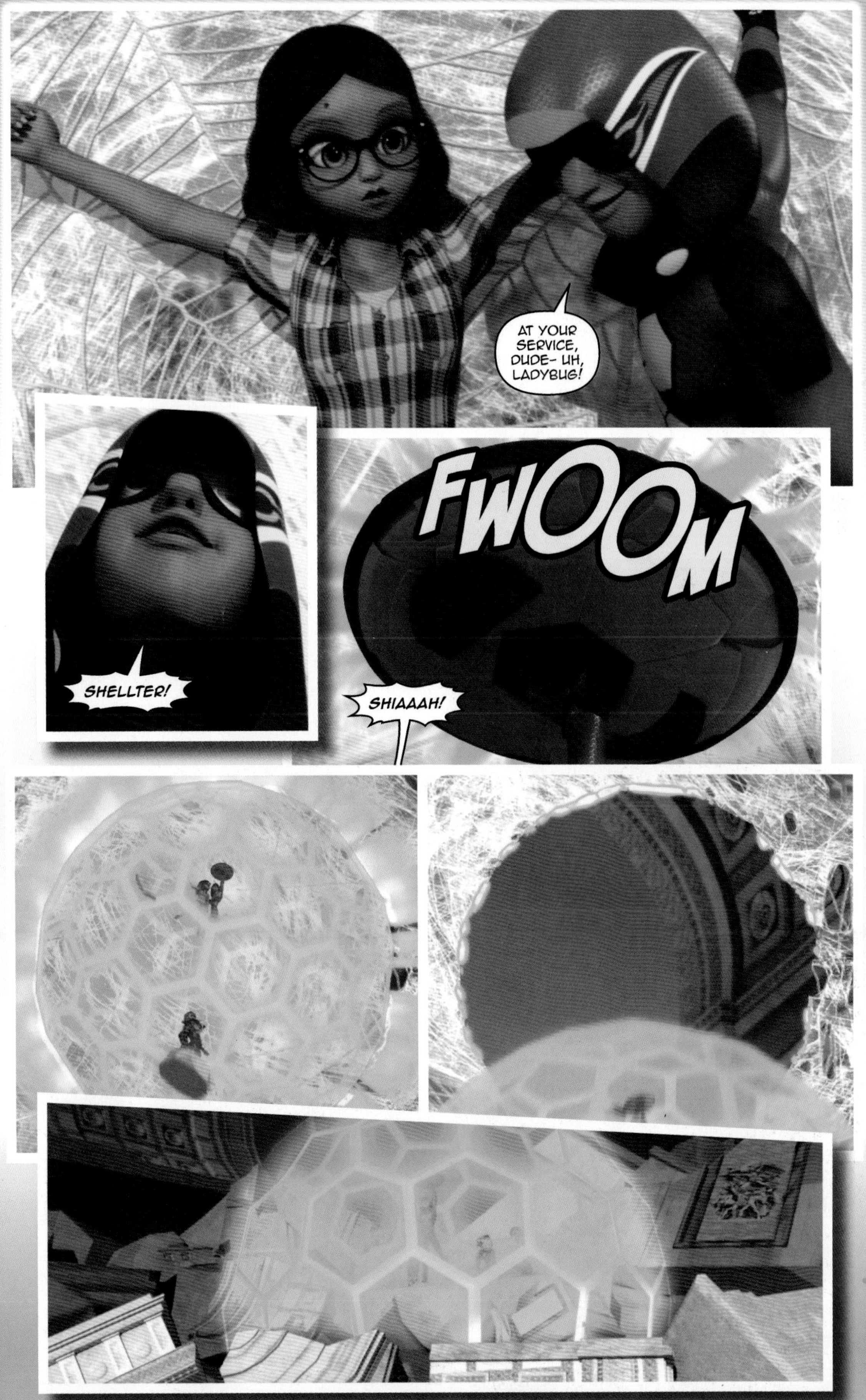
AT YOUR SERVICE, DUDE- UH, LADYBUG!
SHELLTER!
FWOOM
SHIAAAH!

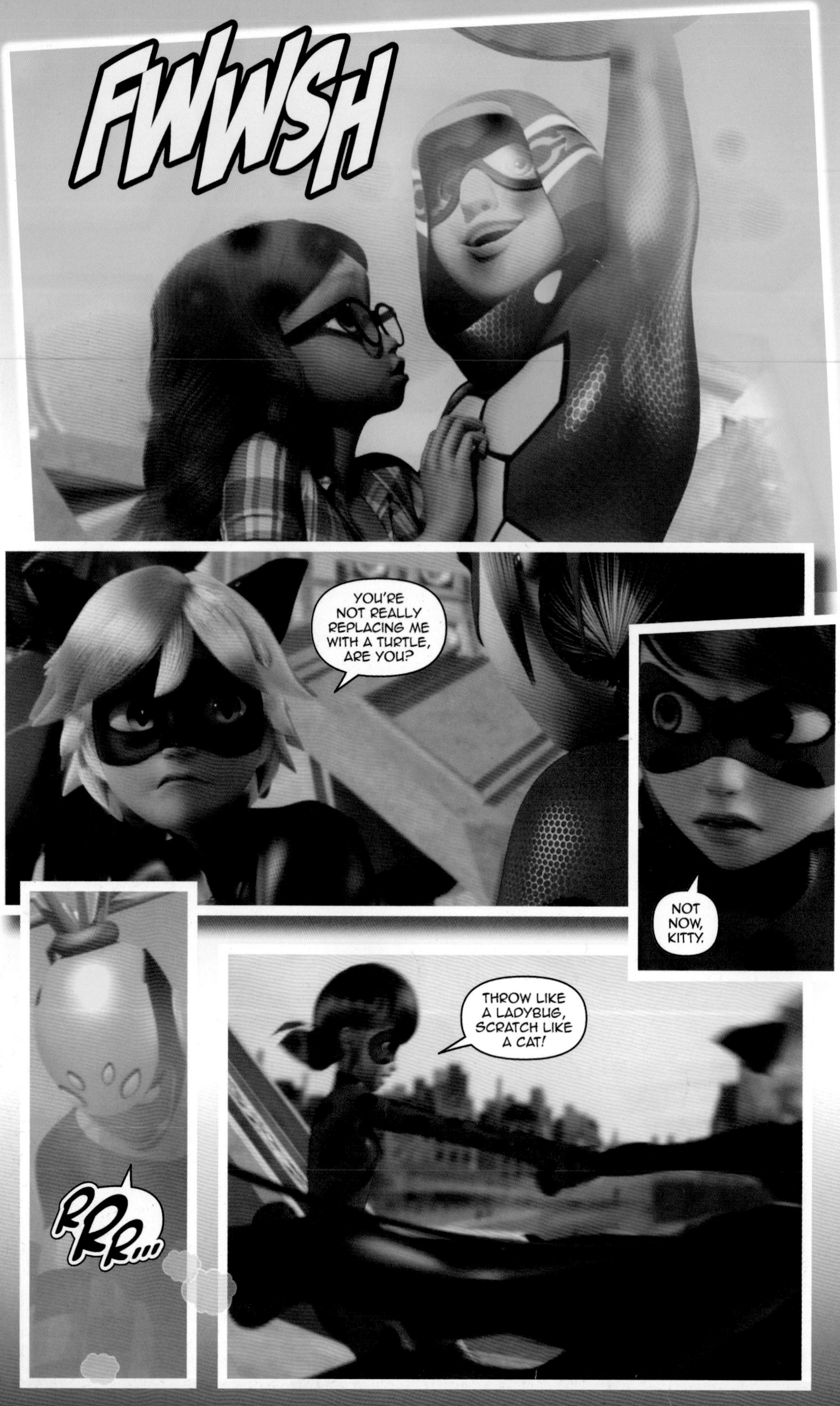
FWWSH
YOU'RE NOT REALLY REPLACING ME WITH A TURTLE, ARE YOU?
NOT NOW, KITTY.
RRR...
THROW LIKE A LADYBUG, SCRATCH LIKE A CAT!

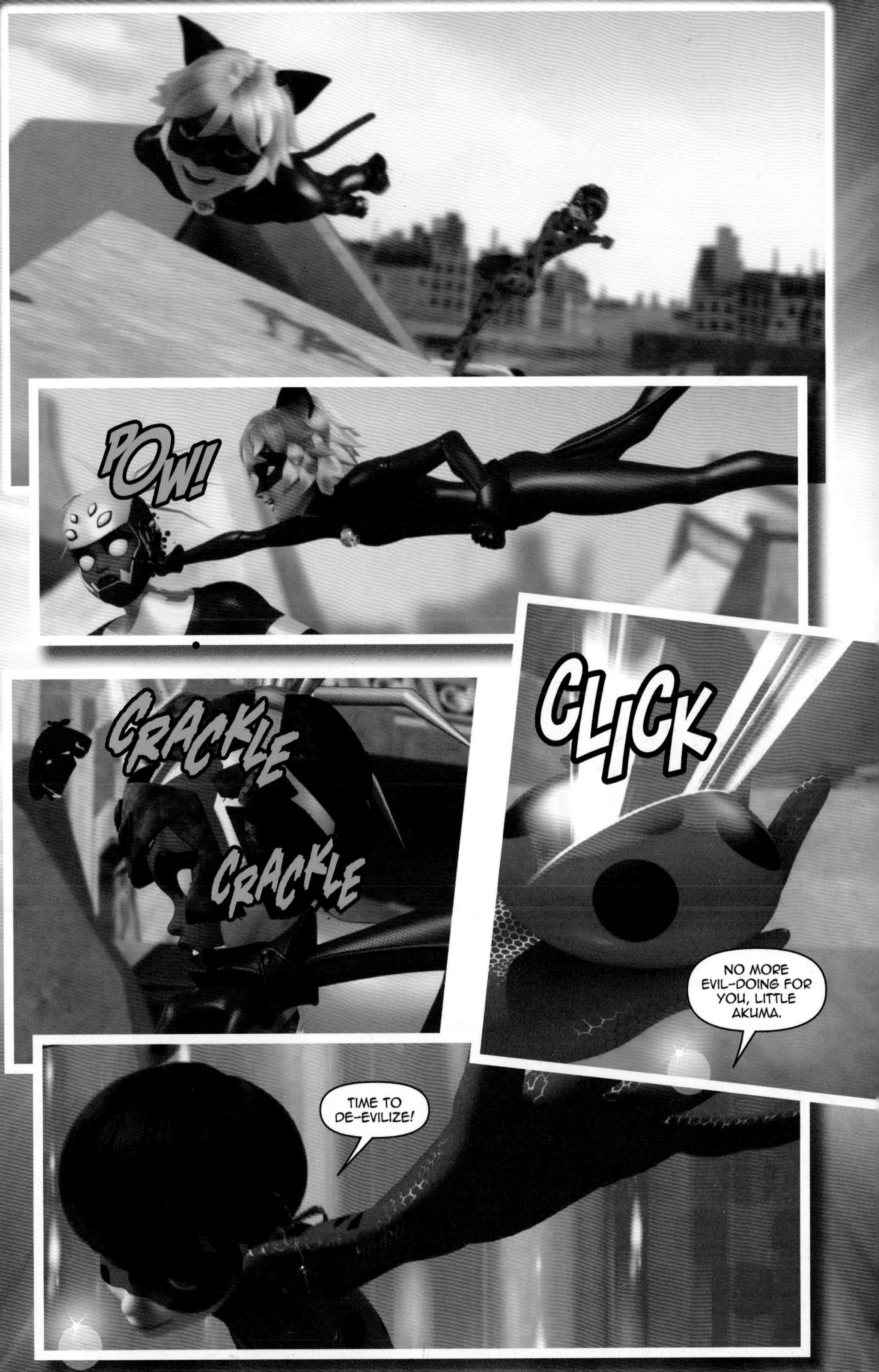
POW!
CRACKLE
CRACKLE
CLICK
NO MORE EVIL-DOING FOR YOU, LITTLE AKUMA.
TIME TO DE-EVILIZE!

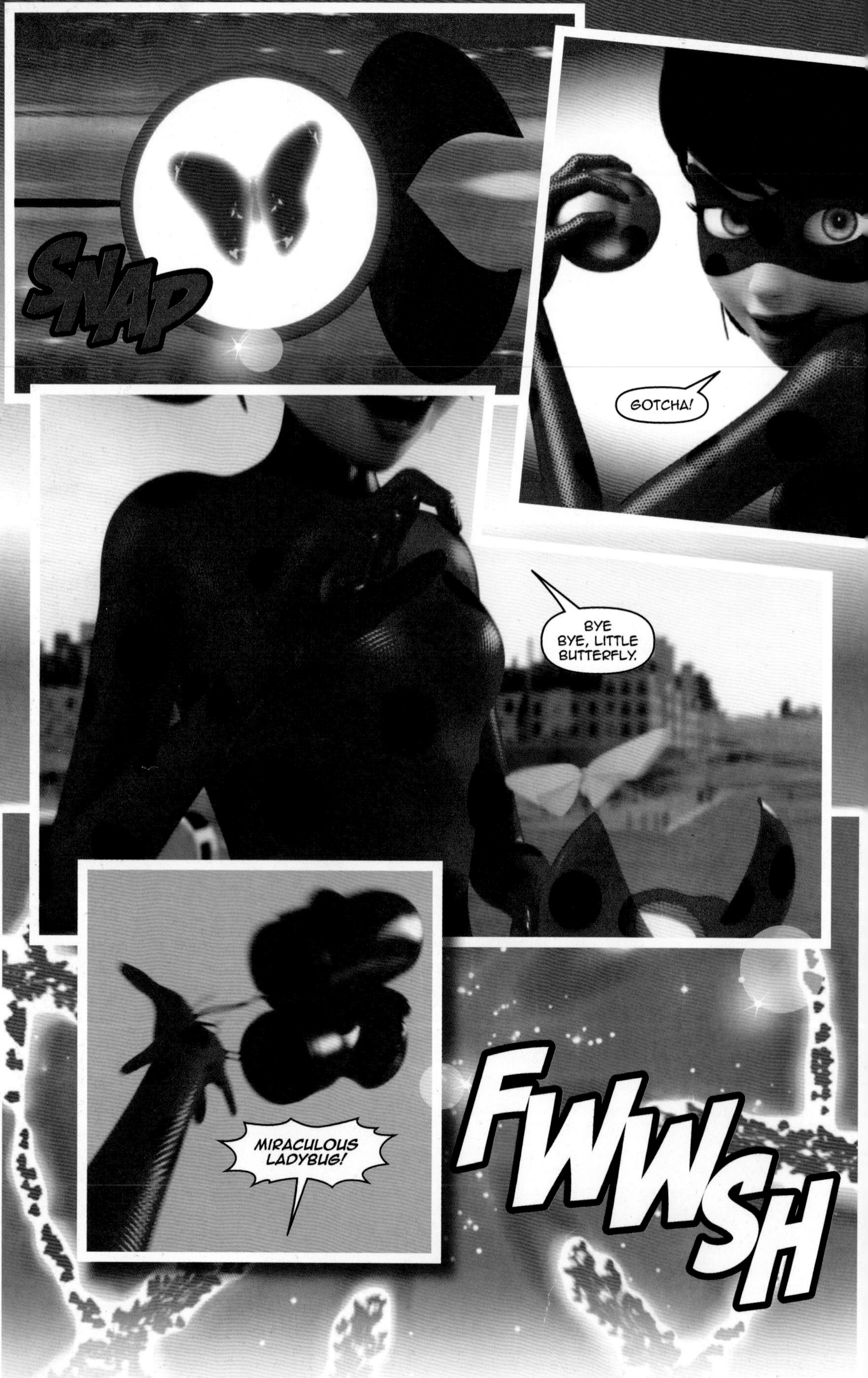
SNAP
GOTCHA!
BYE BYE, LITTLE BUTTERFLY.
MIRACULOUS LADYBUG!
FWWSH

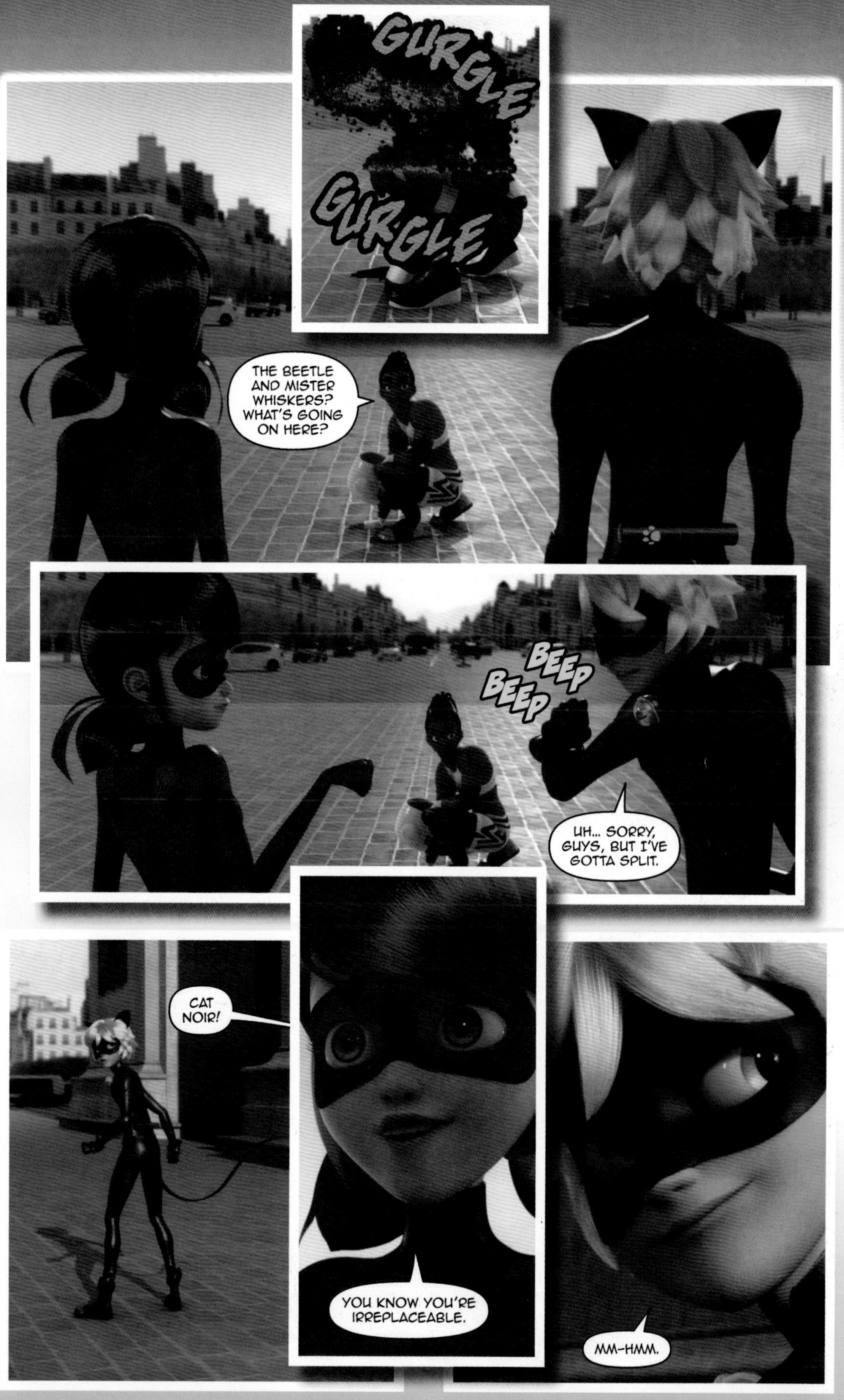
GURGLE
GURGLE
THE BEETLE AND MISTER WHISKERS? WHAT'S GOING ON HERE?
BEEP
BEEP
UH... SORRY, GUYS, BUT I'VE GOTTA SPLIT.
CAT NOIR!
YOU KNOW YOU'RE IRREPLACEABLE.
MM-HMM.

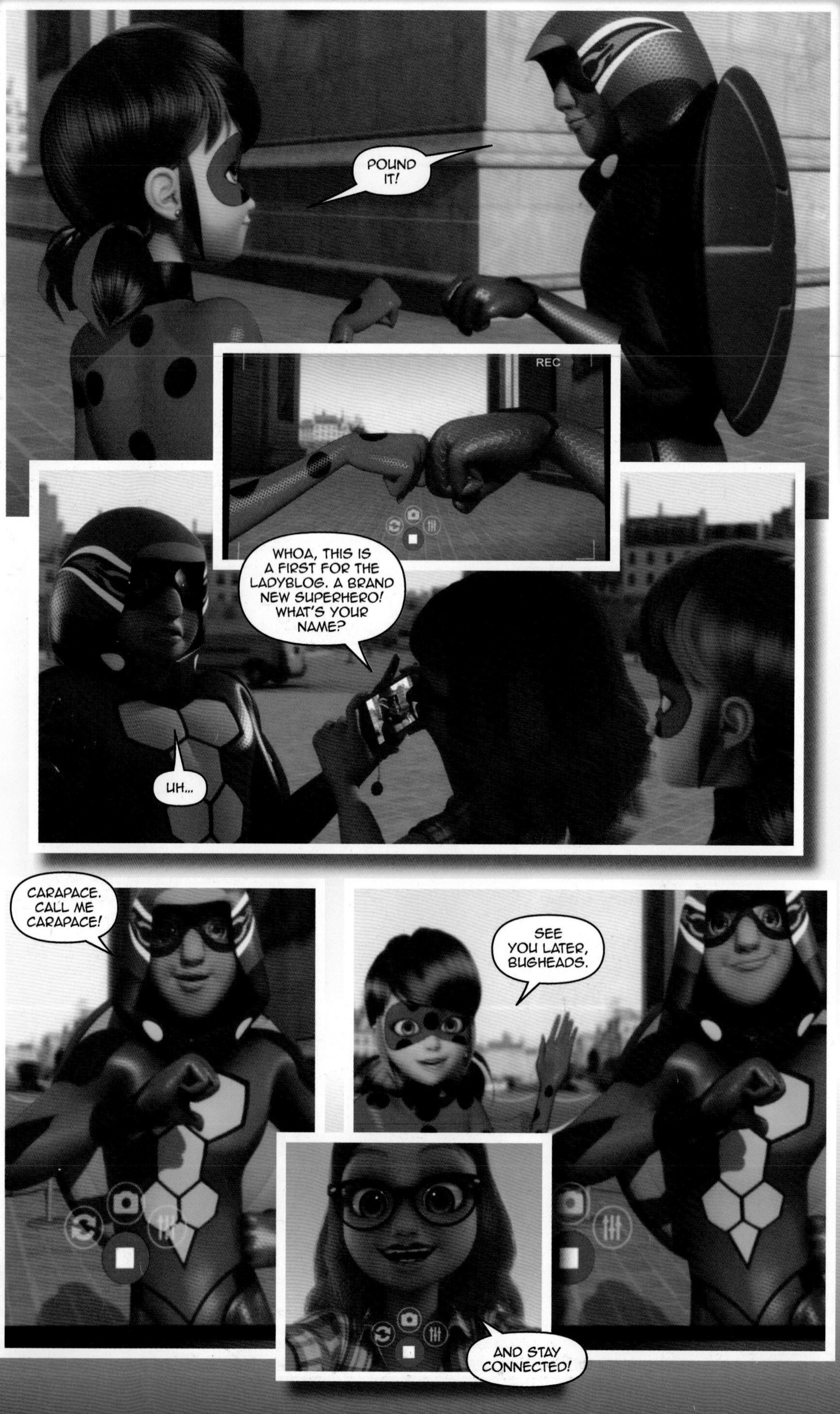
POUND IT!
REC
WHOA, THIS IS A FIRST FOR THE LADYBLOG. A BRAND NEW SUPERHERO! WHAT'S YOUR NAME?
UH...
CARAPACE. CALL ME CARAPACE!
SEE YOU LATER, BUGHEADS.
AND STAY CONNECTED!

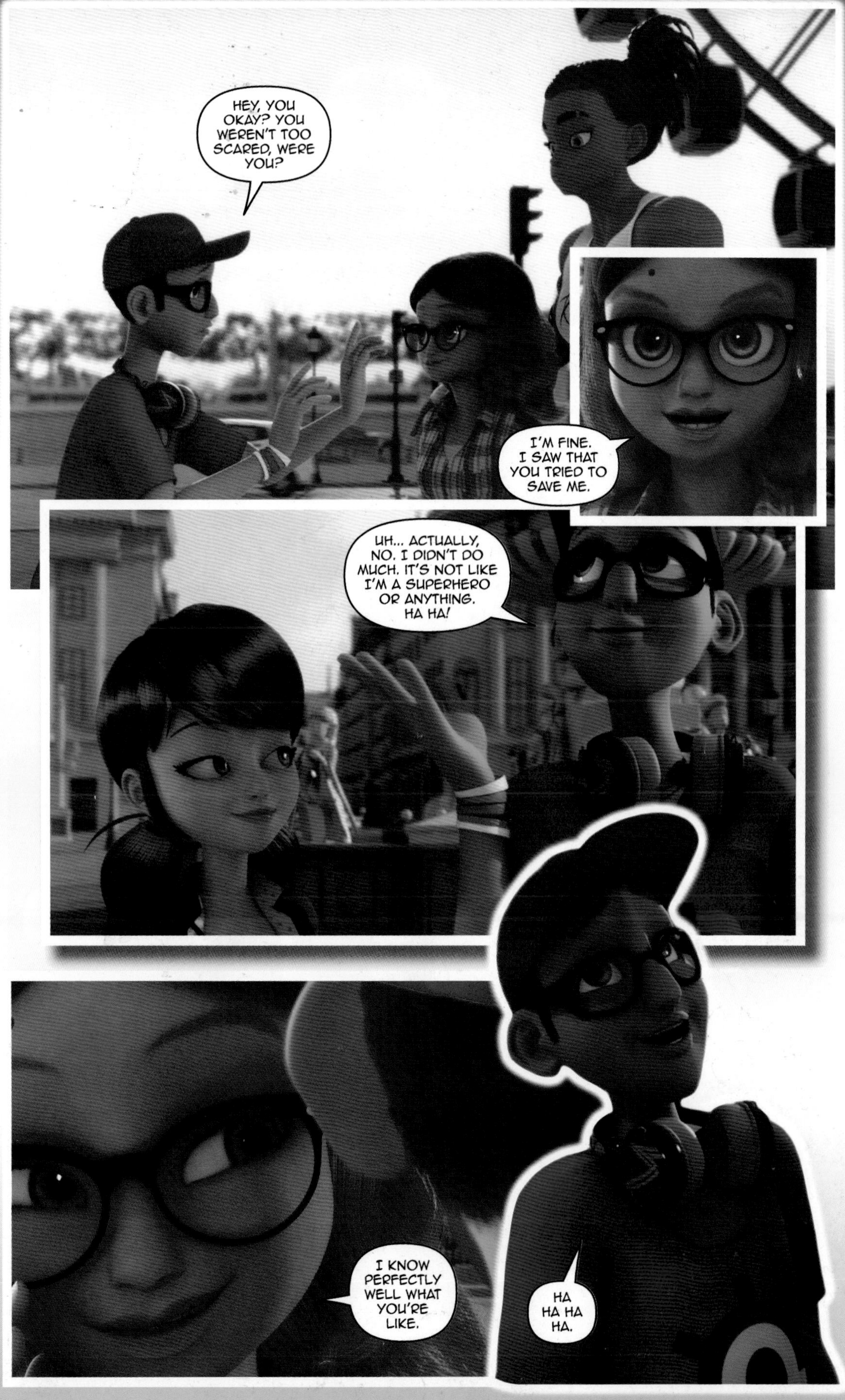
HEY, YOU OKAY? YOU WEREN'T TOO SCARED, WERE YOU?
I'M FINE. I SAW THAT YOU TRIED TO SAVE ME.
UH... ACTUALLY, NO. I DIDN'T DO MUCH. IT'S NOT LIKE I'M A SUPERHERO OR ANYTHING. HA HA!
I KNOW PERFECTLY WELL WHAT YOU'RE LIKE.
HA HA HA HA.

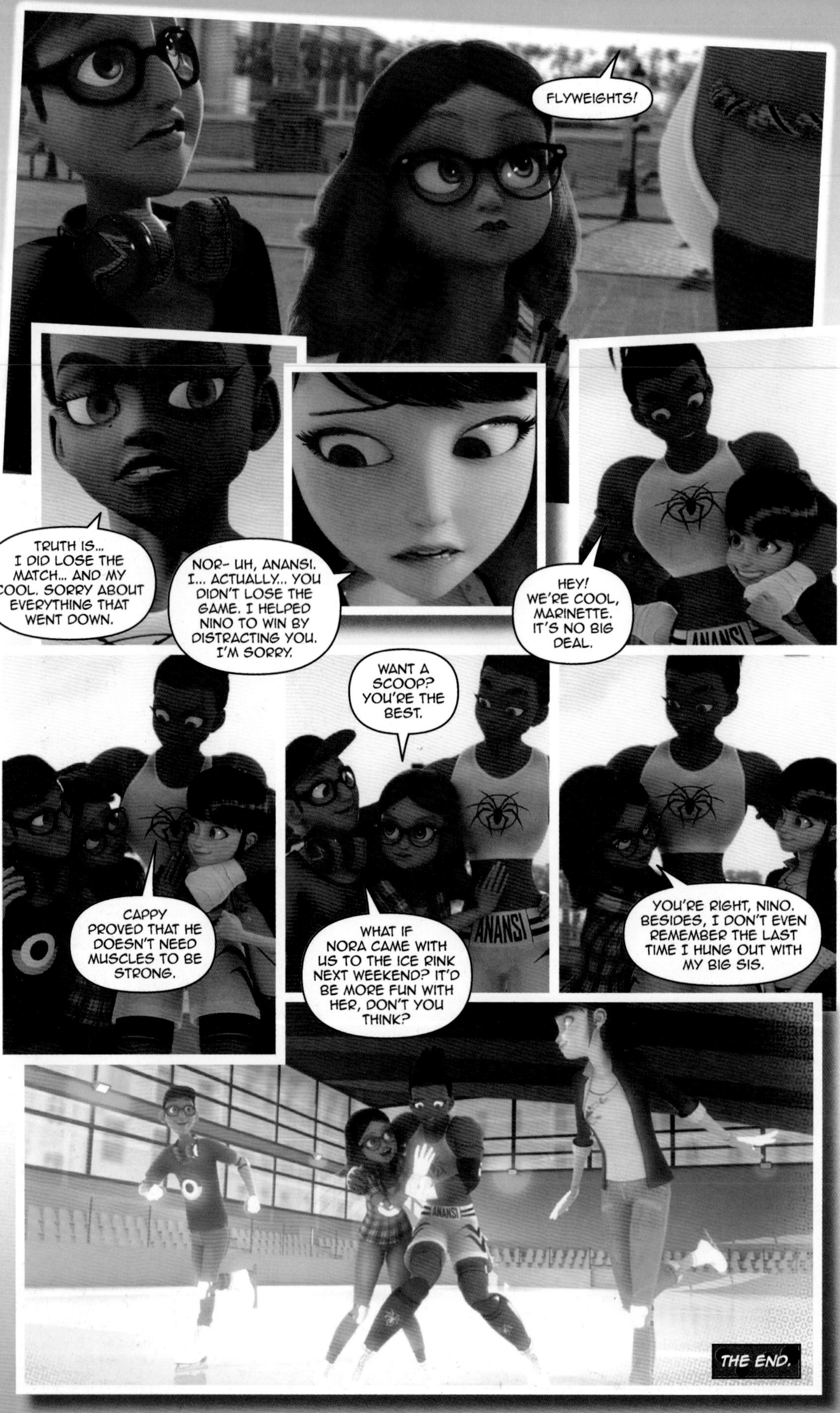
FLYWEIGHTS!
TRUTH IS... I DID LOSE THE MATCH... AND MY COOL. SORRY ABOUT EVERYTHING THAT WENT DOWN.
NOR- UH, ANANSI. I... ACTUALLY... YOU DIDN'T LOSE THE GAME. I HELPED NINO TO WIN BY DISTRACTING YOU. I'M SORRY.
HEY! WE'RE COOL, MARINETTE. IT'S NO BIG DEAL.
CAPPY PROVED THAT HE DOESN'T NEED MUSCLES TO BE STRONG.
WANT A SCOOP? YOU'RE THE BEST.
WHAT IF NORA CAME WITH US TO THE ICE RINK NEXT WEEKEND? IT'D BE MORE FUN WITH HER, DON'T YOU THINK?
YOU'RE RIGHT, NINO. BESIDES, I DON'T EVEN REMEMBER THE LAST TIME I HUNG OUT WITH MY BIG SIS.
THE END.

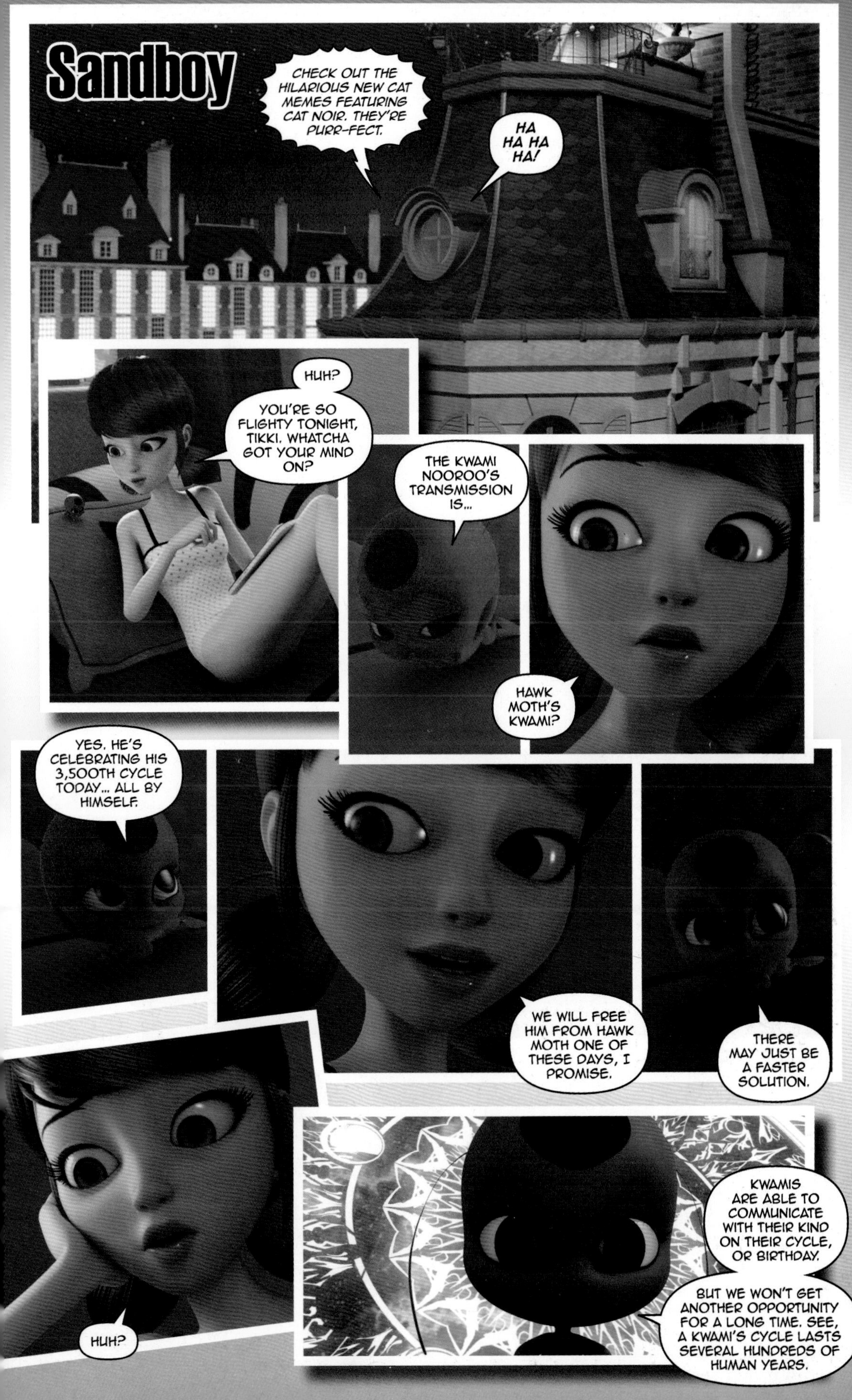
Sandboy
CHECK OUT THE HILARIOUS NEW CAT MEMES FEATURING CAT NOIR. THEY'RE PURR-FECT.
HA HA HA HA!
HUH?
YOU'RE SO FLIGHTY TONIGHT, TIKKI. WHATCHA GOT YOUR MIND ON?
THE KWAMI NOOROO'S TRANSMISSION IS...
HAWK MOTH'S KWAMI?
YES. HE'S CELEBRATING HIS 3,500TH CYCLE TODAY... ALL BY HIMSELF.
WE WILL FREE HIM FROM HAWK MOTH ONE OF THESE DAYS, I PROMISE.
THERE MAY JUST BE A FASTER SOLUTION.
HUH?
KWAMIS ARE ABLE TO COMMUNICATE WITH THEIR KIND ON THEIR CYCLE, OR BIRTHDAY.
BUT WE WON'T GET ANOTHER OPPORTUNITY FOR A LONG TIME. SEE, A KWAMI'S CYCLE LASTS SEVERAL HUNDREDS OF HUMAN YEARS.

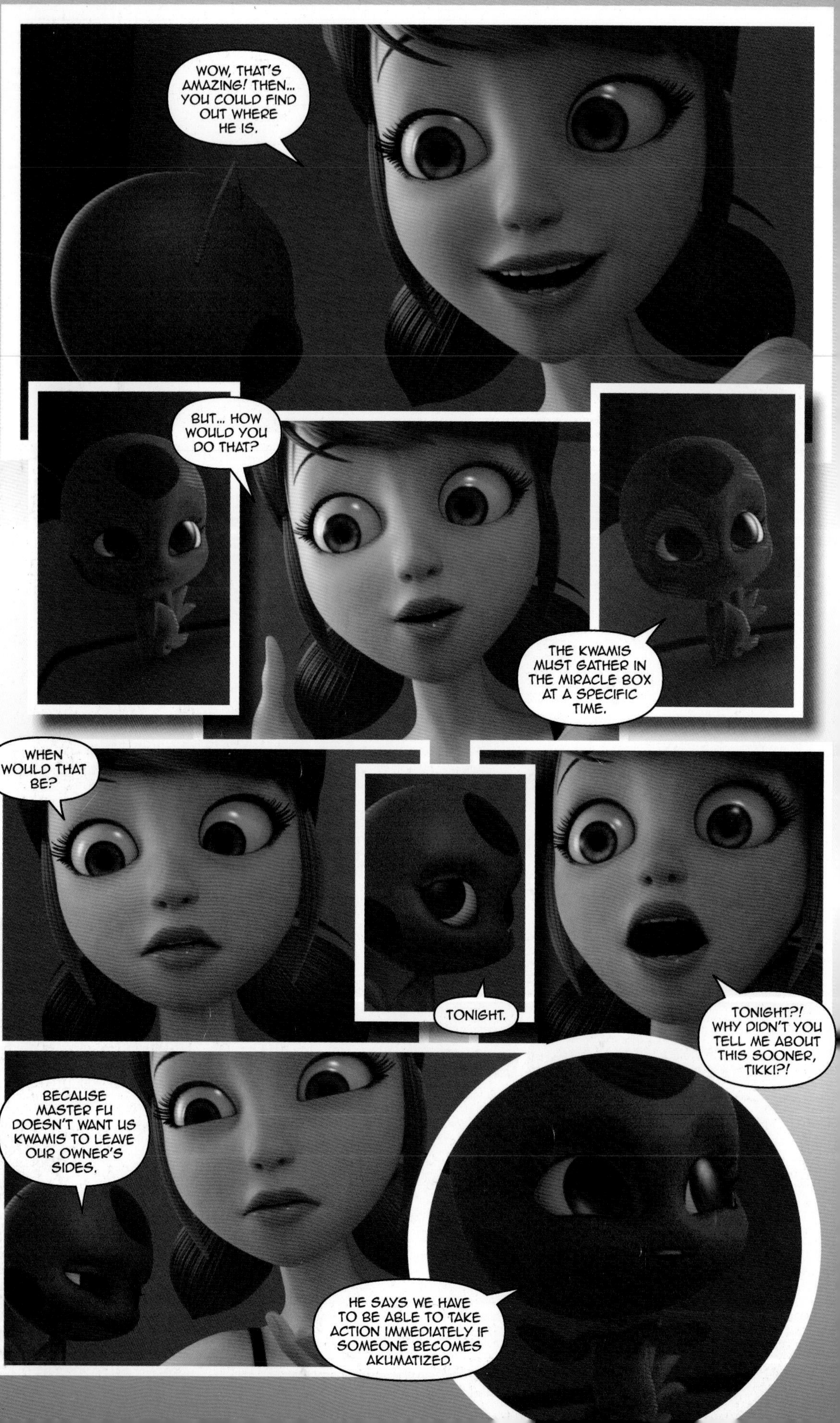
WOW, THAT'S AMAZING! THEN... YOU COULD FIND OUT WHERE HE IS.
BUT... HOW WOULD YOU DO THAT?
THE KWAMIS MUST GATHER IN THE MIRACLE BOX AT A SPECIFIC TIME.
WHEN WOULD THAT BE?
TONIGHT.
TONIGHT?! WHY DIDN'T YOU TELL ME ABOUT THIS SOONER, TIKKI?!
BECAUSE MASTER FU DOESN'T WANT US KWAMIS TO LEAVE OUR OWNER'S SIDES.
HE SAYS WE HAVE TO BE ABLE TO TAKE ACTION IMMEDIATELY IF SOMEONE BECOMES AKUMATIZED.

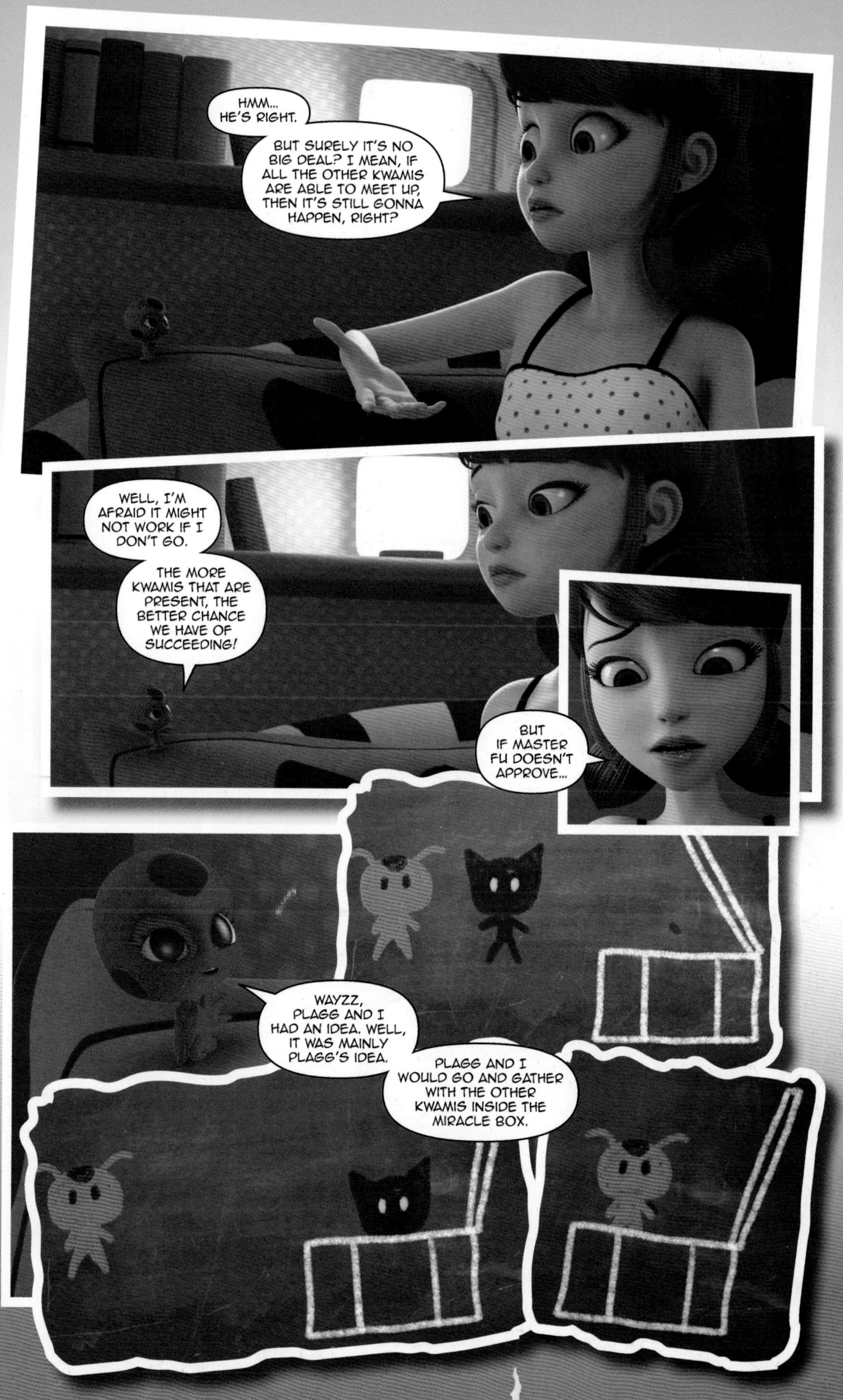
HMM... HE'S RIGHT.
BUT SURELY IT'S NO BIG DEAL? I MEAN, IF ALL THE OTHER KWAMIS ARE ABLE TO MEET UP, THEN IT'S STILL GONNA HAPPEN, RIGHT?
WELL, I'M AFRAID IT MIGHT NOT WORK IF I DON'T GO.
THE MORE KWAMIS THAT ARE PRESENT, THE BETTER CHANCE WE HAVE OF SUCCEEDING!
BUT IF MASTER FU DOESN'T APPROVE...
WAYZZ, PLAGG AND I HAD AN IDEA. WELL, IT WAS MAINLY PLAGG'S IDEA.
PLAGG AND I WOULD GO AND GATHER WITH THE OTHER KWAMIS INSIDE THE MIRACLE BOX.

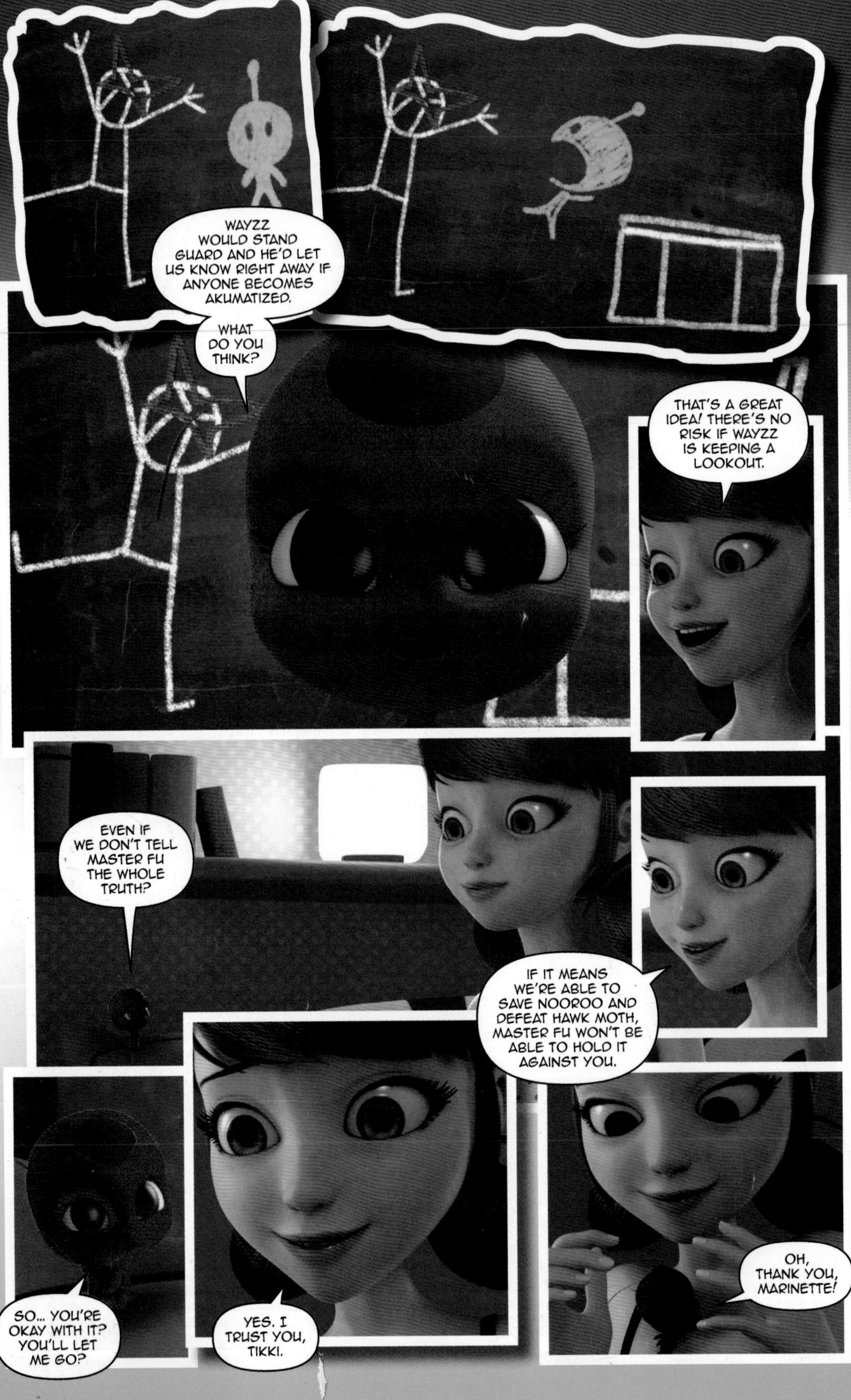
WAYZZ WOULD STAND GUARD AND HE'D LET US KNOW RIGHT AWAY IF ANYONE BECOMES AKUMATIZED.
WHAT DO YOU THINK?
THAT'S A GREAT IDEA! THERE'S NO RISK IF WAYZZ IS KEEPING A LOOKOUT.
EVEN IF WE DON'T TELL MASTER FU THE WHOLE TRUTH?
IF IT MEANS WE'RE ABLE TO SAVE NOOROO AND DEFEAT HAWK MOTH, MASTER FU WON'T BE ABLE TO HOLD IT AGAINST YOU.
SO... YOU'RE OKAY WITH IT? YOU'LL LET ME GO?
YES. I TRUST YOU, TIKKI.
OH, THANK YOU, MARINETTE!

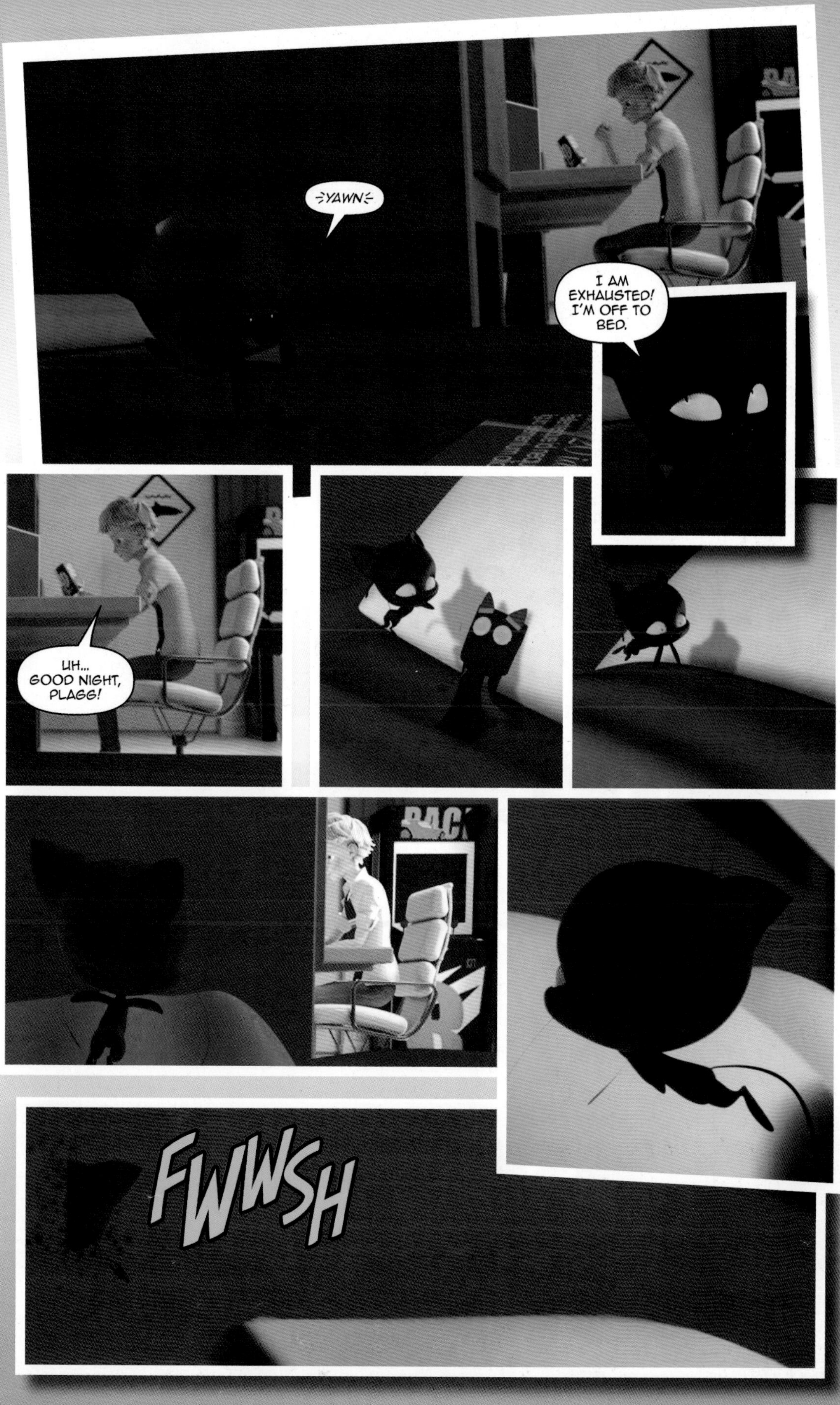

YAWN
I AM EXHAUSTED! I'M OFF TO BED.
UH... GOOD NIGHT, PLAGG!
FWWSH

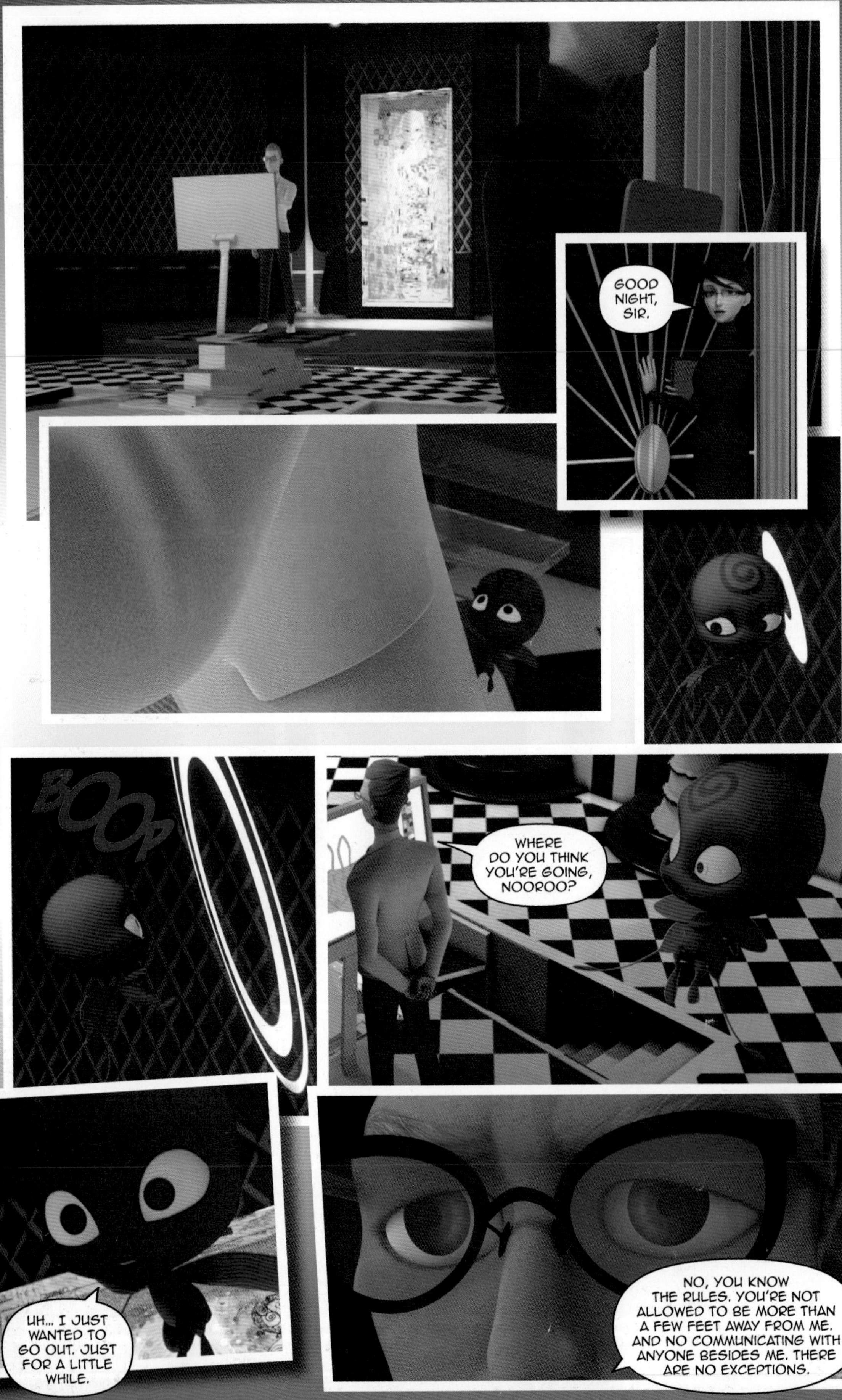
GOOD NIGHT, SIR.
BOOP
WHERE DO YOU THINK YOU'RE GOING, NOOROO?
UH... I JUST WANTED TO GO OUT. JUST FOR A LITTLE WHILE.
NO, YOU KNOW THE RULES. YOU'RE NOT ALLOWED TO BE MORE THAN A FEW FEET AWAY FROM ME. AND NO COMMUNICATING WITH ANYONE BESIDES ME. THERE ARE NO EXCEPTIONS.

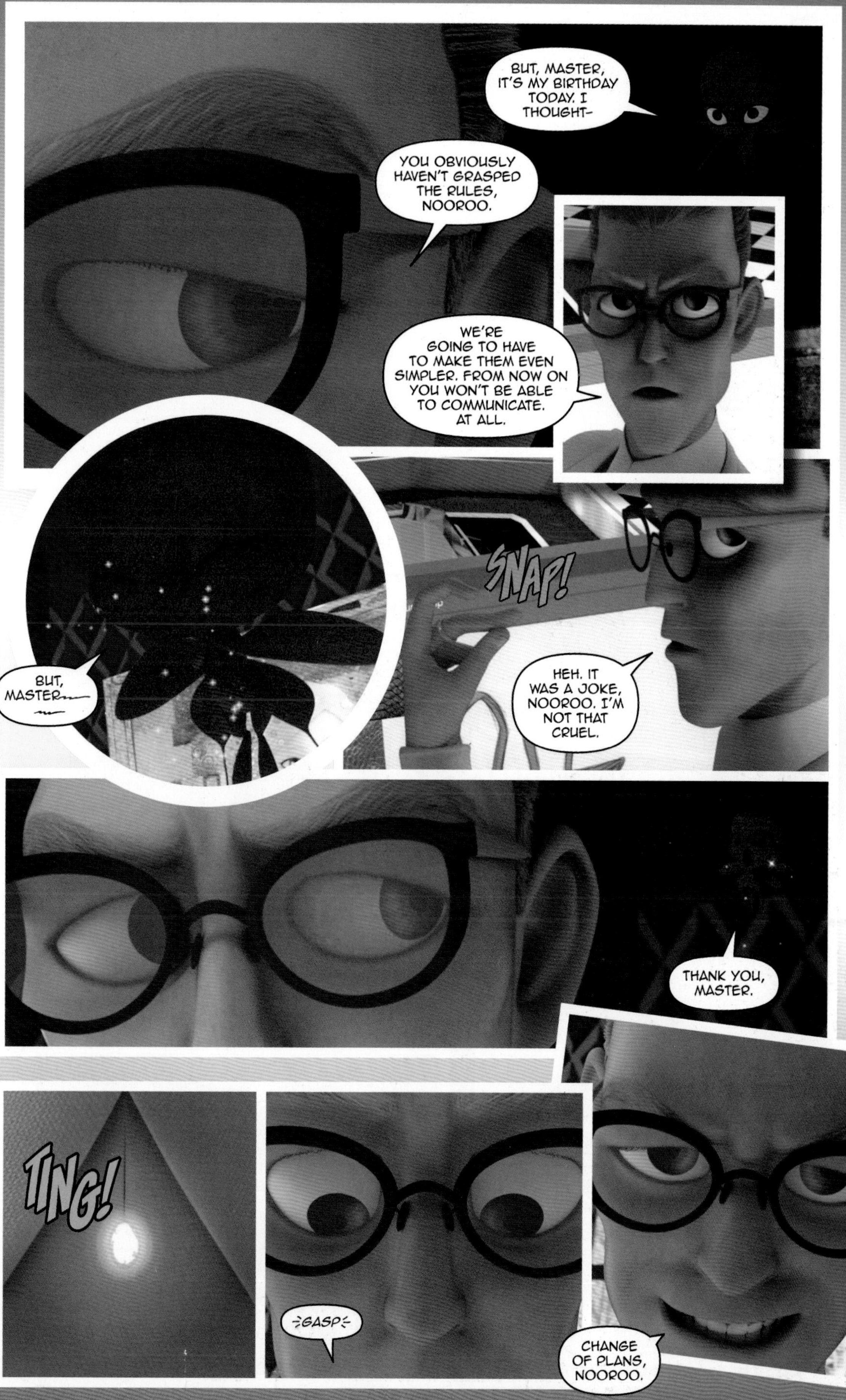
BUT, MASTER, IT'S MY BIRTHDAY TODAY. I THOUGHT-
YOU OBVIOUSLY HAVEN'T GRASPED THE RULES, NOOROO.
WE'RE GOING TO HAVE TO MAKE THEM EVEN SIMPLER. FROM NOW ON YOU WON'T BE ABLE TO COMMUNICATE. AT ALL.
BUT, MASTER
SNAP!
HEH. IT WAS A JOKE, NOOROO. I'M NOT THAT CRUEL.
THANK YOU, MASTER.
TING!
GASP
CHANGE OF PLANS, NOOROO.

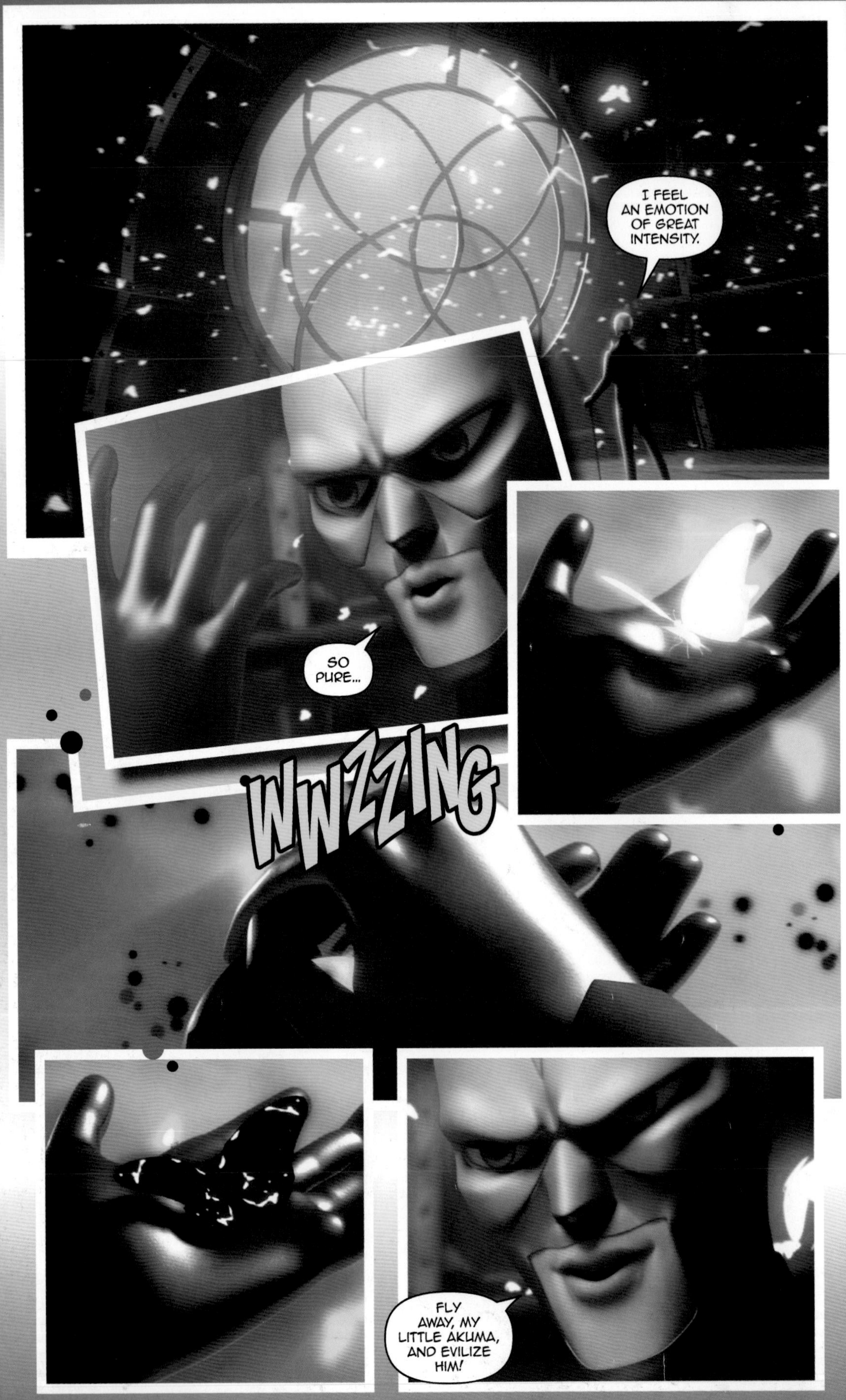
I FEEL AN EMOTION OF GREAT INTENSITY.
SO PURE...
WWZZING
FLY AWAY, MY LITTLE AKUMA, AND EVILIZE HIM!

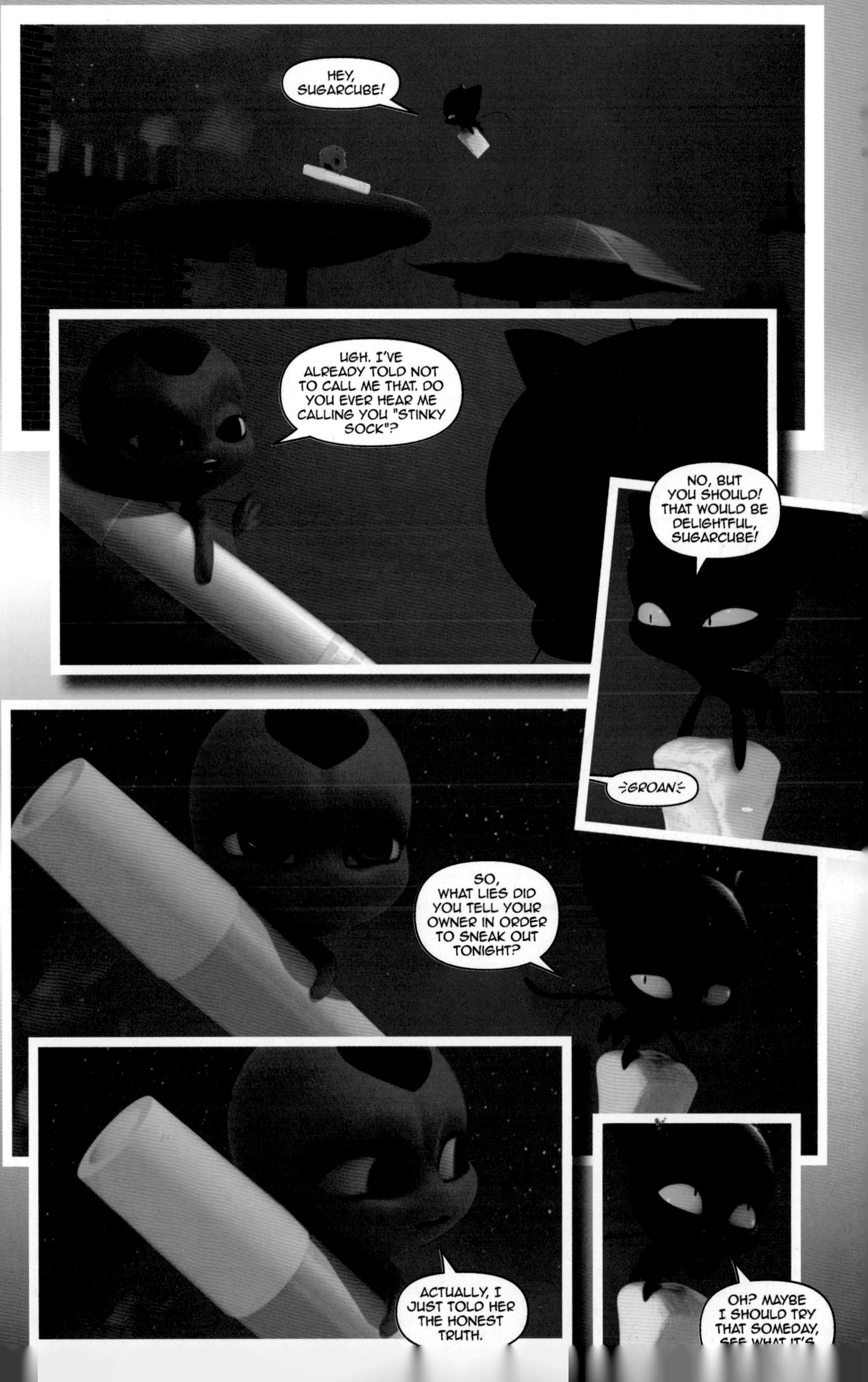
HEY, SUGARCUBE!
UGH. I'VE ALREADY TOLD NOT TO CALL ME THAT. DO YOU EVER HEAR ME CALLING YOU "STINKY SOCK"?
NO, BUT YOU SHOULD! THAT WOULD BE DELIGHTFUL, SUGARCUBE!
GROAN
SO, WHAT LIES DID YOU TELL YOUR OWNER IN ORDER TO SNEAK OUT TONIGHT?
ACTUALLY, I JUST TOLD HER THE HONEST TRUTH.
OH? MAYBE I SHOULD TRY THAT SOMEDAY,

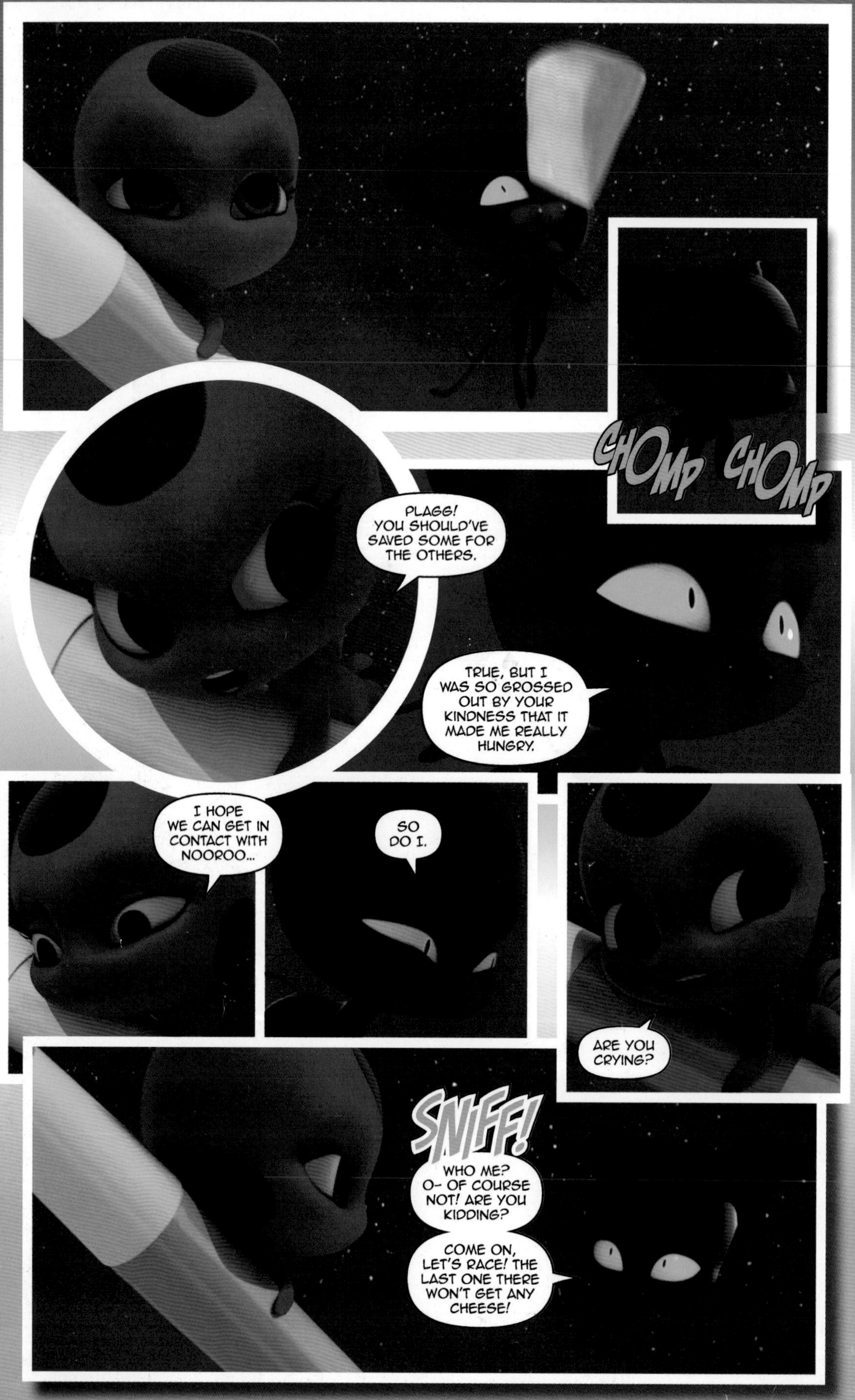
CHOMP CHOMP
PLAGG! YOU SHOULD'VE SAVED SOME FOR THE OTHERS.
TRUE, BUT I WAS SO GROSSED OUT BY YOUR KINDNESS THAT IT MADE ME REALLY HUNGRY.
I HOPE WE CAN GET IN CONTACT WITH NOOROO...
SO DO I.
ARE YOU CRYING?
SNIFF!
WHO ME? O- OF COURSE NOT! ARE YOU KIDDING?
COME ON, LET'S RACE! THE LAST ONE THERE WON'T GET ANY CHEESE!

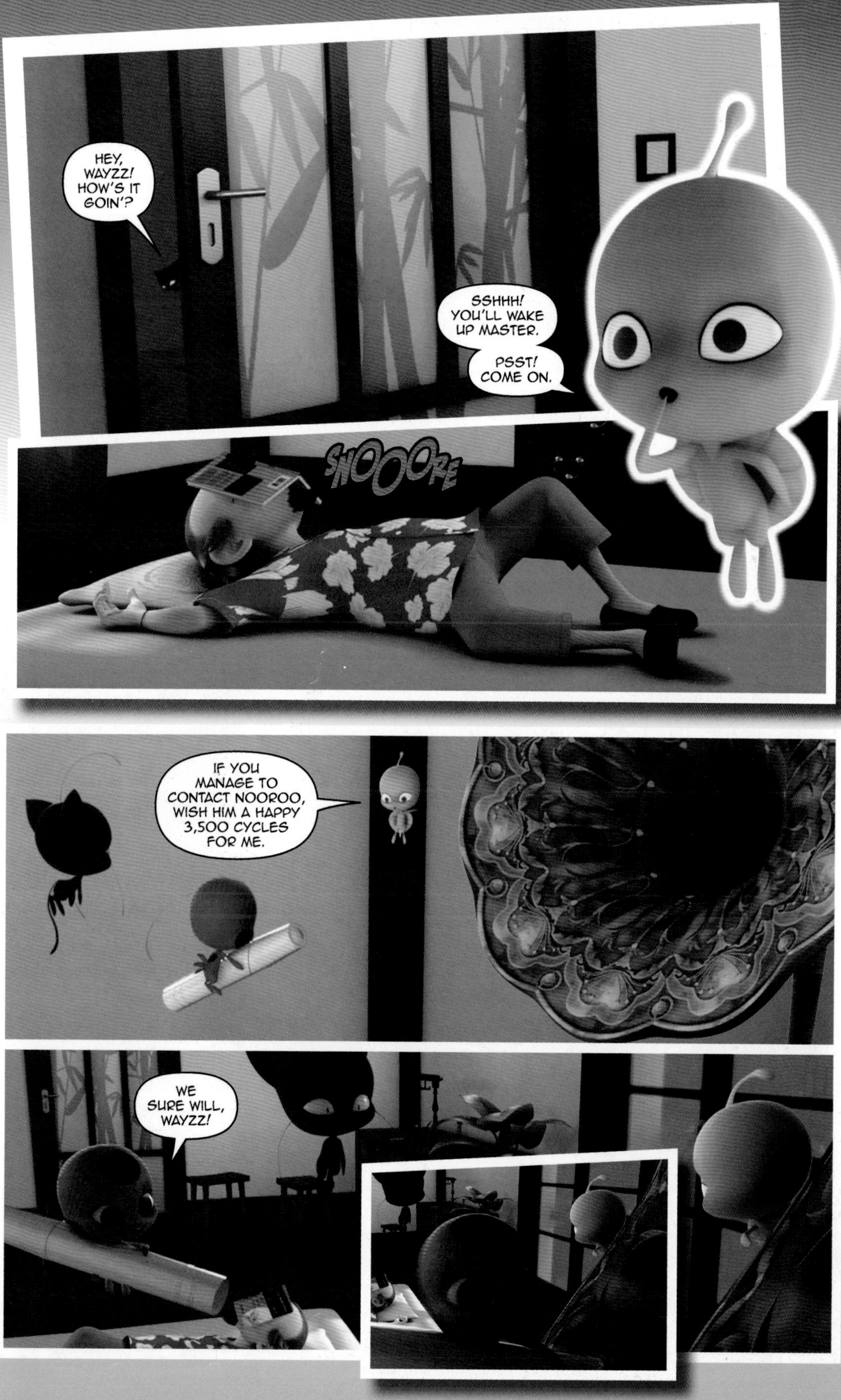
HEY, WAYZZ! HOW'S IT GOIN'?
SSHHH! YOU'LL WAKE UP MASTER.
PSST! COME ON.
SNOOORE
IF YOU MANAGE TO CONTACT NOOROO, WISH HIM A HAPPY 3,500 CYCLES FOR ME.
WE SURE WILL, WAYZZ!

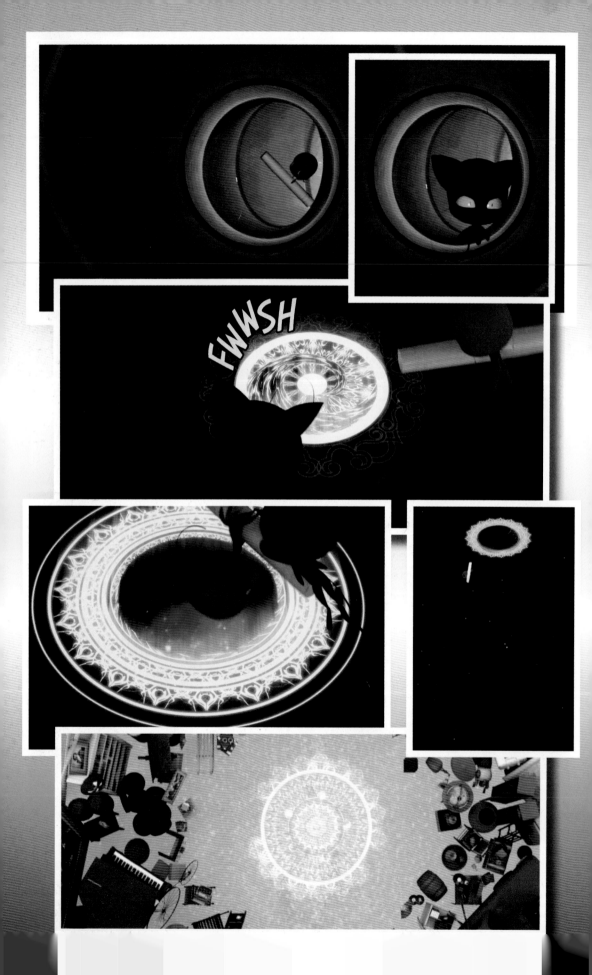

FWWSH

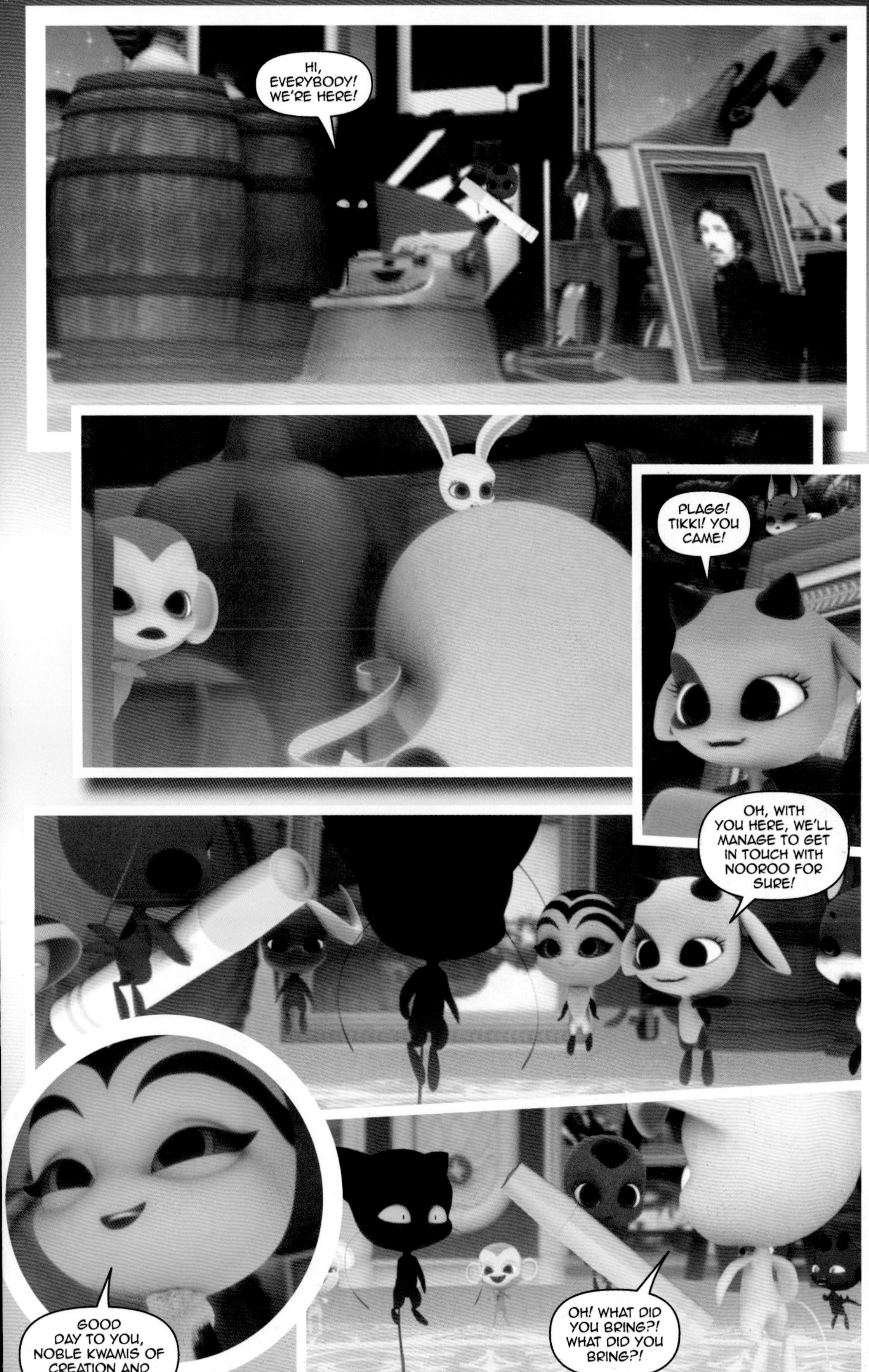
HI, EVERYBODY! WE'RE HERE!
PLAGG! TIKKI! YOU CAME!
OH, WITH YOU HERE, WE'LL MANAGE TO GET IN TOUCH WITH NOOROO FOR SURE!
GOOD DAY TO YOU, NOBLE KWAMIS OF CREATION AND DESTRUCTION.
OH! WHAT DID YOU BRING?! WHAT DID YOU BRING?!

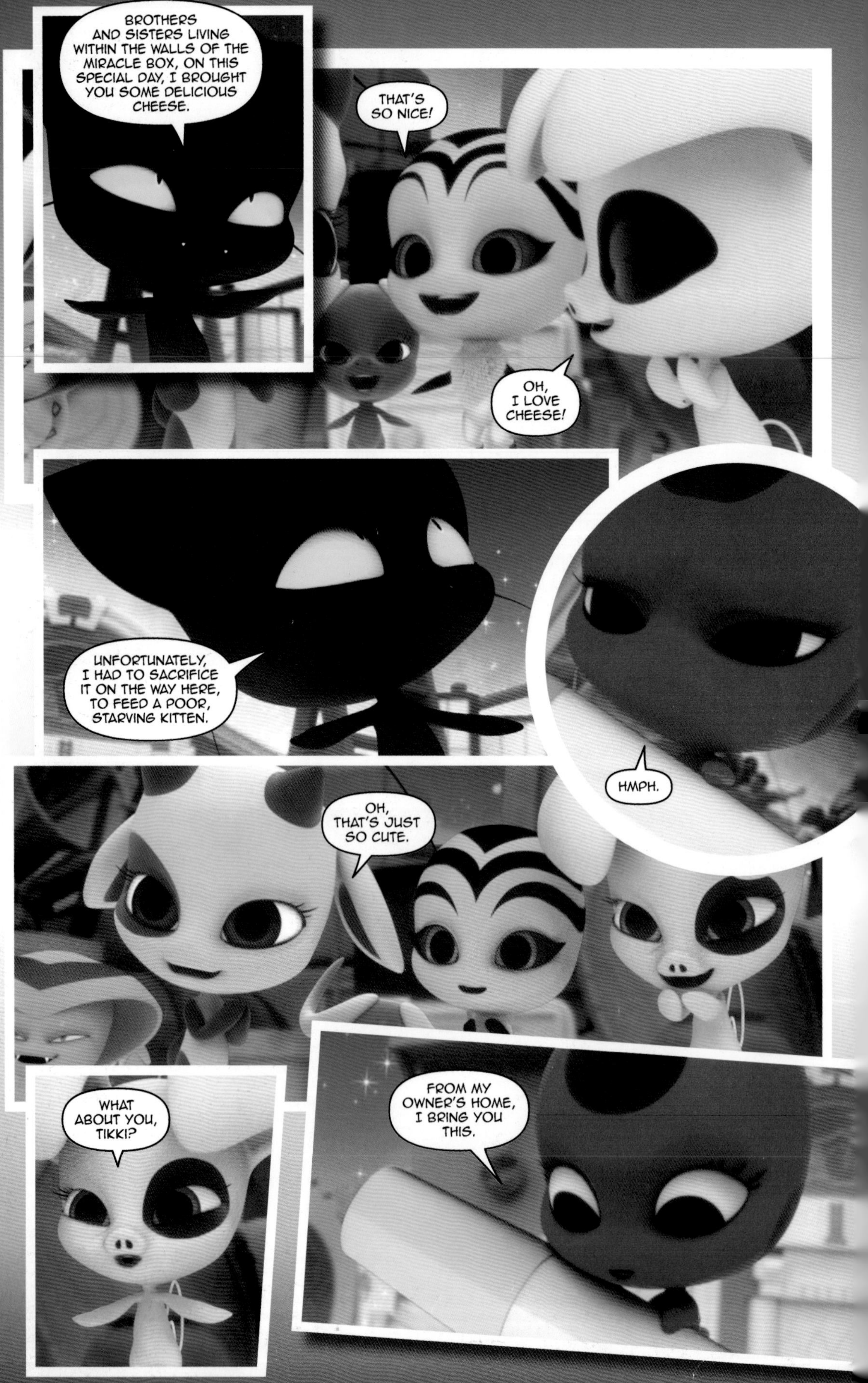
BROTHERS AND SISTERS LIVING WITHIN THE WALLS OF THE MIRACLE BOX, ON THIS SPECIAL DAY, I BROUGHT YOU SOME DELICIOUS CHEESE.
THAT'S SO NICE!
OH, I LOVE CHEESE!
UNFORTUNATELY, I HAD TO SACRIFICE IT ON THE WAY HERE, TO FEED A POOR, STARVING KITTEN.
HMPH.
OH, THAT'S JUST SO CUTE.
WHAT ABOUT YOU, TIKKI?
FROM MY OWNER'S HOME, I BRING YOU THIS.

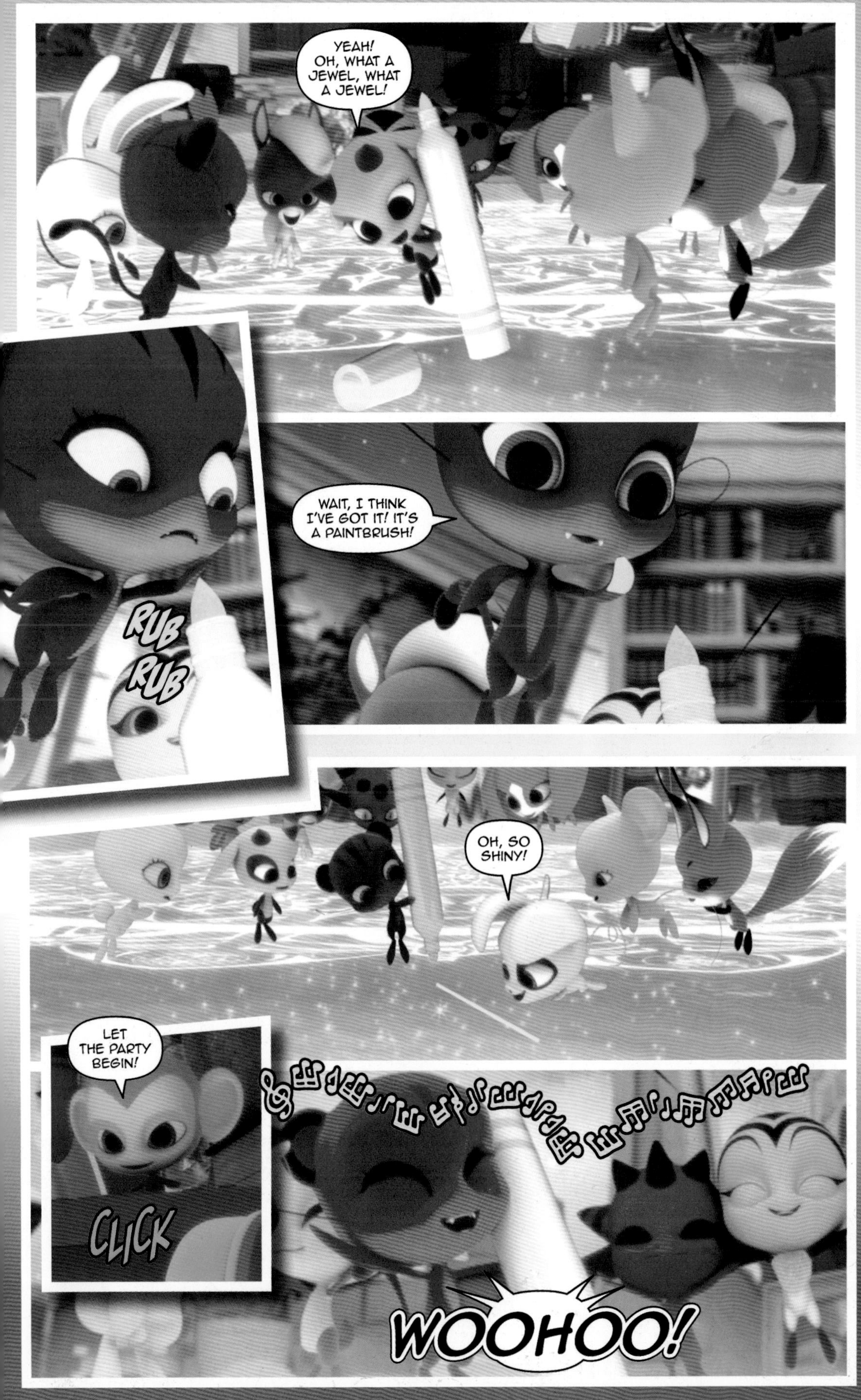
YEAH! OH, WHAT A JEWEL, WHAT A JEWEL!
RUB RUB
WAIT, I THINK I'VE GOT IT! IT'S A PAINTBRUSH!
OH, SO SHINY!
LET THE PARTY BEGIN!
CLICK
WOOHOO!

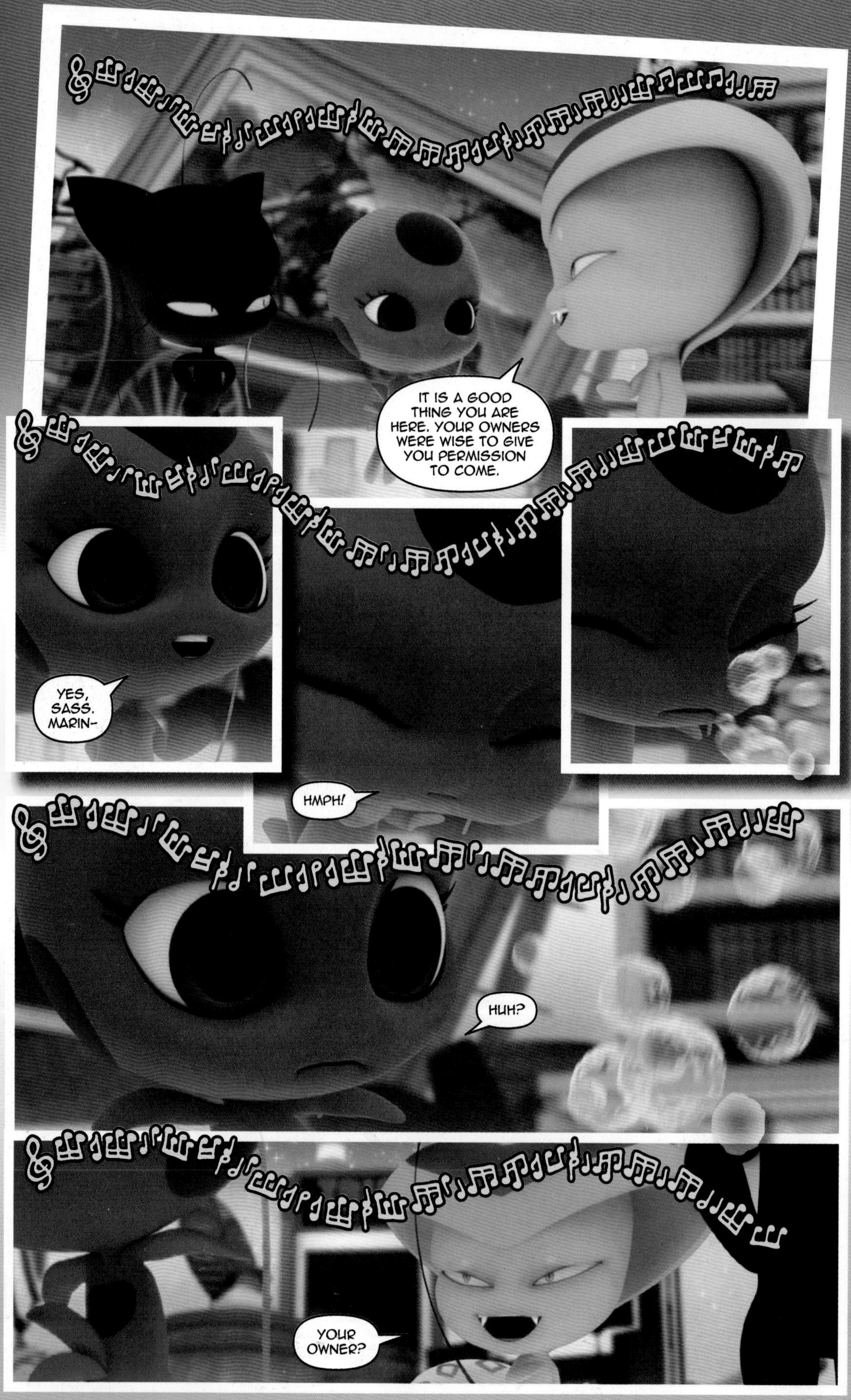
IT IS A GOOD THING YOU ARE HERE. YOUR OWNERS WERE WISE TO GIVE YOU PERMISSION TO COME.
YES, SASS. MARIN-
HMPH!
HUH?
YOUR OWNER?

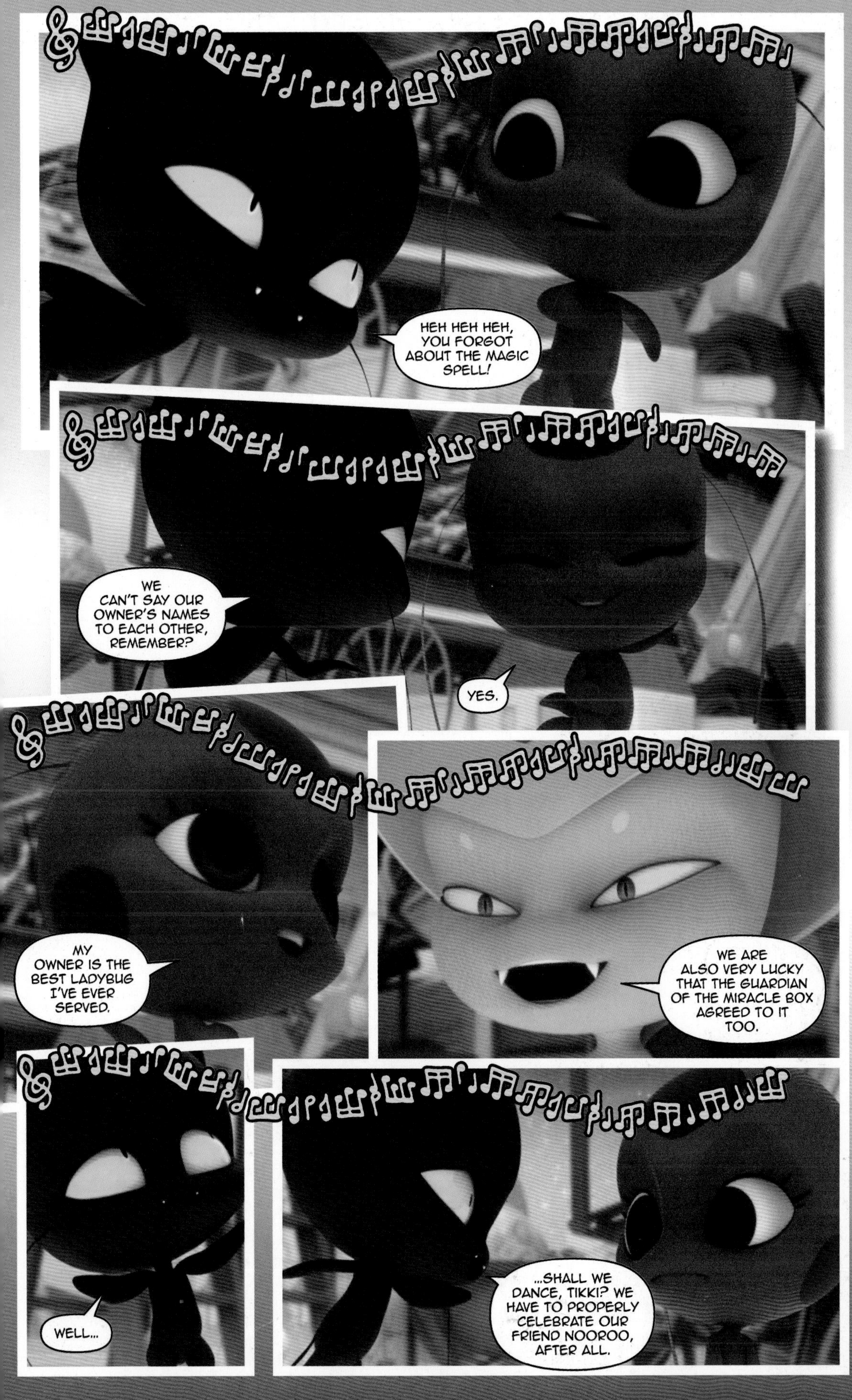
HEH HEH HEH, YOU FORGOT ABOUT THE MAGIC SPELL!
WE CAN'T SAY OUR OWNER'S NAMES TO EACH OTHER, REMEMBER?
YES.
MY OWNER IS THE BEST LADYBUG I'VE EVER SERVED.
WE ARE ALSO VERY LUCKY THAT THE GUARDIAN OF THE MIRACLE BOX AGREED TO IT TOO.
WELL...
...SHALL WE DANCE, TIKKI? WE HAVE TO PROPERLY CELEBRATE OUR FRIEND NOOROO, AFTER ALL.

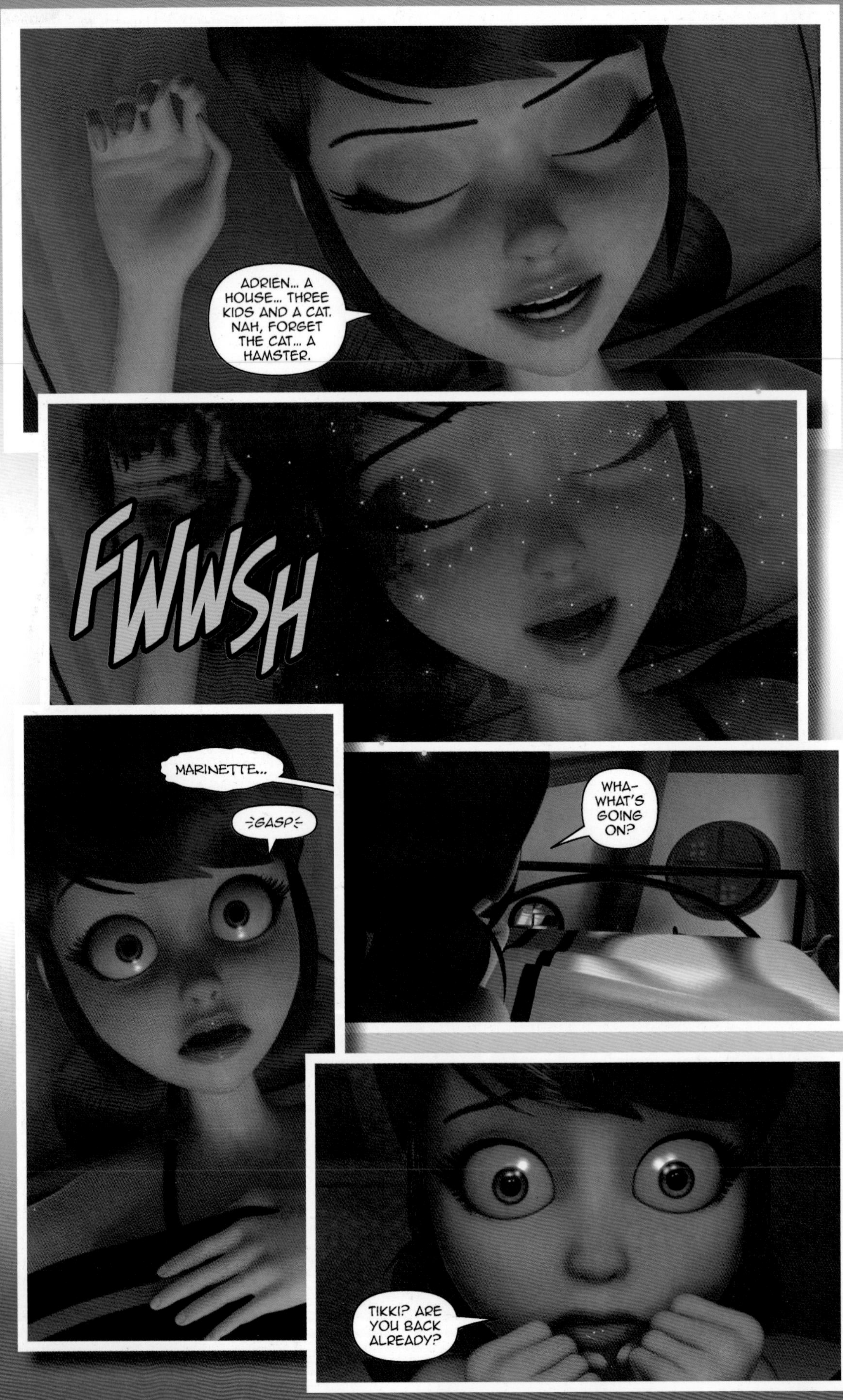
ADRIEN... A HOUSE... THREE KIDS AND A CAT. NAH, FORGET THE CAT... A HAMSTER.
FWWSH
MARINETTE...
GASP
WHA-WHAT'S GOING ON?
TIKKI? ARE YOU BACK ALREADY?

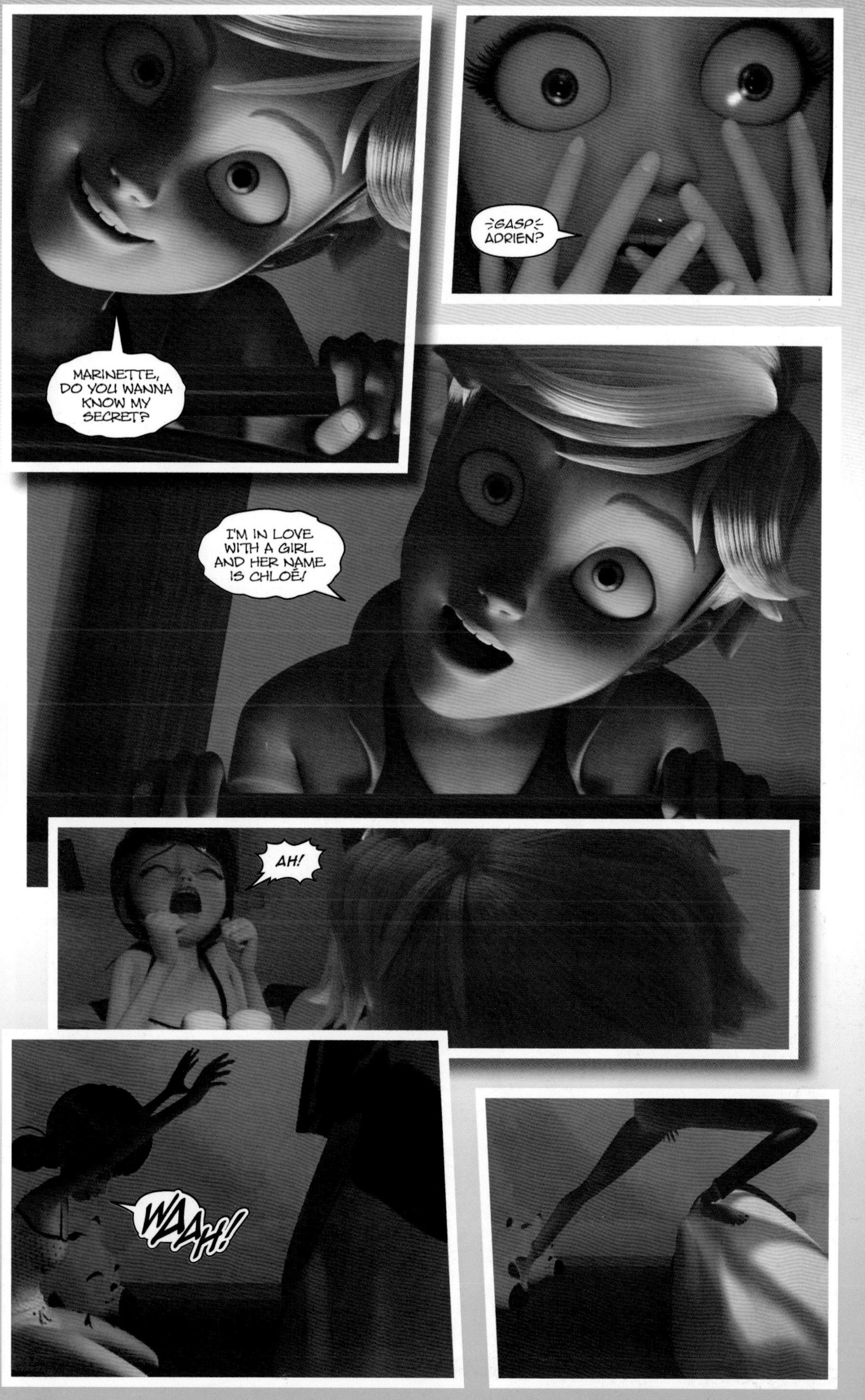
MARINETTE, DO YOU WANNA KNOW MY SECRET?
GASP ADRIEN?
I'M IN LOVE WITH A GIRL AND HER NAME IS CHLOÉ!
AH!
WAAH!

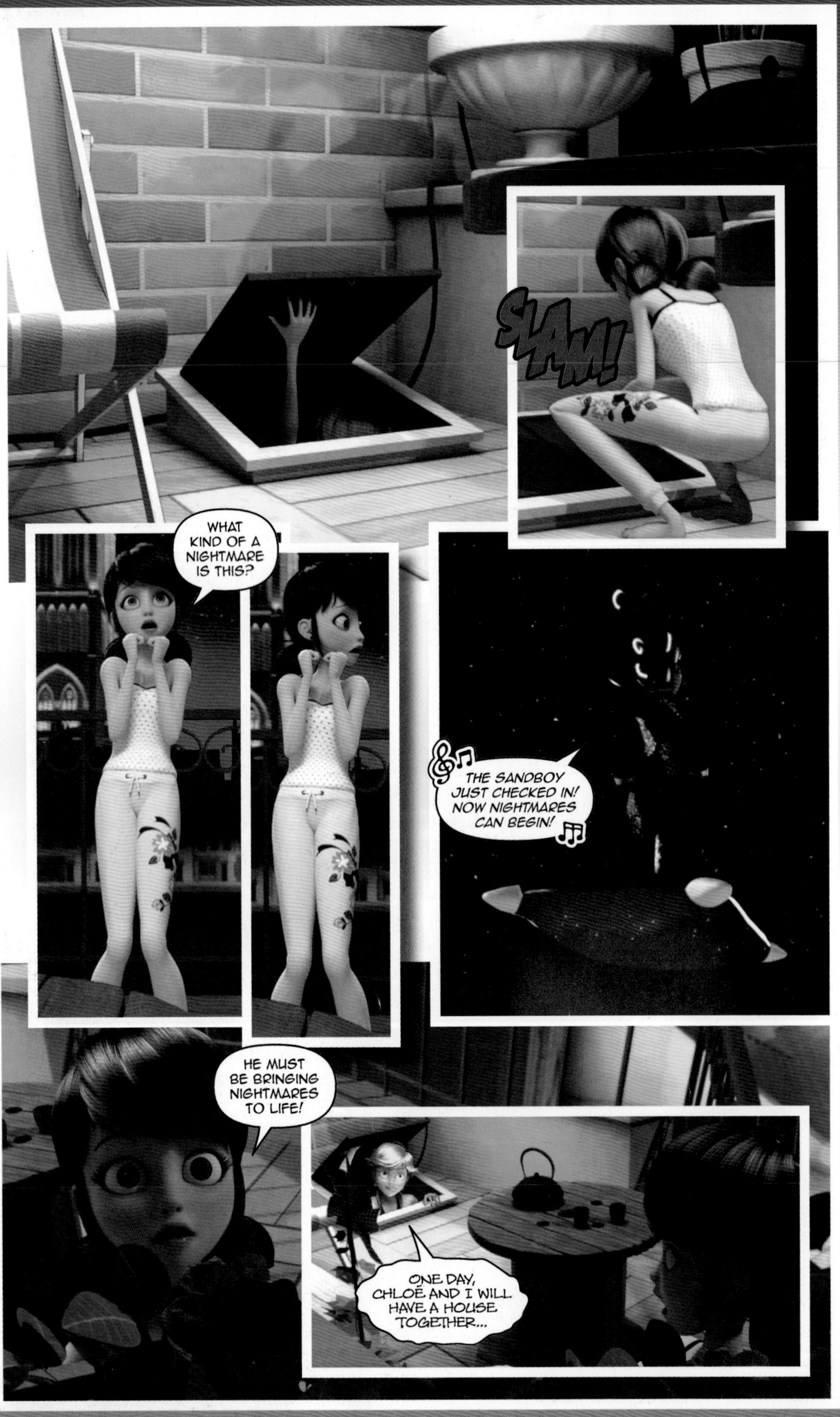
SLAM!
WHAT KIND OF A NIGHTMARE IS THIS?
THE SANDBOY JUST CHECKED IN! NOW NIGHTMARES CAN BEGIN!
HE MUST BE BRINGING NIGHTMARES TO LIFE!
ONE DAY, CHLOË AND I WILL HAVE A HOUSE TOGETHER...

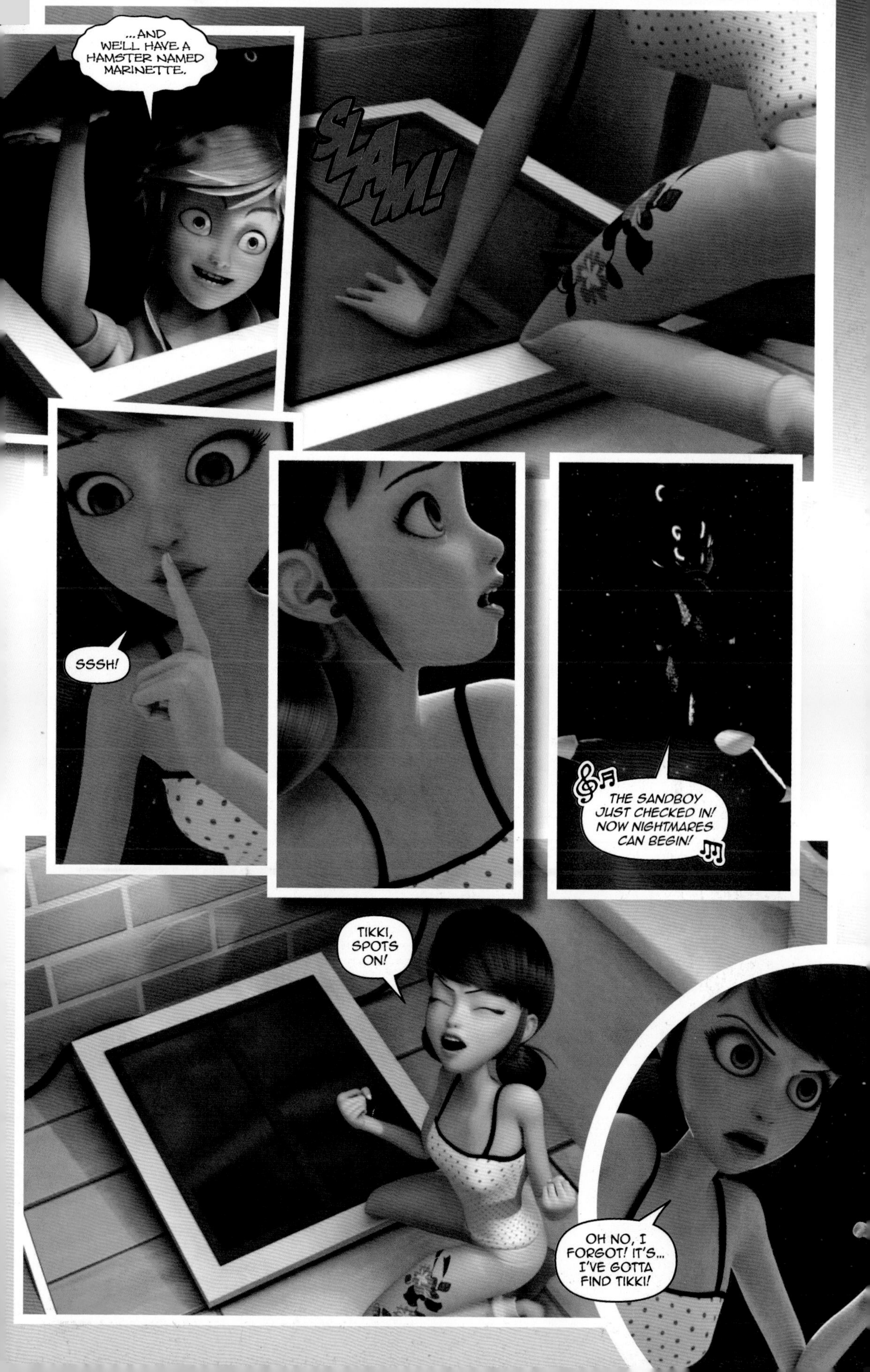
...AND WE'LL HAVE A HAMSTER NAMED MARINETTE.
SLAM!
SSSH!
THE SANDBOY JUST CHECKED IN! NOW NIGHTMARES CAN BEGIN!
TIKKI, SPOTS ON!
OH NO, I FORGOT! IT'S... I'VE GOTTA FIND TIKKI!

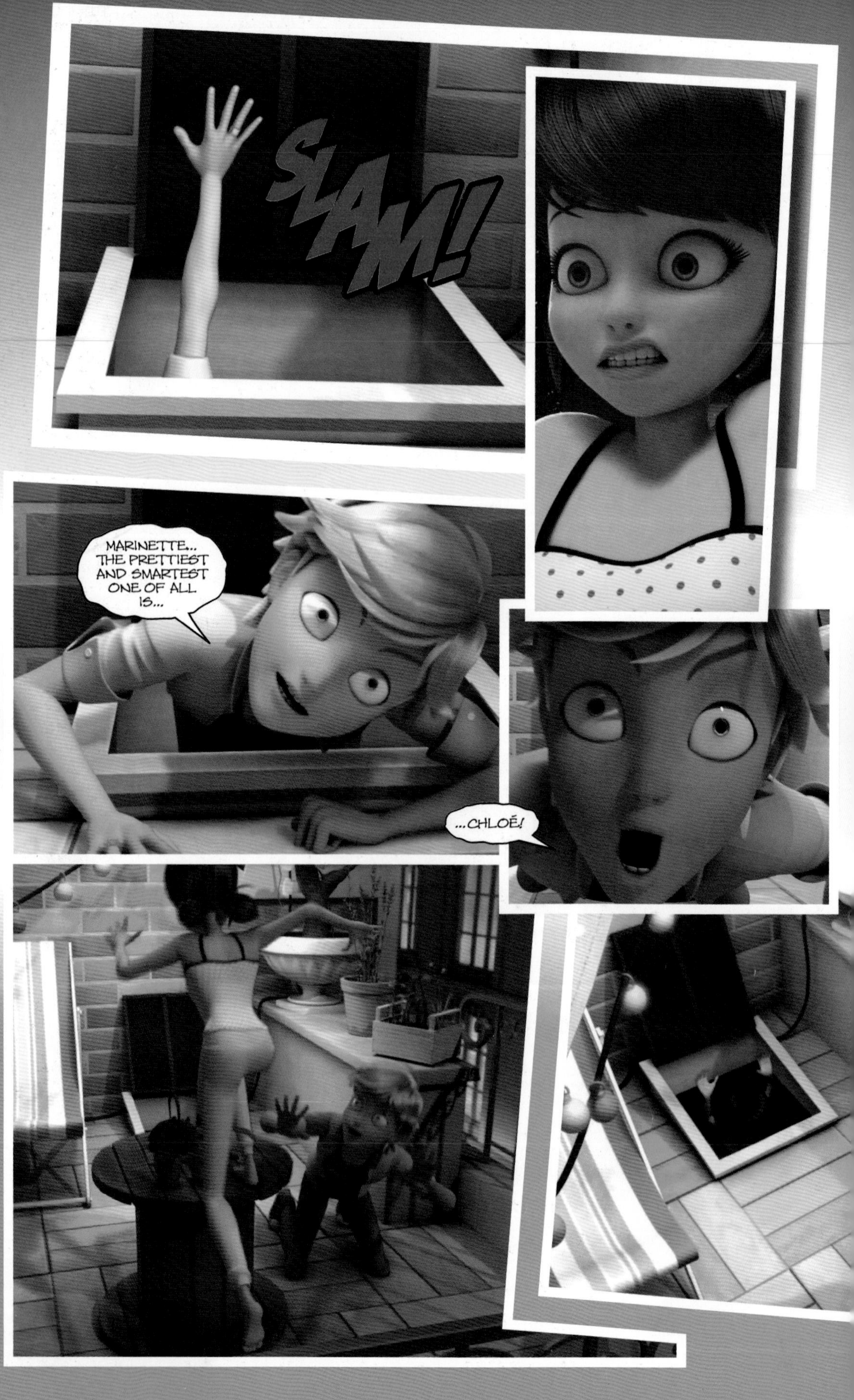
SLAM!
MARINETTE... THE PRETTIEST AND SMARTEST ONE OF ALL IS...
...CHLOÉ!

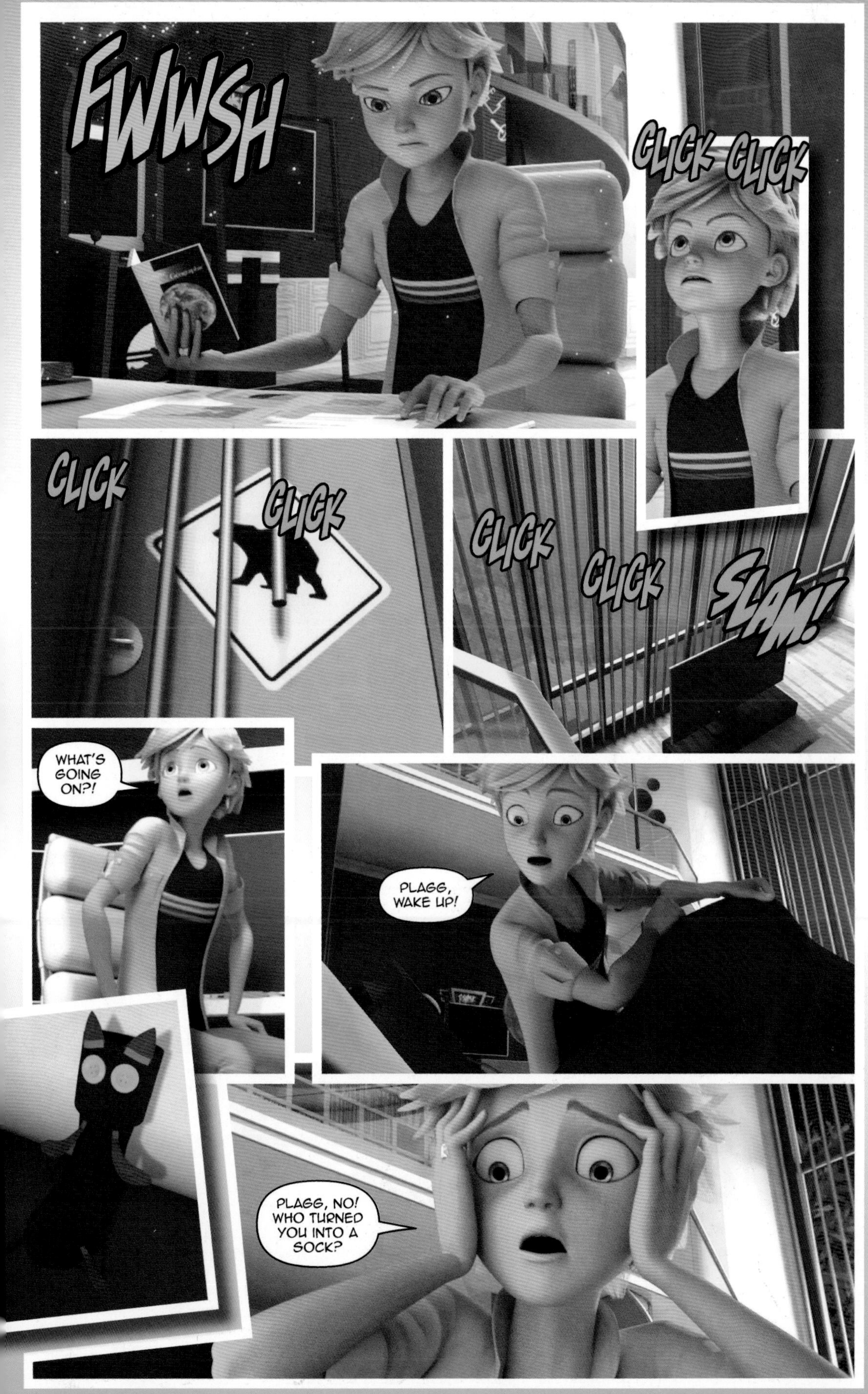
FWWSH
CLICK CLICK
CLICK
CLICK
CLICK
CLICK
SLAM!
WHAT'S GOING ON?!
PLAGG, WAKE UP!
PLAGG, NO! WHO TURNED YOU INTO A SOCK?

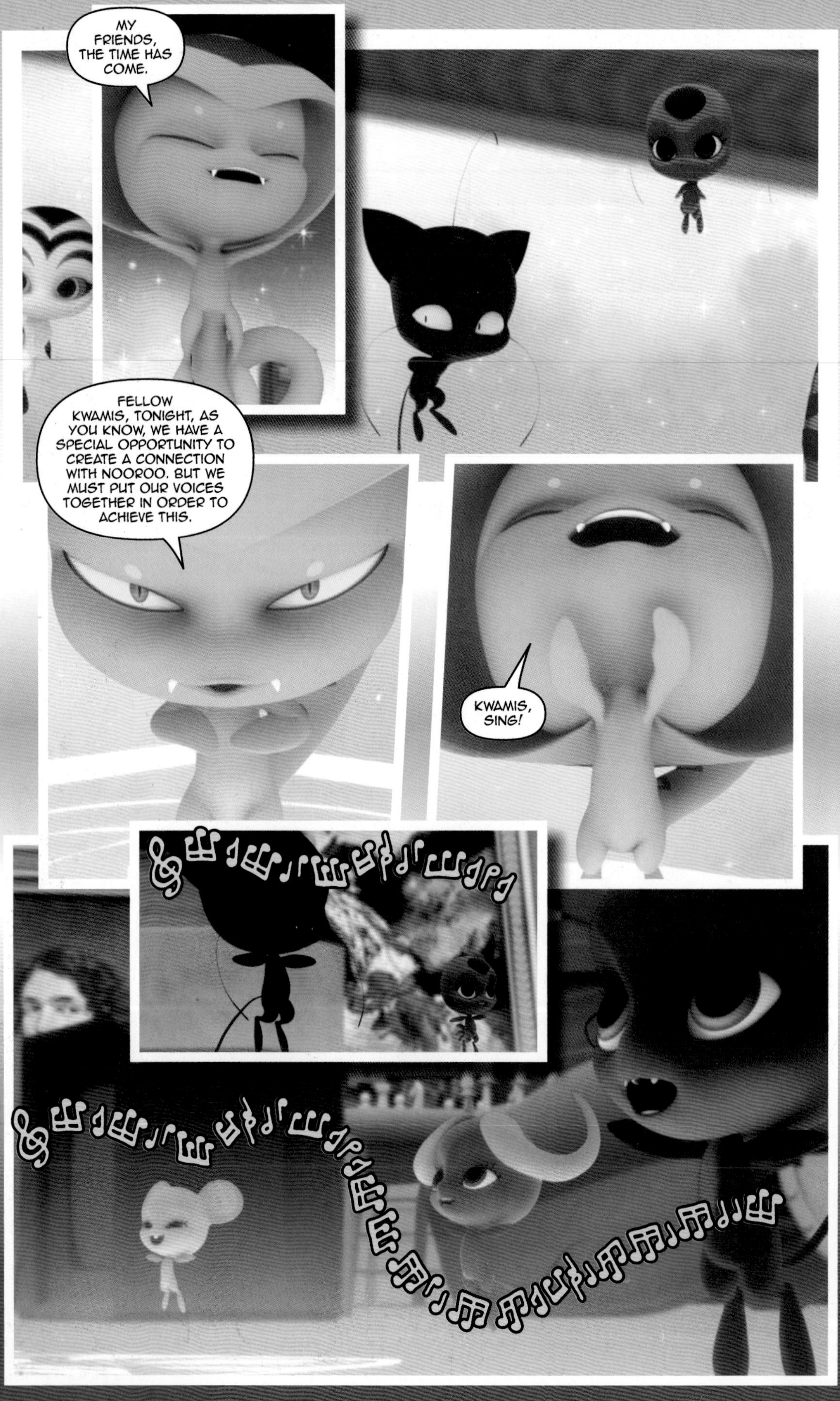
MY FRIENDS, THE TIME HAS COME.
FELLOW KWAMIS, TONIGHT, AS YOU KNOW, WE HAVE A SPECIAL OPPORTUNITY TO CREATE A CONNECTION WITH NOOROO. BUT WE MUST PUT OUR VOICES TOGETHER IN ORDER TO ACHIEVE THIS.
KWAMIS, SING!

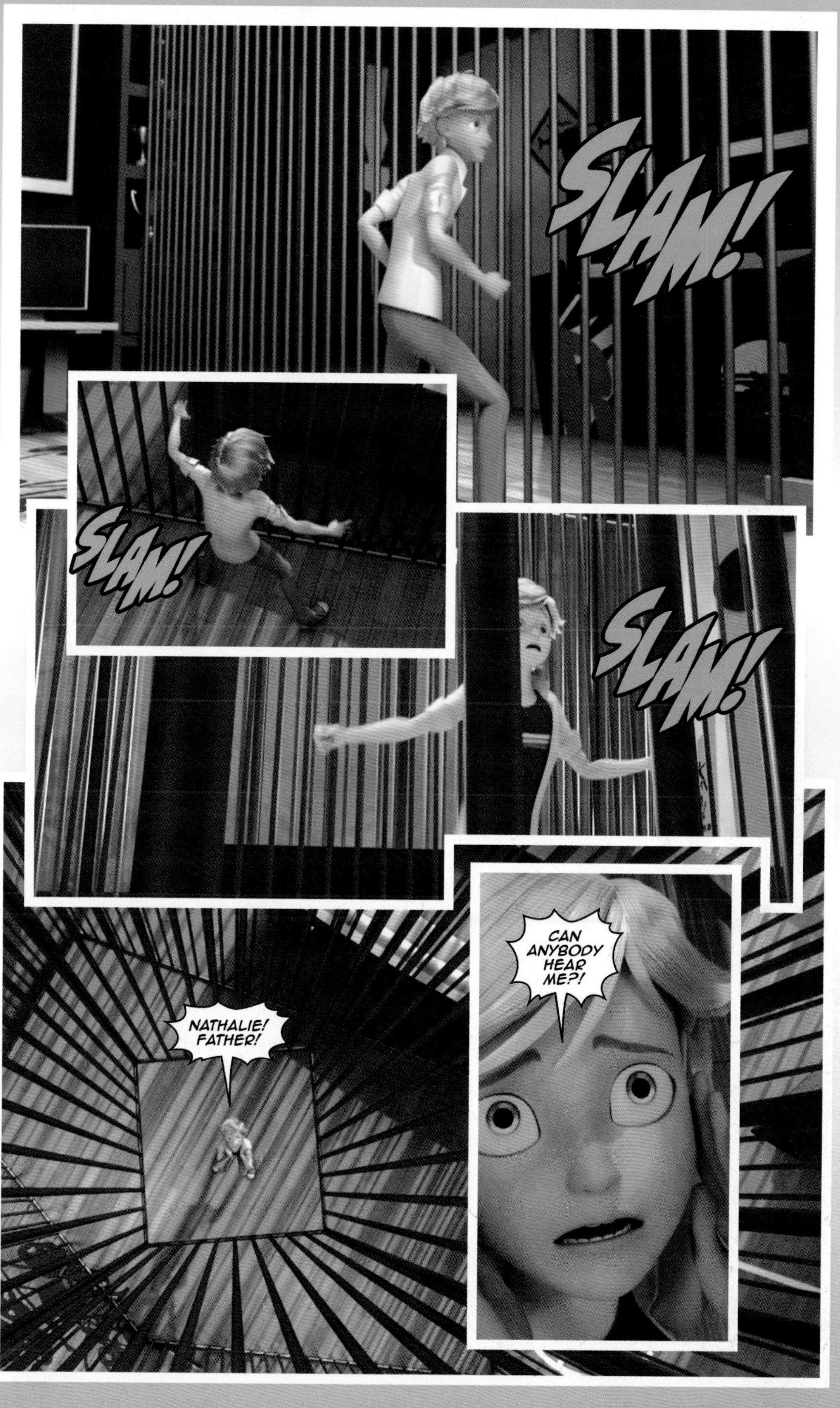
SLAM!
SLAM!
SLAM!
NATHALIE! FATHER!
CAN ANYBODY HEAR ME?!

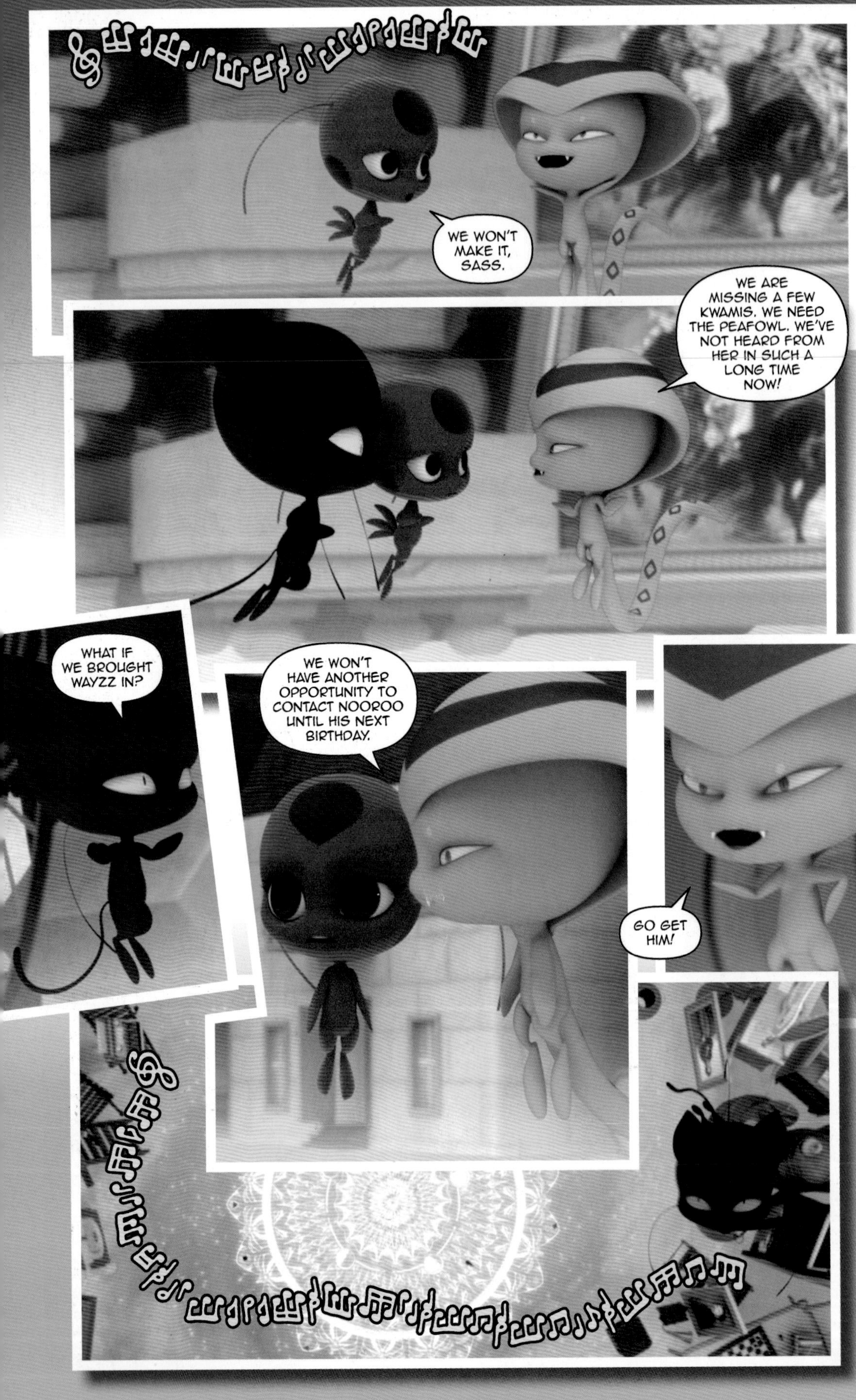
WE WON'T MAKE IT, SASS.
WE ARE MISSING A FEW KWAMIS. WE NEED THE PEAFOWL. WE'VE NOT HEARD FROM HER IN SUCH A LONG TIME NOW!
WHAT IF WE BROUGHT WAYZZ IN?
WE WON'T HAVE ANOTHER OPPORTUNITY TO CONTACT NOOROO UNTIL HIS NEXT BIRTHDAY.
GO GET HIM!

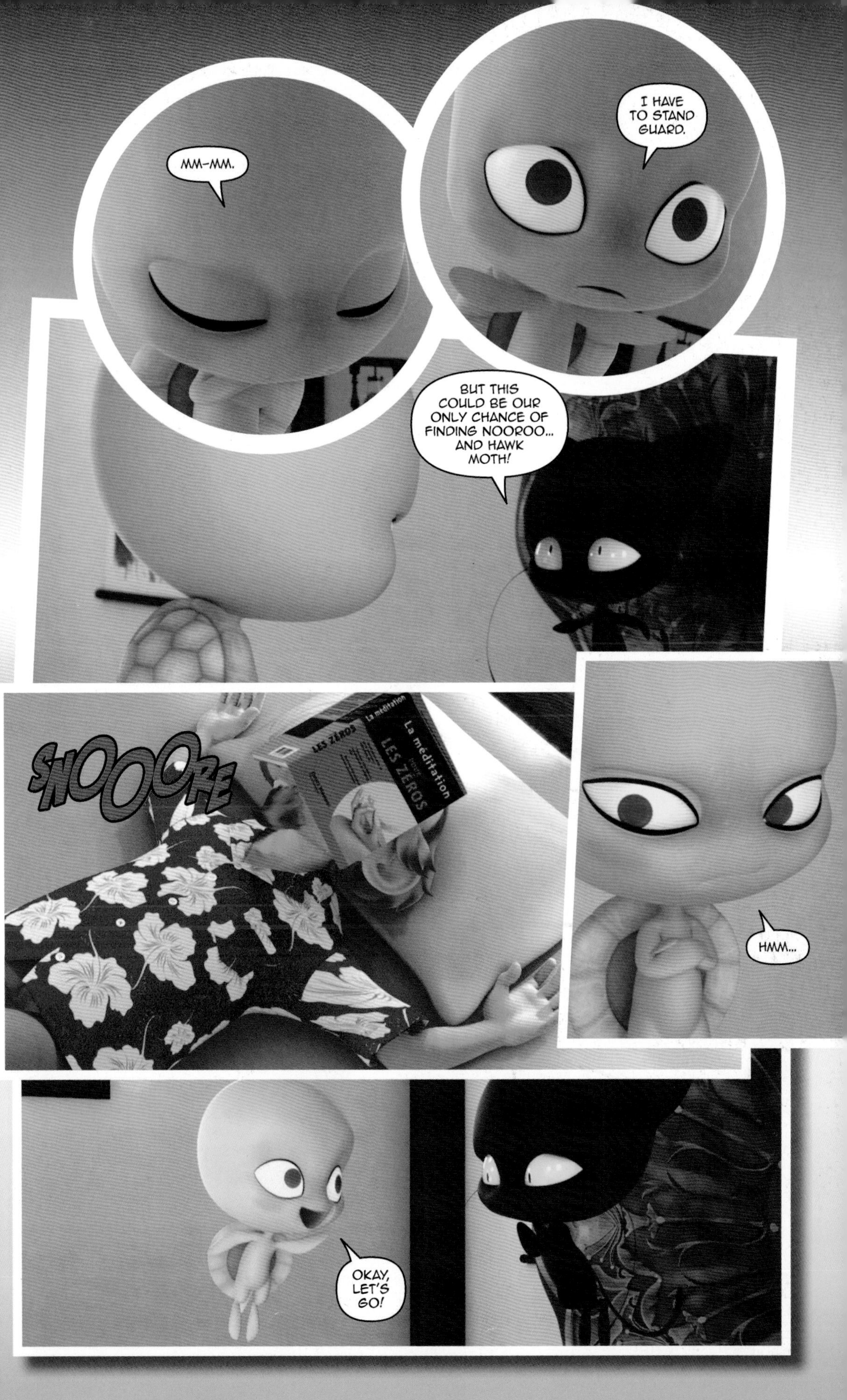
MM-MM.
I HAVE TO STAND GUARD.
BUT THIS COULD BE OUR ONLY CHANCE OF FINDING NOOROO... AND HAWK MOTH!
SNOOORE
La méditation
LES ZEROS
HMM...
OKAY, LET'S GO!

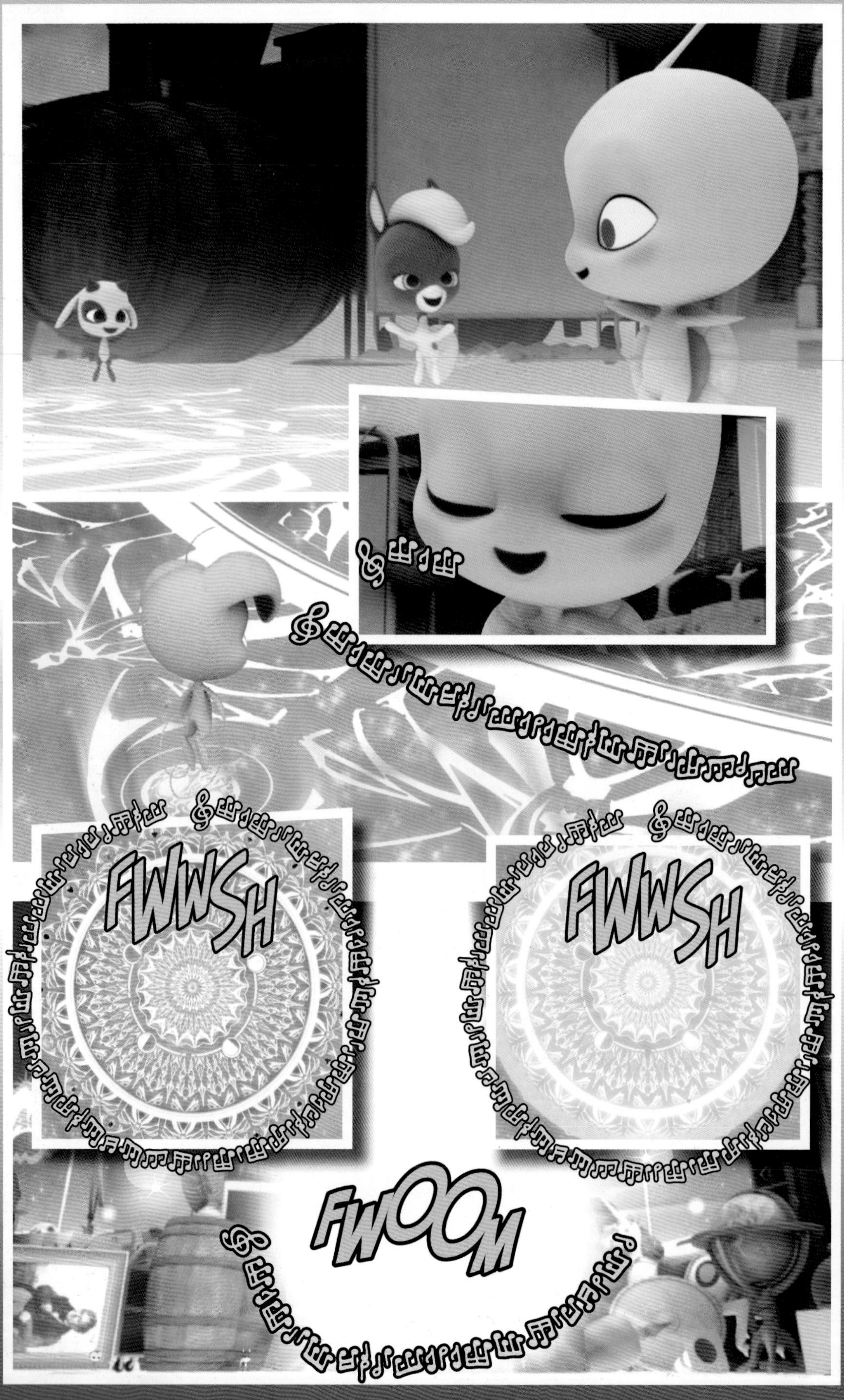
FWWSH
FWWSH
FWOOM

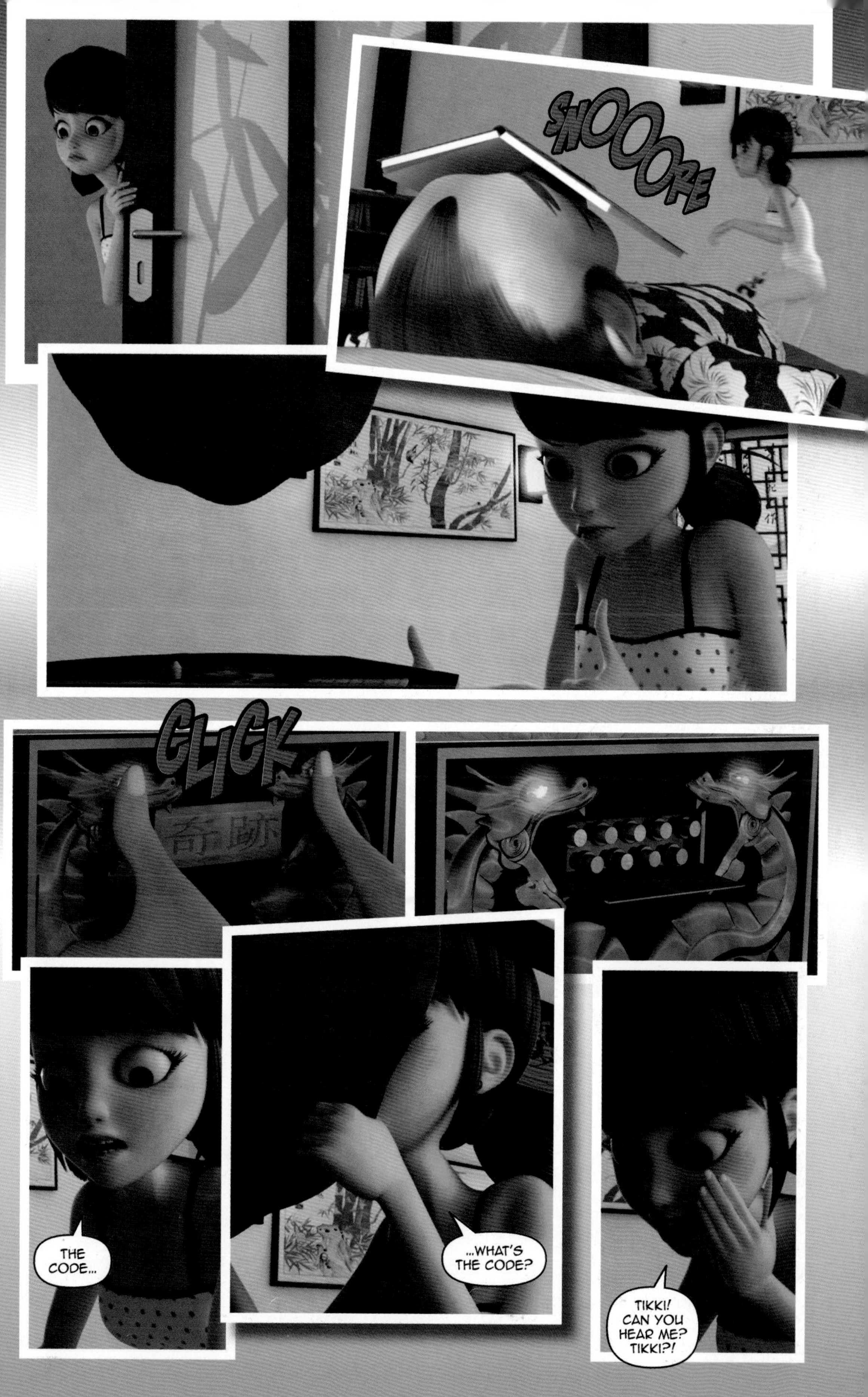
SNOOORE
CLICK
THE CODE...
...WHAT'S THE CODE?
TIKKI! CAN YOU HEAR ME? TIKKI!?!

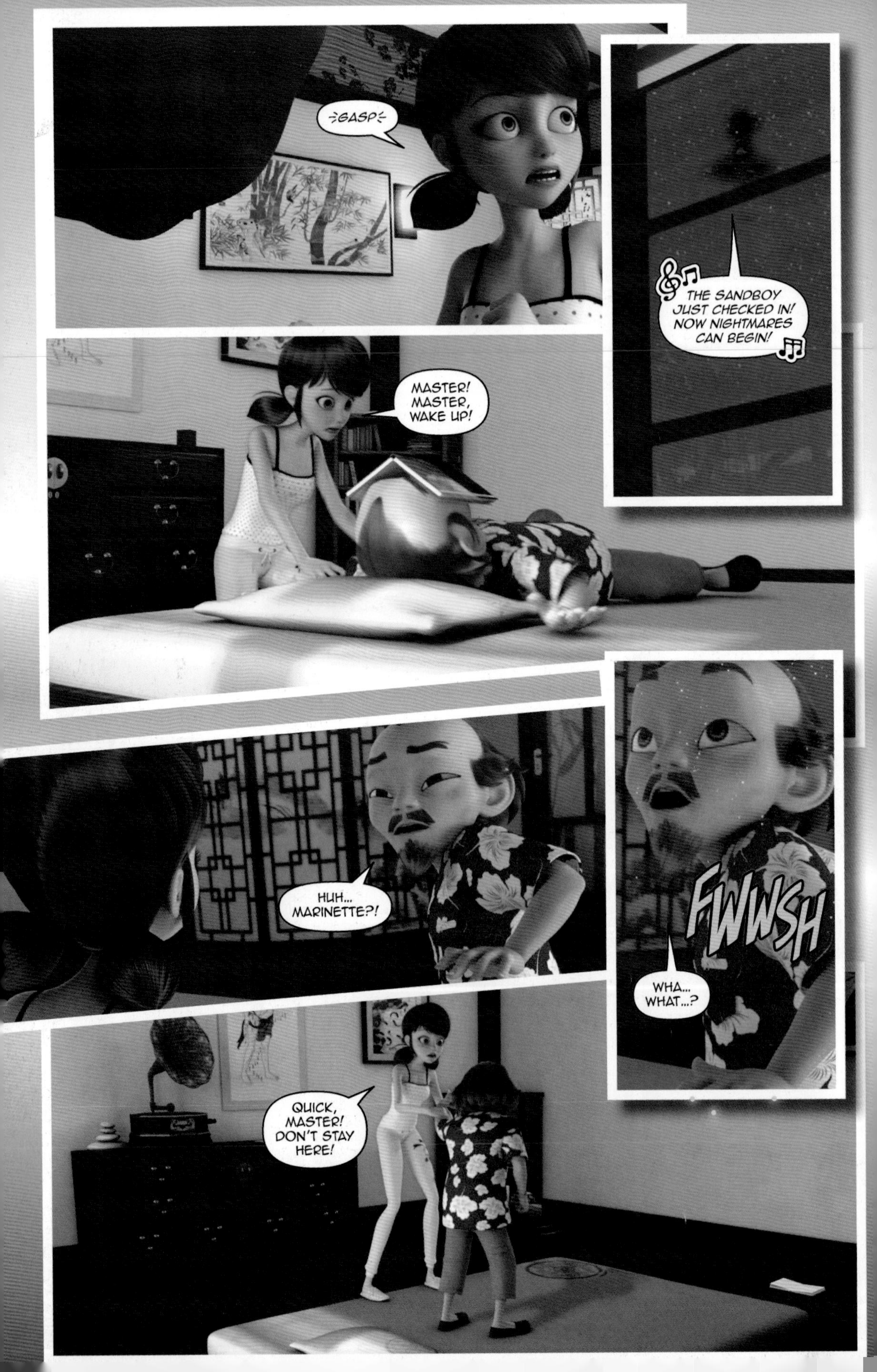

GASP
THE SANDBOY JUST CHECKED IN! NOW NIGHTMARES CAN BEGIN!
MASTER! MASTER, WAKE UP!
HUH... MARINETTE?!
FWWSH
WHA... WHAT...?
QUICK, MASTER! DON'T STAY HERE!

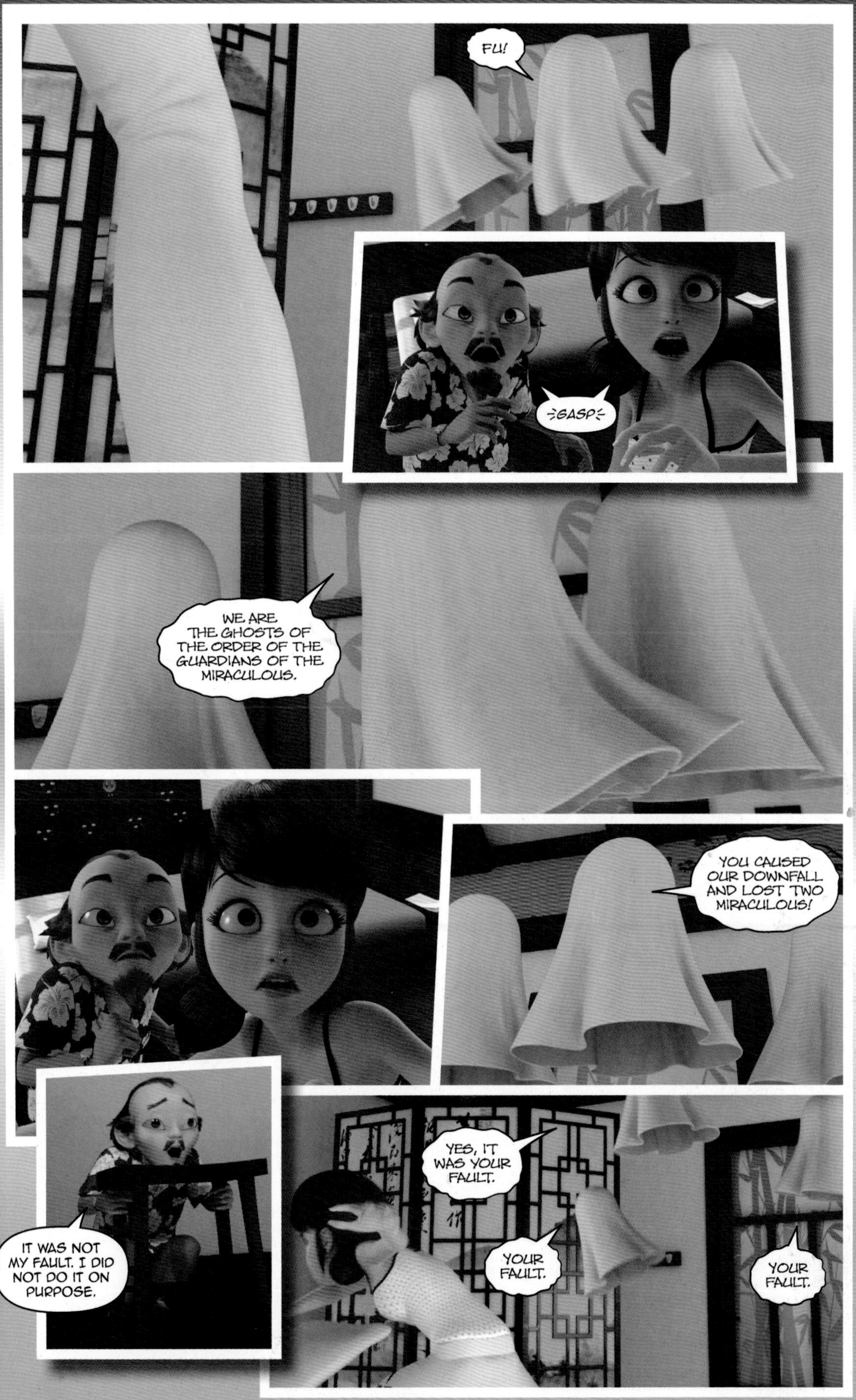
FU!
GASP
WE ARE THE GHOSTS OF THE ORDER OF THE GUARDIANS OF THE MIRACULOUS.
YOU CAUSED OUR DOWNFALL AND LOST TWO MIRACULOUS!
IT WAS NOT MY FAULT. I DID NOT DO IT ON PURPOSE.
YES, IT WAS YOUR FAULT.
YOUR FAULT.
YOUR FAULT.

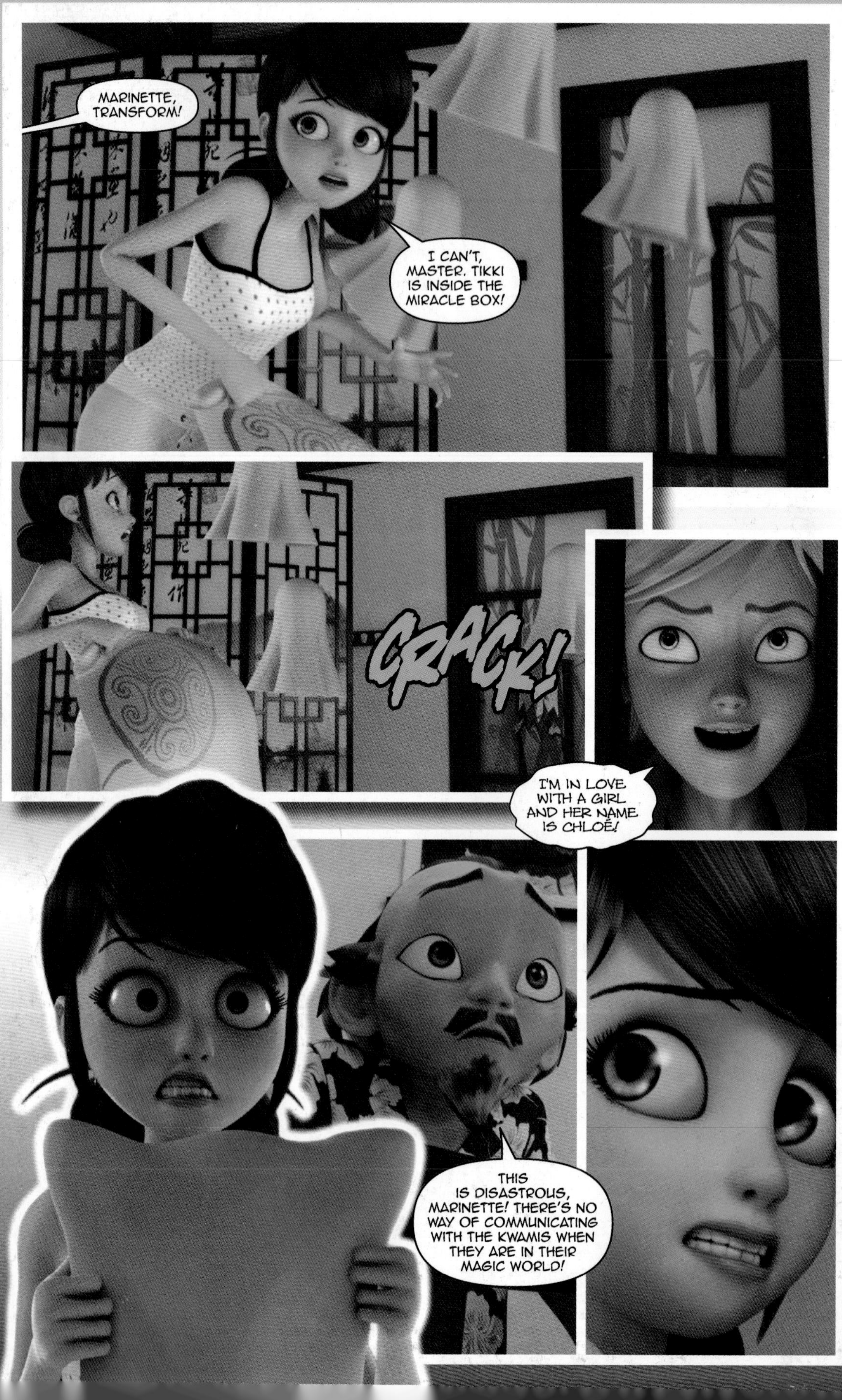
MARINETTE, TRANSFORM!
I CAN'T, MASTER. TIKKI IS INSIDE THE MIRACLE BOX!
CRACK!
I'M IN LOVE WITH A GIRL AND HER NAME IS CHLOÉ!
THIS IS DISASTROUS, MARINETTE! THERE'S NO WAY OF COMMUNICATING WITH THE KWAMIS WHEN THEY ARE IN THEIR MAGIC WORLD!

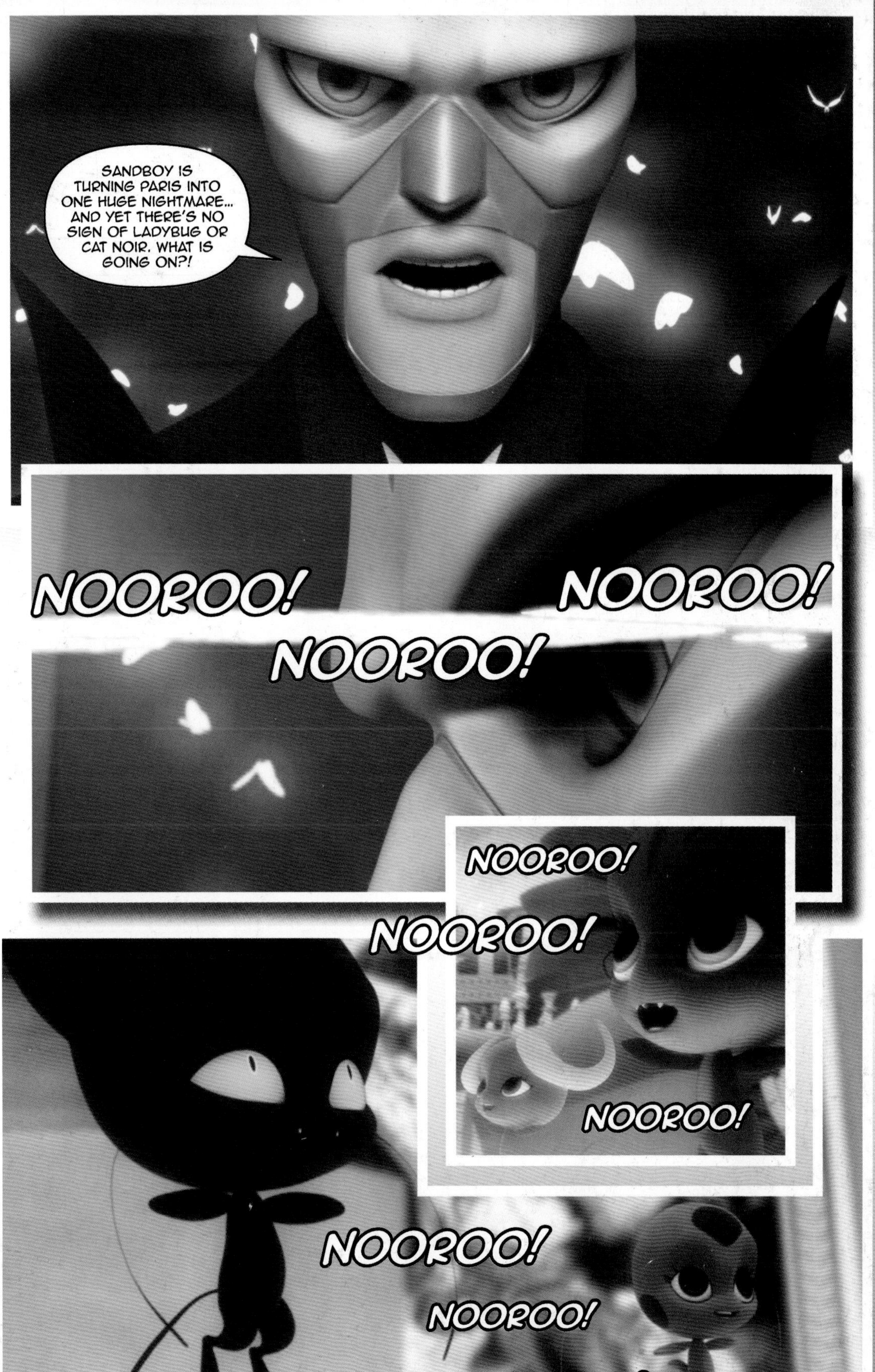
SANDBOY IS TURNING PARIS INTO ONE HUGE NIGHTMARE... AND YET THERE'S NO SIGN OF LADYBUG OR CAT NOIR. WHAT IS GOING ON?!
NOOROO!
NOOROO!
NOOROO!
NOOROO!
NOOROO!
NOOROO!
NOOROO!
NOOROO!
NOOROO!

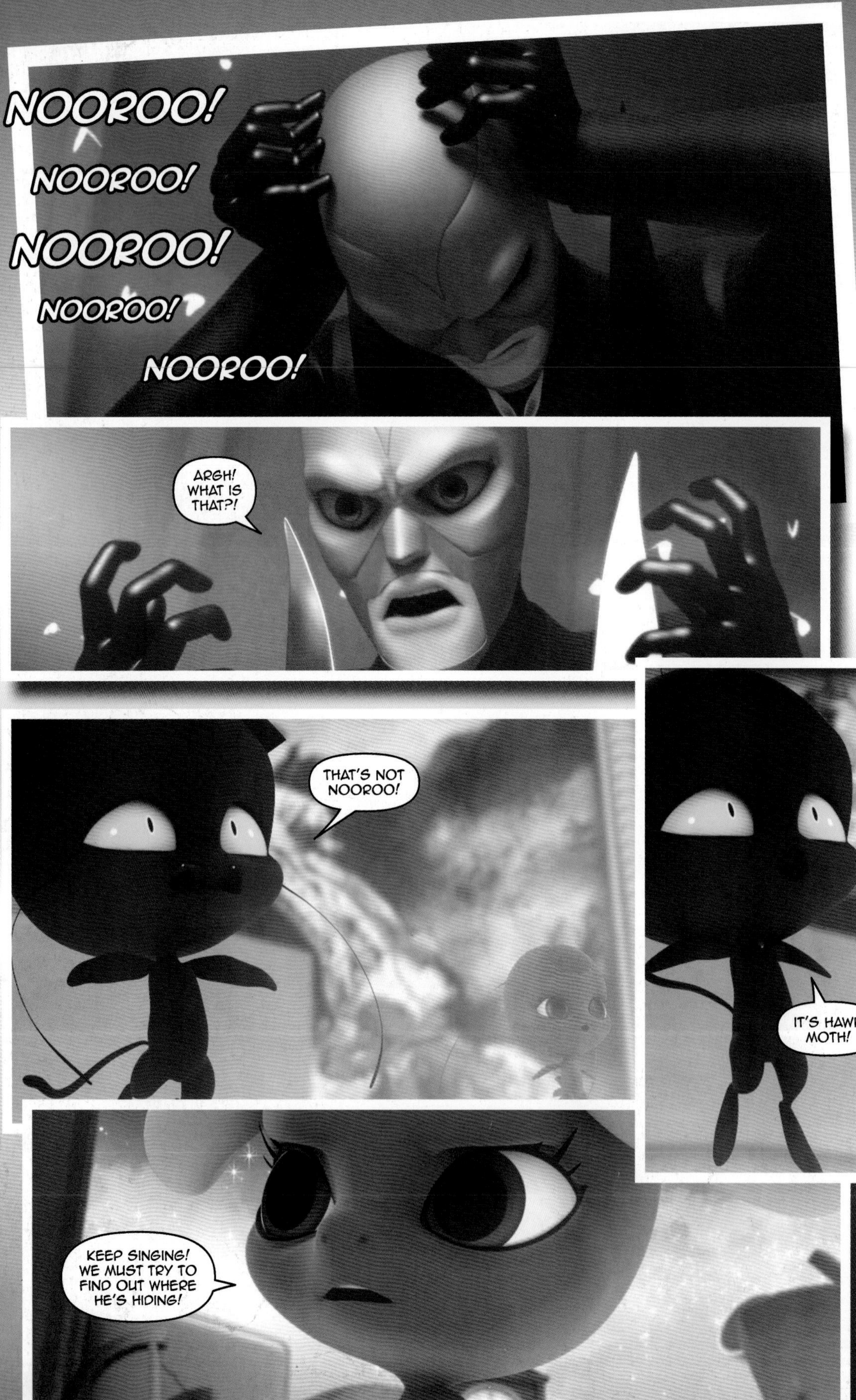
NOOROO!
NOOROO!
NOOROO!
NOOROO!
NOOROO!
ARGH! WHAT IS THAT?!
THAT'S NOT NOOROO!
IT'S HAWK MOTH!
KEEP SINGING! WE MUST TRY TO FIND OUT WHERE HE'S HIDING!

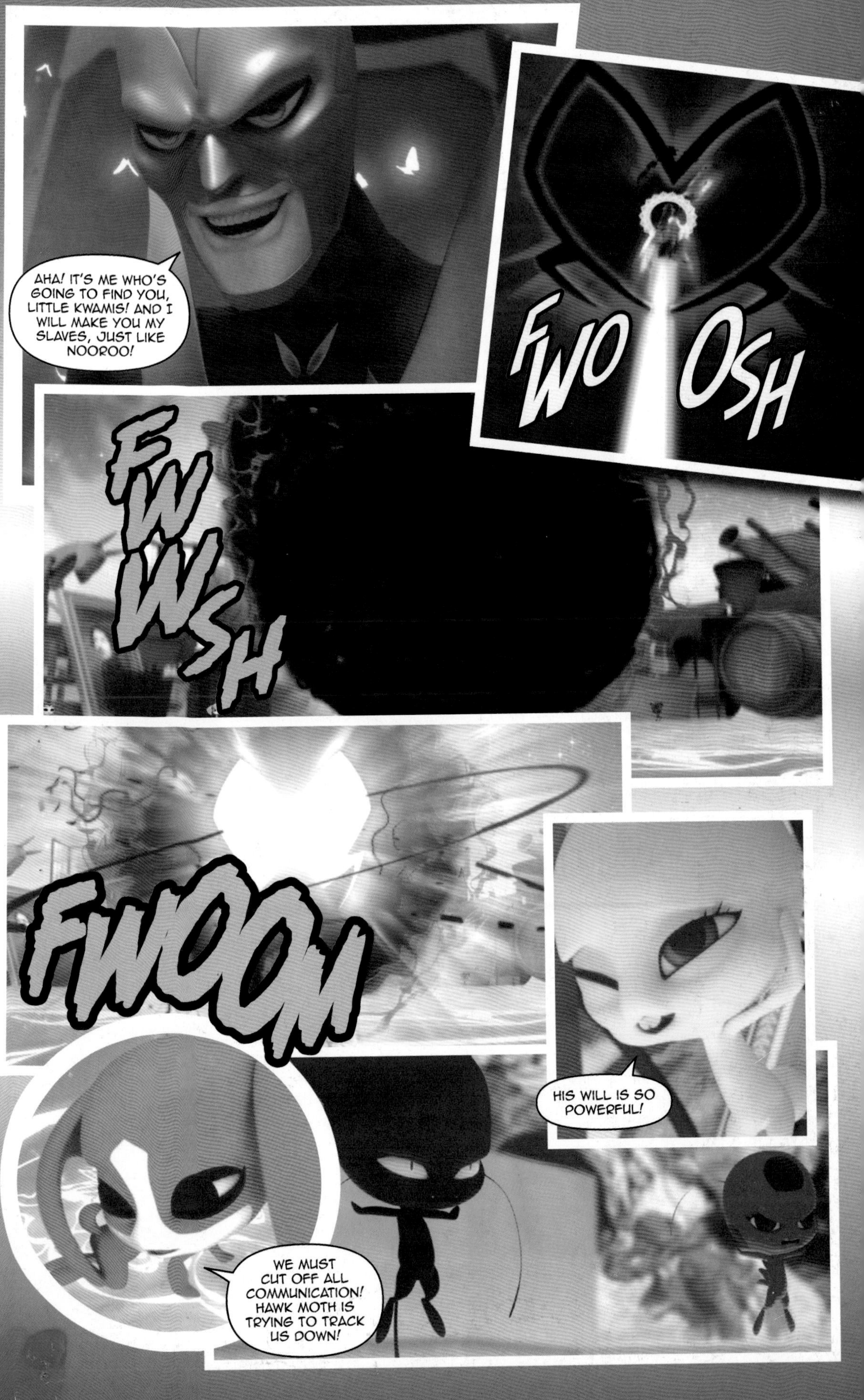
AHA! IT'S ME WHO'S GOING TO FIND YOU, LITTLE KWAMIS! AND I WILL MAKE YOU MY SLAVES, JUST LIKE NOOROO!
FWOOSH
FWWSH
FWOOM
HIS WILL IS SO POWERFUL!
WE MUST CUT OFF ALL COMMUNICATION! HAWK MOTH IS TRYING TO TRACK US DOWN!

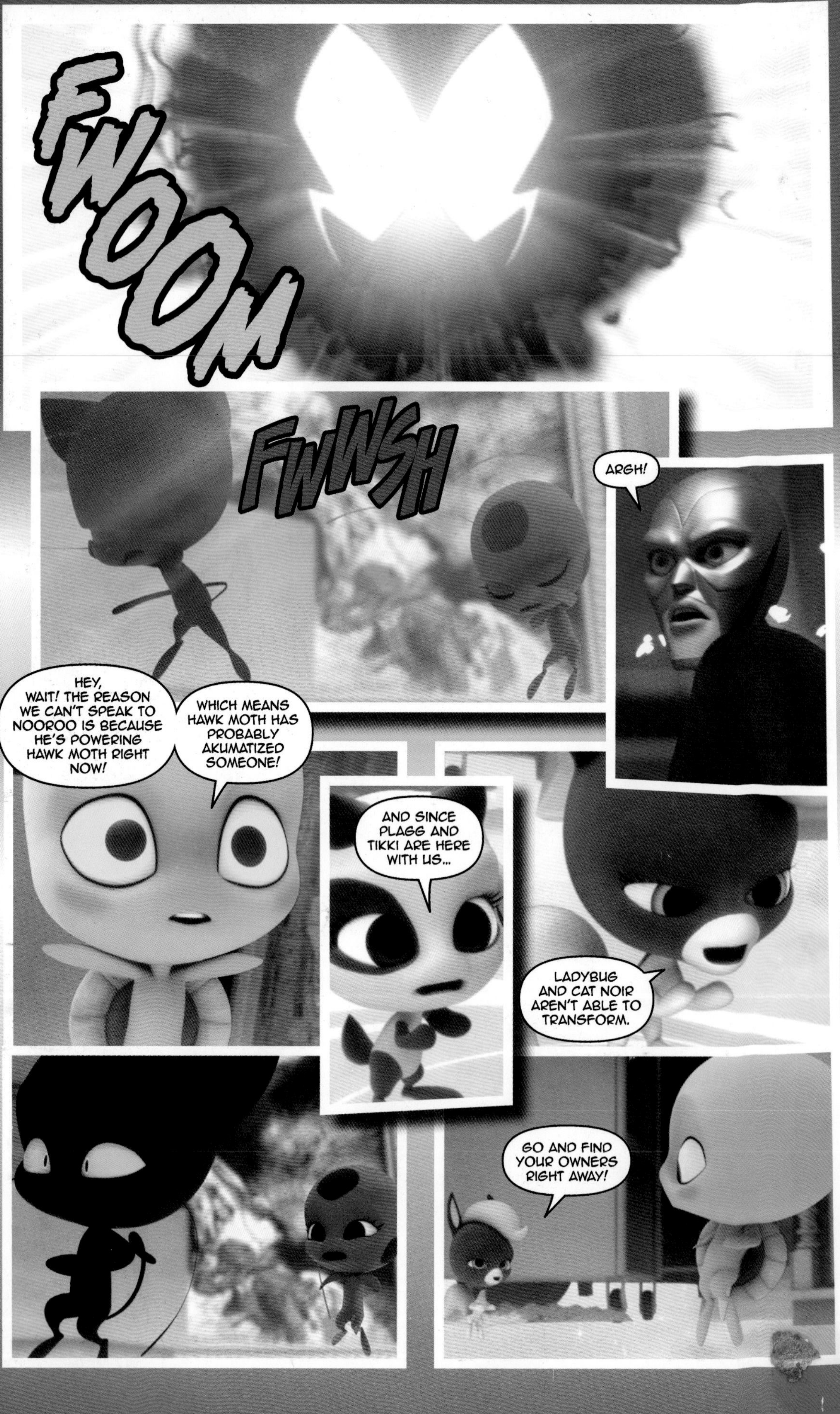
FWOOM
FWWSH
ARGH!
HEY, WAIT! THE REASON WE CAN'T SPEAK TO NOOROO IS BECAUSE HE'S POWERING HAWK MOTH RIGHT NOW!
WHICH MEANS HAWK MOTH HAS PROBABLY AKUMATIZED SOMEONE!
AND SINCE PLAGG AND TIKKI ARE HERE WITH US...
LADYBUG AND CAT NOIR AREN'T ABLE TO TRANSFORM.
GO AND FIND YOUR OWNERS RIGHT AWAY!

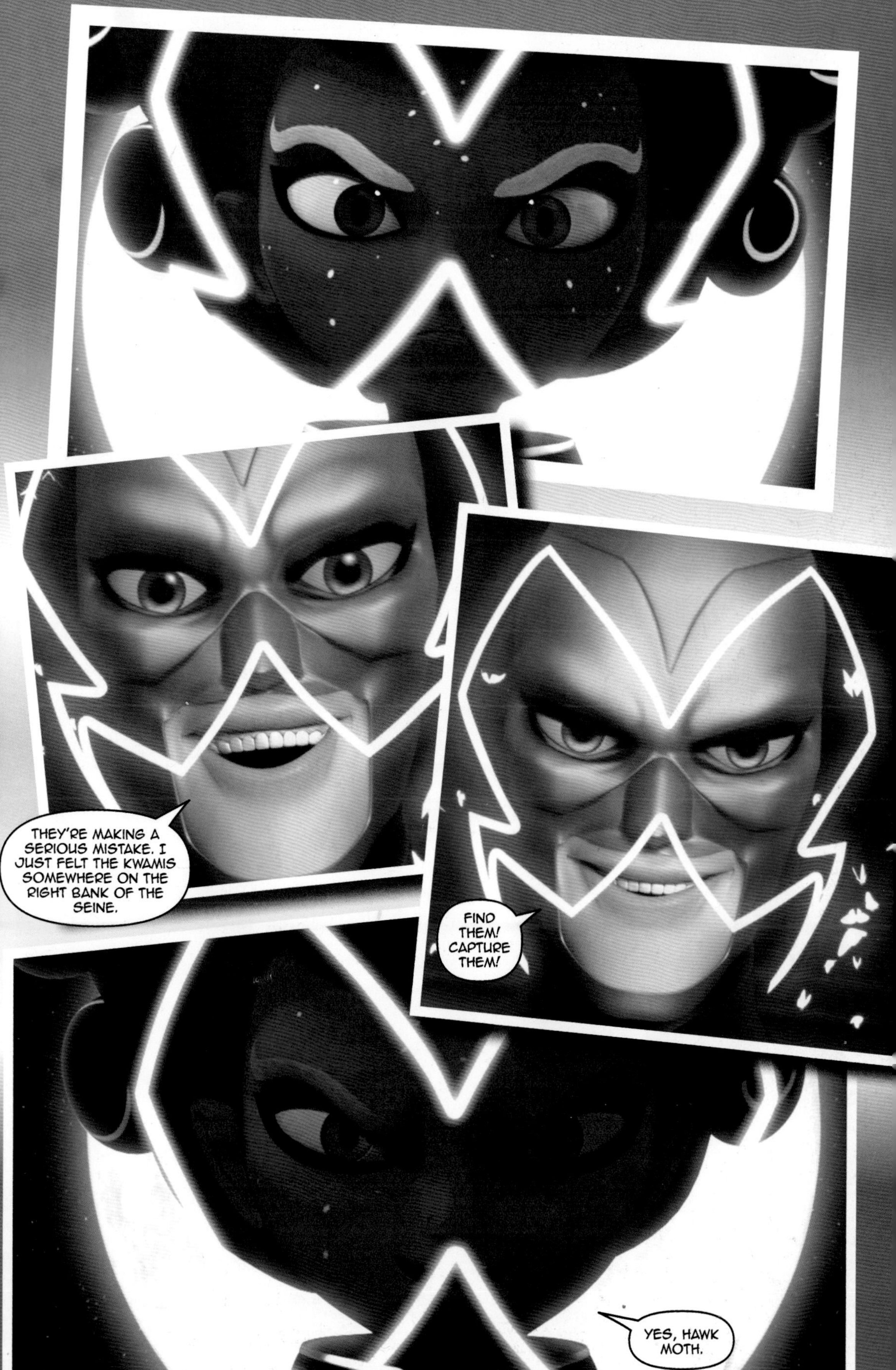
THEY'RE MAKING A SERIOUS MISTAKE. I JUST FELT THE KWAMIS SOMEWHERE ON THE RIGHT BANK OF THE SEINE.
FIND THEM! CAPTURE THEM!
YES, HAWK MOTH.

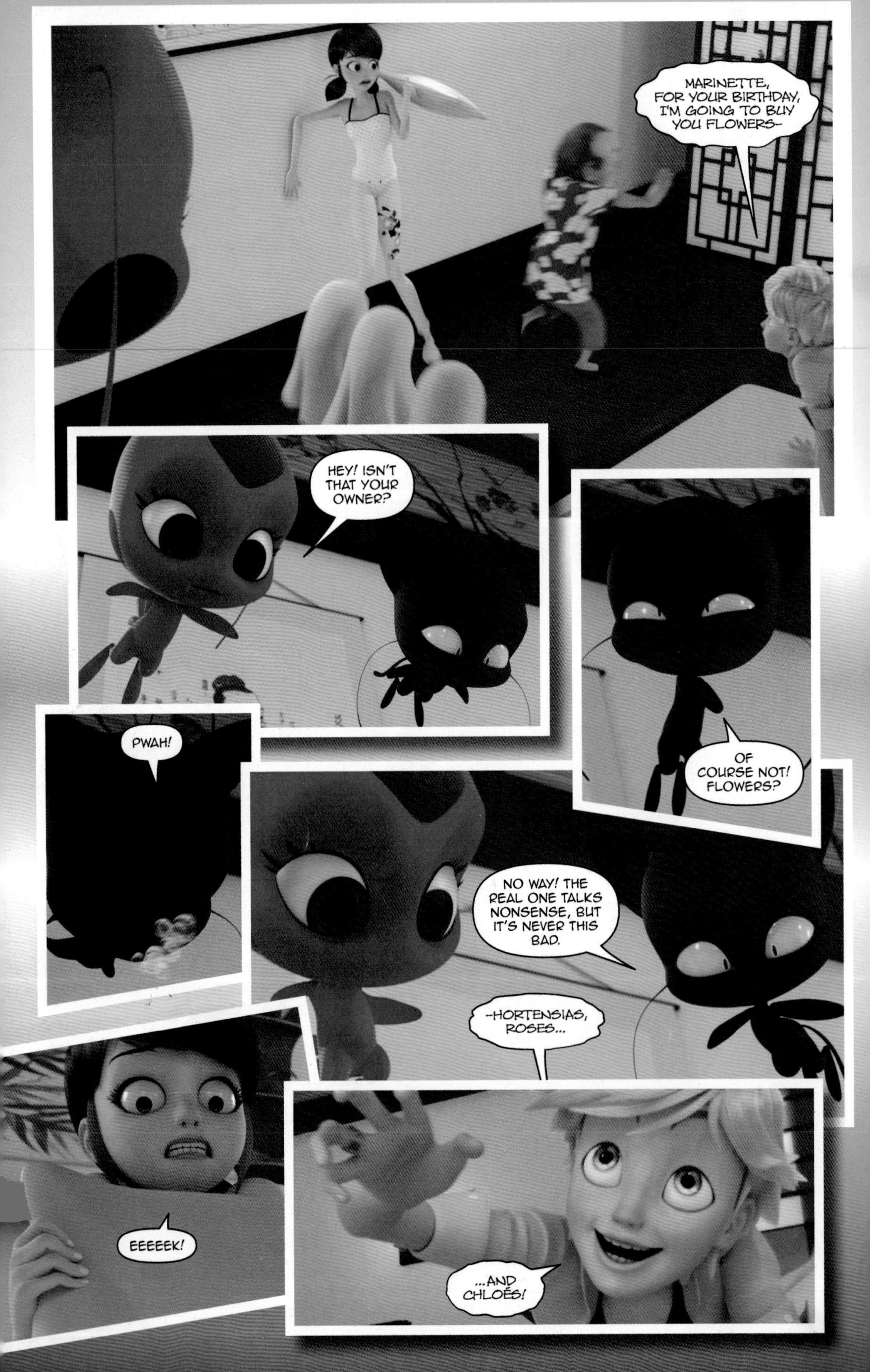
MARINETTE, FOR YOUR BIRTHDAY, I'M GOING TO BUY YOU FLOWERS-
HEY! ISN'T THAT YOUR OWNER?
OF COURSE NOT! FLOWERS?
PWAH!
NO WAY! THE REAL ONE TALKS NONSENSE, BUT IT'S NEVER THIS BAD.
-HORTENSIAS, ROSES...
EEEEEK!
...AND CHLOÉS!

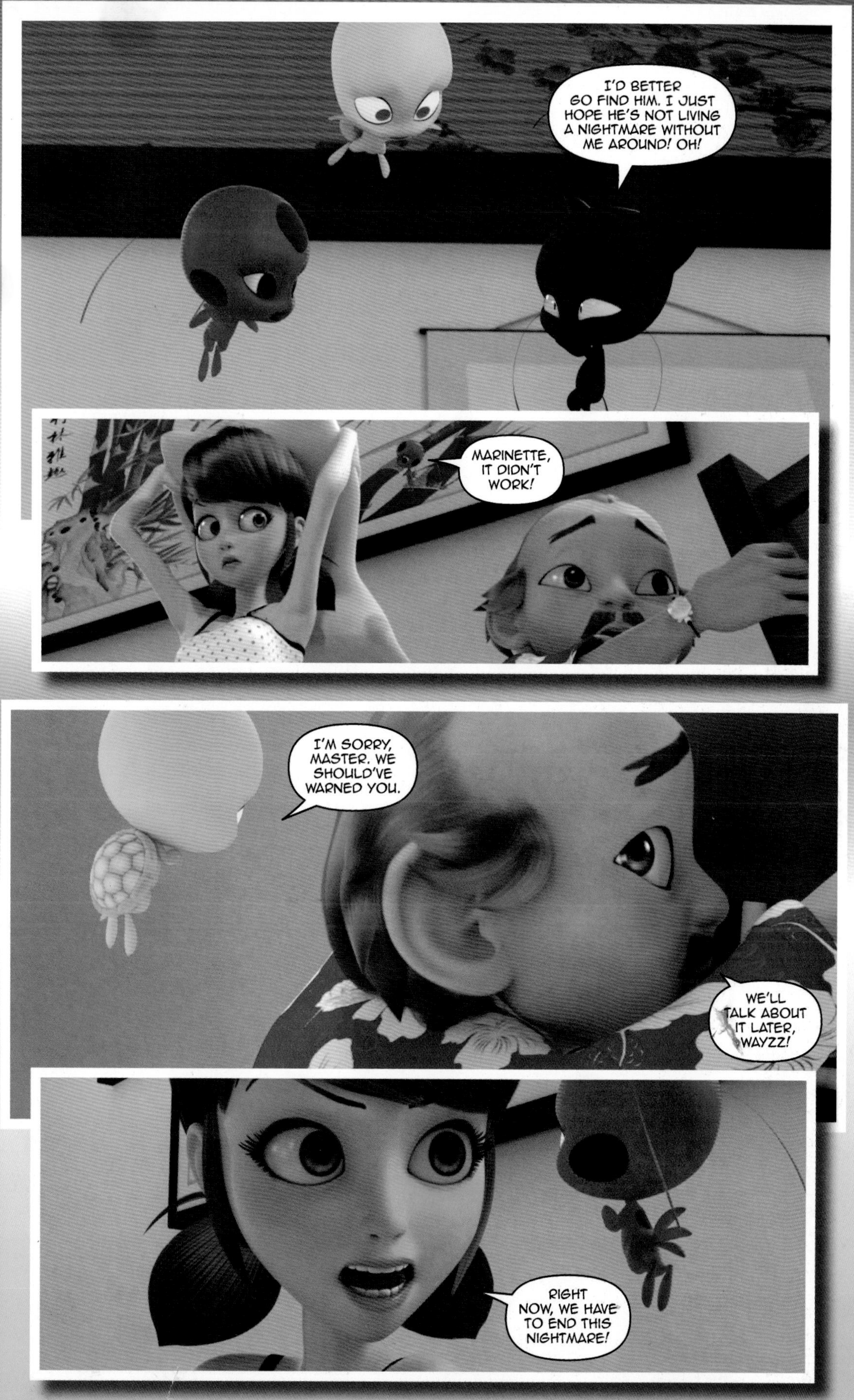
I'D BETTER GO FIND HIM. I JUST HOPE HE'S NOT LIVING A NIGHTMARE WITHOUT ME AROUND! OH!
MARINETTE, IT DIDN'T WORK!
I'M SORRY, MASTER. WE SHOULD'VE WARNED YOU.
WE'LL TALK ABOUT IT LATER, WAYZZ!
RIGHT NOW, WE HAVE TO END THIS NIGHTMARE!

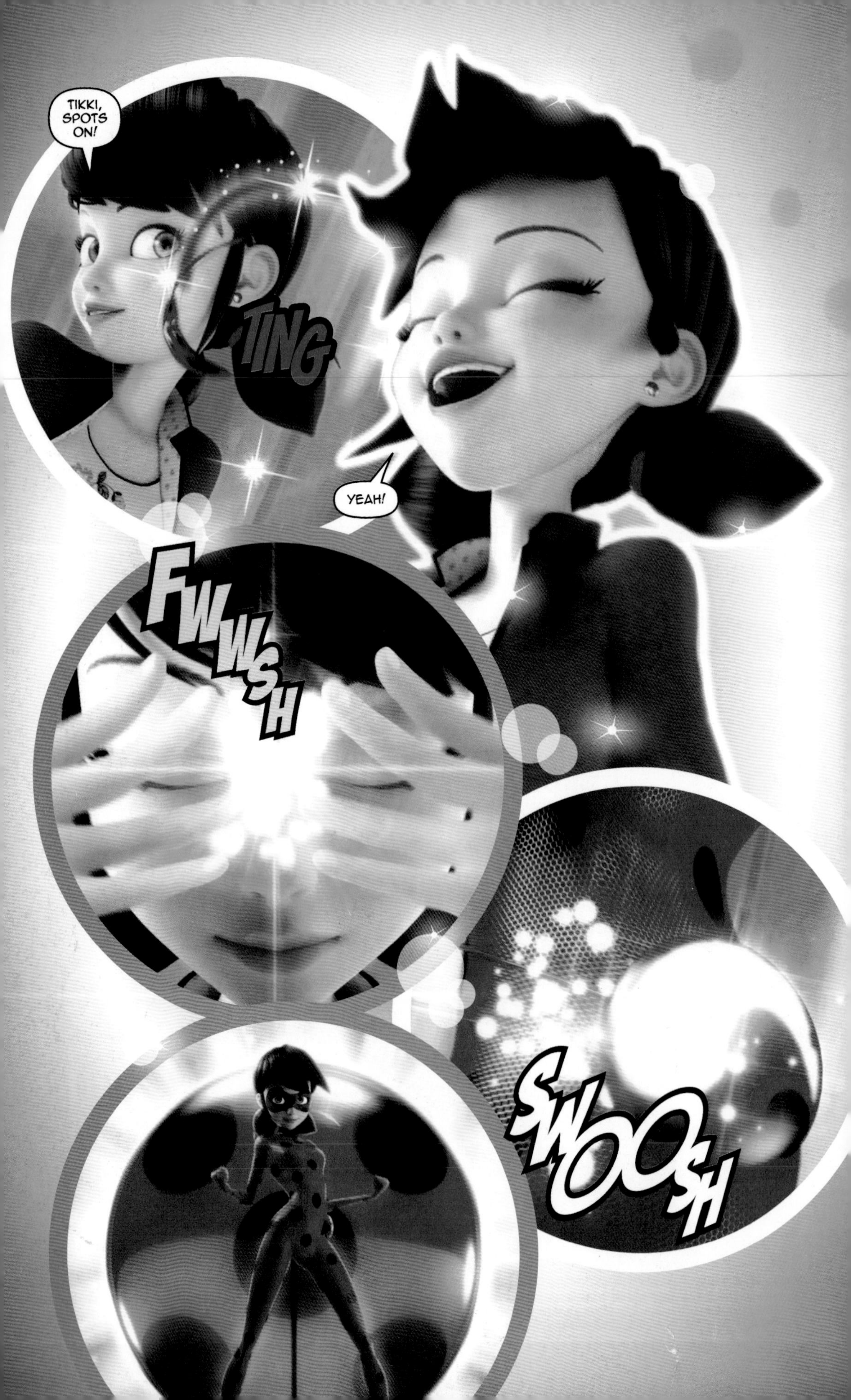
TIKKI, SPOTS ON!
TING
YEAH!
FWWSH
SWOOSH

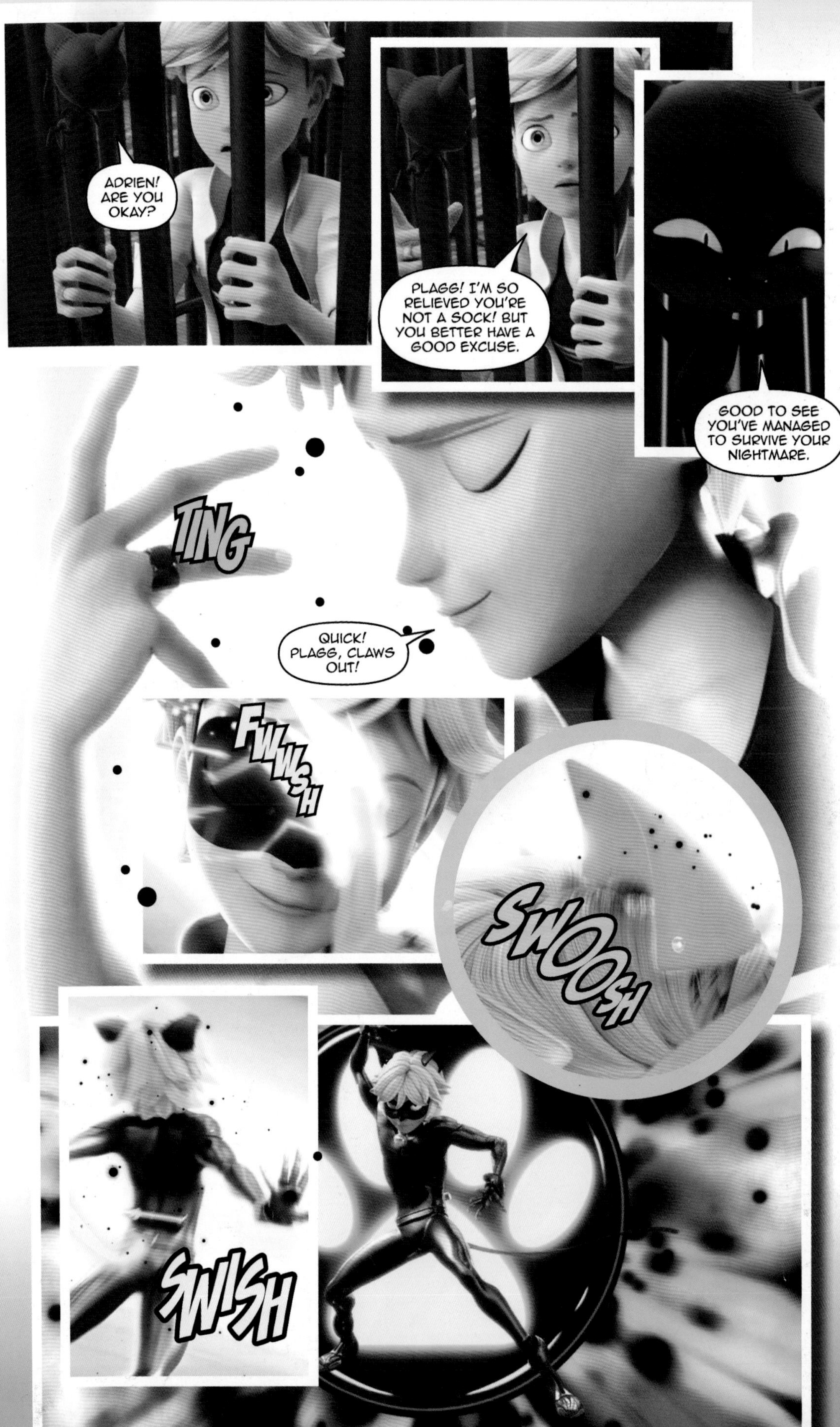
ADRIEN! ARE YOU OKAY?
PLAGG! I'M SO RELIEVED YOU'RE NOT A SOCK! BUT YOU BETTER HAVE A GOOD EXCUSE.
GOOD TO SEE YOU'VE MANAGED TO SURVIVE YOUR NIGHTMARE.
TING
QUICK! PLAGG, CLAWS OUT!
FWWSH
SWOOSH
SWISH

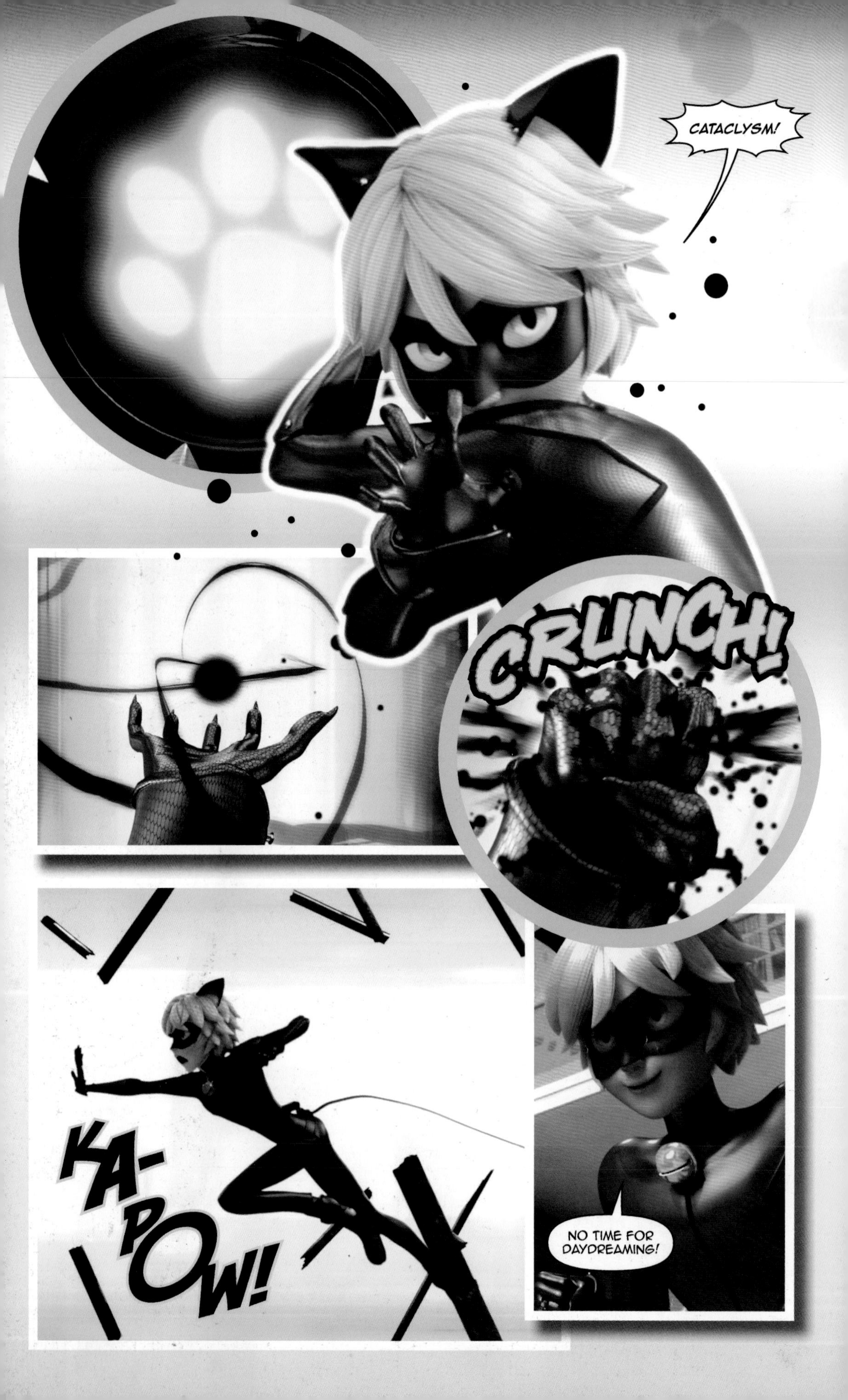
CATACLYSM!
CRUNCH!
KA-POW!
NO TIME FOR DAYDREAMING!

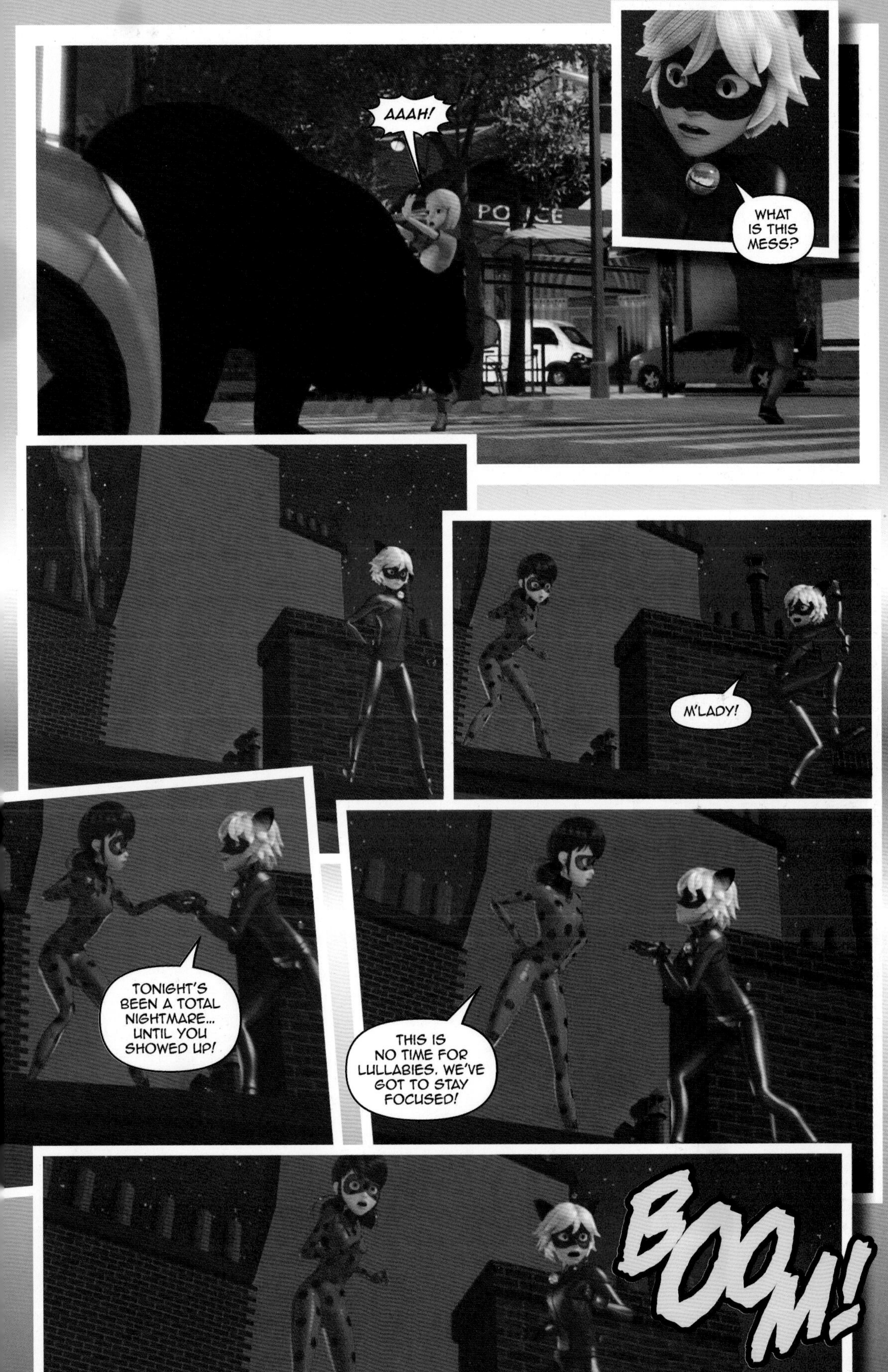
AAAH!
POLICE
WHAT IS THIS MESS?
M'LADY!
TONIGHT'S BEEN A TOTAL NIGHTMARE... UNTIL YOU SHOWED UP!
THIS IS NO TIME FOR LULLABIES. WE'VE GOT TO STAY FOCUSED!
BOOM!

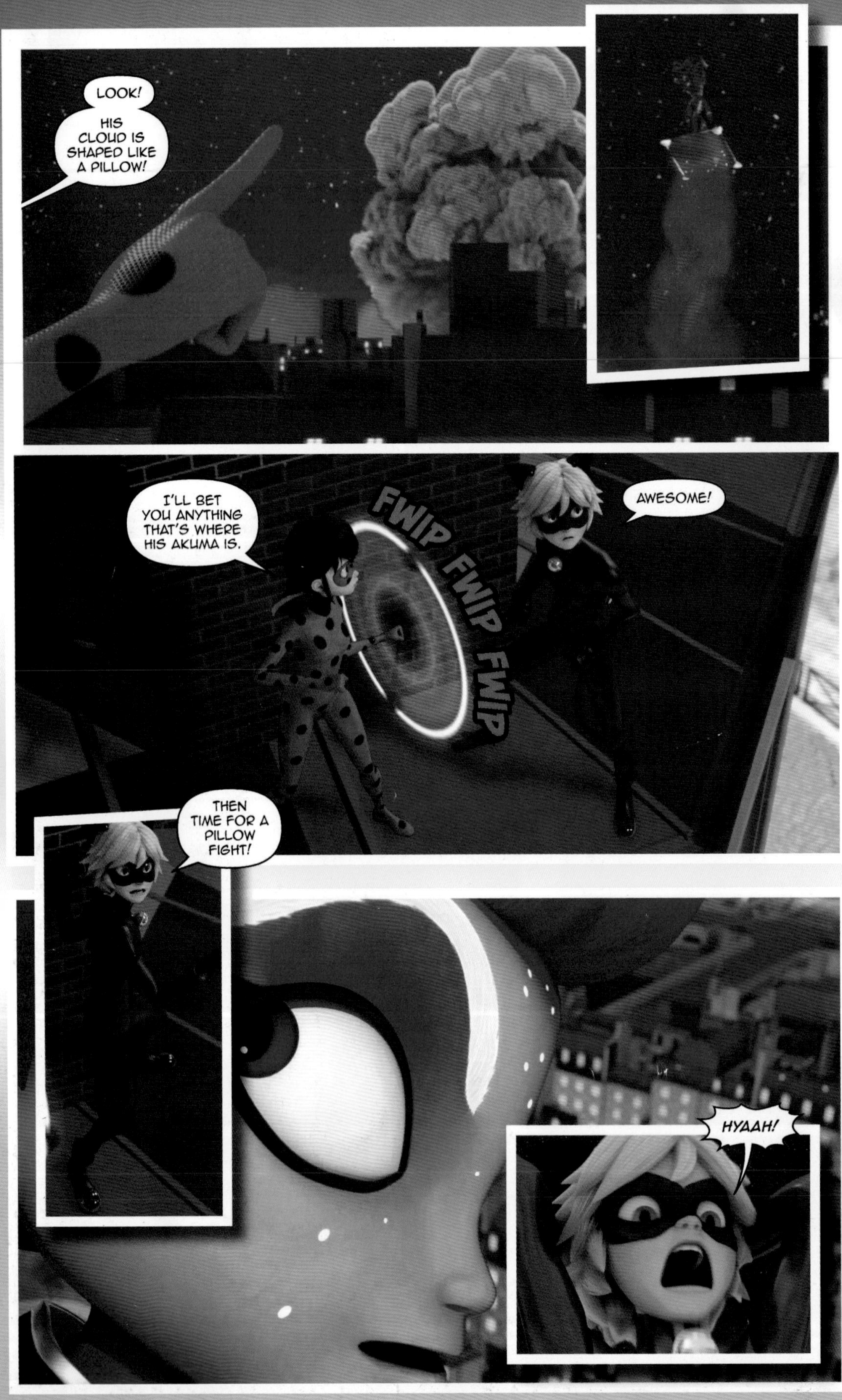

LOOK!
HIS CLOUD IS SHAPED LIKE A PILLOW!
I'LL BET YOU ANYTHING THAT'S WHERE HIS AKUMA IS.
FWIP FWIP FWIP FWIP
AWESOME!
THEN TIME FOR A PILLOW FIGHT!
HYAAH!

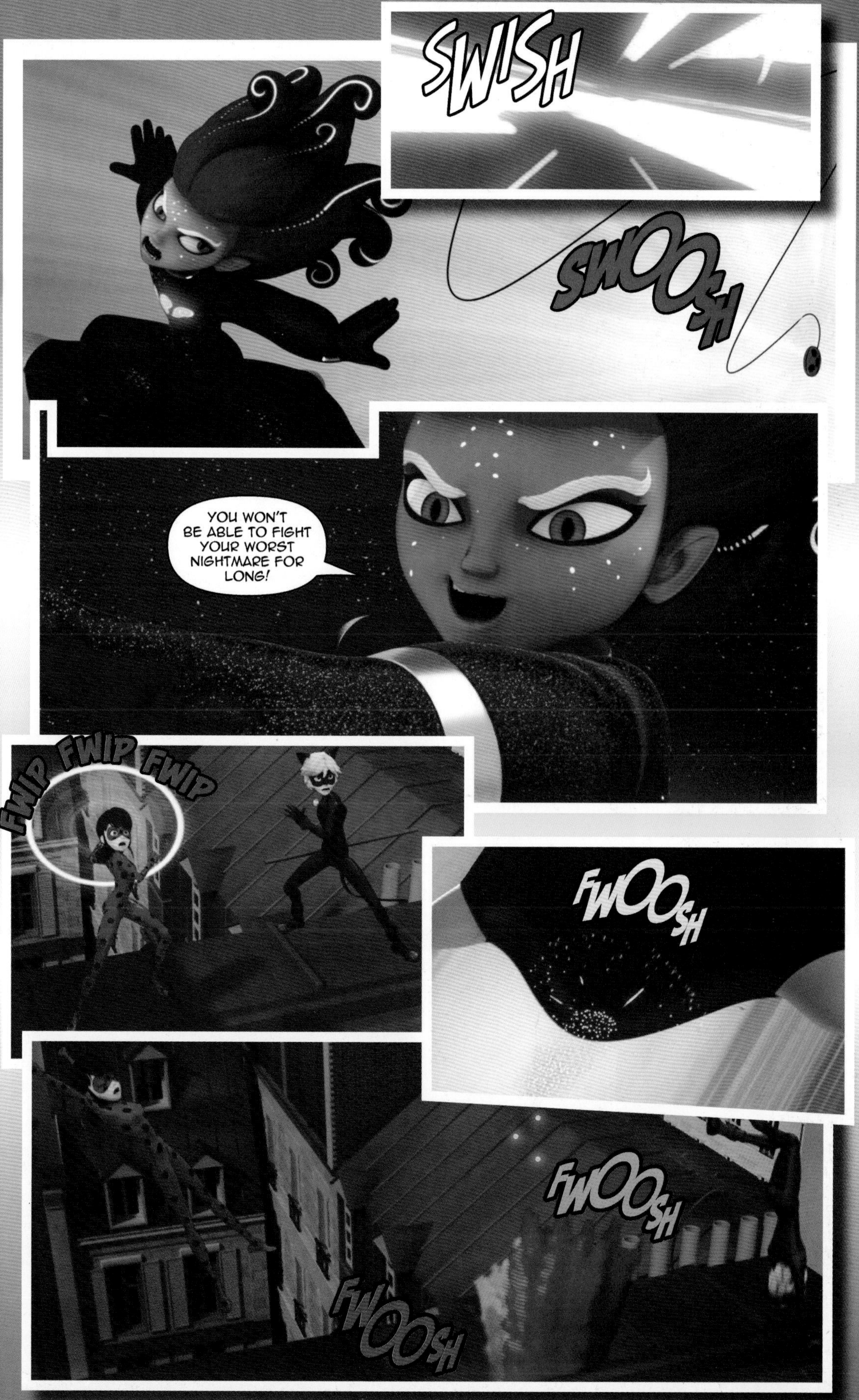
SWISH
SWOOSH
YOU WON'T BE ABLE TO FIGHT YOUR WORST NIGHTMARE FOR LONG!
FWIP FWIP FWIP
FWOOSH
FWOOSH
FWOOSH

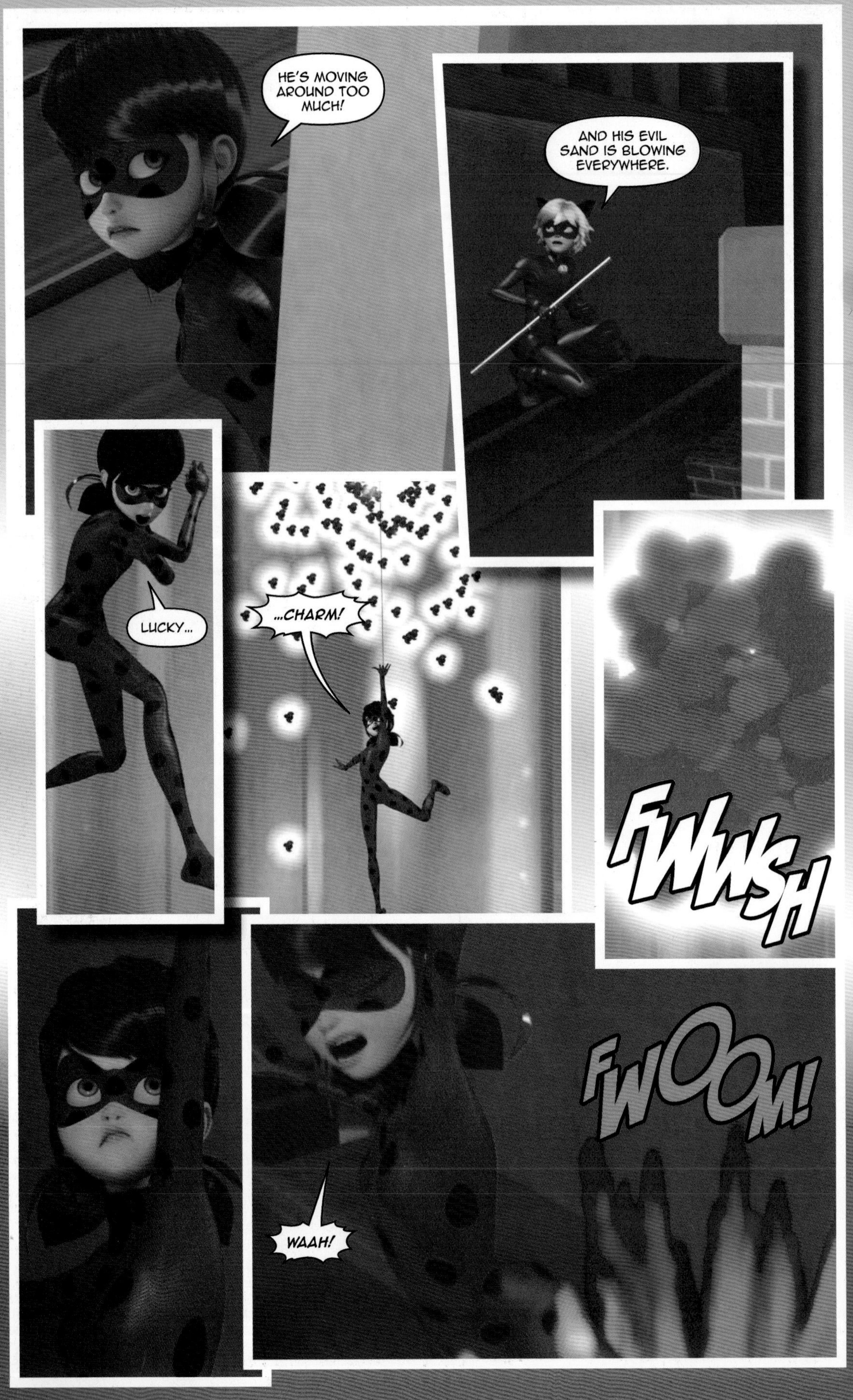
HE'S MOVING AROUND TOO MUCH!
AND HIS EVIL SAND IS BLOWING EVERYWHERE.
LUCKY...
...CHARM!
FWWSH
FWOOM!
WAAH!

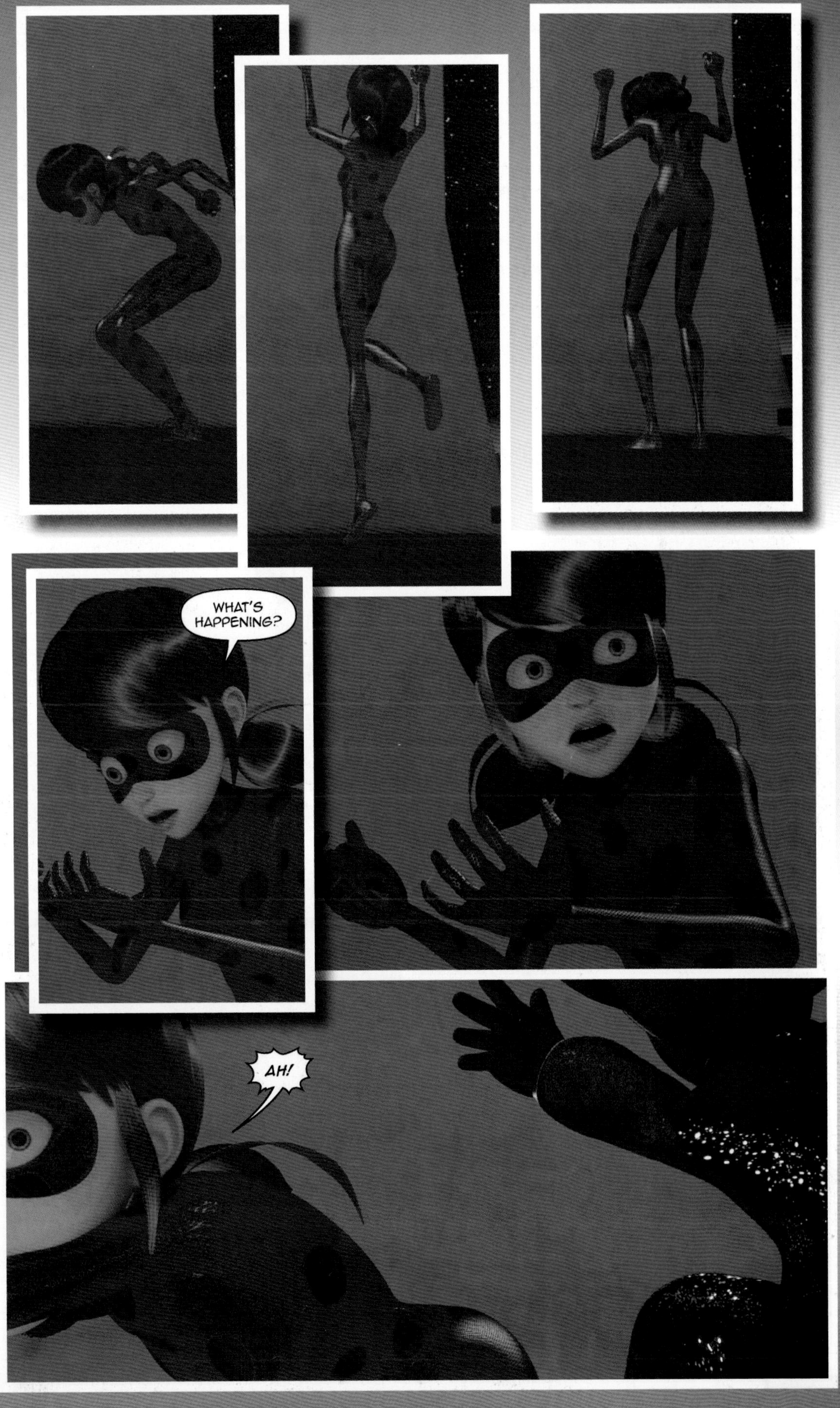
WHAT'S HAPPENING?
AH!

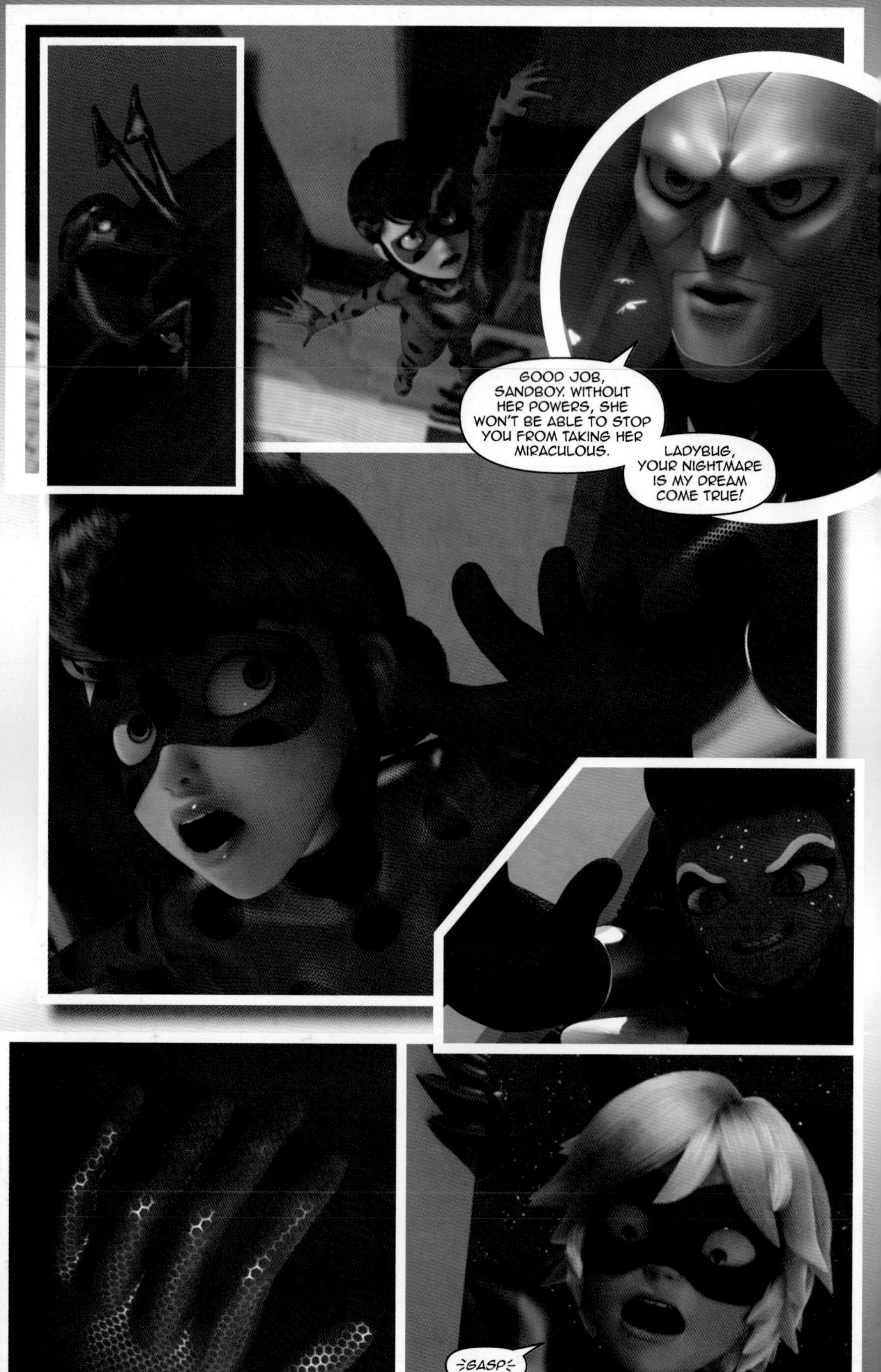
GOOD JOB, SANDBOY. WITHOUT HER POWERS, SHE WON'T BE ABLE TO STOP YOU FROM TAKING HER MIRACULOUS.
LADYBUG, YOUR NIGHTMARE IS MY DREAM COME TRUE!
GASP

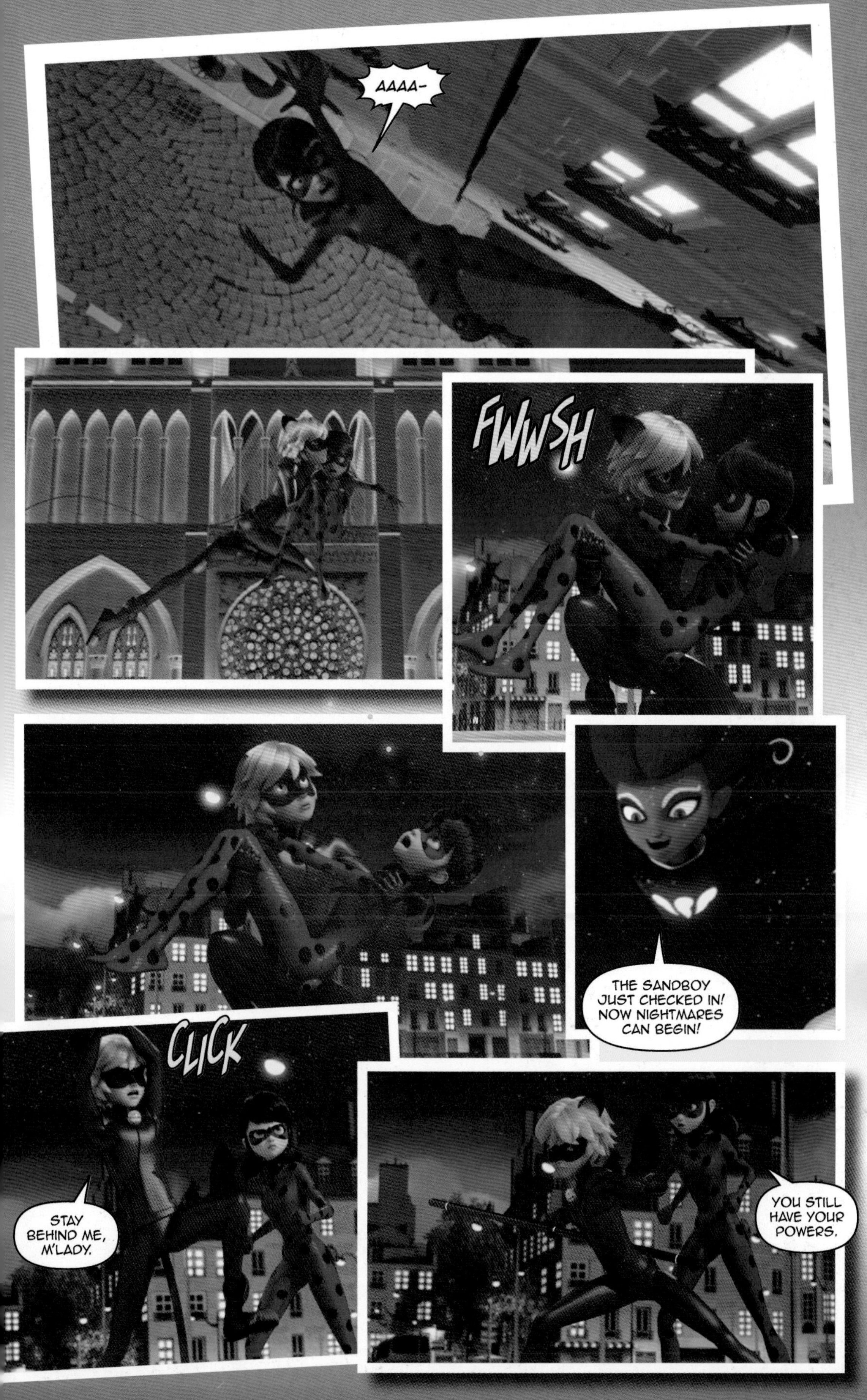
AAAA-
FWWSH
THE SANDBOY JUST CHECKED IN! NOW NIGHTMARES CAN BEGIN!
CLICK
STAY BEHIND ME, M'LADY.
YOU STILL HAVE YOUR POWERS.

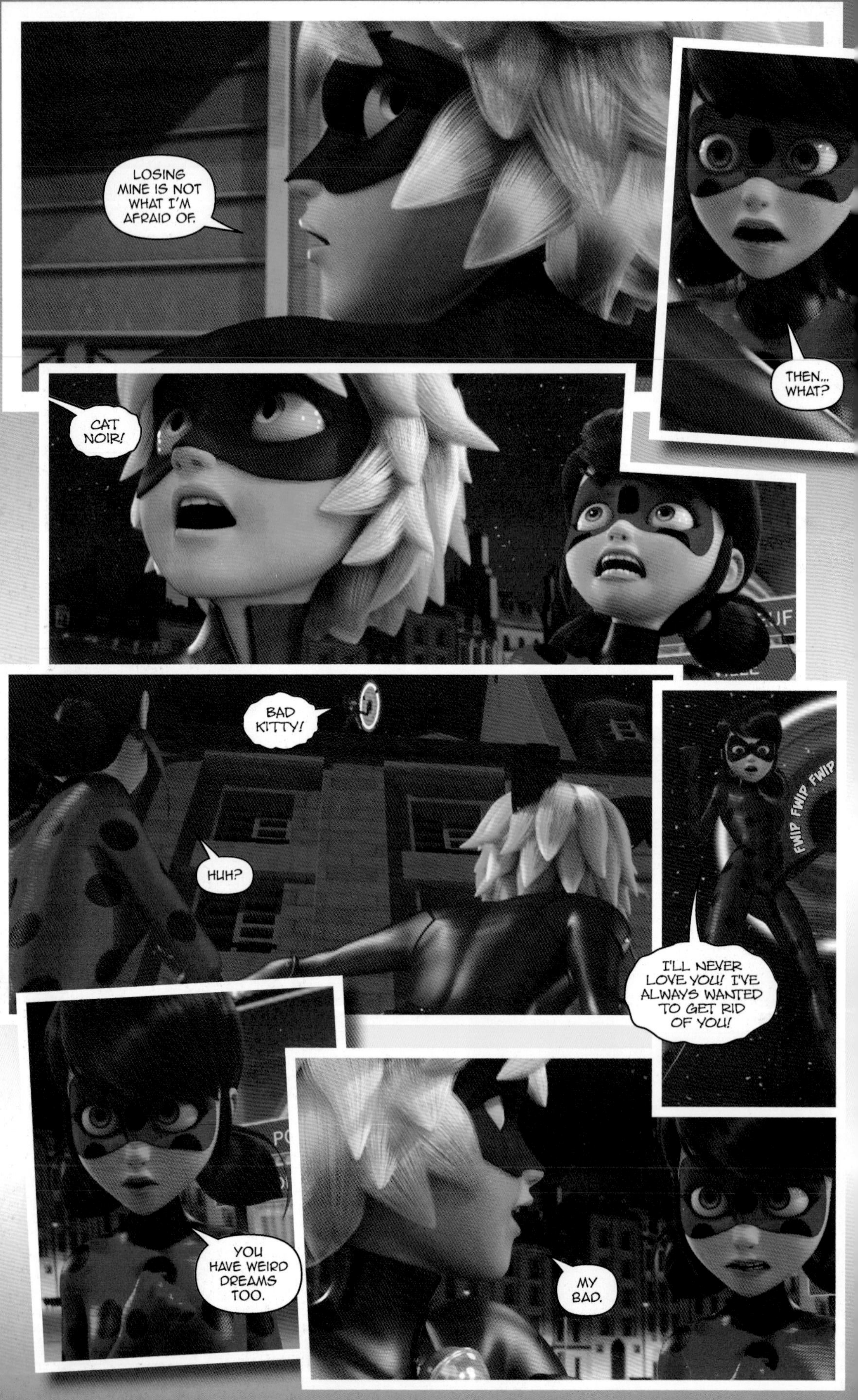
LOSING MINE IS NOT WHAT I'M AFRAID OF.
THEN... WHAT?
CAT NOIR!
BAD KITTY!
HUH?
FWIP FWIP FWIP
I'LL NEVER LOVE YOU! I'VE ALWAYS WANTED TO GET RID OF YOU!
YOU HAVE WEIRD DREAMS TOO.
MY BAD.

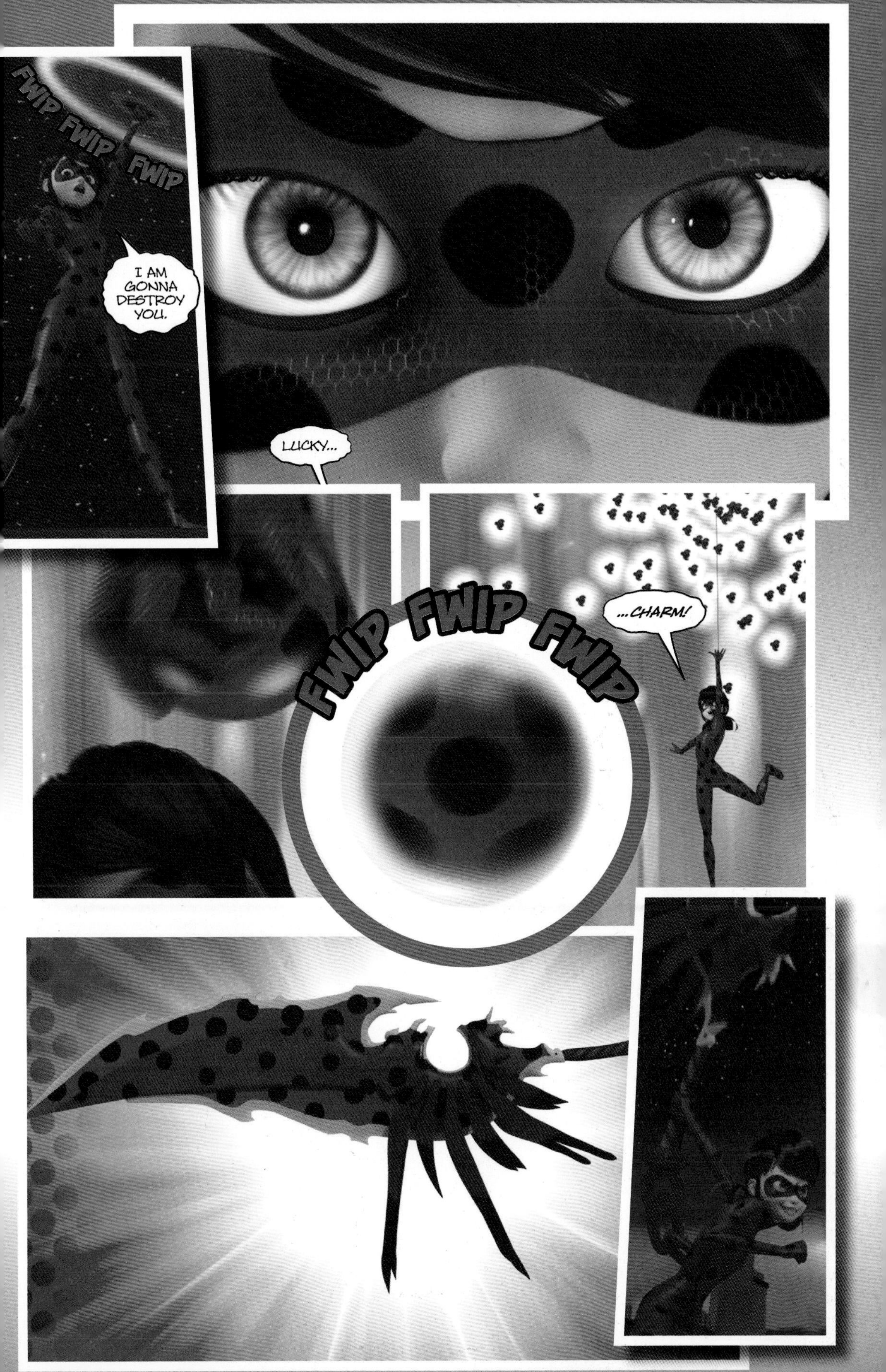
FWIP FWIP FWIP
I AM GONNA DESTROY YOU.
LUCKY...
FWIP FWIP FWIP
...CHARM!

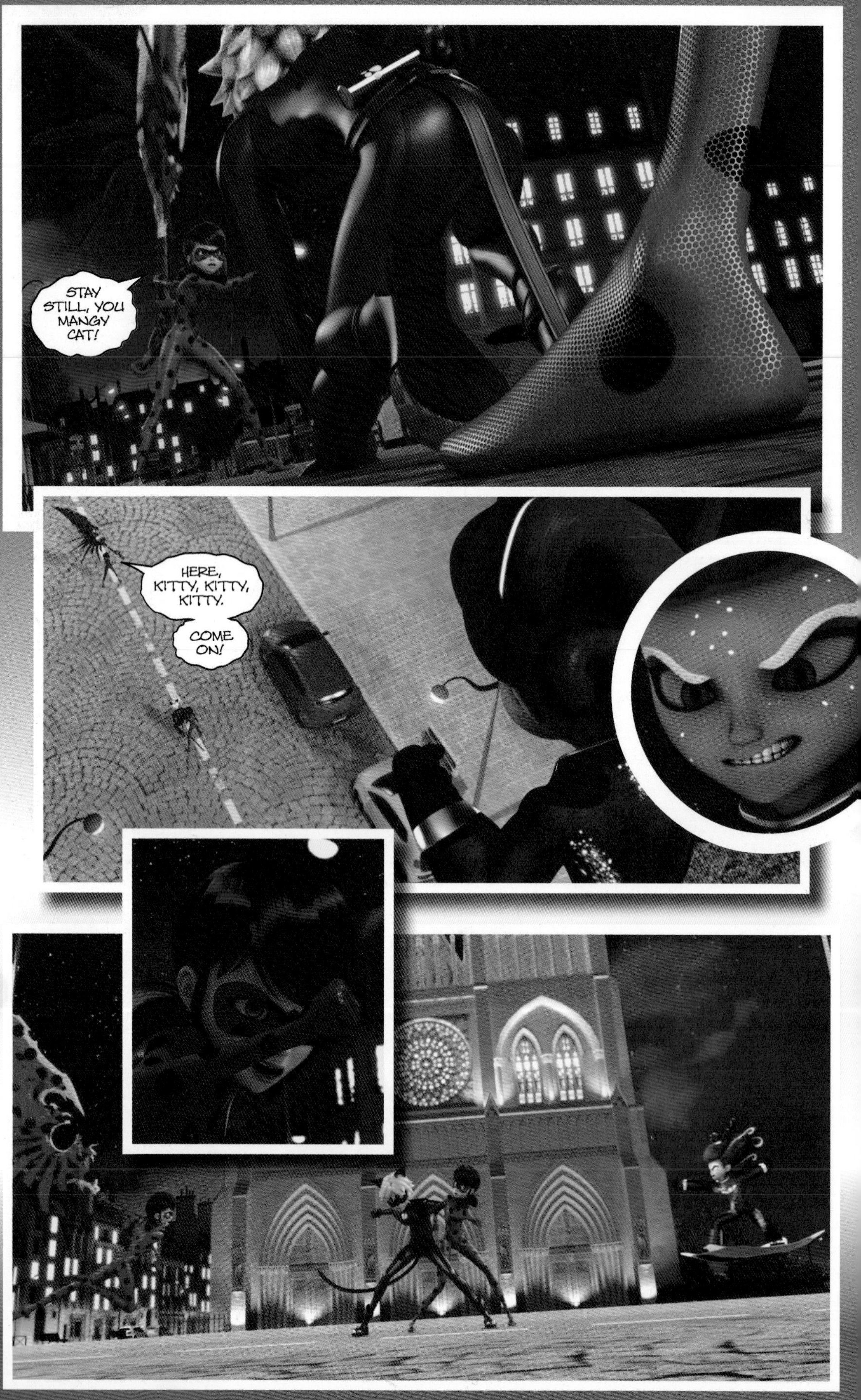
STAY STILL, YOU MANGY CAT!
HERE, KITTY, KITTY, KITTY.
COME ON!

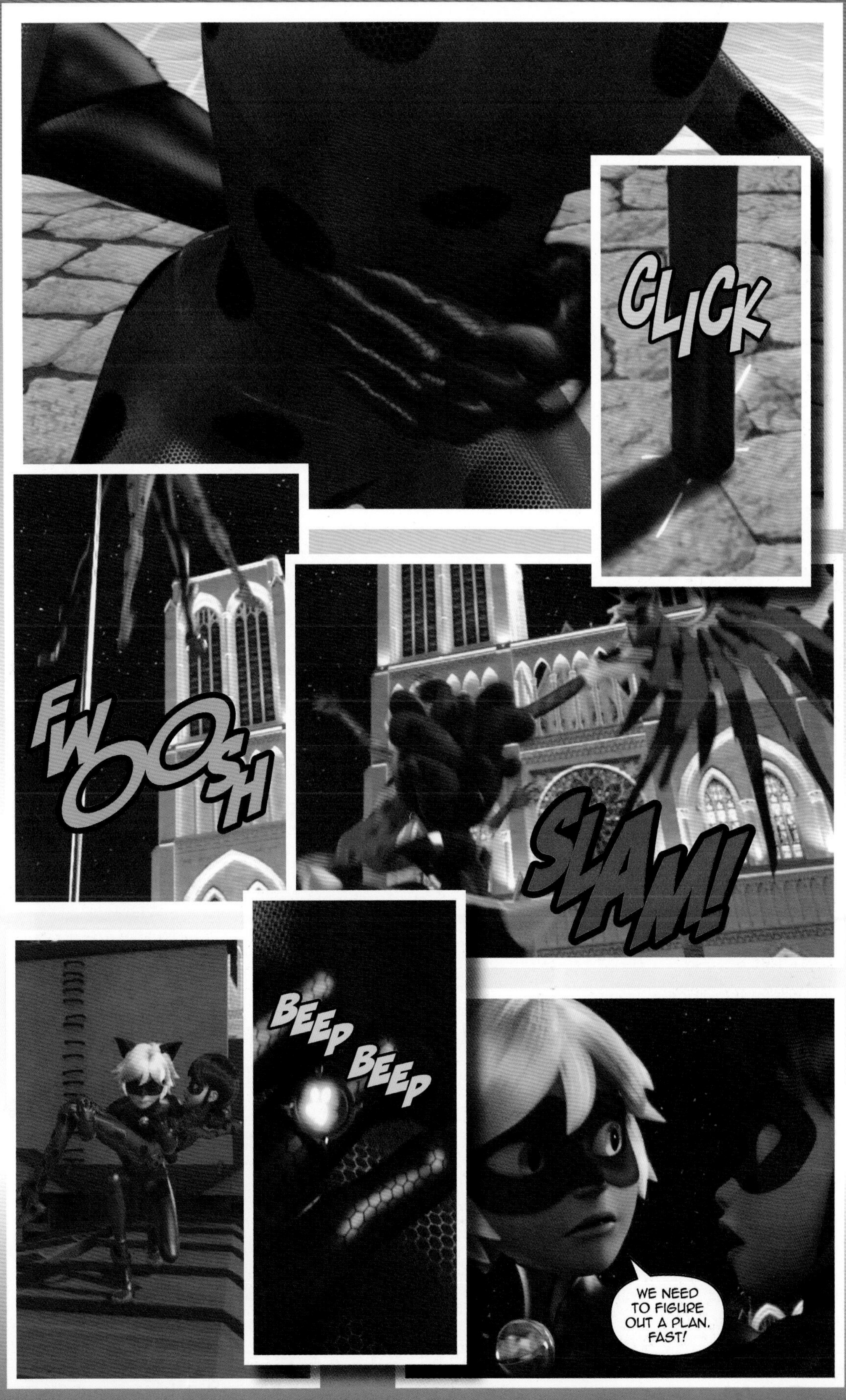
CLICK
FWOOSH
SLAM!
BEEP BEEP
WE NEED TO FIGURE OUT A PLAN. FAST!

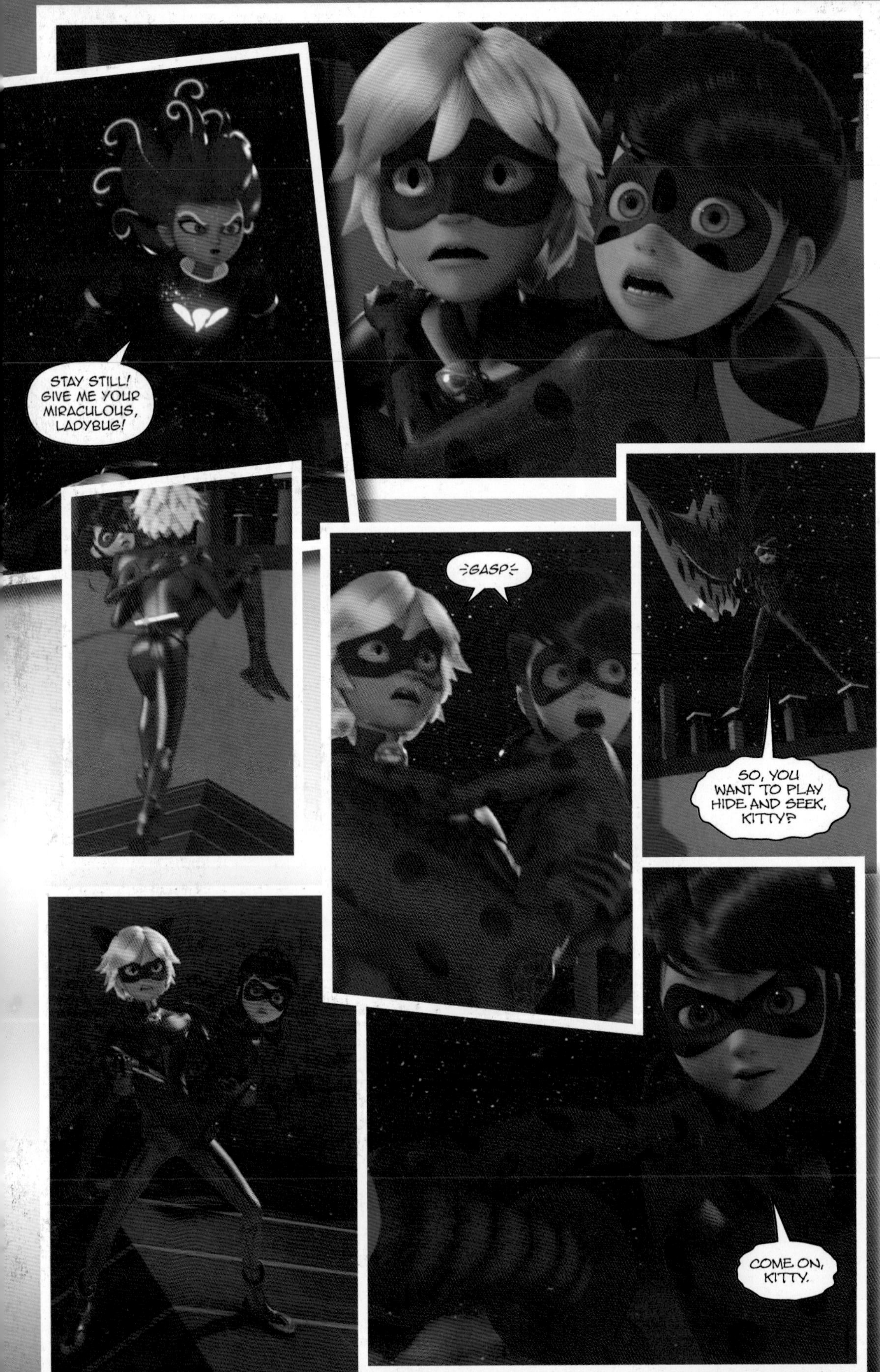
STAY STILL! GIVE ME YOUR MIRACULOUS, LADYBUG!
GASP
SO, YOU WANT TO PLAY HIDE AND SEEK, KITTY?
COME ON, KITTY.

WATCH OUT, LADYBUG!

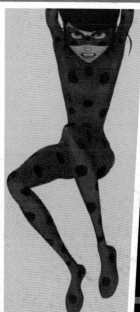

CLANG!

HYAH!

CLANG!

LADYBUG, I'M ABOUT TO TRANSFORM BACK! ANY IDEAS?

LOOKING!

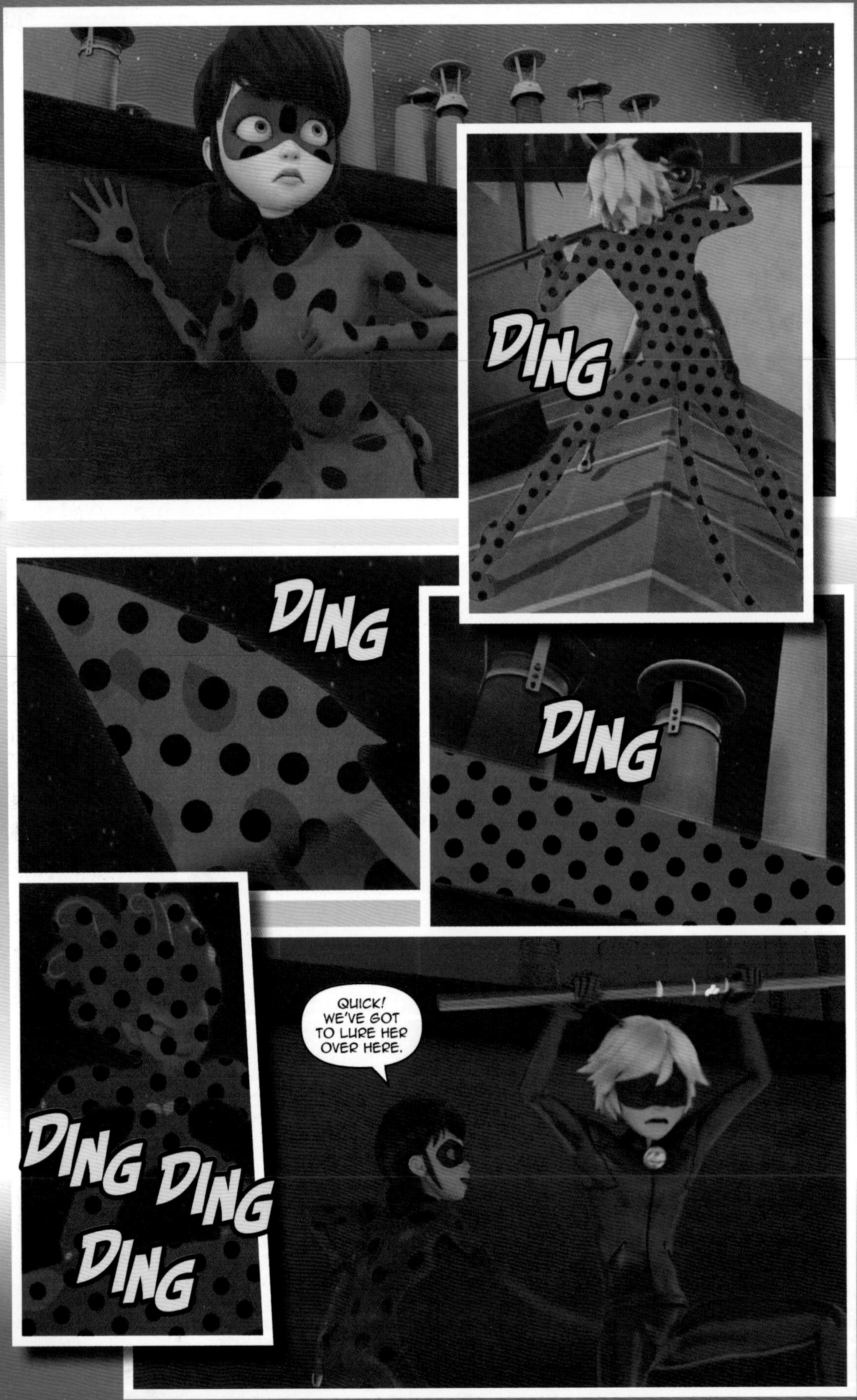
DING
DING
DING
QUICK! WE'VE GOT TO LURE HER OVER HERE.
DING DING DING

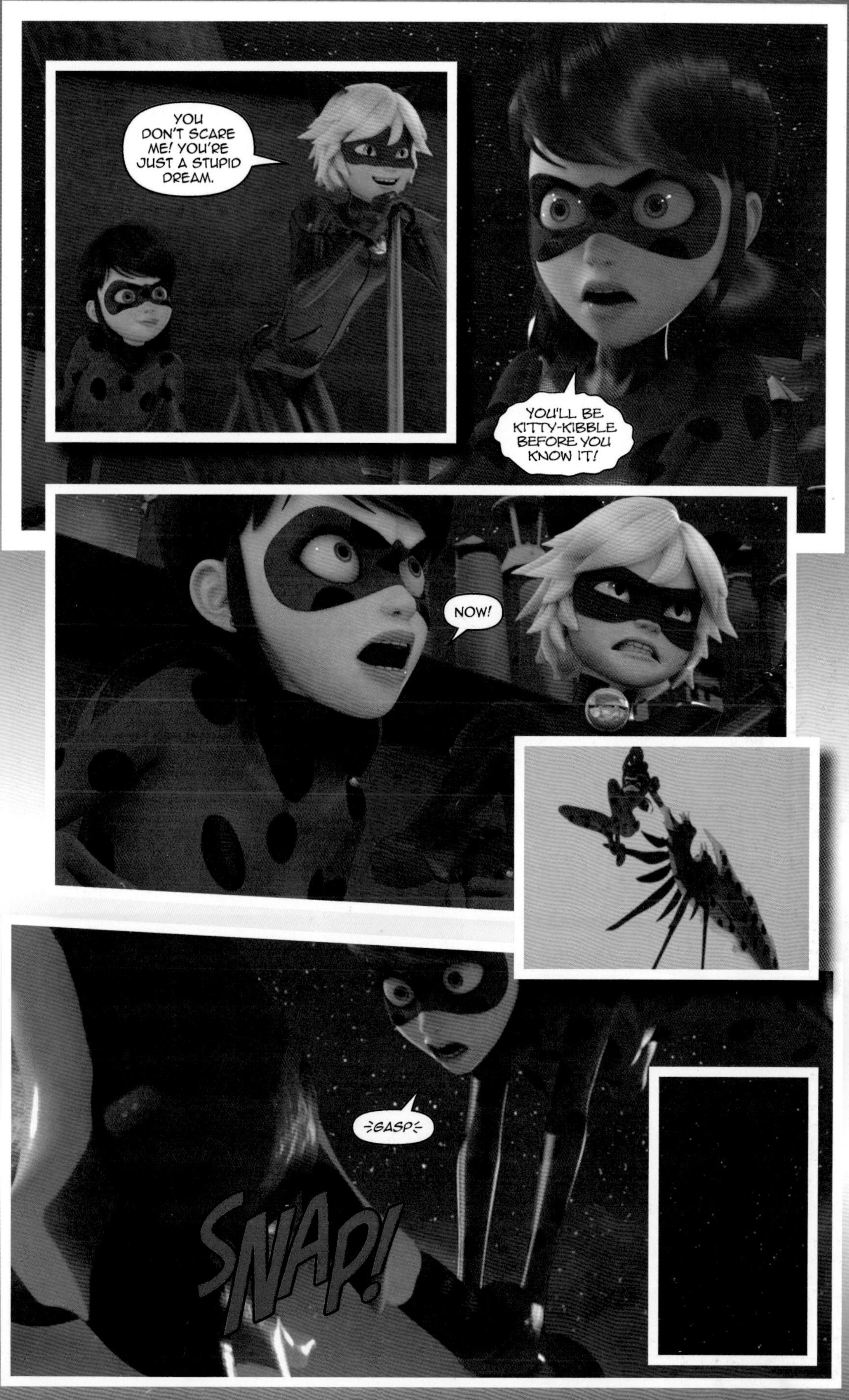
YOU DON'T SCARE ME! YOU'RE JUST A STUPID DREAM.
YOU'LL BE KITTY-KIBBLE BEFORE YOU KNOW IT!
NOW!
GASP
SNAP!

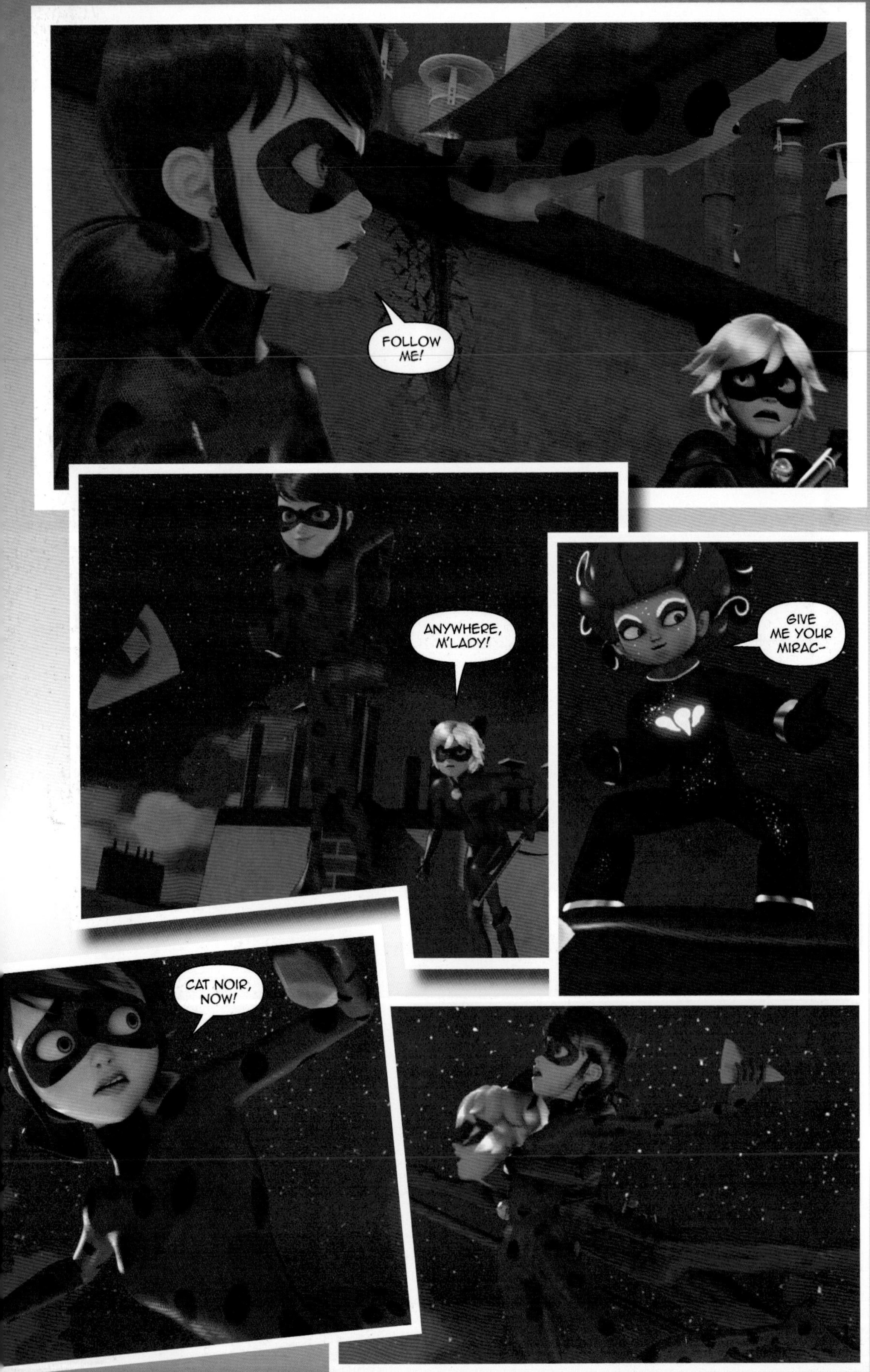
FOLLOW ME!
ANYWHERE, M'LADY!
GIVE ME YOUR MIRAC-
CAT NOIR, NOW!

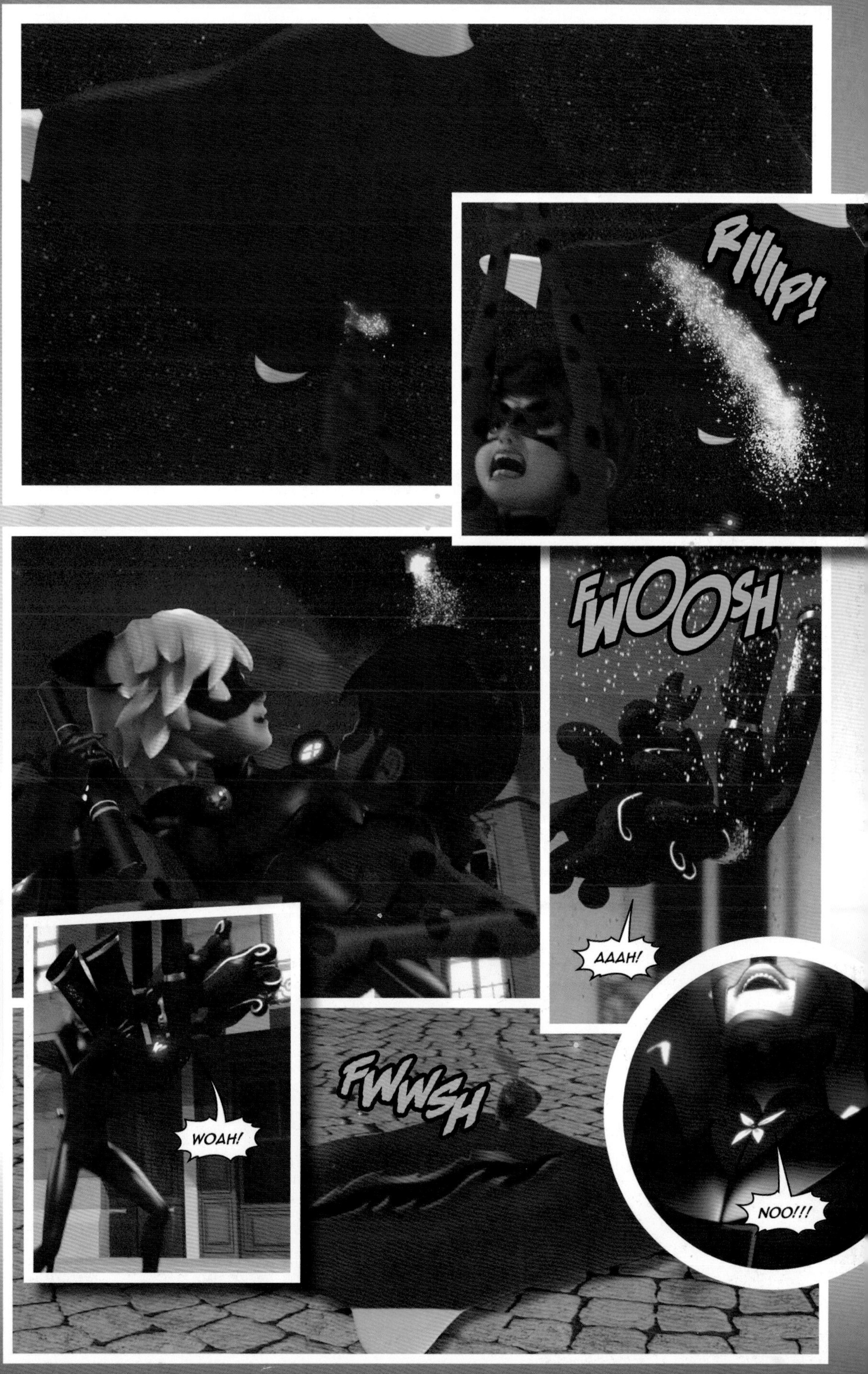
RIIIIP!
FWOOSH
AAAH!
WOAH!
FWWSH
NOO!!!

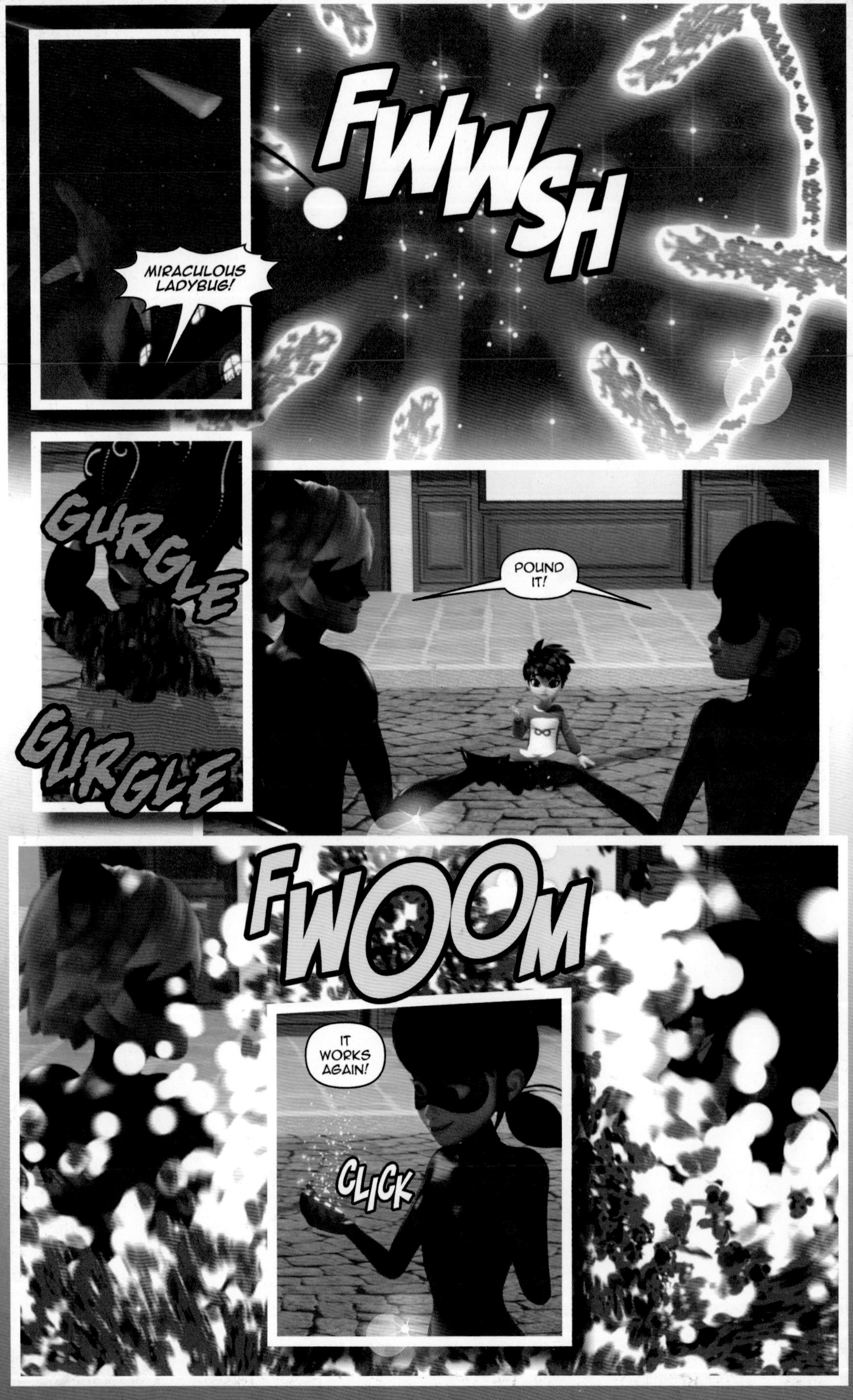
MIRACULOUS LADYBUG!
FWWSH
GURGLE
GURGLE
POUND IT!
FWOOM
IT WORKS AGAIN!
CLICK

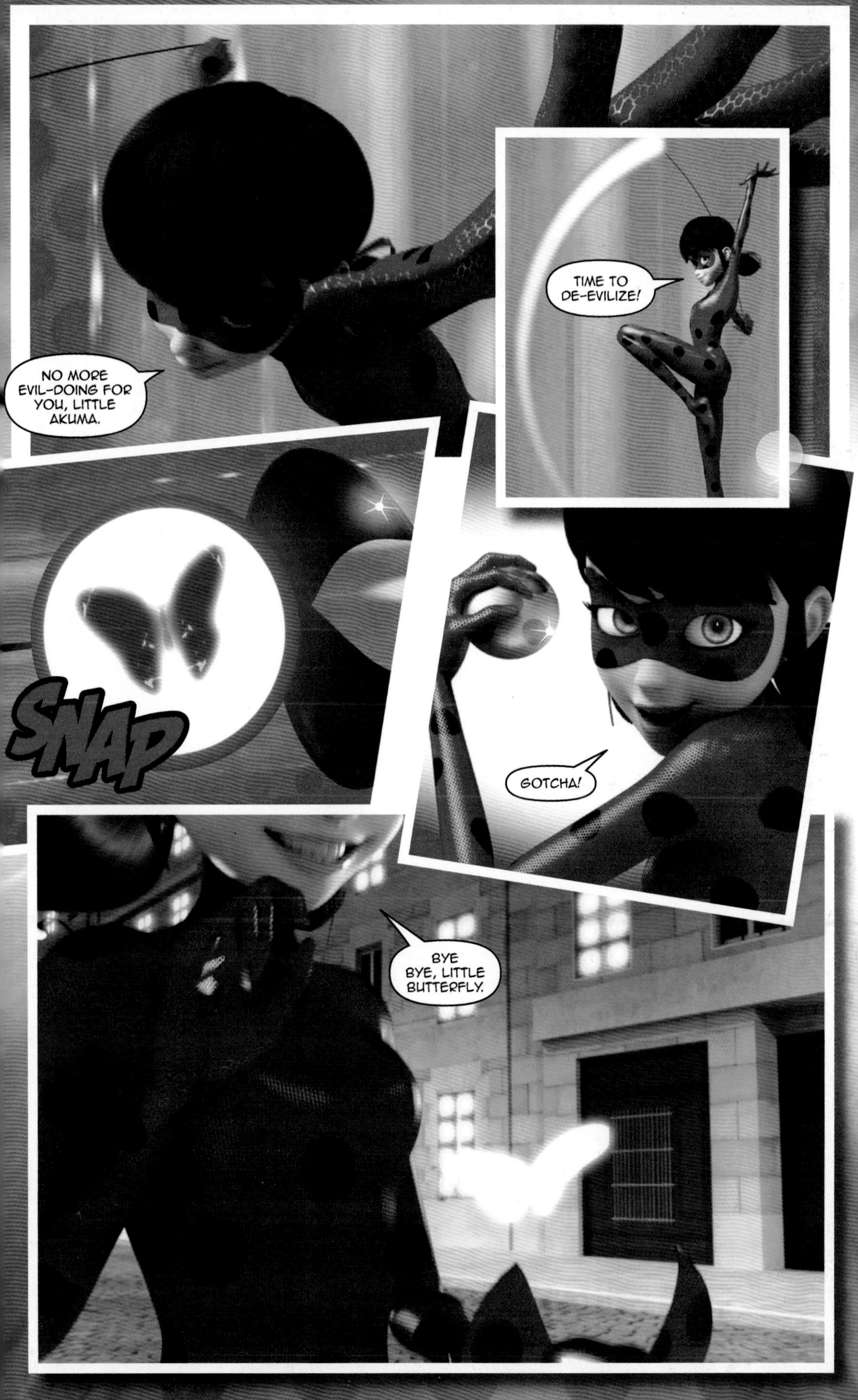
NO MORE EVIL-DOING FOR YOU, LITTLE AKUMA.
TIME TO DE-EVILIZE!
SNAP
GOTCHA!
BYE BYE, LITTLE BUTTERFLY.

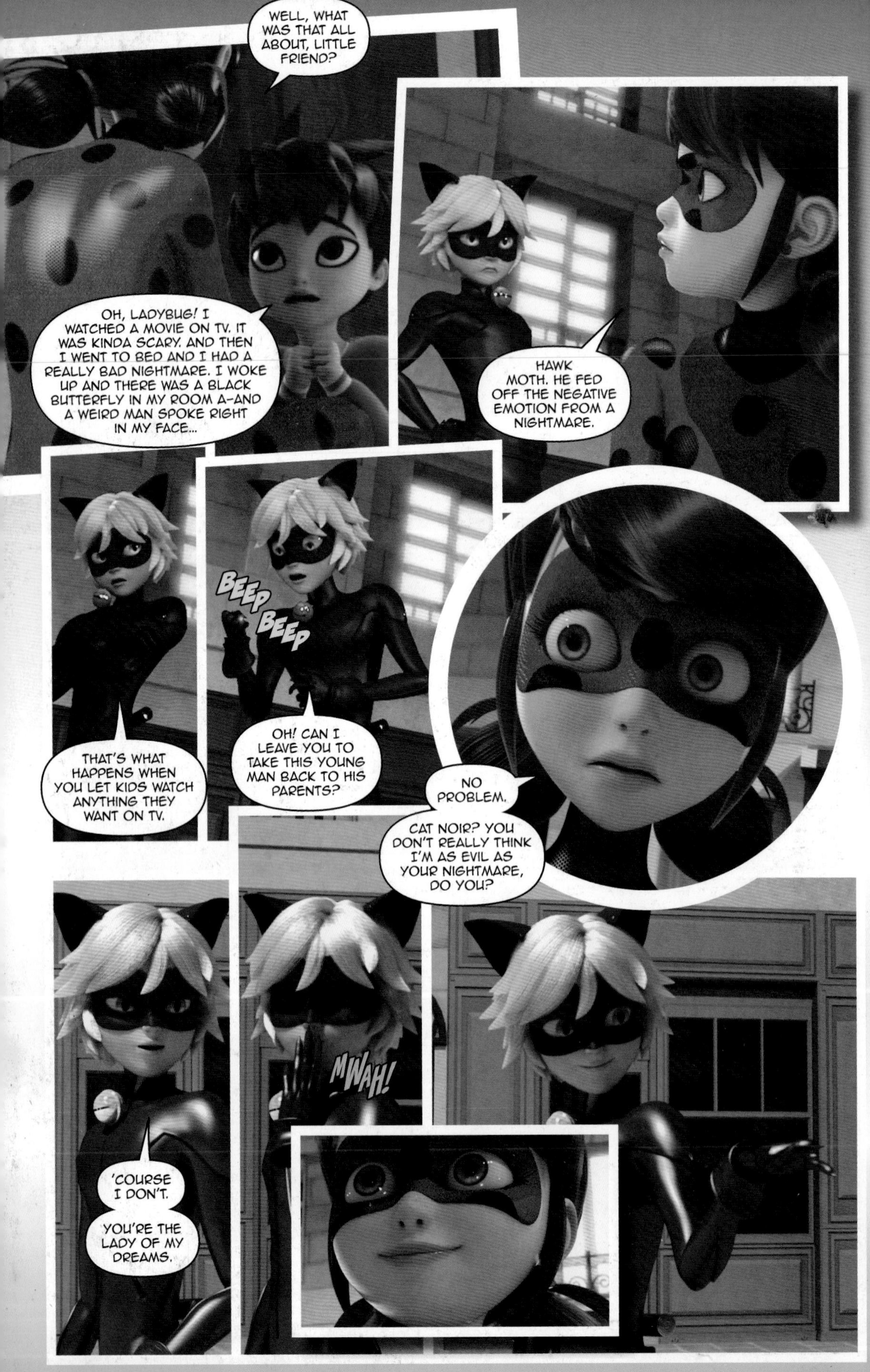
WELL, WHAT WAS THAT ALL ABOUT, LITTLE FRIEND?
OH, LADYBUG! I WATCHED A MOVIE ON TV. IT WAS KINDA SCARY. AND THEN I WENT TO BED AND I HAD A REALLY BAD NIGHTMARE. I WOKE UP AND THERE WAS A BLACK BUTTERFLY IN MY ROOM A-AND A WEIRD MAN SPOKE RIGHT IN MY FACE...
HAWK MOTH. HE FED OFF THE NEGATIVE EMOTION FROM A NIGHTMARE.
THAT'S WHAT HAPPENS WHEN YOU LET KIDS WATCH ANYTHING THEY WANT ON TV.
BEEP BEEP
OH! CAN I LEAVE YOU TO TAKE THIS YOUNG MAN BACK TO HIS PARENTS?
NO PROBLEM.
CAT NOIR? YOU DON'T REALLY THINK I'M AS EVIL AS YOUR NIGHTMARE, DO YOU?
'COURSE I DON'T.
YOU'RE THE LADY OF MY DREAMS.
MWAH!

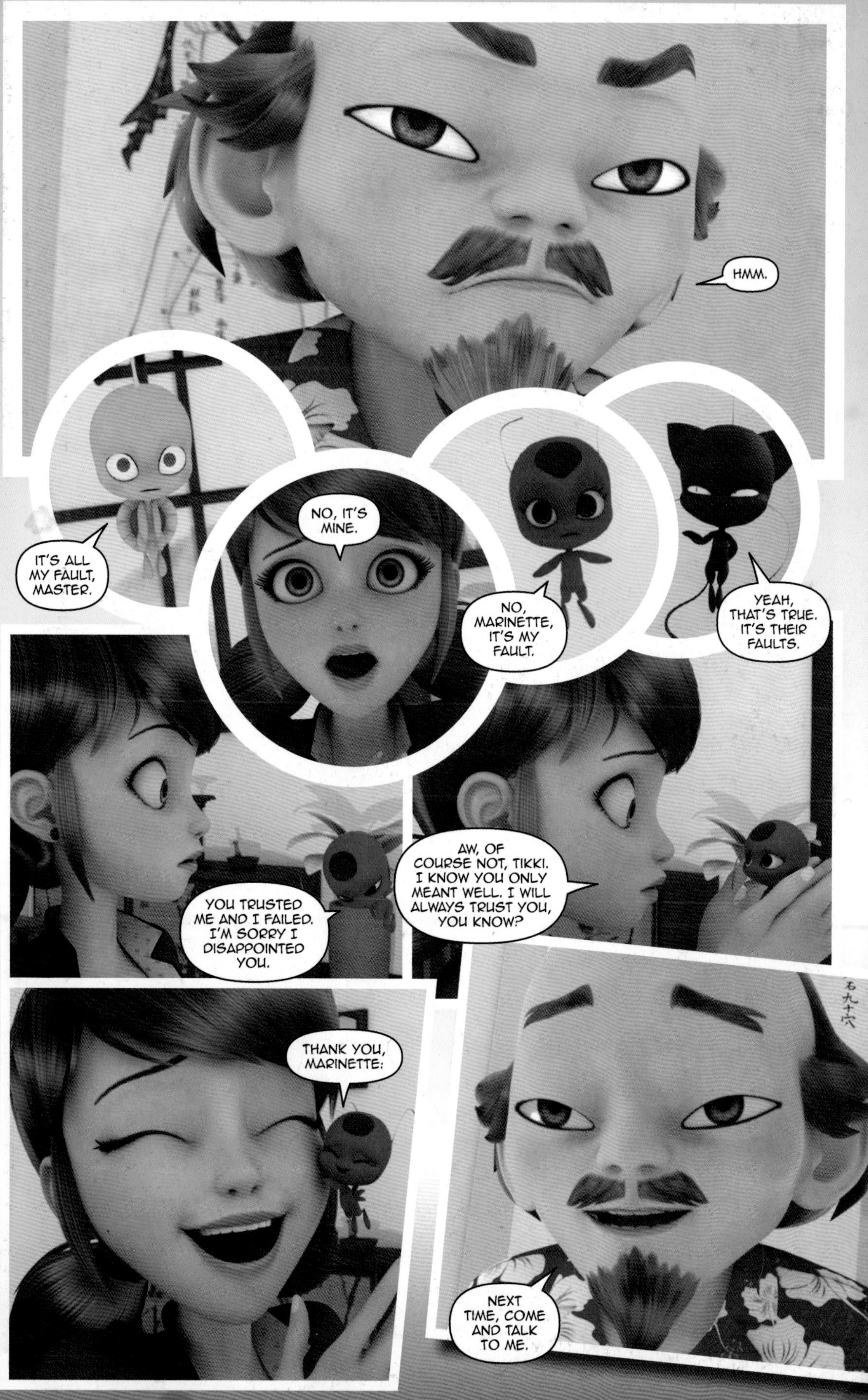
HMM.
IT'S ALL MY FAULT, MASTER.
NO, IT'S MINE.
NO, MARINETTE, IT'S MY FAULT.
YEAH, THAT'S TRUE. IT'S THEIR FAULTS.
YOU TRUSTED ME AND I FAILED. I'M SORRY I DISAPPOINTED YOU.
AW, OF COURSE NOT, TIKKI. I KNOW YOU ONLY MEANT WELL. I WILL ALWAYS TRUST YOU, YOU KNOW?
THANK YOU, MARINETTE.
NEXT TIME, COME AND TALK TO ME.

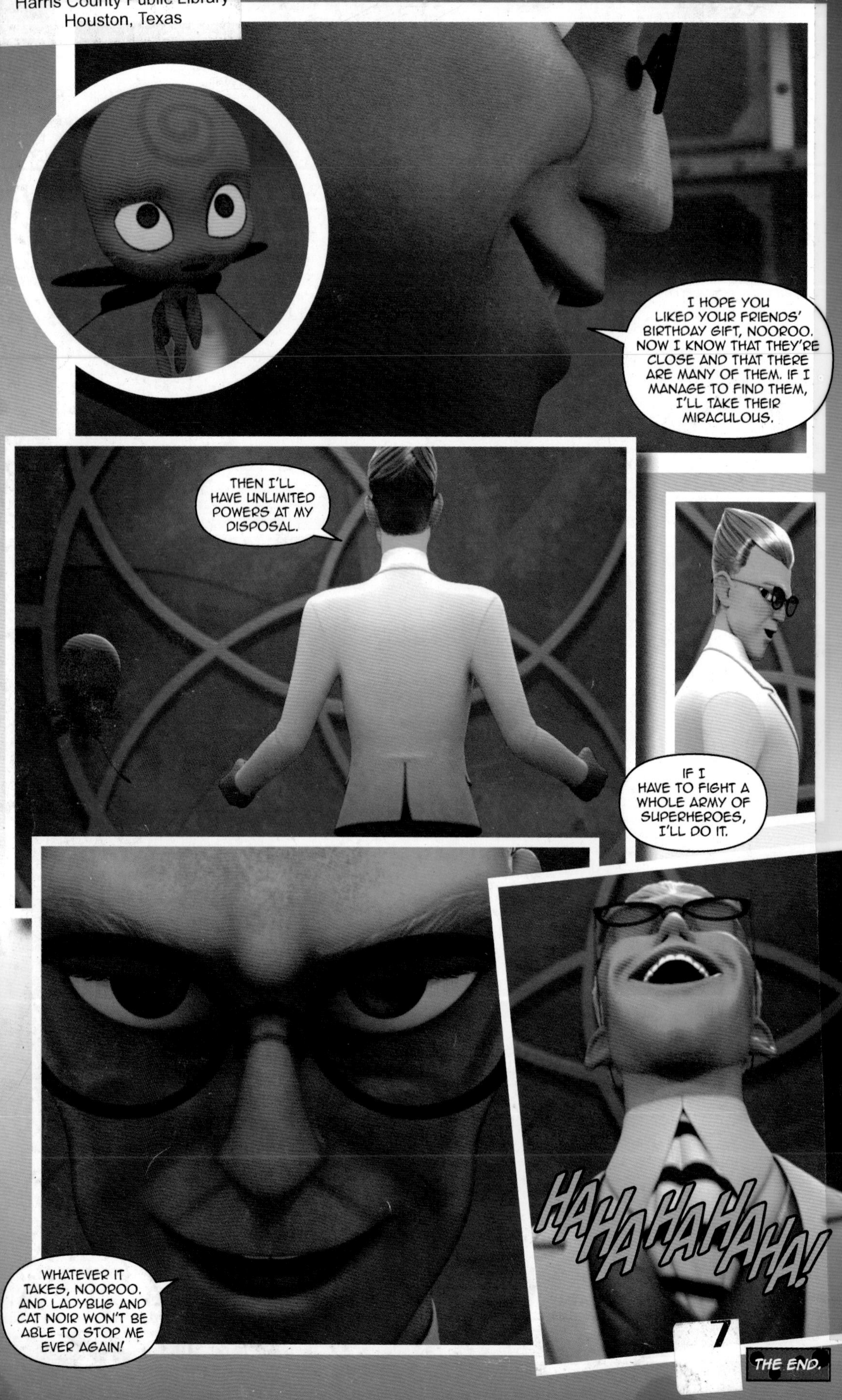
I HOPE YOU LIKED YOUR FRIENDS' BIRTHDAY GIFT, NOOROO. NOW I KNOW THAT THEY'RE CLOSE AND THAT THERE ARE MANY OF THEM. IF I MANAGE TO FIND THEM, I'LL TAKE THEIR MIRACULOUS.
THEN I'LL HAVE UNLIMITED POWERS AT MY DISPOSAL.
IF I HAVE TO FIGHT A WHOLE ARMY OF SUPERHEROES, I'LL DO IT.
WHATEVER IT TAKES, NOOROO. AND LADYBUG AND CAT NOIR WON'T BE ABLE TO STOP ME EVER AGAIN!
HAHAHAHAHAHA!
THE END.